CRUCIBLE

ALSO BY JOHN SAYLES

Pride of the Bimbos

Union Dues

The Anarchists' Convention

Thinking in Pictures: The Making of the Movie Matewan

Los Gusanos

Dillinger in Hollywood

A Moment in the Sun

Yellow Earth

Jamie MacGillivray

To Save the Man

CRUCIBLE

A NOVEL

JOHN SAYLES

MELVILLE HOUSE
BROOKLYN • LONDON

Crucible
First published in 2026 by Melville House

First Melville House Printing: November 2025
Distributed by Penguin Random House LLC,
1745 Broadway, New York, NY 10019 USA.
www.penguinrandomhouse.com

Melville House Publishing
46 John Street
Brooklyn, NY 11201
and
Melville House UK
Suite 2000
16/18 Woodford Road
London E7 0HA

mhpbooks.com
@melvillehouse

ISBN: 978-1-68589-227-2
ISBN: 978-1-68589-228-9 (eBook)

Library of Congress Control Number: 2025944674

Designed by Beste M. Doğan

Printed in the United States of America
1 3 5 7 9 10 8 6 4 2

A catalog record for this book is available from the Library of Congress

To Maggie

CRUCIBLE

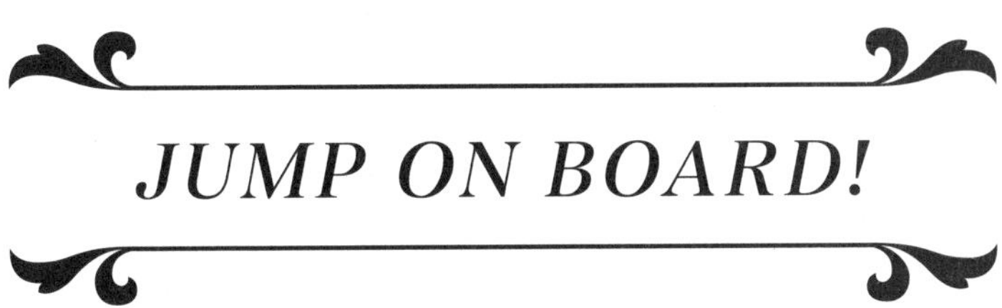

JUMP ON BOARD!

THE NEW FORD offers many advantages to the woman who uses an automobile constantly for quick trips to the Country Club, for shopping, the theater, for the many social and business activities of a busy day. Rarely is there to be found such an ideal combination of charm and utility.

In addition to its beauty of line and color, the New Ford brings you an unusual degree of mechanical excellence and good performance. You will drive with a new feeling of confidence because of its safety and ease of operation.

COME SEE THE NEW FORD NOW!

THE DRIVER DOES NOT SPARE the whip. Despite the rutted roads, the patches of unfrozen mud, the eddies of snow swirling up and over the windshield, he keeps his foot on one of the additions to the New Ford Car—a gas pedal—and tips the odometer past sixty a few times, all the while babbling the Company spiel—'standard gearshift, four-wheel brakes, hydraulic shock absorbers, automatic windshield wiper' and a host of lesser innovations having to do with things Smitty does not understand and does not wish to. He hears Breen from the *Times* making little gasping noises in the back seat, and is comforted to know somebody in the automobile is more terrified than he is.

"How'd you like it?" grins the young buck at the wheel when they careen back into the lot at the Engineering Laboratory.

"Son, you've made a Christian of me," Smitty answers, then staggers to join the other inkslingers in their quest to grab a few quotables from the Woeful Prince and the aptly named Liebold. They've got Edsel surrounded, his back up against a spanking-new Tudor Sedan in what the Company handout says is 'Niagara Blue.'

"Mr. Ford—over here!"

"Mr. Ford!"

"Give us a big smile—"

"Look in the lens, Mr. Ford—"

"They say she'll do sixty miles an hour, Mr. Ford—"

"In *reverse*," says the heir apparent, grinning, and the newsmen laugh.

"Rumor has it," calls Smitty, "that your dad wanted to just keep making the Model T."

The Sage of Dearborn is allegedly 'out of town' for this important sneak peek, a hint, perhaps, that he really did oppose the redesign as long as was fiscally possible, occasionally applying wrathful bootheel and lug wrench to the bodies of early prototypes. Yes, the Founder held out for a planetary transmission, whatever that is, and resented being forced to modify the brakes due to new government regulations, but Smitty figures he's just a stubborn old cuss used to being right about everything.

"My father became aware," says Edsel evenly, always the diplomat, "that the public has become desirous of more *frills* on their automobiles—"

"You mean like windshield wipers and a real gearshift?"

A chuckle from the reporters, and the Royal Pain-in-the-Ass, Liebold, leaps in, wielding his steely Company smile-

"This new model is still *cheap*er and more durable than any other car on the road. Three hundred eighty-five dollars buys you the basic model—you can put one-third down and schedule twelve more payments—"

"And how do your line workers at the Rouge like making it?"

Smitty likes to feed the humorless flack a curveball now and then.

"No different than when they were making the T," says Liebold without an eyeblink. "They're grateful to be employed."

"Tightening the same nut four thousand times a day."

The smile disappears. "All that Mr. Ford requires of his employees is that they do sufficient work to pay the overhead on the floor space they occupy."

Ever the charmer, Liebold is quoting the Old Man word for word, but with a dose of venom for a former employee, Liebold having fired Smitty off the *Dearborn Independent* shortly after the Old Man bought it to push his philosophy, fired him even before the worst of the anti-pork-dodger tirades began. Liebold still runs the paper, exhibiting a somewhat less virulent but extremely dim view of the Jewish people, and watches over the Old Man's bottom line with his owl-like gaze.

"The Ford Motor Company remains committed," he states, "to making a fine automobile that any of its assembly-line workers can afford to *pur*chase. We'll be showcasing the New Car for the public tomorrow at the Convention Center, with sixty Ford dealers on hand to take orders. I'm afraid the demand is already overwhelming, but we'll do our best to meet it."

Smitty waves to get Edsel's attention. When the Old Man bought or forced his investors out of the Company back in '19, he installed his only son as president, ceding him nearly half the stock as well. Already one of America's wealthiest citizens, and by all reports happily married, there is much conjecture regarding the younger Ford's consistently wistful countenance.

"Edsel, I hear this is your baby, like the Lincoln."

The rueful smile. "Father makes the decisions."

"But *you*'re the president of the Company—"

"The company that Father started."

"That you will someday inherit—"

The smile again, like a man with a nail in his shoe making the best of it. "Perhaps."

The Company stopped producing new Ts in April, shedding an army of stunned workers onto the street and leaving their dealers around the country only used buggies to sell for over six months. Though most of King Henry's competitors have been rooting for a debacle, Thomas Edison, Will Rogers, and a couple hundred thousand less celebrated citizens have already signed up for delivery, sight unseen, and Smitty, catching the reflection of his own envious face on the brilliant 'Arabian Sand' exterior of the chariot beside him, wishes he could afford to do the same.

"So, Edsel," he asks, tentatively laying a hand on the ivory-hued hard top, "what's all this about buying Brazil?"

For whatever reason, Henry tells Rufus to drive down Miller Road instead of looping around on Schaefer to get to Administration today. It's the way the workers who have cars—all of them Model Ts—come in to the vast parking lots, and you can see new construction off to the left.

People want the automobile, he thinks. *But to make it in quantity and in an efficient manner, you need capital—money from banks and investors—who then sit back and do nothing but enjoy your profits.*

"What's that?" he asks when he notices.

"The new coke ovens," says Harry Bennett, sitting in the rear beside him as always.

"Who ordered new coke ovens?"

"Your son. He thought, with the New Model coming, it would be more efficient for the foundry if—"

"What does Edsel know about the foundry? He fools around with that bunch who dream up pictures of automobiles we don't build—"

"The designers."

"Is that what they call themselves?"

But if you sell enough automobiles and still make the investors' lives miserable, you can get rid of them.

"I never go up there, Chief, you know that. Not my purview."

"A collection of desk jockeys. With rulers and adding machines."

Automobiles are made of wood and glass and steel and rubber.

The people who have those things can't be trusted, they form cabals, and one day are certain to put the screws to you.

Harry has been looking for the right moment to drop Edsel's coke ovens into the conversation, guessing that the Chief won't approve, but didn't want to seem to be telling tales. Luckily the Chief doesn't miss anything for long-

"Pull them out," says Henry.

"He won't be pleased—"

"Screw Edsel. What right has he got to order new ovens?"

"He *is* the president of the Company, Chief."

If you need wood, why not cut down and mill your own trees?

And what is glass but sand and heat? Why not make your own?

What is steel but iron ore crushed, then heated with coke fire, with the impurities skimmed off?

Why not mine your own coal and iron ore, and find a use for the slag?

"I'll tell you what," says Henry with a grin. "When will they be finished?"

"The ovens? A couple days, maybe—"

"Wait till they're finished, *then* pull them out."

"Yes, sir."

They drive in silence for a moment, passing under the bridge the workers use to cross from the main parking lot to the factory.

"Sorenson deals with the work-flow," says Henry Ford. "If he thought we needed more ovens he'd have stuck them there."

Once wooden wheels are outmoded, what are tires but tubes of rubber?

Rubber bleeds from trees.

Why not grow your own?

• • •

There is nothing whiter in the world.

Not clouds without even a hint of a *tempestade* in them, not the cotton the doctor used to dab at the infected cut when Flavio was brought into Belém so he wouldn't die, not the white of the linen sheets of wealthy people, which he has seen hanging to dry on thin ropes behind their houses. When it bleeds out of the cuts his father makes in the sides of the *castanha do pará* tree, running down the center groove and dripping to fill the cup, it is the purest, brightest white that can be imagined, truly *ouro branco* that needs only to be smoked and sweated till it hardens into the dense black balls, some weighing nearly as much as Flavio does, balls that his mother is patiently making, layer by layer, back where they have camped.

Flavio struggles to keep up with his father, lugging the pails—one full and the other nearly up to half—his skinny arms held as wide as he can manage to keep from bumping them against his legs and causing a spill. You don't spill white gold. One of his jobs is to carefully dig out the clotted, spongey bits of rubber that have hardened and cling to the bottom of the cups on the trees.

You can leave it in the tree, his father always says, but never on the ground.

It is still dark and cool when they leave on the route, Flavio holding the kerosene lamp as high as he can while his father makes the cuts, leaving the lamp, when the sun finally fights through the jungle canopy, at the base of one of the trees they'll revisit to collect *seiva de borracha* from. Flavio is trusted with the pails then, his father carrying his *facão* to hack away at vines and underbrush that have snaked into their narrow pathway overnight, and lately the Winchester in his other hand, having come upon the remains, just hide and bone, of a tapir at the edge of the river.

They come to the next tree on their circuit, Flavio's father pouring what has run into the cup into the half-full pail.

Time to cut the other side, he says.

Flavio loves to watch this process, his father using the hook-ended scoring knife he keeps in his belt to make diagonal cuts, each one just below and parallel to the next in the untapped side of the tree, gouging out little curls of bark with a bit of pith, working carefully till there is inscribed something shaped like a palm leaf, the two sides of parallel slashes channeling into a central, vertical stem. By the time his father has hung an empty cup at the bottom of the channel, the liquid *borracha* is already weeping from the wounds and running downward, and Flavio, every time he sees this, is thrilled.

There is nothing whiter in the world.

João worries about the boy. Flavio is watchful and obedient, a good helper if it doesn't call for too much strength, but it is clear now that he will be their only child, and for Beatriz he is the world. She insisted on coming out with them this season, saying it was to smoke the *bolas* while they were gone tapping trees, but he knows it is because she can't bear not seeing her scrawny wisp of a son every night, often leaning close to the boy's mouth while he sleeps to feel his warm breath on her face. Beatriz is sure she was cursed by the old woman who lived next to them when João worked on the dock in Manaus, the old woman whose scabby vicious dog she would keep at bay by throwing rocks. That was when Flavio was a baby to be carried and since then there have been no more. João promises her every evening never to let the boy out of his sight, but there are snakes in the *selva* waiting in tree branches and underbrush, everywhere there are mosquitos they say will give you the *malaria*, and, if what the doctors say is true, there are even smaller things you can drink or breathe that can kill you.

And maybe now a jaguar hunting on their route.

When Flavio's leg was cut, just a fall when climbing a tree, and swelled so big and turned an ugly color, they thought they would lose him. If Dom Fernando had not advanced the money to bring him to the doctor—it is not worth thinking about. João already owed Dom Fernando for kerosene and coffee and his rifle and the *fogão de borracha* Beatriz will be sweating rubber over till they get back to camp. João's father, a tapper his whole life, had died still owing Dom Fernando for years of supplies, a debt João has not yet paid.

A *seringueiro* toils his whole life, his father was fond of saying, and at the end his hands hold nothing but smoke.

They are halfway to the next tree, closer to the river, when João hears the chopping.

Hide the pails in there, he tells Flavio, pointing to the buttress roots of a huge ceiba tree, and stay behind me.

João hands his son the *facão* so he can keep both hands on the Winchester, and steps down the path toward the sound. There has been no sign of other *seringueiros* here, and there is an understanding that any tree recently tapped belongs to the man who cut it. But there are poachers sometimes, desperate or just bold, and you have to protect what you've staked out or they'll take everything.

There are two men chopping at the base of a mature Brazil nut tree, one on each side, and now, faintly, João can hear more chopping, lots of it, spreading out in the distance closer to the river.

The man closest, no shirt, dark skin glistening with sweat, barely glances at João despite the rifle, instead flicking nervous glances up into the high branches, wary of the coconut-sized nut pods coming loose to smash his brains out.

What are you doing? João asks him.

What does it look like?

But why? This tree will give nuts for years. Even if you sell the wood, it will never—

"Senhor For' está chegando," states the man with the axe, as if it is a very well-known fact.

It is the one word in English that Flavio, who does not read or write, knows for sure. He has even traced it with his fingertip, within the oval on the grill of a Model T parked on a street in Belém, and could squat and draw the same shapes in the dirt if asked.

It would look like this-

FORD

"Senhor For'?" asks his father, not understanding.

"O rei do automóvel," says the man with a glance above before he slams the head of the axe into the V-shaped notch he's cut. The other worker chops without breaking his rhythm.

Why would he come here?

To put you lousy *seringueiros* out of business. He bought land here to plant rubber trees.

Plant them?

That's right.

He must be a very patient man—it takes six or seven years for an *árvore de borracha* to give up rubber.

Very patient and very *rich.* You won't believe how much land he's bought.

All the way to the river from here? asks Flavio's father, the rifle forgotten in his hands now.

The man with the axe looks up past the branches of the Brazil nut tree to a patch of blue sky where a trio of hawks are circling.

If you were one of those birds up there, he says, you still couldn't see all the land he's bought.

Does he own the trees we've been tapping? Flavio asks, not sure if the idea is terrifying or just exciting.

He'll cut those down, says the man, chips flying as he attacks the *castanheira* again. Cut them down and grow better ones.

• • •

Beatriz tosses a few more of the soaked palm nuts into the earthenware chimney till the smoke blows out thick from the top again, then lifts the paddle by the thin end, holding the fist-sized lump of rubber she has built up on it over the heat, rotating it slowly a few times, then carefully ladles a thin stream of yellowing liquid *borracha* onto the lump as she turns it, forming sticky strings that adhere and add to the bulk of the *bola*. It would be steady, almost soothing work if not for the smoke, which leaves her red-eyed and coughing every evening. There are a half-dozen of coconut-sized *bolas* already made, blackening with exposure to air and sunlight, and it is still very early in the season.

Beatriz hears her husband's voice then, and grips the paddle tightly, afraid to turn her head. It's too early for them to be back— something must be wrong-

When you're done with these, says João to her as Flavio lays two buckets full of liquid gold next to where she is kneeling, we are finished.

Finished? she asks. Both husband and son are smiling. How can we be finished?

João waves a piece of paper with writing on it. Because I've just been hired by the wealthiest and most brilliant of Americans, he says. Who will pay me three times more than I can make bleeding these trees.

Pay you to do what?

Clear the land, put seeds in the ground. And when I have enough cash money, I will go put it in the hand of Dom Fernando, so that I can tell him to go park his behind on an anthill.

Flavio laughs at this, his eyes sparkling. Her husband does not look or smell like he has been drinking.

Do we have to move? asks Beatriz, again spinning the growing *bola* in the hot smoke.

Only to the river, says João. To Fordlandia.

• • •

They started Kaz upstairs on the T back at Highland Park, dipping fenders in paint and hooking them up by the bolt-hole on the overhead rail, metal done dripping as the line edged forward to accept the next piece. One of the simplest starter jobs, maybe due to the misunderstanding that Kaz only spoke Polish like his father did when he started, but once that was cleared up and they saw he could handle a wrench he was brought downstairs on the chassis, lining up spacer washers and inserting fender-to-running-board bolts, sliding lock washers onto bolt ends and tightening nuts over them, a grumpy Lithuanian who never uttered a word mirroring him on the other side of the conveyor. Now that he's at the Rouge and they're making the New Ford Car, Kaz is on Tudor body assembly, bending and bolting and crimping and tightening and every day there's another guy in a white shirt putting a stopwatch on him. Molly thinks it's just a stomach bug, but Kaz believes the job itself may be making him sick.

When he first started at Highland Park it was exciting, being a part of a gigantic, thousand-armed machine that spat out automobiles, seeing a shiny new Lizzie rolling down the street and knowing he'd had a hand in making it. Then the dreams started. Not nightmares really, just anxious extensions of the day, dipping fenders at first, and then the rolling parade of running boards to bolt, one after another after another after another. Nothing stands still in his dreams now, everything rolling, rolling past and behind and overhead—and it has dawned upon Kaz that this is *it*. The same motions, unit after unit, hour after hour, day after day. On the Ts there was only black, and now there's a little lift, a solid five minutes of extra energy when the body coming at you is suddenly gun-metal blue instead of gray.

But his stomach isn't fooled.

There is something wrong with the new baby, Sonia. She has a hard time nursing, like she can't even suck, and it's eight months already and she can't sit up. Dr. Green says they have to wait and see, but Molly says she can tell it's not right. The twins are fine, three now, and climbing everything in sight, but having a baby who isn't normal-

Kaz waves down the line to catch the eye of the relief man and tries to look desperate enough to be allowed a dash to the toilet.

Dipping fenders you could let your mind wander, and he'd think about Molly, who was pregnant with the twins then, or sing songs in his head or even daydream. But climbing in and out to clinch the pressed-steel body pieces together you have to pay attention, you have to be as much like a machine as you can, no switching hands with the tools or moving so your back and knees don't feel the load. He's tried counting down units, calculating, if there are no stoppages, how many are left to come before lunch break or quitting time. He's tried making a dance of it, muttering the number of each step to himself, but that just seemed like added work. He's caught himself going unconscious, waking up in the middle of the process and worrying that he may have missed doing something on the last dozen units that passed on, the ones he wasn't really there for.

It is a boring, repetitive job and you have to do it for a seemingly endless eight hours and there's no more chance of him getting bumped up to foreman than there is of the Tigers winning a pennant.

Psacharopulous, the relief man, who they call Sourpuss, takes the wrench from his hand and nudges him out of the way as the belt rolls forward.

The bathrooms are far enough away that you want to make a show of walking fast. Grimes, the carriage-assembly foreman, doesn't seem to look as Kaz passes, but one of Harry Bennett's Service Department spotters peels off to follow him into the john. There are no doors on the stalls and he should be used to it by now, but it makes it hard to go when the guy is standing right there—nothing comes out. The explosion he felt was about to blow turns out to be just the same dull ache. He makes a few of the appropriate noises, flushes, pulls up his pants, and steps out. The spotter, a squash-nosed lunk named Klopf who fellas say did a year in Jackson for strong-arming dry cleaners for protection money, leans back against a sink with his arms crossed on his chest, staring dully at Kaz.

That guy gets paid at least as much as me, thinks Kaz, and feels sick again.

Kaz hurries to the sink next to the lunk, pats his face with water, uses paper towels, not too many, to dry his hands, and steps out, hearing Klopf step out behind him. Bud Novak, who works two buildings away in Glass, says all the shadowing is so nobody can meet in there and talk to each other. If that's how they want it, thinks Kaz, I will *stroll* back to my station. It doesn't feel so slow, what with a cable hung with glistening running boards rolling in the opposite direction, but Grimes is glaring at him now and takes over from Klopf in following him.

Kaz ducks in under the hard top to grab the wrench from Sourpuss, who moves up the line to relieve another assembler. Grimes raps a knuckle on the side door frame-

"You okay, Pilsudski?"

Kaz knows he's one of the lucky ones who they sent straight from Highland Park to B Building here to start retooling for the New Car, more than half the faces on this assembly line new to him.

"Stomach had the wobblies," he tells the foreman, already inserting the split pins. "I'm good now."

He could be out on the street like his father. Hell, he could be over at the foundry with the colored-

The longer the shank, the more muscle you got to use when the ladle is full up. But, then, the longer the shank, the further away you are if that hot metal spits or spills out some or the sand mold got a fault in it and pops at you. Goggles will take care of your eyes, but every man in the foundry building remembers the day Elton Reeves caught that drop of melted steel between his shoe and his ankle and couldn't pull the laces off fast enough.

So Zeke wears the strap-on leggings that cover your shoe tops, something like a baseball catcher's shin guards, even though they start to dig in after an hour or two. He knows a mite about what happens before him—cupola cars bringing molten iron direct from the smelter to the foundry, no pig-iron ingots like back at Highland Park anymore—and then coking carbon and other kinds of molten metals from the control furnaces mixed with it in the crucible of the transfer ladle and dealt out to the line.

But Zeke is only a pourer.

When Zeke pours, he pours rock-steady, whoever is doing it right next to him got nothing to worry long as they be sure to swing those poles in rhythm. Zeke has tried wearing gloves, only your hands sweat so inside them and the grip isn't as good, but dipping with a long shaft you're not likely to burn your hands. Right now it feels like twenty-five, thirty pounds of the hot stuff fill up the ladle for this casting. Those two-man bull ladles might slide along on a hoist, but when you tip them it's right over your legs and that heat come up on your face-

There's no way to be sure about it, cause you don't be wearing any *watch* up near the furnaces, but Zeke would bet good money these molds are sliding up faster than they did last week. He was always good at numbers, got half the way through high school before he had to quit and come to Ford, and like he explained to Willis on the streetcar headed home to Inkster, if they speed the job up just one *sec*ond for every minute, that adds eight whole minutes of production to the shift. Do that once or twice a month and pretty soon Mr. Ford got a dozen more automobiles roll out for him to sell without an extra penny leaving his pocket.

"That Mr. Ford," Willis said, impressed, "he gonna bottle our *sweat* some day and sell it back as lemonade."

It's one thing to speed up on Willis and the others further down the line doing shake-out, busting the cooling castings out of the molds—you just whale away with your sledges and crowbars a mite faster with no worry about getting *burnt*. But try to hurry pouring molten steel out of that ladle-

As it is, Mavis got to rub his arms and shoulders down before sleep every night with her mix, smell like it got camphor in it, and if there's not a seat on the streetcar coming home it hurts awful to reach up for a strap. Zeke was a pretty fair hurler back in school, but now he couldn't throw a hen's egg across a bicycle path.

"It sounds like Hell," Mavis said when he first described the foundry job to her.

"In Hell you got all Eternity to burn, and you can take your time," Zeke corrected her. "Mr. Ford got us on the *clock*."

They sent him to the rolling mill when they first left off making the T, kept putting out sheet metal for whatever come next, which is lucky since now Mavis's shiftless little brother Whitley come up from Montgomery and has moved in. And them already with Zeke, Mavis, and the three little ones underfoot, crammed into three tiny rooms with the outhouse behind, better than some in Inkster but the roof leaks and the walls are too thin for a Michigan winter. Whitley been weeks looking without finding a job or anything with a roof on it he can afford to rent, unless it's boarding with people got dirt floors and no electric or water.

"It's not much," Mavis says of their own little box, "but it's not Ala*bam*a."

Zeke keeps a rag stuffed in his pocket and has just enough time to wipe the sweat from his eyes before taking up the pole again. This new layout along the river is further from Inkster than Highland Park was, which adds to your day. Everything is on a bigger scale here, the stacks and the presses and the cranes, but at least in the foundry the Service Department sluggers don't like to come so close to the heat.

"Afraid their brass knuckles will melt," says Willis, who passes on stories from his brother who puts tires onto wheel hubs over in B Building all day. The foundry men joke about how easy it would be to nudge some bossy cracker into the hot stuff and how little would be left of him, but you still have to be careful who you lock eyes with on the way in and out of the

Rouge. Ford is the best money a colored man can make up here, the only big auto shop that will hire you for something that doesn't need a mop and a bucket, and it doesn't pay to rock the boat.

Zeke dips, lifts, and holds it steady, shaft bending ever so slightly with the weight, till Flournoy next to him has done the same, then they swing the poles around in unison, a three-step pivot, heat off their faces and onto their backsides for a moment now, then carefully tip the smoking, orange-glowing liquid into the molds as they creep past on the belt.

At *least* a second faster, maybe two.

• • •

The Rouge is a beast.

The Rouge is a beast grown so big it has hunkered down alongside the river, never to move again, a creature worshipped and feared, serviced by an army of myrmidons feeding it coal, coke, petroleum, scrap metal, electric power—the creature purring, buzzing, clattering, roaring with satisfaction as it spews smoke and ash from its hackle-like towers and excretes a shiny stream of automobiles to be carted away by trains, barges, trucks. It is a beast that never sleeps, for whenever the feeding and excreting are paused a smaller legion appears to maintain its organs, sweeping, cleaning, polishing, oiling, the beast quieted now but the hunger within it growing-

The Rouge is not a factory, it's a *city*.

Hours early for his appointment, Jim Rogan wanders among the long, low brick buildings, showing his visitor's badge and asking directions when he's challenged, asking questions, dodging the supply trains constantly rolling this way and that—there must be a hundred miles of track when you add it all up. Sure, there's the three-story B Building where they put the cars together, there was a film of it, made by the Company, that they showed before *The Son of the Sheik* when he took Norma to the pictures in Iron Mountain. But he didn't know there was a steel mill and a foundry and a cement mill and a safety glass plant and a building where scrap paper is made into carboard that is fed to the box factory, and there is a tire plant and a rolling mill and a building for tool and die manufacture and an open hearth furnace to reclaim scrap iron and junked cars and a press shop where they stamp out the body parts and even a canal that comes off the specially-channeled river for Mr. Ford's ore boats to unload.

Jim Rogan, chief of a crew of twelve at the sawmill, feels very small.

Back in Pine Camp he knows the names of every one of the boys on the job, knows the wives and kids of the married ones, even knows the couple families that have nothing to do with cutting down and milling Mr. Ford's trees. But here he's heard one of the tour guides that come past say there are five thousand employees who do nothing but clean up. The complex is, in fact, surprisingly clean, and amazingly *organized*—the mountains of coke and slag and scrap metal haven't just been dumped somewhere, they're in constant flux, trucks and railcars shifting material to wherever it will find a purpose. And the noises—at the sawmill Jim keeps beeswax handy for his ears when they get the big blades spinning, and wishes he had thought to bring some here, each building with its own particular racket, and that's only on the outside. What it must be like to work on the assembly floor in B Building-

A hulking security guard, this one not in a uniform, blocks his path.

"What's the story, pal? You the Wandering Jew they talk about?"

"I was only looking. It's so—"

"If you're not with a tour you don't get to *look*. Either you got business or you don't."

"They sent me this—"

Jim shows him the telegram and the man reads it with a scowl on his face.

"I have a meeting with Mr. Bennett."

"Probly to get your keister fried," says the man, gripping Jim's arm and pulling him away. "I'll steer you there."

Once inside the Administration building it is quieter, mostly people at desks in smallish rooms, but still a bit of a search, leading him finally down to the basement floor. He has to ask a colored janitor up on a ladder replacing a light.

"Excuse me—Mr. Bennett's office?"

The janitor looks down at him as if he's a condemned man.

"What you mess up?"

"I don't—I was just told to come see Mr. Bennett. I drove down from the UP—"

The janitor points. "Last one on the left. And be sure you *knock* before you step in there."

Moving down the hallway, he tries to think of what he could have 'messed up'. The model village is up and running, no problems at the mill, nobody caught drinking or smoking that he knows of-

He thinks he hears a gunshot from the last room on the left.

"Somebody snitched," Norma, who always looks on the dark side, assured him as he left the house before sunrise. "Blew the whistle because we bought those tomatoes in Iron Mountain instead of growing our own."

Jim knocks on the door. Another gunshot. Jim knows what a gunshot sounds like.

"Come in."

A youngish secretary at one of two desks—it seems like a reception area. She looks up at him-

"Jim Rogan? From Pine Camp? For Mr. Bennett?"

She pushes a button, speaks into a machine. He's heard of these but never seen one in action.

"Mr. Bennett? A Jim Rogan to see you?"

A tinny voice from the machine. "He's early."

Jim raises his voice, talking toward the machine, not sure if it can hear him without the secretary's finger on the button. "I know, sir, but outside they—"

"Send him in."

The secretary nods to a door across from her, goes back to her typewriting.

Jim steps through the door.

A man in his mid-thirties wearing a gray suit and a red bowtie leans back with his feet on his big oaken desk, a .32 Colt in his hand. He cocks his head sideways.

"Remind me—"

He's a little man, short and solid like a lightweight boxer, like Benny Leonard, who Jim once saw manhandle some poor stiff in the ring at Benton Harbor.

"From the sawmill up in Pine Camp? You sent me a telegram—"

Bennett lays the Colt flat on the desk and grins. "Paul Bunyan!"

"Who?"

"The lumberjack."

"Yes sir, I—"

"Move over by that map."

There are a couple garish paintings of lions and tigers hung on the wall, and then a large map of the world, red pushpins stuck in it, which Jim guesses are to mark Ford dealerships. He moves to the map-

"Hold right there—no, a little to your left—half step—that's it—"

Bennett swiftly raises the pistol and BLAM! drills a hole in the map, laughing as Jim jumps away from it.

"That was close!"

"Not bad, huh? Take a gander at where the bullet went in."

Jim cautiously moves back, finds the hole-

"Whad I hit?"

"Uhm—it's like a big river, part of the Amazon maybe? In Brazil—"

"That's where you're headed, buddy."

"I am?"

"Boat sails in a day or two."

"Why would you send me to—?"

"Why would Mr. Ford let Harvey Firestone or the fucking British hold us over a barrel? *Rubber.* We make our own steel, right? Why not grow our own rubber."

"I don't know anything about rubber."

"And I don't know jack shit about making automobiles, but every single man and woman employed here at the Rouge, the hiring goes through *me*, Harry Bennett. Before we grow the new trees, we got to clear the land of what's already there, right? A task for the mighty Paul Bunyan. Think you're up to it?"

Jim is relieved. He hasn't been fired and he hasn't been shot.

"Yes sir. Brazil—"

"Two days. You go back to the north woods there, pack up what you need, say goodbye to your blue ox, then—say, do you drink?"

It is not only a federal law but a Company rule, one that he has been ordered to enforce at the mill and in the tiny community, checking in the footlockers in the bunkhouse for the unmarried men, giving the married ones a lecture. But on trips to Iron Mountain-

"Well, sir, not so much that—"

"If you do, keep it to yourself. What goes for Dearborn goes for the boat trip and down there in Bananaland."

"Yes sir."

"Discretion is the watchword, my friend. That's all."

Jim tries to move to the door without turning his back to Bennett, the Colt still in the little man's hand. Jim has one foot in the hallway when the head of the Service Department calls out again-

"Oh, Rogan—"

Jim turns to look at him.

"Family man?"

"Yes sir. I've got—"

"Once you got it squared away, Mr. Ford will expect your family to join you down there. Can't have a troop of bachelors going native in the jungle, can we?"

• • •

Poor sap.

When the Chief gets a bug up his bottom—soybeans, waste paper, folk dancing, you name it—there is no stopping him. Harry has tiptoed around it with him, acting the ignoramus, knowing that even in the jungle it's got to take a while to grow a new tree out of the ground, and what do we know about rubber trees? But the Chief hands him his line about anybody can be taught to do anything, what did I know about making steel or glass when I built Highland Park, blah, blah, blah. Only when he put up the first foundry he didn't bring some hick lumberjack down from the north woods to do it. As far as Harry knows, the Chief, with his usual contempt for 'experts,' hasn't hired a single tree specialist—arborist? botanist? tree surgeon? to go down there and play Johnny Rubberseed.

Which you don't go pointing out to the Sage of Dearborn.

The locals here, reads the telegram from Blakely on Harry's desk, *are of three main stocks, Portuguese, Indian, and Negro, though the admixture has gone on so long that it is near impossible to distinguish the different types. They are not possessed of the stolidity of the Orientals, but have enough of the white race in them to long for the better things—*

Mildred buzzes from the outer office.

"Two gentlemen to see you, Mr. Bennett. Rabbi Franklin and a Mr. Winkler."

Jew business.

"Give me five and then have them come in."

Harry tucks the pistol in his desk drawer. Kid gloves with these people—the rabbi a neighbor and 'friend' of the Chief's ever since the apology. That one really stuck in Harry's craw, even if he only had to read it over the phone.

"I frankly confess that I have been greatly shocked as a result of my study and examination of the files of The Dearborn Independent *and of the pamphlets entitled* The International Jew—*"*

As if the Chief hadn't bought the paper expressly to warn the world about them after he bought that *Protocols* bunk from the Russian, as if he didn't dictate his own words of wisdom to Liebold or that lush Bill Cameron and instruct them to 'gussy it up some.'

"I deem it to be my duty as an honorable man to make amends for the wrong done

to the Jews as fellow-men and brothers, by asking their forgiveness for the harm that I have unintentionally committed—"

The gussying in this case was written by Louis Marshall, big shot New York lawyer and head of something called the American Jewish Committee, who the Chief had Harry track down and hire. That, after Harry had already engineered a mistrial in the slander lawsuit and was ready to fix another in the retrial-

"It's pretty bad," Harry told the Chief over the phone when Marshall delivered the goods.

"Just settle it."

"Let me read you some—"

And he got maybe a third of the way through it before the Chief repeated-

"Just *set*tle it, Harry," and he hung up.

With some finessing—Harry got the Chief's old pal Arthur Brisbane to break the story in New York and set the tone for the press reaction—the whole thing blew over in a couple days.

It was mostly Liebold and Bill Cameron anyway, always piddling in the Chief's ear, the Jews this, the Jews that, till they give him the fever. Like that public bet he made, "Show me one Jew who's a farmer," that he had to quietly pay off the day after. Sure, there's plenty shysters and bankers and business *goniffs* you got to watch out for, but there were Jewish boys on Harry's ship who'd get their hands dirty, guys you'd trust to come through in a pinch, and look at the fighters—Abe Attell, Benny Leonard, Battling Levinsky—you can't juggle numbers in the ring. The best thing about the whole sorry mess is that the Chief let Harry personally tell that fastidious prick Liebold the *Independent* was out of business, something he'll be able to relay to these fine Hebrew gentlemen, whatever their beef is-

Mildred on the box.

"Are you ready, Mr. Bennett?"

"Send them in."

The rabbi he's met before, a bit stuffy but not a bad egg, and the other is a long drink of water with a proboscis that won't quit. If you drew him in a cartoon the AJC would be crying foul in two seconds.

"Gentlemen, sit down, please, what can I do for you?" he says after the hand pumping is dispensed with. "You seem to be in a pleasant mood."

"We've just seen the New Car," says the rabbi. "It's a beauty."

"It is that. Mr. Ford and young Edsel are very high on it, and I believe the customers will agree."

"I'm a Packard man myself," smiles the tall one—Winkleman? "But viewing these new models, I might have to convert."

"It will take you a while to get ahold of one—the advance orders have been tremendous."

"Sight unseen?"

"Hey—they're *Fords*."

The visitors laugh, then the rabbi puts on a serious face-

"What we've come to you to discuss—"

Harry goes to the watch-

"Oh dear—I'm so sorry—could you gentlemen excuse me for a moment? There's one little thing I have to deal with right away—"

Always good to keep the other guy off balance. That was Harry's main skill when he put on the gloves—change your rhythm, jab, jab, feint, step on their toes before the uppercut-

"Uhm—certainly—"

Harry up and almost to the door.

"I promise I won't be long—make yourselves at home."

Mildred gives him a look as he shuts the door behind, and he points to her typewriter so she'll make with the keys. He sits in at his listening desk, slips the headset on.

Harry has a microphone placed behind the portrait of his daughter hung on the wall—some of his best work with the brush, people being much more difficult to capture than the big cats.

Mildred begins to type and Harry begins to listen to his guests. Left alone, people feel free to converse.

"Is that a *tar*get of some kind?" asks Winklestein.

"Ah—yes. Mr. Bennett has a pistol down here, and I suppose when things are slow—"

"There are holes in the map, too."

"He can't be that bad a shot. Perhaps choosing new territories for Mr. Ford to conquer."

"Like our poor little township."

"We don't know that Mr. Ford is behind the consolidation effort. When he came to a meeting the idea seemed new to him—"

"I fake that kind of surprise every time somebody tries to buy a diamond at three-quarter price."

Harry has the lengthy one pegged now, runs a jewelry shop over in Dearborn Township, the one Big Chet LaMare hit when he was still pulling strongarm jobs. And they're not here on Jew business, just worried about the move to combine Dearborn, Dearborn Township, and Fordson into one burg, which means that two out of three of their public officials will be yanked, squealing, away from the trough.

And yes, the Chief, with his hatred of waste, is the driving force behind the whole idea.

"Well, if Mr. Ford is as involved as you believe, I'm sure Harry Bennett will pass on our concerns."

"He is a bit of a *runt*, isn't he? I mean, I've heard all the stories—"

Harry is on his feet, headset tossed aside, heading back in. He's heard enough, and peace treaty with the Children of Israel or no, somebody is aching to have their beak busted-

• • •

Her face, only slightly distorted in the bathroom mirror, isn't exactly unattractive, it's just—ex*treme*. With jet black hair her brows are probably too thick—who but cinema heroines and the congenitally vain have the time to pluck them into fine arches every few days? Her mouth is acceptable, though what comes out of it is seldom deemed appropriate for a young lady, as was constantly pointed out to her in high school, and her gaze, no matter how she tries to soften it, is considered too intense—often told she's staring when she is only looking, putting people she's just met on the defensive. And the nose—ah, well. Papa says it gives her face character, and if so, the character is resolutely not American. Rosa has been taken for Italian, Greek, Lebanese, and, of course, what her weisenheimer brother Ira calls 'a daughter of the Tribe'.

Which goes down well in many of the shops near their little cell of an apartment on Hastings, *hondlers* of various stripes returning to their old neighborhood to run their businesses, their groceries and pharmacies and pawn brokerages and second-hand clothing emporiums, selling to the colored who have become the majority in Black Bottom and Paradise Valley.

"Darling," they call her.

"*Leebele.*"

"*Hertzele.*"

And lately, when leaving their stores, the little bell over the door tinkling, calling "You be careful out there," which Rosa resents, an insult both to her and to her colored neighbors.

Who mostly ignore her.

Except for the boys who gather outside the ice cream parlor at Hastings and Brewster, who look her over coming and going, evaluating. Approaching, one will announce, "Here come the Jew Girl," and she makes sure to meet their eyes with her maybe-too-intense gaze as she passes. Going, they are civil enough to hold their comments till she's out of earshot.

She imagines that white boys would do the same.

There is a pounding on the bathroom door.

Ira never knocks, he *pounds*.

"I'm dying out here," he calls.

"Just a moment—"

"In a moment, the waters burst forth—"

"You're such a ham."

"A Jewish ham—I could be in *Ripley's*."

"You should be in a carnival sideshow. Here—"

Rosa steps out and Ira rushes in past her, ducking his head and slamming the door behind him. They are on the top floor of the Rose Apartments, where the builders ran out of headroom, so everything including the doorsills are low. At least once a week, Ira, a beanpole, cracks his noggin on one of them.

Papa is ensconced in his chair, watching her.

"You don't wear makeup," he observes.

"I'm not on the stage."

"Most girls your age—"

"Most girls my age have cotton candy for brains. I'm sorry, but it's true. None of my *friends* wear makeup."

Papa spends most of the day in that chair, everything he needs in reach with the wooden grabber, not steady on his feet since the beating.

"I was only thinking—she doesn't wear makeup, but she spends hours in the bathroom in front of the mirror—"

"You're exaggerating."

"I'll get a stopwatch and time you some day. Pretend I'm a foreman on the breakdown line."

Papa was strong before, able to hoist a whole side of beef up onto a hook-

"If you need to use the bathroom, Papa, just—"

"I'm not complaining, I'm just curious. Your mother, bless her soul, looked in a mirror the morning of our wedding and never again."

"She worked like a slave, Mama."

Papa frowns. "That was the times. To feed children, to put a roof above your head—"

"Those times are still here, Papa. Our neighbors—"

"Like sardines, they pack them in. I tell this to Bachman—"

Bachman is their landlord, who only appears when the rent is due.

"'Compared to where they come from,' Bachman says, 'this is Paradise.' So I tell him that in Paradise the heating works and the toilets flush, but he has a heart of stone."

Rosa pulls on her jacket. "We're protesting an eviction today."

"Mazel tov."

Papa worries, she knows, but never says "be careful out there." You don't change the world by being careful.

"Can I bring anything home?"

"You're going near the library?"

"Not really, but—"

"I'll have Ira do it then."

"I might be in pretty late."

"Then be sure to eat something. Fighting landlords, you need your strength."

She crosses to her father and kisses his cheek, then hurries out. Missing the struggle, he loves to hear what she and Ira are up to out in the world.

The stairway is getting riper, especially on the second floor, like maybe an animal has died under the boards. Rosa tries to hold her breath till the bottom landing, then closes her eyes with her hand on the doorknob, summoning her byword before stepping out onto Hastings and facing the day-

Forward!

• • •

Blakely has soaked through his shirt already and the sun is not nearly overhead. Harry Bennett pitched this caper as a move up the ladder, said that down here he'd be the head instead of the tail for a change, told some tales about the dolls in Rio, which might as well be off on the moon from this hellhole. Gomes, who he picked up in Santorém and sort of savvies English, has mustered the clearing gang for his inspection, lining them up with the Tapajós at their backs. Blakely points to the spot he's chosen, just behind them.

"We build the dock here."

"*Sim, patrao.*"

He knows by now that this means 'Yes, boss', but wishes Gomes wouldn't keep grinning like an idiot and saying it before he's heard something to agree with.

The two-dozen-odd men and one little boy who spread out before him look like the world's most pitiful pirate crew, smallish and scrawny, dressed in what his mother would call 'mere rags', some with open sores, and among them every color from white ash to deep mahogany, looking uncertain with their axes and machetes in hand. He'll need hundreds more to get a thousand acres planted before the deadline the Brazilian government set as part of the land sale. He's been told by their officials to avoid hiring Indians, who aren't 'tame' enough for salaried work, and so far nobody with tribal scars and a bone stuck through their nose has showed up-

"Think your boys here can handle that?"

"Sim, patrao."

He gives his *segundo* a hard look.

"You tell," says Gomes, "they do."

"And that sorry excuse for a little village—" he points across the river and up-

"Boa Vista—"

"They can't live there. I need to keep an eye on these characters—tell them they can throw up their shacks and lean-tos closer to here—"

"Sim, patrao."

"And once there's a dock we'll bring in a cooking barge—"

"Sim, patrao."

João and Flavio watch, trying to read the American's face, ready to jump into action, whatever it might be, when ordered. They try to talk without moving their mouths-

Is that Mr. Ford? whispers Flavio.

No.

Are you sure?

Does he look like a great man to you?

Flavio considers this. "No, he does not.

Blakely strolls past the workers like a general surveying his troops, Gomes at his heels.

"And no more shitting in the river," he says. "They'll have to use outhouses. You know what an outhouse is?"

"Sim. Para cagar—"

"And let them know they'll have to use the Company hammocks—we take that out of their wages."

"Company—?"

"The hammocks I bought in Santorém. Six hundred *reales* a pop."

Gomes knows that the *patrao* only paid four hundred for each hammock, but says nothing. Blakely halts his inspection, turns to face him.

"Exactly what kind of niggers are these?"

Gomes hesitates, eager to please but confused by the question-

"Quite a *mix*, actually," answers a man approaching across the stump-studded ground they've had time to clear. Blakely puts him at sixty, healthy-looking, a sunburned white man wearing a white linen jacket despite the liquid heat. "Down here the African, the Indian, and the European have come together in various percentages—*pretos*, *brancos*, *indios*, and *amarelos* joining their bloods to become *pardos*, or here in Amazonia, *caboclos*."

"And what are you?"

"I, sir, am a *confederado*," says the older man, offering his hand. "David Riker."

Blakely shakes cautiously. "You're an American."

Riker smiles. "Born in South Carolina. But my father gave up his citizenship, preferring not to dwell beneath the Yankee banner, shortly after the Capitulation. A good number of us came to Brazil and became citizens, and I assumed responsibility for my father's estate some years ago. I understand, from the dimensions of your Mr. Ford's purchase, that we are neighbors."

"You speak Brazilian?"

"Portuguese. Yes, I am fluent, as well as a few words in many of the local tribal languages."

"How'd you like a job?"

Blakely has done recruiting for Harry Bennett—more like screening, as you've got to beat the hungry joes away from the Rouge with a stick—and knows the direct approach is best.

"I might be of some service to you, if we can come to terms."

"You know anything about growing rubber trees?"

The old *confederado* smiles again. "Of course. My family's fortune was *built* on rubber."

• • •

The wives are out in front of their picture-perfect houses, hands on hips, peering down the street or across the little man-made pond they encircle, wondering what Jim can be doing. The shift isn't over, their men at the mill planing logs, and he's here loading his Ford for what seems a lengthy trip, with Norma and little Kerry looking desolate on the lawn. They know he was summoned down to Dearborn the other day, but Norma has been all mysterious about that, saying that even Jim didn't know what the summons was about.

But Jim helped build the village, or 'model community' in Mr. Ford's literature, and he's in charge of the sawmill and in the absence of elected officials serves as mayor, budget manager, and police department. If he's going somewhere, it affects them all.

"You must have done something wrong," says Norma, arms crossed over her chest, frowning.

"I'll be getting paid double—"

"To live in the jungle."

"I'm not sending for you till we've made a clearing and—you know—built a town—"

"A town in the middle of a jungle."

"We're in the middle of woods already—"

"But we don't have *mon*keys," Kerry interjects, mostly upset that she's not getting to go along.

"And we don't have snakes that can swallow you whole," adds Norma, "or jaguars, or quicksand, or tropical diseases that—"

"Those movies always exaggerate." Jim is taking all his clothes but the heavy winter wear, with no idea of what will be required. And his thermos, a tent, his hunting gear-

"And you're always complaining about how boring it is here."

"At least here there's no cannibals."

"What's a cannibal?" asks Kerry.

"Something that's only in the movies—"

"The movies got the idea from somewhere," says Norma. "From *Brazil*."

"But there *will* be monkeys, won't there?"

Kerry has spent most of her young life here in Pine Camp, something of a tomboy, and has only recently accepted the fact that wild raccoons have no desire to become pets.

"I haven't even seen a photograph of the place, honey, I can't tell you for sure what's there."

"Your father is leaving us to go off on an ad*ven*ture," says Norma.

"I'm going off to build a town for us to live in," he tells his daughter.

Norma, usually such a trooper, looks miserable. "Is there even a sawmill down there waiting for you?"

Jim, just too young to enlist in the Great War, has only been out of the state of Michigan once, on a fishing trip to Thunder Bay in Canada. He turns to face his wife and daughter.

"I'm sure Mr. Ford has everything worked out."

• • •

The *Lake Ormoc* is one of the rusting tubs the King of Dearborn bought cheap from the War Department, seaworthy enough to have escaped being taken apart for machinery and scrap like the others. He and the Rueful Prince and the squarehead captain, Olafson, are posing on the deck for Snaps Wiley and the other shutterbugs, flanked by some other Company honchos who they'll get names for in case they can't frame them out of the picture completely. King Henry doesn't believe in titles, so other than Edsel, who is officially Company President, it's hard to keep a scorecard on who's who. The captain is a tall, stoop-shouldered character with a thick accent and no sense of humor, like most old-country Swedes Smitty has met. Or is he Norwegian? He'll have to check, as it's the kind of detail that will put Editorial on your back. Print the big lies that can't be avoided due to politics or the threat of lawsuits, but make damn sure everybody's name is spelled right.

The sky over the lake is bright enough that the picture-taking lacks that firing squad crackle and smell you get with flash powder, and the camera boys step back to let the copy hounds take over.

Smitty tosses the first easy one.

"Are you personally going to be heading down to Brazil with this outfit, Mr. Ford?"

The Sage, owner of the bucket and the several thousands of tons of equipment stuffed in its hold, has a twinkle in his steely gray eye.

"No, but I'll be there soon enough."

"Have you ever sailed down the Amazon, Captain Olafson?" asks Curtis from the *News*.

"This I have not done," answers the captain, "but I am foreseeing no difficulties. First we must reach New Jersey."

A laugh from the scribes. Olafson plows ahead-

"There we are taking on board more supplies for the plantation. Once this is done, depending on the weather, we will in five, perhaps six weeks be reaching the Tapajós River."

"You planning to go nose-to-nose against Firestone?"

Smitty again, who knows that the Sage and Harvey Firestone are bosom pals and traveling companions.

"Mr. Firestone and I," Ford responds, "are both concerned about the British forming a monopoly in the rubber trade and driving up prices for our consumers."

The British are included on the long list of things King Henry dislikes—bankers, socialists, drinkers, smokers, Jews, Catholics, fat people, jazz, Hollywood films, taxes, and waste.

Oh yes—and anybody named DuPont or Rockefeller.

Perhaps the white man's magic will transform the area, Smitty wrote in his first article about the venture, which included a rundown on former president Teddy Roosevelt's nearly fatal expedition to the nearby River of

Doubt. But TR was only there in the interest of knowledge and adventure, whereas Ford is out to complete his monopoly-

"When do you expect to be producing rubber?" asks Breen from the Hearst paper.

"We're already putting trees in the ground," says Henry, "and if there's a way to make them grow *fast*er, my people will come up with it."

• • •

The trees have been cleared back a full acre from the river, Blakely strolling parallel to the water with Gomes and David Riker trailing him, weaving around the stumps that have been left till a tractor can be obtained, passing two smoldering wood dumps that are still shoulder-high despite the gallons of fuel sacrificed to their burning. Riker said it was still too wet in June for bonfires and the Confederate son of a bitch was right, damn it, and then when the piles dried out sufficiently—well, you couldn't exactly call it a forest fire, but it did get out of hand. Lots of snakes and little furry things burnt to a crisp. They come to what he likes to think of as the battle front—men chopping, slashing, hauling, a few sitting or kneeling on the ground looking exhausted. Sitting is grounds for dismissal at the Rouge plant, of course, as is talking on the line or being caught with your hands in your pockets. But here, despite his learning the Brazilian equivalent of the Ford motto—'Faster! Let's move it!'—the *trabalhadores* work at their own pace, steady but flagrantly unhurried, and go to ground or find a stump to sit on when they're tired.

"At least the wood is getting drier," he observes.

"*Sim, patrão,*" parrots Gomes.

"And the water level is dropping," says Riker, "as it does in this season. As it recedes we'll have puddles, which can be dangerous."

"We've had plenty of puddles already."

"But it's been *rain*ing. The rain disturbs the water surface and the mosquitos can't deposit their larva. No rain along with puddles means more mos*quit*os, which brings more malaria, which means even more men not showing up for work."

The old *confederado* is full of these cautions, his family having adjusted to the place in some sixty years of residence, and in his version, fought it to a draw. This whole mish-mash of a country is a jumble—too big to govern, its wilderness allowed to stay wild, so many of its people not even speaking the official language. They pass a man clearing underbrush with a small boy, maybe seven or eight years old, helping to drag away what has been cut.

"Are we paying that kid?"

"No," Riker assures him, "but he helps his father."

João has decided they are clearing land for an automobile factory, not a plantation. This idea that they'll clear so much land and then plant rubber trees can't be true—if rubber trees wanted to stand beside each other they would have found a way to do it by now. No, this is a trick of *Senhor* Ford's—so many other, useful trees can only have been sacrificed for something even more valuable, like the wonderful machines that roll upon the streets of Belém.

"*Pressa! Vamos!*" calls *Senhor* Blakely as he moves away with the *capataz* and the *velho confederado* behind him, and João and Flavio exchange a look.

They *are* hurrying.

• • •

The jungle is excess itself.

Too much sun, too much wet, too much growing and rotting, bountiful and poisonous, screaming with parrots, its rivers twisting upon themselves, a vast tangle of too much-

Jim stands unsteadily on the deck of the motor launch, wondering how there can be anything left in his body to eliminate. He has been careful since docking in the country, but eventually you have to eat and drink *some*thing, and now whatever is left of it is determined to escape and doesn't care which end it leaves from. The tiny excuse for a donicker, surrendered now to the flies, was a stinking horror even before he stepped on board in Santorém, and luckily the crew, three harbor rats of some mixture that Jim, familiar with Ojibway and Cree people if not Negroes, has no idea what to call, politely look the other way when he or Pringle have to grab onto one of the cables holding down crates of equipment, drop their trousers and let loose, their aft quarters hanging out over the river.

Curtis Pringle, a deputy sheriff up in Copper Harbor before joining the Company as a foreman in the rolling mill, seems like a steady character, perhaps more able to laugh at their predicament.

"When we get there," he says to Jim as he rebuckles his belt for the fourth time this afternoon, "I can be head of the Fertilizer Department."

The Tapajós River meanders through an unchanging jungle-scape, unfamiliar trees and a tangle of creeping vines solid on both sides of the water, each bend revealing more of the same. Jim searched the upper branches for monkeys at first, thinking of Kerry, sighting only a few colorful birds, and had the barefoot first mate point out something far too thick and far too long undulating alongside of them.

"*A serpente*," grinned the mate, showing an upper palate with only two yellowed teeth remaining.

It has been smooth and steady so far, despite the pilot's mimed warning when the crated millworks were being swung onto the deck by an alarmingly screechy crane. The man pointed to the crates, then made squatting motions to indicate weight before raising a horizontal palm up and up, past his shoulders, past his eyes, and finally over his head before shaking it dolefully.

He is worried they're overloaded.

But everything on board is needed, is in fact long overdue according to Blakely's blunt telegram.

Up to our ears in lumber. Where the hell are you?

Translation is a problem, and then the rapid inflation that the sight of a white American seems to trigger—he's glad Pringle was there to back him up in Santorém, there to take his arm and make loud noises and pull him away as if they were leaving to either find another transport or to take the big ship back to the states. They ended up paying only one-and-a-half times the price originally contracted by the Company's man in Rio, and Jim hopes none of the overage will be docked from his pay.

The pilot steps back to them, making up-and-down roller-coaster gestures with his hand.

"Corredeiras à frente."

"I think there's rough water ahead," says Pringle. "Or else it's a mountain range."

The pilot leads them toward the prow and plants them between two of the bigger crates, indicating that they should hang on to the lashings for balance. The ride is getting choppier, and they can hear the tearing sound of white water ahead.

"We'll be fine," Jim says to Pringle when the pilot leaves them to guide the boat.

"Can you swim?"

The lakes have always been too cold when Jim has spent time near them. He can dog-paddle in a pinch.

"Not really. You?"

"I just don't want some damn crocodile chewing on me."

The deck seems to fall out from under them then, before the hull slams back into the water, the tearing sound suddenly roaring now as they see between the crates that the boat is descending a long, terraced section of shoals, jagged rocks jutting out here and there and floating logs sticking up where they've been jammed between close-set boulders. Spray flies over the bow and the lashings snap taut as the boat thumps its way down through the rapids. The big ship following them, thinks Jim, will never get through here until the water rises twice as high-

Pringle whoops.

"We survive this," he calls over the sound of the crashing water, crouching low with a tight smile on his face, "we'll have some stories to tell!"

• • •

Teitzel and McTeague are waiting on the dock, both in their late thirties, dressed in permanently-rumpled white linen suits and battered straw hats. Though not quite bearded, they are always unshaven. Victor, one of the Brazilian foremen, and a dark-skinned young man who will serve as their cook wait in the thatched-roof motor launch they'll take upriver to find and buy rubber seedlings.

"*Guten Morgen, Herr* Bossman," says Teitzel, who seems to be the less hung-over of the two.

"It's afternoon," says Blakely.

Teitzel looks to the sky, so much more of it visible since the clearing began. "*Ja*—dis is very well observed."

Blakely has serious doubts about the men, but at least can speak with them directly.

"You sure you understand the job?"

McTeague, a Scot, has angry gin blossoms on his face and a nose that is peeling with sunburn. "We're tae travel upriver, tell the Indians we meet tae find us wee rubber trees," he holds a flat palm by his knee—"this height or lesser, and on our way back they bring them tae us."

"And how do you pay?"

"*Mit der* cash-money only," says Teitzel. "Brazilian *reis*."

Dearborn has been adamant about this—no credit, no barter.

"You think you speak enough of their lingo?"

"If we dinnae have the tongue fer it, we'll employ our *hands*," says McTeague, wiggling his fingers. "When fowk are keen fer trade, they'll ken what yer aboot."

Blakely points to a rubber tree seedling in a pot, sitting on the dock between them.

"And you'll show them this so they know what we're looking for—"

"Ah doot we'll need it. There must be hundreds, mebbe thoosands of trees oot here, and they've a *name* for every ane of them."

"We're not looking for just a couple boatloads of seedlings. The point is to get them to be part of the work force, to start *nurs*eries."

"*Natürlich*," says Teitzel. "Dis dey can do."

Back at the Rouge these two might pan out as spotters or snitches in

Harry's Service Department, but to send them off loaded with cash on a trade mission—he's had Gomes supervise the packing of their boat to be sure there's no liquor on board.

"I gotta tell you, you fellas fuck this up, I'll have your *heads*."

Teitzel grins again, flashing two gold teeth. "If we are fucking dis opp mit der natives" he says, "dey will already haf been taken."

"I've had numerous dealings with those gentlemen," says David Riker as the boat disappears around a bend in the river. "Very resourceful, if unorthodox in their approach."

"They sold rubber to you."

"They contracted labor, mostly, an endless business. The people who have come here to toil at Fordlandia may have a certain financial goal in their minds, and once they have *reach*ed that goal you'll see them no more. Extremely independent of spirit."

"They'd be extremely *fire*d back home."

"These people would prefer not to work at all than to be unhappy in their labor."

"They prefer to starve to death?"

"That has been known to happen, yes."

A dozen green parrots flap over them, heading for the other side of the river.

"But your people made good."

The *confederado* stares into the flowing Tapajós.

"During the so-called Kingdom of Rubber. A time of great confidence and excitement here, as well as excessive cruelty. In certain areas the *seringueiros* were given quotas by their masters, and if they did not meet them, their hands were severed."

"You said people will just leave if—"

"Slavery was not abolished here until 1888, when I was already married and a father of children."

They hear a motor sound then and look upriver to the bend, wondering if Teitzel and McTeague have already given up their quest. But it is a much bigger boat, and not one of the peddlers' crafts that flock around the dock each day to trade with the workers. Blakely shades his eyes, sees a pair of white men aboard.

At first Jim can't imagine this could be the Company's land, the waterfront sections resembling the wake of a hurricane or forest fire more than an agricultural clearing. Felled trees scattered on the surface like matchsticks, enormous, hacked stumps still in place, smoldering heaps of half-burnt boles and branches, and shirtless men with cutting tools toiling haphazardly among it all. Jim runs his logging operations at home like a military campaign, a skirmish line and assault plan mapped out, parameters marked with paint on bark, avenues of retreat cleared for when the big ones topple, and a clear idea of how to move the felled trees to the mill. This—this is *slaugh*ter.

"Welcome to Fordlandia!"

The younger of the two white men, who he assumes is Blakely, calls from up on the newly-built but oddly-tilted pier they are slowing to tie up to.

Jim calls back, hoping this is not the principal entrance to the plantation. "How are we supposed to get these crates ashore?"

The man's feet are well over Jim's head as they come alongside.

"They tell me in the rainy season the water comes up this high."

"But we're here *now*."

The man frowns down at Jim and Pringle. "Which one are you?"

"Jim Rogan."

"The lumber guy—"

"Right. We need a floating dock."

"You'll build us one."

"With what?"

"You got motors, saw blades, all that stuff, right?"

Jim sees that there is at least a metal ladder to climb up. "Most of it is still in the big ship behind us. You're Mr. Blakely?"

“I wish I wasn’t. Why the hell would they send the sawmill guy without the equipment he needs to cut wood?”

Jim has a sinking feeling, and it doesn’t feel like dysentery. “I was hoping you could tell me.”

• • •

The problem with experts, thinks the Colossus of Industry, is that you give them a title, Lord forbid a degree in something, and they’ll spend eternity having meetings and pondering over the drawing board—might as well be a Ouija board—up on Mahogany Row instead of coming down to the shop where they belong and getting a little grease on their knuckles. Give me a fella with some common sense who’s willing to work, and you can teach him how to do pretty much anything.

Henry steps into the Carding Mill, a pair of workers jockeying the centerpiece machine into position. The Celebration is tomorrow and will serve as the grand opening of the Village as well, and several of the exhibits still want a crowning touch. Henry paces to a spot on the floor—

“Set the feeder end right here.”

He has been so consistently present out here that the workers are neither intimidated nor overly impressed when he talks to them in person. He steps back to let the men, a tall one and a chubby one, gently roll the carder into place.

“You boys lift her up and I’ll yank those wheels out from under.”

The men bend their knees, take a careful grip-

“One—two—*three*!”

They lift and Henry pulls the mechanics’ dolly out sideways. They ease the weight down, then step back to look the machine over.

“So, you throw raw wool in here—” says the chubby one.

“And something you can weave with comes out the other end,” says Henry. “I used to bring wool to this very mill with my father, watch Mr. Gonsolly run it through.” He pats the machine. “This was as big a deal as the Model T back in its day.”

The tall one shakes his head. “Looks like a bunch of washing-machine mangles all crowded together.”

Henry drags over the bin of raw wool, fresh off the backs of the sheep that are grazing in front of his relocated boyhood home.

“Not too far off. Only this machine is for separating and straightening, not squeezing.” He runs his open palms together. “When my father was a boy they done it with a couple paddles and a good deal of elbow grease. The women mostly, sitting near a fire if they were lucky, rubbing till their arms like to fall off.”

“So somebody thought this contraption up.”

“First somebody realized if you took the *prin*ciple—one set of teeth moving opposite another—and applied it to a *roll*er that would just keep on moving—course, the first ones were hand cranked, not steam or electric powered—”

“But somebody had to build it.”

“No telling how many versions of this got tried before they came up with one that really worked and didn’t cost too much, didn’t break down all the time. Trial and error, like my automobile. Doesn’t a thing come into this world that isn’t built on what’s come before.”

It is, for Henry, the whole point of the village, to remind people that history isn’t the dates when wars happen, written down in some book, but people finding ways to make their lives better, step by step.

“There must have been some fella, way back when in the Ice Age or whatever, looked at a wild sheep and said ‘Damn if that critter don’t look a good sight warmer than me.’”

He gazes around the shop, neater, perhaps, than it was when he was a boy, and room kept clear for the visitors to come through. “Good smell in here—got the oil from the wool and the oil for the machinery. You boys get her hooked up to the power and I’ll send Martin in to do a trial run.”

Henry steps out and can see a knot of men, some of them holding cameras, out in front of the Print Office and Tin Shop. Reporters. Liebold must have invited the bunch from the Detroit papers over for a sneak peek before the festivities. They'll be on him about Mr. Edison, and the Village, which is fine, but the stock market drop is bound to come up as well, as if he gives a hoot about that nonsense. Have to be careful not to say the word 'Jew', even if everybody knows that's what they're talking about.

"Good afternoon, gentlemen."

He recognizes the faces even if the names aren't worth remembering. They call him Mr. Ford.

"So," begins the one from the *Times*, "The Celebration of Light's Golden Jubilee."

"A golden jubilee is fifty years. Thomas Edison come up with the incandescent light bulb in 1879." Henry spreads his arms to indicate his own legacy, Greenfield Village, all around them. "And here we are."

"You and Thomas Edison share a lot in common—"

"Mr. Edison is an in*vent*or," Henry corrects. "While I am just a *tink*erer who refined and improved other people's inventions. Fellas like me are a dime a dozen."

This earns a laugh from the newspaper boys.

"Do you really think all of America will turn their lights on at the same moment?"

It is a stunt they've worked out with the radio people, a way to honor that Great Man with more than words.

"Won't it be fantastic if they do? If it wasn't for Mr. Edison, you boys would still be scribbling by candlelight."

"You think this is the biggest collection of antiques ever assembled?"

A lot has already been written about his searches for specific household items, for the exact woodstove that heated the family farm, for early glassware and furniture, and how much he was willing to pay to get it-

"An*tiques* are expensive things owned by rich folks in the past and bought for too much money by other rich folks today. What I'm collecting here is a *story*—the story of how just regular folks got from then to now."

"This, uhm—can I call it a museum?"

It is the most annoying of the gang, from the *Free Press*. Smith—Smitty-

"Call it a living history exhibition."

"It must have put you out a goodly sum—"

"I can afford it."

"Even with the stock market falling like a buckshot pheasant?"

He knew they'd get to that.

"Not something I pay a great deal of attention to. My son and I are the only shareholders in the Ford Motor Company—"

"But investors in every other arena are starting to panic, the banks—"

"Look, the whole mess is what you get when you let people who care only about money manipulate the market, and the poor saps too lazy to work for their living choose to gamble on a bunch of numbers they don't really understand."

"When people lose confidence in investments, in industry and banking, they stop spending—"

"Good. A little dose of hard times will be good for America, hardship builds *cha*racter. People have been spending way too much."

Smitty grins like a cat cornering a mouse.

"Even on automobiles?"

"Absolutely. I mean who in his right mind needs to ride around in a LaSalle, or God help us, a Rolls Royce? When all you need is something that will get you from here to there in comfort and safety. I've been seriously considering lowering the price on the Model A."

Edsel and the ear-piddlers around him squealed like piglets when he raised this possibility in the lunch suite the other day, but it makes good sense.

"How can you do that?"

"Improvements in our manufacturing process. If we figure out how to make them cheaper, we'll *sell* them cheaper."

"There is a—let's call it a nostalgic quality to much that will be on display here at Greenfield Village," says the one from the *News*. "And yet your Model T was instrumental in destroying the rural America it harkens back to."

"Nonsense!" Henry begins to walk away. The reporter who can go stride for stride with Henry Ford when he wants to be somewhere else has not been hatched. He turns to call back to them, trying to seem madder than he is.

"You find me a farmer sitting on one of our Fordson tractors and ask him if he misses harnessing a team of mules before sunup. We didn't des*troy* a damn thing. And if somehow we did, it's *values* we want to keep hold of, not *things*."

• • •

It's always a struggle to stay awake for eight long miles on the streetcar. Once you pass through Dearborn most of the white people have gotten off, so there might be a seat open, and there the trouble starts. Once you fall out it's tough to wake up, even with the motorman calling the stops extra loud. And after a shift where you been on your feet for all but fifteen minutes, that little patch of streetcar bench might as well be a feather bed.

There start to be colored faces to see through the windows and Zeke searches among them, not so much to recognize somebody as to stay awake. Ford workers, even ones from the same building, don't talk much in the streetcar to or from the Rouge. Never know if there might be a Company spy on board, listening up for kickers or radicals. Jumbo Withers, who used to keep them laughing when he'd talk like his Hunky foreman in the rolling mill, come in one day to find his big black self had been dis*missed*.

"You know why," they told him, and it wasn't anything he'd done on the job.

Finally they pull up by Zeke's stop, bell ringing, motorman shouting, and he climbs out. Home is right, Maceo's is left. He heads for Maceo's.

Good beer is harder to get up here than good hard liquor, which they ferry across the river from Canada every night.

"Bottles are easier to hide than barrels," Maceo always says when he's out of brew, which he claims happens cause he won't sell the home-made stuff. "And I make it a rule to never poison my customers. Bad for business."

Maceo's place was a carriage barn back when, and you walk down a little alleyway to come in the back. There's a horseshoe nailed on one of the big doors that haven't been used for years, and if you see it's been turned so it makes a U then Maceo has been told by whoever he pays off to lay low for a spell.

No problem today.

"Must be near four o'clock," Maceo calls out from behind the counter. "For E*ze*kial is among us."

A half-dozen no-job regulars and DuPree, who works in the scrap metal and must have caught an earlier streetcar, turn from tables and stools to greet him, Maceo already pulling a beer. It's twenty cents a mug in here, worth it because the man keeps his kegs on ice.

Zeke hangs his heavy coat on a hook, sits in on a stool next to DuPree.

"Like to freeze you to death out there," says DuPree, settled behind a glass of whiskey. "The *ic*icles got icicles, and the man drinkin cold beer."

Zeke nods to DuPree's drink. "I put one of those down my throat, I be out for the count."

The first gulp of brew is like rain in the Sahara. Zeke closes his eyes as he swallows.

"Been waitin on that all day."

"You been *warm* all day."

DuPree drives a rig that pulls old Fords in from the rail siding to be stripped, crushed, then fed to the open hearths to make more steel. He turns to the men at the other side of the counter. "Zeke here was *white* before he gone to work at that foundry," he says. "They done *smoked* the man."

Maceo leans across the scarred countertop. "We have a conundrum that awaits your adjudication, Ezekial. The Mule or the Turkey?"

Maceo is a race man and a scholar—always has copies of the *Chicago Defender*, the *Messenger* and Garvey's *Negro World* free to look at in his place, reads books without pictures in them, and unlike Zeke, lets everybody know it, slinging his vocabulary at whoever wanders in.

"Baseball season gone past now."

"This does not resolve our dispute. One camp puts Turkey Stearnes forward as the brightest sepia star on the diamond, others vouch for Mule Suttles."

"Both power hitters," Zeke muses, considering, "both with good speed—even if Turkey looks like he'll shake himself apart getting from third to home. Good fielders, bat for a good average—"

"'Good average' is a contradiction of terms."

"A *nice* average—always over three hundred—"

"I seen Mule put one out of Mack Park last year," says DuPree. "I mean *out*, bouncing down Beniteau Avenue."

"Turkey hit some long ones too. Of course, him being a lefty—"

"And being our hometown hero—"

"He's toiling over at Briggs at the present," says Maceo, "providing Model A bodies for Mr. Ford at half the pay Ezekial here receives."

"Briggs hires colored?"

"Not for his *Tigers*," says Zeke, drawing a laugh from the regulars, all of them Detroit Tiger fans even if it is a white ballclub. "But on his assembly line there's a few."

"Speaking of which, Ezekial—" Maceo nods to a teenaged boy who sits at a table behind Zeke, no drink in front of him. "This young man would like a word with you." He motions for the boy to come up to them. "Don't be shy, Junior."

He is dark and spindly and has cottonfield stamped all over him. Zeke, a refugee from Arkansas, scoots around on his stool to put his back to the bar and get a look.

"I don't know you, do I?"

"No suh," mumbles the teen boy, eyes not quite meeting Zeke's. "I only heard you was over at the Fode—"

"And you want to get on there."

"I needs a job."

"Don't we all. But you asking the wrong man, son. You want the *Rev.* What's your name?"

"Johnsie."

"Well, Johnsie, get yourself down to the Second Baptist Church on Monroe Street in *De*troit—"

"'The Home of Strangers'" Maceo intones-

"Smack in the middle of Greektown—" adds DuPree-

"-and you ask for Reverend Bradby. Now he might be out and about, politicking or saving souls—"

"Or berating the lushes in dens of iniquity such as this to mend their ways," says Maceo-

"-but the Rev will fix you up if he can. There's only two colored men with a line to Harry Bennett, who does the hiring at the Rouge—one is Reverend Bradby, and the other you don't want to be messing with."

"That aint so—Donald Marshall the one who got *me* in to see the Little Man," protests DuPree.

Donald Marshall, sometimes referred to as Old Black and Blue, was a city patrolman before he went to work for Ford, and rumored to still be the man to keep happy if you want to operate a gin mill in Black Bottom or Paradise Valley.

"But you're not a fine young example of Southern manhood like we have here, DuPree," says the bar owner. "Damaged goods like you have *got* to go to Marshall."

"What I got that's damaged?" asks DuPree.

"At the time of your interview, if I recall, you and Bernice were no longer co*hab*iting. Crockery had been hurled—"

"Yeah, and Marshall fixed that up with Bennett—"

"For a modest fee."

DuPree shrugs. "He let me pay it back on time. Dollar a week—"

"You come even yet?"

"It come out fine. I could be slaving over at Briggs, or got no work at all."

Zeke points to the thin, worn denim jacket the Southern boy is wearing. "And you ask Miss Ella who's always there to get you a proper overcoat—don't be proud. Young man that's froze to death don't need employment."

"I told you he was the gentleman to talk to," says Maceo. "If Ezekial Crowder does not know it, it is not worth *knowing*."

Maceo has the idea that Zeke is a wise man just because he nearly finished high school in the north and doesn't have to wrestle words off the page.

"Now you go catch that inbound rattler and see the Rev before your morals are corrupted by my clientele," says Maceo. "Have you got streetcar fare?"

Johnsie just looks at him, not knowing what streetcar fare into the city might be. Maceo digs in the bowl he keeps under the counter and holds out a palm full of small change. "Go on now," he says. "Receive this and flee from wickedness."

The men in the blind pig all share a laugh when he is gone.

"Raised on buckwheat and molasses."

"And more like him coming every day."

The South is only a smell in Zeke's head now, a screen door banging when his father come in from the fields, cornbread from a skillet. But it is a shadow on so many people here, a threat, and there are days in the glowing hot heart of the foundry when he thinks "That's where I come from, and it could claim me again."

"Stearnes," he says suddenly. "Turkey Stearnes is our man. The Stars are our team, and it's our duty to back them up."

"Amen to that," says Maceo, pulling him another mug.

It is dark when Zeke leaves Maceo's place, the streetlights on Chestnut off for a couple weeks now, something about Inkster village owing Edison Power, and he can read the relief in his wife's eyes when he steps in from the cold. Mavis never says anything, is used to him stopping by Maceo's for one or two most nights, but he knows she worries that one night he might not show. There are fights, things happen, men get discouraged and drift away, or just drift away for the hell of it. But he is a money-on-the-table man like his father before him, and though in the winter he never sees his children in the light of day, he likes it that DeWitt, almost nine now, won't go to bed till his father steps in the door. They are crowded in the little back room, DeWitt and Earline, and Alvin now that he's trained to the little commode Zeke has rigged up, sleeping in the same bed, head to foot to head, with Whitley out on the sorry excuse for a couch.

"Come sit by the coal grate, baby, thaw yourself out."

Zeke stuffs the rolled newspapers back in the crack under the door. He's wedged cardboard in the gaps between the wallboards, laid in a hip-high pile of coal under a tarp in the yard, nailed the west-facing window shut, but there's still times they can see their breath puffing out white inside the little house.

"You get some players today?"

Mavis has been handling action for Jarvis Stokes who controls the number in Inkster, something she took up after the Ford sociological people said they couldn't keep and sell chickens because it was dirty. Sometimes she makes near as much for a week as Zeke does, keeping all of the Stokes business in a little blue notebook she hides in the pantry.

"We got to hope 381 don't hit."

"What's that in the book?"

"Lights."

"Dreams about lights?"

"You know how they talked about that celebration for the light bulb man—Edison—on the radio the other night—"

"Everybody in America gonna turn their lights on at the same time, but Inkster still be in the *dark*."

"Well, people dreamed about light bulbs, and 'Lights' is 831 in the dream book. Folks been coming by all day long, shaking from the cold, still they got to get out and lay some money on 381."

"If it hits, Jarvis got to pay off, not you."

Mavis shakes her head as she crosses to the stove to put his dinner in the oven. "Jarvis don't want any of us taking more than thirty dollars on any number—"

"And you took in—?"

"Fifty-three."

"Why you do that?"

"Cause we keep ten cents off every dollar I take in for him, and it *won't* hit."

"We *hope*."

"If you look at the odds—"

"Odds, nothing, what about the *lights*? That many people dreamed about them, it must mean—"

"You don't believe in none of that."

Zeke's Aunt Hannah won big on a number that went with a dream she had about a spotted horse, but Zeke has never played. Better to spend your nickels on beer than miracles-

"If 381 comes in, Imonna *start* believing it and we're gonna be awful sorry."

"We got bigger things to worry about."

Zeke, halfway off with his work shoes beside the coal grate, snaps his head around toward the back room.

"They all right?"

"The children are fine—"

"Where's DeWitt?"

"He's down the block having snowball wars. What's wrong is the water come out brown again."

They used to fill buckets from a pump in the yard, but Mavis wanted indoor water, with a heater so you don't have to boil it on the stove—

"But the water's still coming out?" Zeke asks, stalling. "It's not frozen—"

"It's coming *out* but it's brown with rust or something and you can't drink it and I can't wash clothes with it."

"Keechie getting brown water too?"

Keechie is Mavis's best friend and lives four houses away.

"Uh-huh."

"Then it's not *our* pipes, it's the village."

"Right. So could you talk to somebody at work?"

"What would I do that for?"

"The Company built some of these houses—"

"And that's the last they want to know about them. You want those Sociologicals in on us again?"

Mavis makes a face. "Well, if the coffee taste bad, don't be looking at *me*."

• • •

There's a lot of education to be had outside of books. So even if Dot Cummings gets over her influenza by next week it won't hurt Kerry to miss a couple days. With all of them crammed into the same little schoolhouse, wee ones mixed with giants in their teens all facing Dot at her desk next to the woodstove, it's no wonder they get sick every winter and then pass it on to the teacher. And then Norma is so darn steamed at Jim, off on his adventure and leaving them stranded in the deep woods in the bleak winter—yes, it's a model community, but you can bet Mr. Ford never spent an October listening to the sawmill whine all day and the squirrels holding a square dance on your roof every night. Norma has been so down in the dumps that some days she waves Kerry off for her two-minute walk to school and then crawls back into bed till the sun actually rises.

Pine Camp is laid out as a long oval, single-family cottages built with lumber planed at the mill, with the church, schoolhouse and garage for the fire truck at one end. The bunkhouse for the unmarried men is on the road to the sawmill, along with the general store and combination barber shop/post office. There is a little playground and a big pond, safe for swimming when it's warm enough, in the middle of the oval of cottages, so Norma's neighbors make jokes about there being an East Pine Camp and a West Pine Camp. Though Mr. Ford does not believe in titles, Jim was something like the manager and foreman of the mill, giving Norma a degree of status in the town that has diminished since he was sent to Brazil. As a virtual widow with only a single child to do for, there is little to fill her days, and the nights-

The nights in the winter begin before six o'clock and never end.

So they leave before sunup on the first day of their adventure, Kerry making both peanut butter and bologna sandwiches for the road, Norma okay with driving the old T once it's started. There are so many things to pull and twist in the proper order, but at least you no longer have to use the crank, which terrified her. After about an hour on the rutted dirt road east from Pine Camp she has the hang of the throttle, getting to almost forty miles per hour at one point, and then the sun comes up, slanting through the tall pines and Kerry is singing songs she learned at school and it is glorious. They are both bundled up, the automobile closed but certainly not heated, and Norma worries all the way to Mackinaw City where she's relieved to see that the lake is not frozen yet. The ferry is supposed to run till the end of the month, but a couple really cold nights will lay a crust on it and nothing has been done about getting an ice breaker or two to bust the way clear in the winter months. Because when it does ice up you really feel *stuck* in the Upper Peninsula, like it's an island the rest of the world has forgotten about.

A boy who should still be in school waves a rag to guide them up the ramp to the upper deck parking of the *Straits of Mackinac* and she and Kerry eat their sandwiches looking out the window of the crowded passenger cabin, gray, choppy water passing below them. Kerry has never been out of the UP, so this feels like they're off to discover a new world.

"I can feel my toes again," Kerry observes.

"Do they burn?"

"No—they just tingle a little bit. Do these ever sink?"

Norma was just wondering the same thing. "I don't think so," she says. "*Boats* have, though—this passage can get pretty rough. But if it's really bad weather I think the ferries wait till it's over before heading out."

"Are we going to cross a time zone?"

"No—if we'd gone the other way toward Wisconsin we would have."

"Can we see a movie when we get there?"

"When we get to Detroit? I suppose so—it depends on what they're showing."

Back in Pine Camp, the Company sends films made by their own picture unit, some about the automobile factory, but others about American history or everyday life. Many of these are now supposed to have sound, but the projector at the Town Center can't play them.

Kerry counts the cars once the ferry is loaded, and reports that over forty of the eighty are Fords, and a dozen of these Model As. She takes pride in being the daughter of an important employee, and pins Jim's old Ford sawmill badge onto her coat whenever they go out. There is only an Episcopal Church in Pine Camp, Catholics like the Rogans traveling all the way in to Iron River on Sundays, and though Kerry has had her First Communion and knows the sins and sacraments, her deepest worship is at the altar of the Almighty Automaker.

"My Daddy works for Mr. Ford," she will tell strangers with very little prodding. "Daddy runs Brazil for him."

Once on the other side, the same boy guides them down the ramp, a long line of cars winding quickly through what there is of St. Ignace and on to their destinations. They reach Cheboygan and Maxine's house a little after dark.

Though Maxine and Tom live right on the river, it smells more like the sawmill Tom works at. It smells like home.

"You ladies have had quite a day," says Tom at dinner. While he cuts the roast Kerry tries hard not to stare at his left hand, missing three fingers from a slip at the mill.

Norma worries some about Maxine, just starting out with a fellow careless enough to get hurt like that. Even if he jokes that you're not really handicapped unless you lose a thumb, it isn't a good omen. Maxine is still so young and has never been that sensible and might go having a huge family like so many soft-hearted Catholic women do, their real teeth gone by the time they're forty.

"We crossed the lake on the ferry and Mom felt sick but didn't upchuck," Kerry informs her uncle cheerfully.

"It was choppy," Norma explains. Tom is a fishing fanatic, and there are several trout and pike trophies mounted in the dining room. Norma and Maxine and Betty grew up with their father's moose head staring down at them, an animal he claimed to have charitably dispatched, as it was afflicted with the circling disease. Norma feels fortunate that Jim has never killed anything he wanted to nail to the wall.

"What do you hope to see in Detroit?" Tom asks them as Maxine passes the platter of potatoes down.

"I want to take a tour of the Rouge factory, but Mom says we have to go shopping."

"She's grown out of all her clothes."

"That was never a problem for me," Maxine explains to Kerry. "There were always my older sisters' hand-me-downs."

"I don't have a sister," Kerry tells her, with no regret, "but I'm going to have a monkey."

Norma is bundled in the same bed with her daughter tonight, but that isn't why she can't sleep. It's always tough on her being with Maxine.

Norma's voice was no longer a little girl's as early as ten, an attribute that made her stand out from the other kids in town. Mr. Fitzwilly at St. Joseph's declared it a 'gift' when she came in as a freshman, giving her more and more difficult solos to learn as the choir drew attention and began to be invited to statewide songfests. That her God-given talent provided the chance to travel, even stay overnight somewhere that wasn't home, made her popular with the other kids.

Mr. Fitz called her "my little songbird."

He was a good-looking man, young compared to most of the priests and nuns teaching at the school, married to a mousy woman who remained childless, which led to a certain amount of clucking and head shaking among the Sisters of the Sacred Heart.

They started their special relationship when she wasn't quite fourteen.

Fitz was quite a taskmaster with the music, and she spent so much time and effort trying to please him—he was in her head night and day. As for the furtive part of it, she couldn't tell between what was exciting and what was terrifying.

Maybe he'd been told he was at fault for having no children, had been told he was sterile-

It was early in her senior year that her mother noticed from the wash that Norma's flow had stopped. She started gaining a little weight, "filling out nicely" as her father said, and one day when she felt too nauseous to go to school her mother cornered her for the inquisition and the die was cast.

A cousin in Battle Creek was invented, Norma and her mother off for a visit that went on and on, till her mother returned, lo and behold, with a late baby, and Norma followed two weeks later having allegedly finished school in Battle Creek and with nothing to sing about.

Jim was in town then, surveying a nearby forest for a lumber outfit, and her dad brought him home for dinner one night and parked him next to Norma. It wasn't a rapid courtship, Jim shy and gentlemanly and soon called back to his company's headquarters, so she was around baby Maxine for over a year, her mother allowing her some care-and-cuddle time if no outsiders to the family were present.

Mr. Fitzwilly had taken a position in Grand Rapids.

Norma and Jim honeymooned at a lake resort on the Leelanau Peninsula, then moved to a little town just as isolated but much less romantic, where there were plenty of trees to cut down. In the early years together her greatest fear was that the doctors in Battle Creek had made some mistake at the birth or she'd somehow damaged herself by starting so young and she'd remain barren. Kerry, when she came, was a blessing, one that has not, for whatever reason, been repeated.

In letters her mother always wrote that '*your little sister Maxine is thriving*'.

Kerry is a restless sleeper, mumbling and squirmy, but once or twice Norma gets to hold her like when she was really little.

They start in the dark again the next morning, a sack full of Maxine's roast beef sandwiches smelling good in the narrow seat behind them, only a dusting of snow here and there. Norma has the young man at the 'full service' filling station put some oil in and check the radiator as well as fill the tank, which Kerry seems fascinated by, maybe believing only her father could perform these tasks. On the drive to Saginaw she entertains her mother with facts she has learned about the Amazon River.

"Despite its length," she recites, "there are no bridges across the Amazon, chiefly because there are so few roads in the rain forest that grows around it. Canoes and ferries make the crossing where necessary, and if one chooses to swim, one might be joined by river dolphins, giant otters, caimans, which are a species of crocodilian, or the aggressive, flesh-eating piranha fish."

"If we ever go there," Norma tells her, "we stay in the boat."

The roads are all paved here, in good condition, and several times they are passed by faster Chevrolets, Hudsons, and Chrysler-Plymouths, Kerry calling out each model as it goes by. Only two of the speedsters are Model As.

"Luxury cars," Kerry huffs at the non-Fords, sounding like her father, but is able to rattle off all their innovations and advantages.

"We only need something that gets us there," Norma assures her.

"Gets us there and back home," adds Kerry, who has voiced a fantasy of driving home over the frozen-solid lake.

Betty, oldest of the Kilmurray girls, lives in a two-story house in the center of Saginaw, her husband Bill a manager at Grey Iron Foundry, making engine blocks and cylinder heads for GM cars, which Kerry views as a brand of treachery. He is a red-faced, heavyset man, given to lectures and the open consumption of private-stock whiskey before dinner, something Kerry, raised in a Ford model town, has never witnessed.

"The Old Man got caught napping," he boasts as they wait for the roast to leave the oven. "First, he got jealous of some of his best people and fired them—that's who's running *our* outfit these days. Then he thought the old Tin Lizzie would tickle the public forever. How was it today, pushing that tractor down the road?"

"We did forty-five more than once," Kerry announces loyally.

Bill laughs. "And at times so many were passing it looked like you were backing up."

Betty has worn a pained, patient smile on her face for several years now. Their boys, Randy and Andy, are in high school and communicate in grunts and nods. Norma has always wondered if Betty knows the real story behind Maxine, but has never dared asked her.

"I have to admit, the Old Man's A is a sweet-looking car, but it's only one of many these days."

"You can't beat the price," says Kerry.

"You should run a Ford dealership. You're heading for the big city tomorrow—"

A statement, not a question-

"And staying in a hotel." Kerry can't hide her excitement. She has seen the two hotels in Iron River, but never set foot within.

"Well, you want to be careful down there. Detroit has a—let's call it a somewhat combustible *mix* of citizens. Beware of which neighborhoods you wander into."

"We aren't *wan*dering anywhere," Norma tells him. "I have everything planned."

"The Old Man is throwing that shindig for Edison tomorrow, but I suppose that will be mostly up in Dearborn."

The shindig is Light's Golden Jubilee, Mr. Ford celebrating the fiftieth anniversary of the invention of the light bulb, as well as officially opening his new historical village and museum.

"Mr. Ford brought Edison's whole laboratory from New Jersey and put it there," Kerry announces proudly.

"As well as the birthplace of the author of *McGuffey's Eclectic Reader*," adds Bill, pouring himself a second glass of Canadian whiskey. "From which your parents and I were taught to read." He closes his eyes, quotes—"*A fat hen. A big rat. The rat runs from the box. Can the hen run?*"

"What was the rat doing in the box?"

"I shudder to think."

More roast beef sandwiches in a sack, again departing in the dark the next morning.

"The adventure continues," announces Kerry, a very early reader. She has become devoted to the *Oz* books, which go back to the last century and offer a new story each year.

It is a cold, windy, rainy mess of a day.

Norma finds herself rigid in the driver's seat, dealing with the brake, the clutch, and the throttle as they crawl along through the downpour, Kerry helpfully cranking the single windshield wiper and swiping the fog off the inside of the glass with a handkerchief every few minutes. It feels like they have entered a long, dangerous tunnel, the road mostly straight but constantly disappearing from view. Other vehicles not only splash past them, but many drivers blat their horns as they do.

"We only need to get there," Kerry reassures her.

Then there are so many buildings and so many cars, and people without umbrellas darting across in front of them and Norma has Kerry call out the names of the streets if she can see them through the rain on the windows. She thinks they are headed right for the LaSalle Hotel at Woodward and Adelaide when a policeman in a slicker waves them aside for a detour. She slows as she passes him and has Kerry crank down the side window.

"It's the parade, lady," he shouts in at them. "Keep moving!"

And then they are truly lost, nobody on the sidewalks to ask directions from, and it isn't long before Norma notices that the people huddled in the doorways looking out at the downpour are all colored.

"Look, Mom," says Kerry.

"It's not polite to stare."

"I'm not *star*ing. And if I was they can't see in here."

As far as Norma can tell, her daughter has only seen colored faces in *The Story of Little Black Sambo*, set in India, but the drawings make the characters blacker than anybody she's ever witnessed in her few visits to the big city. They spoke of the book recently, Norma having to explain that there were no tigers and no ghee to make pancakes with in Brazil.

Though she's not so sure about the tigers—

Finally a man, a colored man, steps up while they are at a crossroads wondering which way to turn, and before she can warn her not to, Kerry has cranked her window down again.

"Where you trying to get to?"

"Uhm—the LaSalle Hotel?"

The man nods, raindrops bouncing off that tight-curled hair they have, Kerry clearly fascinated, and he instructs them on which way to go, though cautioning it may not be clear.

"President Hoover is speaking out front of City Hall," he says, "and then it's a parade."

"A parade for ducks," says Kerry, and the man laughs and Norma thanks him politely before he runs back from the curb to shelter.

They soon come to another blockade of people stuck in their automobiles, and when Norma climbs out into the rain she can see streetcars stopped across the opening of the street with dozens of people who have climbed on top of them to watch what, from the music and the shouting, must be the parade going past. Other cars pile up behind them so there is no backing out and it's at least an hour sitting there, the motor off but Kerry still working the windshield blade now and then so they can see the car stuck in front of them.

"The music sounds *wet*," she announces. Sometimes the things she says frighten Norma a bit, in her experience too much intelligence never good news for a girl. The nuns at school, in fact, put a premium on decorum and silence and always cautioned Norma and her sisters "not to get any big ideas."

Finally the parade is past and policemen come to move the barriers and sort out the streetcars and automobile traffic. They are only a few blocks from the hotel and Norma manages to find a parking space just across the street. They have only one suitcase each, Kerry's a little cardboard thing with a picture of a horse on it, and manage not to get too soaked rushing into the lobby. There are men bringing in some kind of equipment there, and Kerry thinks she recognizes somebody's voice, and, innocent country girl that she is, is not shy about blurting it out.

"You're Jerry Buckley!"

The young man just smiles.

"We hear you on the radio all the time."

Probably feeling guilty about ditching them in Pine Camp, Jim bought a beautiful 6-tube Model 14 Zenith plug-in radio before he left, and it gets amazing reception.

"I'm honored to hear that."

"What were you doing out in the rain?"

"Recording the president's speech. We usually broadcast from a room on the top floor here."

Jerry Buckley is shorter but even better-looking than Norma would have thought from his voice, and shows a lot of teeth when he smiles.

"We're on an adventure," Kerry tells him. "I've never been to Detroit before."

"Ah—the Paris of the West."

Norma is relieved that Kerry doesn't ask Buckley what Paris is. He has a strong, sympathetic voice on the radio and she likes a lot of what he says about taking care of old people and people without jobs, but isn't sure she cares to be referred to as one of 'the common herd'.

"I see more people in this room," says Kerry, scanning the crowded lobby, "than there are in the whole town where I live."

"And but for a few politicians, whom I shall not point out," says the radio star, "they are all well worth meeting."

Their room is comfortable and well-heated, nothing extravagant, and after Kerry finishes with her bed-bouncing they both take a nap, too exhausted from the drive to go search for lunch. Norma has so rarely spent the night in a rented room. There was her honeymoon cabin with Jim at the lake resort, no traffic noise outside, pretending to be a virgin-

-and there was her first night in Battle Creek, pregnant and miserable.

It is five o'clock when the desk calls to wake them, a shock to remember the telephone in the room, and a glance out the window reveals that the rain has abated. It is not a long walk to the massive Fox Theater building, and they stroll around its periphery looking into the shop and restaurant windows till Kerry makes a choice.

"Is sea food different than lake food?"

Assured that this is the case, they settle in behind some clam chowder, which Kerry, whose palate never ceases to amaze her mother, dumps a shocking amount of pepper onto.

"You'll ruin the taste."

"I like it spicy."

Kerry finishes the entire bowl and is delighted when Baked Alaska can be produced before the show starts at the Fox.

The multiple, gleaming brass doors and uniformed greeters do not prepare Norma for the lobby—it goes up and up, six stories in all, decorated with lions, butterflies, peacocks—and she hears Kerry's gasp as she takes it in. They purchase their tickets, fifty cents for Norma and fifteen for Kerry, immediately handing them to another uniformed young man to tear, Kerry saving both the stubs, then wait in a line at one of the refreshment counters, buying a large cardboard box of popped corn to share, and, as Kerry wheedled a Coca Cola at dinner, asking for two cups of cold water to go with it.

The main auditorium is another revelation, thousands of seats in three tiers, with elaborate pillars and colorfully-lit decorations—Tibetan? Persian? Indian? Chinese?—along the side walls, and somehow *clouds* moving peacefully across the ceiling. They pass between a pair of plaster lions with jeweled eyes to ascend the grand staircase, entering the mezzanine level and settling near the front. They are early enough—seats only a quarter full—to afford them time to study their surroundings. The main floor is fronted by the orchestra pit, a squadron of well-dressed musicians warming up their instruments, and if Norma and Kerry turn around, they can wonder at the enormous Moller organ above the balcony.

The sizable orchestra—Kerry counts them and reports thirty members—begins to play before all the audience is seated. Songs popular on the radio like *Blue Skies, My Blue Heaven*, and *My Baby Just Cares for Me* as well as one of those long ones where all the horns and even the drummer seem to take a solo. They don't have a vocalist, something of a disappointment to Norma. She steals a look at Kerry, who is beaming, and feels like the hardships of the road have been worth it. Once a month when the Ford movies arrive in Pine Camp, Agnes Waller accompanies the dramatic silent films on an almost-tuned piano, but she knows very little secular music and is of little use except for wedding and funeral scenes. Beside the Ford short subjects, there is usually something with Kerry's favorite, Mary Pickford, who persists in portraying adolescent girls though she is clearly twenty-five if she's a day. But this, this *palace*, this 'showcase of the world' as they bill themselves, must be overwhelming for a little girl from the deep woods.

Which is what Norma has always considered herself.

The advertised feature is not, thinks Norma, the kind of thing she'd ordinarily pay money to see, but it at least does not list that Lupe Velez in the cast. Señorita Velez appears regularly in Norma's worst fantasies, cavorting with her husband Jim in steamy Brazil, wearing very little and looking far too *ripe*. It is a ridiculous obsession, she knows, but once the actress's come-hither smile was planted in her imagination-

Another gasp from her daughter when the orchestra ceases playing and sinks into the pit, the house lights dimming and the curtain, a vast wall of red velvet, spreading open to reveal a white sand beach dotted with orange beach umbrellas tilted forward so they make perfect circles facing the audience, all under a massive azure sky with a sparkling golden sun suspended in front of it. In the program this is listed as *Fanchon and Marco's Beach 'Idea',* an idea that Norma tries to grasp as the umbrellas tip back and the two-dozen Sunkist Beauties beneath, wearing the scantiest of bathing costumes, spring into action.

There are no pauses, no introductions, as the dancing girls strut and wiggle into various geometric patterns, climb onto lifeguard towers that are swiftly wheeled in and out, and dive into tanks of water that seem to appear from nowhere, while the Jazzmonic Rhythm Kings pound out their music from the pit, the girls seamlessly yielding the stage to an adorable, tricycle-riding bear, then a pair of comics who are supposed to be an Irishman and a German and might be funny if you could understand their accents, then a pair of extremely athletic song-and-tap performers in Sambo makeup.

"What's that on their faces?" asks Kerry.

"I think they still use burnt cork—"

"But why?"

"Do you remember those colored people we saw on the street?"

"Yes."

"It's to make them look like colored people while they sing and dance."

Kerry, pondering this answer, watches the men do splits and leapfrog one over the other, all the while singing and waving their straw boaters. Finally she whispers back to her mother.

"Why don't they just get colored people who can sing and dance?"

A question thankfully avoided when the blue-sky backdrop is pushed out into three terraces, with Sunkist beauties, now in white bathers with musical notes printed on them, somehow lying on their bellies singing and stroking while some kind of conveyor belt moves them right-to-left or left-to-right, an illusion that warrants a round of applause from the audience. Norma follows one girl with bright red hair curling out from under her bathing cap as she 'swims' into the wings, then reappears on a higher terrace stroking in the opposite direction.

"I've never seen anything like this," Kerry tells her, more puzzled than excited.

The swimming routine somehow turns into a finale with all the girls and the comics and the blackface dancers in a long line stepping and kicking while palm trees rise from the ground around them and the suspended sun bounces in time with the music. There is applause when it seems to be over and then the curtain closes and the lights come up halfway.

Norma is exhausted already.

"Some of those girls weren't much older than me," says Kerry, exaggerating her age by a decade.

"You want to join the company?"

You can still tease her without causing a snit, which is something to say for living so far from the bright lights.

"No. I'd rather *real*ly go swimming."

The lights go down full and again the curtain parts majestically, this time to display the enormous white screen, rising higher than even the Fanchon and Marco sun.

Kerry, even in her mezzanine seat, has to tilt her head to see the top of it.

At the Pine Camp center it is a little thing you pull down, the same size as the map of the United States that Mrs. Cummings uses for Geography and Civics, and the film projector is making a racket right behind you in the room. This is a white space you could walk into, that you could get lost in-

The cartoon, with sound, is called *Hot Dog* and starts with what looks kind of like a dog happily driving an open coupe, tipping his hat whenever he passes a girl who you figure is pretty even though you can only see their legs, while the music is playing *I Want to Sing Like the Birdies*. Then one of the girls turns and pushes her head forward and she's so hideously ugly the coupe digs a hole in the street with its tires and tunnels them away in the other direction. A policeman on a skinny horse sees this and the horse turns and says "C'mon, give him the works" in a croaky voice and they start galloping after the coupe.

The dog driver now pulls up alongside a young woman dog walking along in a very small dress as the music starts to play *Pop Goes the Weasel* and he whistles and waves at her, then a seat extends out on something like what Grampa Rogan uses to grab things off the high shelf and snatches the girl into the coupe, where the dog driver puts his arm around her. He makes kissy faces and she shakes her head no and then the flower on her hat turns into an arm with a big muscle and a fist which pounds him on the top of his dog head so hard it flattens like a pancake. But heads always pop back into shape in cartoons, and now the policeman and the horse are galloping after them to the music of *The Farmer in the Dell.*

The dog driver and the girl start to wrestle as he tries to smooch and she resists, till you see in a kind of knothole view that her shoes turn into roller skates so she can jump out and gracefully skate away while the dog dives out and swims along on the pavement after her, getting to his feet just as the policeman and horse pop their heads out from an alley and both say “Aha!”

The dog is marched into a noisy, crowded courtroom, where he and the policeman both salute the old judge who sits up high on a podium between two glass balls on little posts and wears those glasses without stems that just balance on your nose. The judge leans forward to say “Weeeeeeell?” and you can see from behind the podium that he’s only wearing his unders instead of pants.

The dog says “Well, your Honor, y’see, it was this way” and somehow produces a banjo on which he plays a jazzy kind of song Kerry has heard on the radio but doesn’t know the name of, half-happy, half-sad, and right away all the men in the jury box are bouncing along with it and sticking their long tongues out, then lifting up the jury-box so you can see all their feet dancing.

Even the judge starts dancing then, and we see behind that a Chinese man is ironing his pants. A painting on the wall of a blindfolded woman with a sword in one hand and balance scales like at the butcher’s in the other comes to life and raises her blindfold to get a peek at the dog, then starts to dance till her skirt falls down to show her knickers.

The dog stretches his body up to play right under the judge’s face, black tears dropping from his eyes, and when he wipes one away his hand comes out of the glove but the glove keeps strumming the banjo.

Then he’s singing about “Sweet Mama” and then just nonsense sounds, *doo-ey a doo doo e-ya doodleedoo-* which the man taking notes of the trial clicks out on his typewriter, pulling his tongue out long and strumming it for a bit.

Finally the dog jumps down and mounts the banjo like it is a circus unicycle and tips his hat and sings "That's all!" and then cycles out through the swinging doors and away into the distance.

It is the funniest thing Kerry has ever seen, but leaves her wondering—do courtrooms really have swinging doors like the saloons in the cowboy movies?

Then comes the regular moving picture with real people, only they act like they're in a cartoon. It's called *Cocoanuts* and takes place at a hotel in Florida. Kerry knows that Florida is hot and has palm trees just like Brazil, but the movie is so pretend that you can't tell if they really went there. It stars three funny men, one who is an Italian with a hat like an organ grinder and another that can't talk but beeps a horn and is really crazy and the one in charge has black paint on his lip instead of a real mustache and walks funny and is a wiseacre though nobody seems to catch on that he's insulting them. There is a pretty girl who has a good-looking boyfriend and they sing some sappy songs and the Italian plays piano in a funny way and the crazy one plays the harp which almost puts Kerry asleep.

It's been a long day.

Finally everything turns out okay for the people you're supposed to like, even for the big older lady with a giant bosom and a funny voice who is what Kerry thinks Mrs. Henry Ford must look like at one of her society parties.

The lights come up halfway then and the orchestra is playing again and there might be another movie but Mom says it's time to go.

It isn't raining for the walk back to the hotel, the streets well-lit, which you would expect with Mr. Ford and Mr. Edison being such good friends. Norma holds Kerry's hand for the crosswalks and for the pleasure of it, wondering how old her daughter will be when she won't want to cuddle anymore. The movie was funny and Kerry laughed a lot though she certainly couldn't have understood all that was going on, those crazy brothers changing the direction of the conversation so rapidly, and Norma was a little disappointed in the young girl. Maybe more jealous than disappointed—the soubrette's forced vibrato pulled all real emotion out of her songs, and

Norma is as least as pretty. But, of course, the one time, before Maxine, that she hinted to her mother that she might want to try the stage, she was informed that only harlots and morphine addicts entered that wicked world, and that her voice might be outstanding in Copper Harbor, but that obviously wasn't saying much.

And the harlot part turned out to be prophecy.

Back in the room Kerry drops off right away, but Norma finds that her head is too busy to let her sleep. Of all things it is the banjo song from the rather tasteless cartoon that haunts her, the verses coming to her as she rolls from side to side, sung with a Latin accent by Lupe Velez-

St. Louie woman
With her diamond rings
She pull my man around
By her apron strings—

In the morning, Madge, her cousin George's wife, picks them up to shop at the J. L. Hudson department store. Though the weather is clear and it isn't a long walk from the LaSalle, Madge insists on driving them in her Chevrolet Capitol, yellow with black fenders and roof, scandalously luxurious after their ordeal in the old T. It has balloon tires, you adjust your speed with a gas pedal instead of pushing and pulling a throttle by hand, and it comes with a center-mounted rearview mirror in which she can see Kerry in the back seat, avidly looking out at the sights while probably feeling as traitorous as Norma does to be rolling in something other than a Ford.

"George's supervisor at the Exchange has a *radio* in his LaSalle," Madge tells them, "but I think that should be illegal. How can you drive while you're listening to music?"

Madge, for instance, has a good deal of trouble talking and parking the car at the same time, her running commentary on the wonders of downtown Detroit not interrupted by two wheels climbing onto the sidewalk for a moment, then jolting back to the street.

"Last year at this time the piles of snow were *enormous*. But I'm sure it's nothing like you see up there near the border."

Norma chooses not to remind Madge that Detroit is actually *at* the border, a narrow river separating it from Canada. Instead she is awed by the massive block of department store looming above them—twenty-five floors with a mezzanine and four basement levels according to Kerry, who has studied for the trip.

"And it's the same Hudson as the automobile," Kerry says as they climb out of the Capitol. "But they don't make them in this building."

Once past the display windows under the marquis, the big store is as jaw-droppingly grand as the Fox Theater. A bank of gleaming elevators that goes on and on greets them, along with a throng, though it is a weekday morning, of eager shoppers, all who seem to know just what they want and where to get it.

"I have to admit that George has me on a terribly short leash this week," says Madge. "These bizarre fluctuations in the New York market."

"Is he worried?"

"Concerned, I would say, but you know George. After all, he *is* looking after our money."

Norma's cousin George works at the Detroit Stock Exchange, mostly trading local companies, in which he's convinced Norma to invest much of the family's savings. Jim always jokes that if it's not feet-and-inches he's hopeless with numbers, leaving Norma in charge of the bankbook, so when George explained how money in a simple bank account would *keep* but never really *grow*-

"Where do you wish to begin?" Madge asks them.

"There are over seven hundred fitting rooms in the building," Kerry informs them. "It's a world record."

"She always needs clothes. Growing girl—"

"Our Hudson Budget Store is in the first basement," says a nearby elevator operator, a smooth-faced young man dressed like one of the bellhops at the LaSalle. "Then on this floor, Woodward Avenue side, there are blouses, belts, sweaters—" He cocks his head to evaluate Kerry. "Then on the fourth floor we have Girls seven to fourteen and Little Miss Hudson."

The initial shopping is fun, Madge not so much offering her opinion as instructing them on What One Must Have while mentioning the specialty shops also downtown that carry the same items but in superior quality and taste. Not that she has any problem with Hudson's.

"It's such a *com*fortable place," she observes, looking around at the milling shoppers. "One sees people of every level here."

The purchase of a new chemise, some woolen stockings, a lovely green drop waist slip-on dress of Irish linen, and a pair of black Mary Janes for special occasions takes all of the morning, Kerry very particular about her clothes and adamantly opposed to anything too fussy—none of the flounces and furbelows that Madge coos over winning her approval. They ride one of the posh elevators—brass, gleaming wood veneer, a rosy pink light shining down on them—to the thirteenth floor where most of the restaurants are located.

Their table has a view of the city below, traffic never ceasing to flow, tiny pedestrians hurrying along in the cold, and Madge has them order the Hudson specialties, something called the Maurice salad and the Canadian cheese soup. The former has strips of ham, Swiss cheese, and turkey laid over iceberg lettuce, and includes sweet pickles, which Kerry loves, while the soup is a hot, cheddary sludge with plenty of potatoes and bits of crispy bacon that makes Norma want to ride the escalator down to the furnishings level and crawl into one of the display beds.

But there are social obligations to be met.

Kerry, full of butterscotch pudding, mopes a bit in the automobile, heartbroken that their last afternoon here will be spent at the Exchange instead of touring the Rouge complex, but she knows quite enough about automobile manufacturing and very little about finance.

The Penobscot building is on West Congress, five stories of unpolished granite giving way to ashlar blocks with terra cotta trimmings on the upper floors, a structure, thinks Norma, that neither hurricane nor flood could budge an inch. Solid. Dependable-

-and an utter madhouse within. It takes several minutes before they can locate George on the floor, riffling ticker tape through his hands like a demon tailor about to measure a whale. Other men—for it is only men—shout and wave fingers in the air in a manner that indicates—not excitement exactly, but—desperation? Kerry is fascinated by the chattering stock ticker machines, twisted nests of paper kicked about the floor before an old colored man with a push broom can sweep them aside, and has to be dragged by the hand through the gesticulating brokers, Madge plowing ahead like an icebreaker. George, engrossed in the codes on the thin strip of paper as it spits out, does not notice them.

"George!" calls Madge, then shouts even louder, "*George! We're here!*"

He looks up at them with no recognition at first, then a demented smile creases his face.

"Ah," he says. "Just in time to board the *Titanic*."

"The *Titanic* sank," Kerry reminds them.

"As has the market—to the bottom of the *sea*."

Madge seems to pale. "You always say these things sink and rise, sink and rise again—"

"So do drowning men, until they rise no more." George transfers the tape, still spewing out, into the shaking hands of a trader with a gray mustache wearing a bowler hat. Norma points to the coils of paper littering the floor.

"That's the news from New York, isn't it? What's being bought and sold—"

"*Sold*, today. Nothing's being bought."

"But that doesn't mean that in Detroit—"

The stocks George has had her buy are all local—Ex-Cell-O Aircraft and Tool, Vernor's, Eureka Vacuum, Federal Screw, even some Packard-

"It's *gone*, all of it, down so low it isn't worth selling, even if you could find a fool to buy it. Do you still have money in the bank?"

Norma feels a sinking feeling in her stomach, like riding down in one of the express elevators at the Hudson. "Yes, some—"

"What bank?"

"The First National in Iron River?"

"I would get back there as soon as you can," says Norma's cousin George, "and withdraw every cent of it."

Kerry is staring at something. The older trader with the gray mustache is weeping.

• • •

You have to run it full tilt or it doesn't cut.

It is a jerry-built set-up, with a decent, level carriage, improvised pulleys and the only blade not still lying in the hold of the big ship up in Santorém. A blade with teeth that have to be filed far too often. The three locals Jim has trained, who at his insistence answer to Pico, Rico and Tico, have the basics down, Pico feeding, Rico adjusting the log between cuts with a cant hook, Tico dealing with the slabs and the cut boards as they come off. It has been hot, frustrating work, Jim learning to recognize the familiar-looking but incredibly dense woods—*ipe*, *garapa*, *cumuru*, *jatoba*—that seem impervious to milling. The bole in the carriage now, called *baraúna* by his boys, is new to Jim, but he didn't like the heft of it once they'd stripped the bark off. He has them set the log to skim off a very thin slab, listening to the whine as he helps Pico guide the log forward—not a happy blade, but not desperate. He sets the next cut for an inch-thick plank and they begin to push.

At three feet in there is a scream that could wake the dead and the blade seizes, Jim rushing to kill the motor before anything snaps or burns out.

The sound of birds, the sound of axes in the far distance, felling more trees to make his life miserable. And then the clanging-

Because a steam engine capable of generating enough oomph to power a Detroit factory whistle has not yet been delivered, a system of hanging metal sheets has been has instituted, to be beaten at starting, lunch, and quitting time, that time being the same as in Detroit, by order of the Ford

Motor Company. The clearing has expanded enough that a relay signal must be beaten both upriver and inland to reach all the workers. Jim checks his watch—it is neither starting, lunch, or quitting time, either here or in Detroit, so there must be some emergency at the dock. Blakely left them two days ago, saying only that he'd been called back by the Company, and to "carry on."

The cut shows no diving—the wood is just too damn hard. Jim uses his repertoire of hand gestures to tell the boys to stay at the mill, free the blade however they can, pull it off the setup and get busy straightening and filing the teeth. They nod and smile, always happy for an interruption in the work, and Jim starts for the dock.

He's been able to make the dock sturdier, driving in piles made from wood the boys say will last for forty years immersed in water, and replacing the decking with *garapa*. There is already a crowd gathered, half of them from the little shanty town that has grown up at the edge of the cleared land, shifting back gradually as more of the forest is cut down, all of them looking upriver and talking excitedly.

It is the *Lake Ormoc*, finally with enough draft to reach Fordlandia.

As the first of the huge crates is being clumsily transferred, a tall, frowning Swede calls to Jim from the deck.

"Who is in charge here?"

Jim has to think about that.

"I'm not sure. Blakely left just—"

"Mr. Blakely has been relieved of his responsibilities," states the captain.

"Oh." Jim looks around. Pringle is coming down the path from the mess building, while the old confederate, Riker, is watching with the locals at the river's edge-

"Well, you know how it is with Ford—there's not really titles. Everybody kind of does what they're best at."

Captain Olafson's frown deepens as he looks out over the cleared land, sloping up and over a hill, less than a thousand knee-high sticks poking up in carefully-spaced rows.

"This is the planting?"

"Yes, so far. The *clear*ing is going well now, we've been pulling stumps when we can get the tractors going, we're leveling ground, but there's no seed available, really—"

"I have been told there were men sent to buy this seed. Some time ago, yes?"

"They—they haven't been heard from. Well, actually, their cook, a Negro, came back here a few weeks after they left, claiming to have been abandoned by them on an island in the river—"

"You are?"

"Jim Rogan. I run the sawmill—"

"You will find them."

"How would I—?"

"You will go to where they were sent. If you do not find them, you will buy seed."

Jim supposes a captain of a ship outranks the head sawyer, and since Blakely is gone-

"I'll need somebody who speaks Portuguese—"

"Of course. And a vessel adequate to survive the journey. The water is high now. Where are the other buildings?"

There is still only the mess hall, the two barracks for the men who don't sleep over in the shanty town, and the few little cabins Jim has been able to throw together for the Americans, replacing the sweatbox he and Pringle first had to sleep in while Blakely lounged at his rented *fazenda*.

"You're looking at most of them. We've had some difficulty—I'm assuming the whole sawmill assembly is aboard?"

"Of course—"

Jim ordered a dozen blades sent down, but none are any tougher than what they've already been using.

"I think Dearborn may have to come up with a new kind of *steel*."

• • •

Father always likes to have somebody working in the background. And since Liebold hasn't invited the radio people, this can be out where the ore cars rumble in from the dock, the big stacks sticking up behind them, the cold creating a sharp edge to the smoke billowing in the wind. When it is good and hot, Father prefers to stride along as he talks, enjoying the sound of the reporters, especially the fat ones, struggling to catch their breath. Father doesn't like fat people. He is terrific with little Hank, of course, but asks "What are you feeding him?" at least once a week.

Father gets right to the point as usual.

"I been hearing a lot of loose talk about the Company—how we're up against the ropes due to this stock market swindle they're running in New York, how we're struggling to keep our noses above water—and I'd just like to say we're struggling so bad that I've decided to raise the base wage for our fellas in production to seven dollars a day."

The predictable babble of excited questions follows, and it's clear Father is enjoying himself. He dropped this particular bomb at lunch a few days ago and let Sorenson turn red and start throwing numbers around, Father just shaking his head slightly through it all and finally saying "Seven it is. You make the rest of it work."

He does not tell the reporters that in the next month or two nearly a quarter of the workforce will be let go, and those kept on may find themselves making that seven dollars for only two or three days a week of labor.

People are not buying new cars.

Father will squeeze the dealers again, and pulling back on workdays will slow the bleeding—they've been quietly outsourcing some parts of the operation, especially the body work, to other firms in the area, firms that don't pay anything near seven a day. But for the moment he is the People's Tycoon again, bucking the official wisdom of auto-makers and money-manipulators all over the country.

"Sure, it'll bounce back pretty soon, these things always do, the way they got it fixed. But I hope it's not before folks have learned their lesson. They got used to the easy money, gambling on numbers up on a tote board instead of *work*ing for their pay. That won't do it in the long run. Got so your average man won't really do a day's work unless he's caught and can't get out of it."

Edsel sees the one from the *Free Press*—Smith? leaning in for the kill.

"So you think this panic is *good* for us all?" he asks.

"Does it look like *I'm* in a panic?" says Father, and even Edsel has to laugh.

• • •

The old man is making *golabki*.

The smell of boiling cabbage always makes Kaz miss his *matka*, who cooked them on the stove every Saturday for the big family meal, which also meant mashed potatoes and *kolacz* with plum jam filling. Most days it was soup and bread, but Saturdays and Sundays there were family meals, usually at the house of his uncle Stanislas who was the first to come over from Poland and worked in a butcher shop in Hamtramck.

The old man has an incredible head of hair, white now, starting at a point low in the center of his forehead and standing almost straight up on its own. As he cooks he hums Paul Whiteman's *Whispering*, which has become his favorite radio song. He seems in a very good mood for a man who has recently lost his job.

"You know, Pop," Kaz opens, his father never a man to welcome help, "I got way too much coal over at the house right now. I could bring some over—"

"I got coal," says the old man.

"This stock market deal—"

"It serve them right."

The old man turns the burner off, carefully brings the pot to the sink and flips it, boiled head of cabbage plopping with a cloud of steam into the colander set there. It is cold in the kitchen, but no colder than they kept it when Kaz was a boy.

"You let strangers gamble you money, what you think hoppen?"

"Which bank have you got yours in now, Pop?"

"I got money rolled in sock, hide it where I show you later. I die, you know where you find him."

"You keep it in the *house*?"

The old man runs cold water over the cabbage. He is not a patient cook.

"Banks are run by Jew. You let Jew near your money, you *lose* it, like Father Coughlin always is saying."

The old man has been listening to the broadcast since the Radio Priest started on WJR, calling it "better than newspaper." He has the set on whenever Kaz comes by after work, usually tuned to the *Philco Hour* on the Blue Network, or a new show called *Amos 'n' Andy*.

"J. P. Morgan wasn't a Jew, Pop."

"Is what they want you to think."

Kaz has almost two hundred dollars in the Guardian Bank, and Molly, whose people have been here since before the Civil War, says it would be cowardly to pull it out because of a panic in New York.

The old man starts to separate the cabbage leaves and lay them out on a plate.

"They get together, fiddle with nombers. Mr. Ford writes of this in noosepepper."

"He apologized for that."

"Is what they want you to think."

The old man has worked for Ford since Highland Park was new, just short of twenty years helping to fill the roads with Model Ts, and remains fervently loyal despite the fact that at the end of the shift one day his foreman told him, without apology, explanation, or the courtesy of eye contact, "Go collect your time and hand in your ID badge."

Kaz sits in his old chair at the table that always needs a piece of folded cardboard under one leg to keep it from wobbling, tall enough now that his knees touch the underside. Growing up, he rarely saw the old man except at this table.

"Do you know what you're going to do now?"

The old man begins to roll *kasza* and ground meat mix in the wilted cabbage leaves, pondering this.

"Other places are making cars."

"None of them pay like Ford."

The old man shrugs. "*Some*thing is better than empty hand."

At the beginning Pop was fitting engine blocks into chassis, wielding a wrench while sidestepping alongside the line, then on to axle assembly and a half-dozen other jobs, often the man chosen to inaugurate a new procedure, before the move to the Rouge. At the Rouge they'd had him mounting tires, which requires a lot of bending-

"They shouldn't be letting the veteran workers go."

"Mr. Ford has *plan*. I am not part of it."

When Kaz was growing up the Ford people were in the house every other week, the Sociological Department brains—for they were mostly college graduates—telling his mother what and how to cook and checking on school attendance and brushing teeth and table manners and having them read the *Rules for Living* pamphlet and insisting that the old man, who at that time spoke little English and could not read, put his meager savings in a bank that they had already approved of. Most nights after his shift he was expected at their English school, coming home to try his new phrases—*Albert watches the crows* or *See the yellow dog run*—on Kaz and his brother Leon. It was embarrassing at first, but then their *makta* explained *they* were working for Ford too, the whole family, and that the pay—two-and-a-half dollars a day at first and then an amazing five—had to be earned by all. And each week the old man grew a little smarter, no longer just an ignorant *Polak* who muttered at them in a language they devalued and barely understood, but a man with feelings and opinions he could share with them.

On the day of his graduation from the English school there was a ceremony, family members invited to sit in bleachers and applaud as their breadwinners, now considered by the government to have filed their 'first papers' and to have renounced the country of their birth, received a diploma while a band played stirring music. When "Prokop Pilsudski" was called out the old man appeared wearing the striped pants, Cossack boots, embroidered red vest and four-cornered black *krakuska* hat he'd borrowed from his friend Jacek, graduated the previous year, who in turn had bought it from Gombrowicz the baker who'd had it all made for him to march in a Kościuszko Day parade. Pop crossed the boards to the band's shaky *mazurka*, received his scroll, then quickly descended steps into a giant 'melting pot' at the front of the stage, reappearing moments later dressed in suit jacket, high collar, and tie, acknowledging the applause by waving the little American flag in his hand. From that day on he'd correct anyone calling themselves 'Polish-American' with his instructor's admonition—

"That hyphen, she is a *mi*nus sign."

Having then qualified for his 'profit participation' of an extra two-fifty a day, the old man's English was good enough to smugly correct his wife's attempts to speak it, as well as understand that 'citizenship' was not the ocean liner Mr. Ford chartered to sail to Europe and call off the Great War. He now claimed that Poland "was not even a country," while cursing Russia, Germany, and Austria for appropriating chunks of it. And though the Sociological Department was eventually disbanded, he still kept his marriage license framed on the wall and his *wódka* hidden beneath the coal chute in the cellar.

The old man has a sauce he's made from canned tomatoes already warming in a skillet, and he lays the cabbage rolls carefully in this and turns up the flame. Kaz's *matka* used to bake them in the oven, but the old man lacks the patience for this.

"I maybe go to Dodge Main in Hamtramck, ask to work there."

"The Victory Six—"

The old man shrugs, gives the skillet a shake. "Is automobile—I can make."

Kaz has a friend, Grblunis, a Lithuanian kid he knew in high school, who does something with a rivet gun at Dodge. Worse pay, but a more relaxed shop floor according to him, though you can still get called out for 'stealing time' if you stop to scratch your nuts. Kaz can't tell yet whether the old man being let go was just an individual thing or if the Company is reacting to this stock market deal and expecting sales to plummet. Only last winter Mr. Ford announced to the world that he was set to hire thirty-thousand new workers. Kaz's little brother Leon was one of the multitude who showed up in the freezing cold the night before to get in line. It turned into a riot—some men allowed in, others turned away with no explanation, Harry Bennett's Service Department thugs turning a fire hose on the ones who protested and wouldn't go away. Leon mentioned both Kaz and the old man during his very short interview, but wasn't given a job. Bud Novak says it was only a show, a chance for the Company to let a bunch of workers go for a few weeks, putting a scare into them, then hire them back at beginner's wages.

But Bud is always kicking about something.

And Kaz is secretly relieved that his brother, short of temper and loose of tongue since birth, was not hired at the Rouge.

Kaz gets up to grab plates, forks and knives, parked where they always were, and lays them out. Setting the table was his responsibility, guided on a visit by a young Sociological who sighed a lot and insisted a full set of utensils be displayed even if they were only having soup.

"You know, Pop," he ventures again, "if you need anything—"

"You take care of you own family," the old man interrupts, "I am getting by without problem."

On Kaz's sixteenth birthday, the old man brought him to see his foreman, who sent him to see the Little Man in the basement of the Engineering Building. Harry Bennett asked him about his short career playing football at Highland Park High School before putting him on the line as a trainee, starting after lunch.

On Edsel Ford's twenty-first birthday a few years earlier, his father Henry gave him a million dollars' worth of gold bullion. Prokop Pilsudski, who as a young man lived under the Czar, is still pleased by this.

"If you are king, you let world know who is *prince*."

There is a loud knock at the door.

The old man's brother Stanislaus died last year, Leon is in Chicago making tractors—nobody just drops by here on a miserable winter night. The old man turns the flame off and wipes his hands on a dishtowel as he heads for the door, grinning-

"Was mis*take*. I knew this. They have come to give me back badge."

The man at the door, face mostly hidden by a woolen muffler, is canvassing for the upcoming election. The old man, trying to hide his disappointment, asks him in.

"I'm a booster for Bowles," says the visitor.

Kaz, an irregular but opinionated voter, has seen the campaign posters in the city. "The guy who always runs—"

"He beat Lodge in the primary this year. Bowles sees the big picture."

"Which is?"

"Police reform. Do you know how much illegal liquor comes across the river every night?"

"As much as the people can drink."

Michigan went dry even before the Volstead Act turned the nation's taps off, to no one's benefit, in Kaz's mind, except for the bootleggers and the corrupt cops they pay off.

"You're anti-Prohibition?"

Kaz shrugs. You never know when some Service Department spy will be lurking in a speakeasy, taking names, so he drinks, when he does, at the house of his buddy Jake, who's a barge pilot and always has a bottle or two.

"They all say 'police reform,'" he tells the canvasser. "That and extending the streetcar lines."

"The other thing Bowles guarantees," says the man, looking over his shoulder toward the door and lowering his voice as if someone might be eavesdropping, "is to keep the jigs in line."

Now Kaz remembers—this is the candidate of the outfit who wear the pointy-headed robes, who are down on Catholics nearly as much as they are on the colored.

"That's good," says the old man, still moping because the knock wasn't Henry Ford coming to apologize. "Somebody gotta do it."

"Pop, when you ever have trouble with colored people?"

"They shoot you," he says. "Right out from their window."

There was a big case a few years back, a Negro doctor named Sweet who moved into a white neighborhood, and when a mob of unhappy neighbors started throwing rocks through his windows he retaliated, with the help of friends and family, by firing into the crowd and killing at least one of them. Headlines, court cases, Clarence Darrow over from Chicago to help defend the doctor from murder charges. Kaz remembers it dragging on and eventually being thrown out of court.

"What would you do if a bunch of colored come and started throwing rocks through *your* window?"

"I call the cops."

"You don't have a telephone, Pop."

"I don't have rifle neither."

"My man gets to be mayor," promises the canvasser, "we'll have some laws in Detroit about who can move in where, just like they do in Dearborn."

"You're *in* Dearborn."

The man looks stricken, nose red and running from the cold, the snow on his brogans melting on the floor. "You're kidding me."

"One block across the line. They don't hand you people a map?"

The canvasser pulls out a folded piece of paper, unfolds and stares at it.

"Pop votes in Dearborn. When he votes."

"Son of a gun."

Kaz votes, when he votes, in Hamtramck, but doesn't want to get into that with this character. But before he can move to show him the door, the man's head pops up like a hunting dog in a deer thicket.

"Say," says the Boomer for Bowles, "is that *golabki* I smell?"

• • •

There are bananas rotting on the loading dock, broken or bruised in shipping, then just tossed to the side till they draw too many flies or somebody slips on the mess. The Chief, always a stickler for cleanliness in the workplace, would have a conniption. Harry passes some guinea haulers jabbering in their lingo and finds Big Chet LaMare in what passes for an office, a card table and a lot of fruit crates to sit on.

"Harry! Howsa boy?" hollers LaMare over the racket the guys are making. "Unload yourself."

Harry finds a crate with a furniture pad folded on it and sits.

"What brings you to my kingdom?"

Fruit, unlike liquor, goes bad quickly. If your deliveries don't leave the dock or warehouse on time, or get held up between here and there, you're out of business. So a vendor finds it useful to have a partner like Chet LaMare, and partners with muscle tend to become bosses-

"You know how the Chief likes to give fellas who've done a little time a second chance," Harry begins.

"Yeah, I heard that."

"And it's my job to *hire* these fellas, who I mostly employ in the Service Department. But I look at a guy's rap sheet, talk to him a few minutes, what do I really know? Whereas somebody like you, used to own the, what was it—the restaurant—?"

"The Venice. And before that the Workingman's Café—"

"Where, if I'm not wrong, many of these formerly incarcerated gentlemen used to congregate, swap stories, plan extra-legal activities—"

"I'm familiar with a lot of those people, yeah—"

"And therefore would be in the perfect position to advise me of which remorseful former offenders I should hire and which I should avoid."

Harry sees the wheels starting to turn, LaMare figuring if a one-time kickback from a mug for landing him a breezy job is enough, or if an ongoing percentage of the mug's salary will be required-

"I might have an opinion on that," Big Chet allows, then pauses to shout—*"Stai zitto, là fuori!"*

The grape-stompers on the loading dock shut their yaps.

"And then there's your influence on local politics, your ability to reason with people who need to be reasoned with—"

The bootlegger's face goes stony. "Such as who?"

There are only three powers to deal with in the area—the Company, the cops, and the criminals. Ford *owns* the cops in Dearborn, but in Detroit the majority of them seem to be in league with the criminals. There are the tough, crazy Jews in the Purple Gang, the various Italian factions, LaMare's included, and a few Irish and mongrel gangs left, all competing for the illegal liquor bonanza, and then the truly out-of-control outlaws who prey on *them*. Harry knows that gangsters control gambling at the plant, that they are probably behind most of the theft of materials, that Dearborn's finest would be outgunned and outsmarted in any serious confrontation with them-

So why not a strategic alliance?

"Such as who?" he says. "Such as the shitbirds who kidnapped David Cass."

Chet holds his hands up as if to push something away.

"Not my racket. Besides, they already nailed the brains behind that outfit."

"That son-of-a-bitch Laman braced me with a shotgun," says Harry. "Just for asking around."

Chet grins. "Yeah, I heard something like that."

Legs Laman had been set up, collecting the four thousand in cash — down from the initial demand of twenty-five Gs—from the aggrieved father. He ran for it when the cops jumped out, catching some lead in his spine, and is currently hanging on by a thread at Receiving Hospital.

"Now, Inspector Garvin told the papers he thinks they probably let the kid go already, told him to stay out of town—"

LaMare shakes his head. "If they didn't get no money, they didn't let nobody *go*. Back when they were smart and stuck to bootleggers—people who won't go crying to the police—half the kidnappings pinned on the

Purples was actually Legs and his bunch. They made a bundle."

"They know what they're doing?"

"Sure—it's a cinch. You start with a finger man who tails the mark you want to grab, he looks around and chooses the best spot for the pickup. Throw a bag over their head, toss em to the floor of a reliable set of wheels, then off to the *castle*. A good castle they might use a bunch of times—quiet and out of the way or maybe really noisy with traffic, no snoopy neighbors—you ditch the package there with your *keep*ers. They slap a blindfold on the guy, feed him now and then in the first couple days, but give him the silent treatment till the business conversation starts up. Then there's a Voice, the only one the package ever hears, who gives instructions, like if they put him on a phone call to prove he's still ticking."

"And they hold him till—?"

"Till they get the price they think the package is worth. They get a cheap offer, that calls for a little persuasion. Cigarette burns, beatings over the phone, ears cut off, that kind of deal—"

"You think they'll try again with David Cass?"

Big Chet considers this. "Naw, the cops fucked it all up. The Detroit bulls are usually too busy counting their end of the liquor business to pull an ambush like that. Garvin must be running for office."

"Any chance they'll let him go?"

"My guess, they'll get rid of the package where it won't never be *found*. If you don't *habeus* the *corpus*, there's no murder. So, what—you're moonlighting for the father—what's his name—"

"Gershon Cass. He's a friend of the Chief. But I'm more worried about them suddenly going after people who are legit—"

"Like your Mr. Ford or his son."

Harry perks up. "You've heard something?"

Chet LaMare sits back, shrugs his shoulders.

"You snatch somebody and get caught, it don't matter how much money they got or how much you asked for, you face the same amount of time. So why not go for the biggest score? Which in Detroit would probably be that

Edsel, or maybe one of his kids. Make the prize worth the risk."

It's what Harry came here for. He leans closer to Big Chet.

"I'd like you to spread the word that it's *not* worth the risk."

"How's that?"

"Michigan state does not deal out a death penalty," says Harry. "But *I* do."

LaMare raises his eyebrows. "You can back that up?"

"You and I both know plenty people who'd take the job on for a price."

LaMare grins. "Hey, I know a dozen would take out Laman or that fuckin Red O'Riordan for *free*. These characters running around like it's the Wild West, shooting up the town, no respect for what's been built up—who needs em?"

"You'll put it in the wind for me? And add that we're not talking about some quick shot in the back of the head."

Abatiello, an east side bootlegger with ambitions, was apparently not considered worth the two-grand ransom requested from his associates. He was found with multiple burns on his chest and face, both his eyes had been put out-

Big Chet seems dubious. "Why am I suddenly doing favors for Harry Bennett? One has a reputation to maintain—"

"Well, Chet, at the moment we don't have a dealership in Hamtramck—"

LaMare narrows his eyes, smelling money. He is no dumb guinea, had the mayor there in Hamtramck, Jezewski, in his pocket till the Polack got greedy and careless and took a trip to Leavenworth.

"Harry, I gotta tell you, I know more about *steal*ing cars than selling them."

"If you own a dealership, you don't stand out there peddling the tin. You're *man*agement. You're in the fruit business, right—"

"Among other ventures—"

"But you don't push a cart full of bananas down Campau Avenue, do you?"

LaMare sizes him up, suspicious.

"So what do I do to rate a deal like that?"

"You spread the word that it's hands-off on the Fords. You keep me informed."

"For information you could read the papers."

"Look, the slap on the wrist you got for the bootlegging collar? I figure you must be telling tales to *some*body."

Big Chet has stiffened on his seat, reddening a little bit. It's like playing a fish, one of those big pike you hook into on the lake, put up a good fight, but once they've taken the bait-

"You don't want to be repeating that to nobody," says the gangster, dead-eyeing Harry. "Tell them I chop up babies for cat food, but to call a guy out as a *rat*—"

"Am I the cops? We're talking about chitchat between business associates."

More pondering. The ones who think it over a bit last a couple years extra before their friends or rivals shoot them in the back-

"The thing is, let's say I got this dealership—that's no guarantee it makes *mon*ey."

"There's also the commissaries."

"The whats?"

"At the Rouge. Our people get fifteen minutes for lunch, and we got little food set-ups at each of the buildings so the ones who don't bring their lunch can run down and grab something. It could be a piece of your fruit."

"That I sell you—"

"At a reasonable price. We give you the fruit concession, you got tens of *thou*sands of customers stuck there, no competition—not to mention the dietary benefits for our employees."

Big Chet starts to laugh again. Bootleggers are making fortunes boating high quality liquor across the river from Canada, their binocular men keeping track of the Coast Guard and local force patrol boats, a signal system worked out, dozens, if not hundreds of lawmen and customs officials on the take, and LaMare is right in the thick of it. But show me the criminal who can pass up what he thinks is an easy score-

"Think about it, Chet," says Harry, standing up from his crate to go. "We could use you in the Ford family."

• • •

"Model village my royal Irish backside," says Charley White, looking over the furniture he's helped Norma pull out of the cottage and onto the snow in the front yard. "We're all out of *work*—what kind of G-D model is that?"

Norma cuts her eyes to Kerry, wrestling the last of the kitchen chairs out.

"Sorry for the language," says Charley, "but you know what I mean."

"Do you think anyone will use these?" Norma asks, worried that the furniture will linger outside after she and Kerry are off to Brazil, that the Rogans will be badmouthed every time somebody looks out their window.

"That's good Michigan pine, good firewood. By the time you're on the ferry it will be gone."

Norma wrote to Jim to say they were coming even before the Company sent everybody notice that Pine Camp is being 'discontinued' as production no longer requires as much wood. She didn't tell him about their savings lost in the Market, or that she was sick of living like a widow. She can't imagine who will be wanting to buy a seven-year-old Model T, but Betty's husband Bill says that he'll try to sell it and send her the money.

"Did you know," offers Kerry, who bought another children's book about Brazil on their fun trip to Detroit and has been a fount of information ever since, "that there are at least sixteen thousand species of trees in the Amazon?"

"When you see your Daddy," says Charley White, "ask if he needs a good millhand to help cut them down."

• • •

The trip up to Barra is smooth, the river now more of a pathway through a giant, wooded lake, the current against them steady but invisible till deadhead logs and occasional floating islands of debris are encountered. When they have to tie off at night the air pulses with the basso croaking of the giant *sapo-cururu*, a nasty-looking toad that grows the size of an adult groundhog and excretes a venom from its skin that the boys tell Jim is used for poison arrows by the forest Indians. The few *indigenos* they manage to talk to on the way tell Gomes there is indeed a 'rubber-seed king' living to the north, a gringo who will trade valuable goods for only the seeds of the tree rather than the gathered and smoked *borracha*. Gomes seems happy to be away from the plantation and aboard the little steamer, and spends much of the day quietly singing popular songs from the radio. He has a beautiful, high voice, and the song Jim recognizes the best is *Blue Skies*-

Céu azul
Sorrindo para mim

For Jim it is a nightmarish trip, feeling himself ever more lost in the wilderness, Norma and Kerry more like a distant memory than people who might still remember him. Nothing is familiar here. Jim has spent his life surrounded by trees, but these, bringing to mind the word his mother reserved for those beyond redemption, are pro*mis*cuous, in both number and variety. The colors of birds, flowers, and fruits are unnaturally bright, and the mosquitos that form the whining cloud that travels along with them invade your netting at night and fatten on your blood. Fishing off the stern is no great pleasure, as the catch—huge, bright yellow bass with black markings, catfish longer and thicker than his legs, pike-like *picudas*—is so abundant and ravenous there isn't much sport to it, and you have to smear so much bug dope on it makes your eyes water.

Nada mas o céu azul
Que eu vejo

They reach Barra, a three-street river town that passes for a metropolis on the Tapajós, and stay a very pleasant night at the *fazenda* of Barreto, the rubber merchant David Riker told them would know the fate of McTeague and Teitzel if anybody did.

"They went up the Cururu," he tells them, "which branches off from the Tapajós just upriver from here. The *indigenos* who bring me their rubber say they've been trading for seeds, even planting some of them."

"But you don't know where exactly they've camped—"

"I don't—but the Franciscans will."

The Cururu is a much narrower maze through the trees, winding this way and that, vines and creepers crossing their pathway so frequently that one of the boys stands at the bow wielding a sharp blade on a pole that he uses to slash them out of the way. There are times that Jim is sure they've wandered off from the river and are just weaving through flooded jungle, but the pilot is unshaken, guiding the steamer through incredibly narrow spaces.

"É fundo aqui," he reassures Jim, pointing down to the water's surface.

"He tells you is deep here," Gomes translates. "Too *esteito*—too narrow—and we can always cut something away. But too little deep, and we are *fuck you*."

It is distressing to Jim that the locals seem to pick up the worst of the English language from their few *gringo* bosses, but not surprising. Whatever is said with heat and volume is more likely to stick in the mind—he has added *foda-se isso*, handy for whenever a blade sticks in a length of hardwood, to his own vocabulary.

Fuck this.

At one point, on some hummocks sticking up from the water, there are a trio of caimans, unmoving crocodile-looking creatures with yellow and black markings on their long snouts, and Jim has to dissuade the boys from making a stop to kill and skin them.

"Estamos no relógio," he reminds them.

We're on the clock.

The Franciscan monks and their Sisters of the Immaculate Conception are German, and Brother Wilhelm, once he gets over his initial suspicion, speaks to Jim in very passable English.

"These two men, McTeague and the other man, *ein Deutscher*—"

"Teitzel—"

"*Herr* Teitzel, *ja*, I am not thinking well of them. Too much *Alkohol* in the boat."

"You think they're trading liquor to the Indians?"

"Maybe so, but mostly I'm thinking they drink it all by themself."

The Mission Indians, Mundurucú people, are handsome and seem well-fed, wearing modest Western clothing, with the children in school uniforms. Jim remembers collections being taken up at Mass back home for children like these. "*Remember the Innocents*," Father Reilly would say, though as a little boy Jim would regret having to drop one of his own hard-earned nickels into the basket.

"These two are not so many kilometers away, and never do they come back to our mission. But the peoples who come to sell us the rubber, they tell stories."

"You trade in rubber?"

"We are giving the best value on the river, but only trading on the Saturday or Sunday, hoping maybe they will stay for Mass."

Jim stays for Mass, kneeling near the back of the chapel, Gomes standing behind him and singing along with the hymns. All of the children and many of the adults attend, and Jim enjoys the mix of Latin, Portuguese, and Tupi. He sings along as well, adding his bass to the higher, softer voices of the Mundurucú-

Et in terra pax hominibus bonae voluntatis-

A young man named Caetano, who is not only tattooed but has a stripe of black paint across his eyes, putting Jim in mind of a raccoon, is chosen to lead them to the traders, if they are in fact still alive and in the area.

They are led through a half-dozen villages, if they can be called that—away from the mission, the Mundurucú choose to live in much larger, common dwellings, all the males of marrying age, which seems to begin in late adolescence, in one long hut, and the women and children in the other. There are small gardens around the huts, which are set on the highest ground, and a clever series of gutters dug to carry the rainwater to the crops without drowning them. The people here wear fewer clothes, the body parts now revealed intricately tattooed, and look even more robust than their Christianized cousins. Many of the people recognize Caetano, greeting him with smiles and laughter and questions about the *pariwat*, standing very close to both Jim and Gomes to look them over and discuss them like cattle being judged. One of these inquisitors wears a leather quiver filled with very long arrows and has a necklace of what might be jaguar teeth hung around his neck. Gomes has suggested that it is best not to venture forth into Indian territory carrying a firearm, but Jim has his doubts.

"These people trade with the Seed King," Gomes tells him after an exchange with Caetano. "We are very near him."

What they come upon first is not a fort or a trading post, but a nursery.

Hundreds of seedlings, in evenly-spaced rows, stick up from a cleared section of ground. As the entire *savana* is more grass than trees, there are few stumps among them, and the same clever irrigation gutters have been dug. Jim, rain-soaked despite his slicker, is amazed as Caetano spreads his arms to indicate the planting and explains something to Gomes.

"He says the older seeds began to sprout, so the King had them planted."

The trading post is all sticks and thatch, a long counter built out onto the front of it, with McTeague found lolling in a hammock hung under a woven roof in the living quarters.

"Ah've been waiting for ye," he says, slowly climbing to his feet and extending a hand to shake. "Any langer and we'd be tappin the trees we've planted for *borracha*."

"We didn't hear from you."

"Aye, the tellyphone service is dreadful in these pairts. We've sent news wi' a few of the river merchants as go up and doon the Tapajós, but they're an unreliable lot."

"And your partner is still—?"

McTeague points. "Built himsel' a wee *cabana* a short wander from here, dwells there with Connie."

"And you've taken on employees?"

McTeague makes a face at the word.

"We have two or three dozen as will lift a hoe or wield a shovel if it suits them and there's something of ours they fancy. Sugar and coffee is most popular—the rum was finished months ago. Ye've no brought a drap or two by any chance?"

"You were given cash to pay—"

"Ah, weel then," says the Scotsman, "mah pairtner took bad with the dysentery, and here we were, deep in the bush with nae a scrap of *papel higênico* betwixt us—"

"What are you saying?"

"That Heinrich had tae wipe his arse with a few thousand *reales*. Is nae a problem though, as the savages prefer tae barter."

"Which is strictly against Company policy."

"Ah have tae tell ye, laddie," says McTeague, "in this corner of the jungle Heinrich and me *are* the bluidy Company."

Jim takes a breath to retain his composure. "I'll need to take a look at your ledger book."

McTeague pulls a canvas tarp off a quartet of jute bags bulging with something.

"Seeds," he announces. "What we were sent here tae procure, if Ah'm not mistaken."

"I need a record of your transactions," Jim tells him. He hates this, has always hated the financial side of any task, but it is what he has been ordered to do.

"Heinrich's yer mon, then. He's a wizard with the numbers."

The rain lightens some as they walk to where Teitzel is staying. They pass something like a warehouse, sacks and crates of food staples, axes, even a few shotguns kept off the ground and dry, a ramshackle version of

Barreto's trading post by the Barra docks. It is clear that these are used to buy the seeds and pay for clearing and sowing.

"Sharp traders, your *Wuy Jugu*," says McTeague. "But the ones you'll see in these pairts dinna fancy the friars nor their teachings—likely to vex the spirits and bring bad fortune doon on yer noggin. And here we be."

Teitzel's *cabana* is made of woven panels with bamboo flooring and a thatched roof. Squares of mosquito netting, much-patched, cover the windows and there is a little garden to the side, outlined by half-buried liquor bottles.

Nothing is growing in the garden.

Connie turns out to be a nice-looking young woman not dressed like either the mission or *savana* Indians, one of those Brazilian mixes Jim can't even guess at, who watches him cautiously from a few feet behind Teitzel. The German is wearing only khaki shorts and some sort of rope sandals, and he is not a pretty sight, unshaven and red-eyed from either alcohol or the lack of it. He has the ledger book in a small, waterproof pouch, and hands it over to Jim with a small bow.

"Is all *geschrieben* in der book."

Jim notes with some relief that the entries are all in English. He glances at a few pages, each with a date inscribed at the top.

"These numbers are *reales*?"

"Dey are number of *tings*. Bag of the sugar, sack of salt, axe for chopping wiss—"

"So all in trade?"

Teitzel looks to McTeague, standing behind Jim, who just throws his arms out in a defeated gesture.

"*Ja*, dis is how we do it."

"Then I'm afraid I have to relieve you men of your duties here. I'll be taking control of the seeds and the seedlings. I'll give you a few days to leave the area—"

"And ye'll pay us what we're due, laddie, afore we move an inch," announces McTeague. "Ah'll not leave here in a boot filled wi' manioc flour."

Jim has been given Brazilian paper money for this. Though he assumes the two have already pocketed a good deal of cash, the seeds are the priority.

"You'll be paid," he says. These are men who marooned both their river guide and their cook, and, if Baretto is to be believed, used Company money to get drunk, buy perfume and spray it on livestock. If there were anything like a police force in this hellhole, he would have them arrested. He has brought his own account book, and resolves to camp out in the little warehouse tomorrow and take inventory. Some sense of order has to be established-

"Those bags of rubber seeds," he asks sternly, "how many in each one?"

"Ah've nae bluidy idea, laddie. Ye'll need tae count them yoursel'."

Caetano comes to Jim that night and wants to be paid for his services. He won't take currency. Gomes acts as intermediary and eventually they agree on a smallish bag of salt. Jim feels like he's committed a sin. Not a mortal sin, of course, but bad enough, the kind the priests always warn you will accrue and lead to your ultimate damnation.

McTeague and Teitzel are gone in the morning, severance pay in their pockets, along with the eight-foot creekboat that was lashed on the deck of the steamer. Who is not gone is Connie, actual name Conceição, who tells Gomes she belongs to the Ford Motor Company and wants to be taken there.

"They pay her, these men, for *foder*, and tell her she belongs to *Senhor* Ford."

The girl is staring at Jim as he sits in the warehouse. There are three dozen Mundurucú men also staring at him, waiting for orders. He has not been trained for this.

"What we are going to do," he tells Gomes, "is to establish a value in each of these goods for a hundred rubber seeds or a day's work in the field. What should I expect for half a kilo of manioc flour?"

Gomes offers him a sympathetic smile. "This depends on how hungry they are."

Conceição chimes in then with quite a long and exasperated dialogue, Gomes following it carefully, nodding a few times.

"What?" asks Jim when she runs out of steam.

"She say that if you don't want to *foder* with her, she can cook."

At last, some good news.

• • •

There are so many women selling themselves on the Ilha da Inocência.

Hey, *magro*, calls one of a trio of them standing in front of a *cachaça* hut, leave your little boy with my friend Catarina and come with me! She'll take care of him and I'll take care of you!

They laugh and João, embarrassed, steers Flavio away. The *trabalhadores* at Fordlandia have been paid today and a great number of them have crossed the river on the motorized rafts the rum-sellers send over to the dock, eager for customers with loose *reales* in their pockets. The village is swarming with plantation workers and prostitutes and men and women shouting out the name of the things they want to sell—knives, cooking pots, clothing, alcohol, paintings of saints, tamed parrots—there might be more people in the mess hall each day for lunch, thinks Flavio, but there they are spaced apart evenly, like rubber tree seedlings, at the long wooden benches and tables, the waiters hurrying around them with platters of food and always a nervous eye on the clock on the wall. Flavio's father has taught him how to read a clock, which is the way *brancos* divide a day and tell you exactly when you have to go back to work.

Look at these two handsome gentlemen! calls a fat, sweating man with several hats piled up on his head. They must be visiting royalty! But what is a king without his crown?

He tries to put a hat onto Flavio but João waves him away. They've come to buy a new cooking pot for Beatriz and nothing else.

Flavio, who has only once in his few years been to a big city, and then in too much pain to look around much, has to shout over a radio playing from one of the huts. So many crowded together! he says.

I've been told that in São Paolo people live in houses that are one on top of the other, says his father. Twenty or thirty high.

Flavio is not sure he believes this.

But when the ones on top have to pee—

They have special tubes for that.

A man who looks like a *gringo* and has not shaved for several days is pushing through the crowd, staggering in their direction.

Do you have our money hidden? asks Flavio, who is paid in small coins by the workers for fetching water for them throughout the day. A huge tank brought on the ship from Santorém has been set up high on legs to dispense the water which, though treated with something that tastes bad, won't make you sick.

To steal it they'll have to take me apart, says his father. But I don't like carrying it.

Before, with Dom Fernando, he says, instead of coins and paper money there was an understanding. If I needed a new axe, or food in the Dead Time when there is no work, or suddenly you decided to grow out of your pants, he would always give what was needed. Across the river in Fordlandia they measure your work with the clock, only paying once you have done it. And there is no telling how long they will be here.

Flavio finds this thought alarming.

They might leave without telling us?

João smiles. When Mr. Ford comes to visit, he says, you can ask him.

But Flavio has already focused his attention on a stand where they are selling cups of sweet cane juice. At quitting time every evening they are forced to swallow a pill of *quinina* with warm water from the giant tank, a pill which is supposed to ward off malaria but leaves a very bad taste, a taste he still feels in the back of his mouth.

"*Papai*," he says, pulling at his father's arm, can I buy one of those?

• • •

Though the water level has fallen a bit, the jungle is still flooded on the trip back to Fordlandia, most of the deck of the steamer given over to the seedlings, which Jim has laid into large, shallow boxes that he's built rather than individual pots. The Mundurucú have turned out to be excellent workers when they have agreed on a task and the price for it—the head man in the village closest to the nursery, who turns out to be Caetano's father, negotiating for the crew of men to do a wider slash-and-burn clearing, and for the women to actually put the sprouting seeds into the ground. It should be worth another visit in four months, thinks Jim, when new seedlings have had time to thrive and the *Wuy Jugu*—what they call themselves—are running short of some of their staples. They don't do much fishing in the winter rainy season, subsisting on wild game and fruit and manioc, a substance Jim has not yet developed a taste for in any of its many forms. His mother used to serve them tapioca pudding for dessert at least twice a week, his brother Kevin declaring that the little pearls were "fish eyeballs," effectively nullifying Jim's enthusiasm for it. On the days when the rain never lets up, the men sit and weave palm fronds into the sturdy baskets the women carry loads in, a tumpline across their foreheads. Once Jim was accepted as a decent sort of *pariwat*, he was invited to eat with the men, sampling their wild pig, overgrown rodents called *cutia* and *paca*, and several kinds of birds, limiting himself to the well-cooked bits.

He declined, holding his stomach as if too full, when the monkey was passed around.

Connie has netted a huge catfish with black markings that she is cooking on a little stove Jim has rigged up. Since she won't go away, Jim has decided to find a place for her in the mess hall at Fordlandia, where her very basic cooking skills will be useful. Mr. Ford is famous for finding jobs that chair-bound or even blind people can handle, requiring at least one good hand and a willingness to work. Connie seems to be a cheerful young woman, with a broad, flat face and well-rounded body. There are times she makes Jim ache for Norma, and he has had to caution Gomes to keep his distance.

"She works for the Company, not for us."

Conceição has never met a *gringo* who didn't drink. This one, *Senhor* Rogan, not only doesn't drink but doesn't seem to be interested in her, though she's been paid in advance for the rest of the month. Gomes says it's because Rogan has a wife and daughter, but when has that made any difference?

The other two were drunk all the time, the German likely to forget his business and fall asleep on top of her. But they paid real money and because there was nothing to spend it on living with the *indigenos*, she has saved most of it, hiding it where nobody can see. She has been lucky enough to dodge the *sífilis* so far, but luck only runs in your favor for so long, and maybe this fantasy that she is a cook is worth pursuing—she can cook as well as her mother did, which means pulling food away from the fire before it burns and adding salt of you have some.

They've been on the Tapajós for most of the day, and finally the drizzle has ceased and the sky above begins to clear. The jungle around them begins to take color, and suddenly there are a pair of bright pink dolphins swimming alongside the steamer, occasionally diving to reappear on the other side.

"*Boto*!" cries Conceição, pointing excitedly.

Jim feels sun on the back of his neck for the first time in a week. There are several large sacks full of rubber seeds below and hundreds, hundreds of seedlings on deck and now an escort of *dol*phins, dolphins the pink of glazed piggy banks. Olafson brought civilization with him on the big ship—an electrical engineer, a chemist, an accountant, a handful of managers and their wives, Dr. Beaton—and they should have things well in hand at the plantation. He'll sleep in a bed with sheets tonight.

Blue skies—

-he begins to sing-

smilin' at me
Nothin' but blue skies, do I see—

It is less than an hour later when Gomes shouts and points to a tree to the starboard that has been split and blackened by a lightning strike. They passed one like it shortly after leaving the plantation for the trip up the Tapajós.

"Is the same one," Gomes tells Jim. "We are close to being there."

Jim buttons his shirt up. He wonders if Captain Olafson is still in charge. There has been no word from Fordlandia, of course, since they left—a war could have broken out, a gold rush started, the rubber plantation idea abandoned-

They pass the Isle of Innocence first.

Olafson's first act was to enforce Prohibition on Ford property—*nobody addicted to alcohol will be hired*—shutting down the bars and makeshift bordellos that had sprung up at the edge of the clearing, but those hardy entrepreneurs have only moved to this little mound in the middle of the Tapajós, a short paddle from the Fordlandia dock, slapping together huts raised on stilts for when the river rises.

Connie steps to the edge of the deck to stare as several of the denizens of the outlaw village wave and shout. She doesn't look happy with what Gomes explains to her.

Jim hears chopping from the Ford side of the river as they chug around a wide bend, sees how the acreage has increased, spindly little plantlets poking up between blackened stumps that haven't been pulled yet, still hoping to meet the Brazilian government's quota. And then the almost-finished water tower comes into sight, a factory whistle installed on top with the Ford logo already painted on it, and some new wooden buildings, one of them with a smokestack above that must be the powerhouse, and then the floating dock Jim built, a few little trade boats tied alongside, and the metal gongs are struck the moment the steamer is spotted, provoking a stampede of the members of the workers' families who haunt the outskirts of the plantation. Jim squints against the sun, trying to think of exactly how long he's been gone.

At the dock Pringle, the first *patrâo* to reach him, is not smiling.

"You brought seedlings," he observes, staring at the display on the deck.

"And plenty of seeds." Jim points to a trio of smallish coffins among a pile of crates. "What's that?"

"We had some fever. Lost a few workers, a bunch of people in the shanty town. And those—those are Olafson's little ones."

"No—"

"He's taking this back to Santorém as soon as you unload. Leaving for good."

Connie has stepped up to take Jim's arm, maybe shy of the crowd.

"Who's in charge then?"

"I hate to say it buddy, but it seems to be *you*."

Before Jim can think this through he sees something that makes no sense, two white faces, familiar, moving up through the jabbering locals.

Norma and Kerry.

Norma is looking at Connie. Kerry is beaming at him. His wife gets there first, with that look on her face that he dreads.

"Welcome back to Paradise," she says.

• • •

Nobody recognizes him in the café, even when he asks where Mr. Bennett is sitting. More and more these days people tumble when they hear the voice, even when they can't quite place it.

"Do I know you?" or just a puzzled look, or that one doll, couldn't have been more than eighteen, waiting on tables at the Book-Cadillac Hotel coffee shop who laughed and said "You know, you sound just like Jerry Buckley."

The radio deal is starting to roll.

He's on every weekday night now, advertisers fighting to buy time, and his pals at the *Free Press* say their editorial writers are always grousing about the size of his audience. People from both the Republicans and the Democrats have felt him out about running for office, but so far nothing that would give him near as much influence with the common herd as he's got broadcasting. No, the next move, if he's going to make one, will be selling one of the networks on taking him national, like CBS has done for Father Coughlin. A bored-senseless city councilman in Detroit, or your voice in living rooms from sea to shining sea?

Harry is in a booth in the back room, which here is even bigger than the front room, wearing one of his bowties. Harry likes to punch people in the nose, and says a long tie is just an invitation to get yourself dragged around the room or choked. He doesn't bother to stand up to shake hands.

"The Voice of the Common Man."

"I never called myself that."

"And I never called myself Henry Ford's Enforcer, but it's *stuck*, hasn't it."

Jerry worked for Bennett and Liebold shortly after he got out of law school, investigating Truman Newberry after he squeaked by Ford in the 1918 Senate election, finding enough violations of campaign finance laws that the man had to resign before his term was over. It was pure sour grapes, the Titan of the Tin Lizzy probably having bent a few of the same rules himself, but he was one of the richest men in American and accustomed to getting his way-

Jerry looks around—not too many tables, lots of floor space, a drop cloth thrown over the long bar counter as if it's not used anymore.

"They say this place turns into a gin mill after eight."

"Please," says Harry with a grin. "There are blind pigs, there are gin mills, there are speakeasies, and there are establishments willing to rent space for private parties. There happens to be a private party here every night after eight."

Quite a flap just last week, and good outrage fuel for the show—Police Commissioner Emmons, while Mayor Bowles was off on vacation, seems to have raided the wrong juice joint, leading to his dismissal when Bowles returned.

"Stupid move," says Jerry. "You don't fire a lawman for doing his job."

"Perhaps he exceeded his authority."

"Perhaps he thought he was working for a mayor who ran on a dry platform and promised to do away with corruption—"

"They all say that—"

"Yes, but most of them have the decency to let a year or so go by before they show their true colors. Your man didn't wait a *week*."

"Bowles wasn't our man," says Harry. "He was only the least of two evils. We have the welfare of hundreds of thousands of workers to look out for—"

"I've heard you've let half of them go in the last couple months."

Harry stops smiling.

"*Ru*mors, Jerry, you want to check something like that out thoroughly before you go polluting the airwaves."

When Jerry worked for them on the investigation, Ford was still America's favorite tycoon, you couldn't say a bad word about him in Detroit without catching a lecture. But lately-

"I don't think anybody in this town still believes your boss is handing out favors." Jerry has been riding rough on "the industrialists" and on Hoover lately, presenting the stories of men who have worked for Ford or some of the other auto makers for twenty years or more, suddenly tossed away like rusted scrap metal. "If you got me here because I've said the Company should be putting something aside for your men when they retire or are laid off—"

"I heard a show the other day about taking a rocket ship to the moon—just as likely to happen."

"Have you walked down Woodward lately? There's an army of jobless men, growing every day—"

"I need to talk to you about Bowles."

"Because of the move to have him recalled."

It's the kind of thing that needs a lot of signatures to get started. Signatures that can be checked by Harry's Service Department goons, which means nobody working at the Rouge is likely to go on record-

"We don't want that to happen, Jerry."

"A recall only means the guy has to stand for election again—"

"And this time Murphy will run against him."

Jerry grins. "Aha."

Judge Murphy presided at the Ossian Sweet trial, and let Clarence Darrow sweet-talk the jury into letting the Negro go free after he shot a white man from the window of his house. Judge Murphy is not in the pocket of the Italian gangs or the Jewish gangs or even the old Irish gang, and more importantly, not in the pocket of Henry Ford or his pint-sized arm-twister.

"He'd be a nightmare," says Harry, "a disaster for the business climate—"

"Especially the monkey-business climate."

"What do you mean by that?"

The table is wide enough and Bennett's arms short enough that Jerry feels safe for the moment, but he is careful with his phrasing.

"Well, I know you like to keep tabs on our—let's call them entrepre-*neurs*—who float the good Canadian stuff across the river, then have their cutters mix it with coffin varnish to sell to the guests at private parties in places like this. I assume it's part of your job—"

Harry likes to rub elbows with the booze runners, and his pal Chet LaMare just had a few rivals ambushed at an east side fish market-

"Jerry, I say this as a friend—keep your beak out of things that don't concern you."

Buckley has received notes at the recording studio in the LaSalle Hotel, scrawled on butcher paper. Some telling him he'd better lay off Bowles, others urging him to push the recall on his show—*If you know what's good for you*. The best he can figure is that one bunch is using Bowles to protect their own joints and go after the ones run by their rivals. Most likely it's the ravioli crowd jockeying for position—if it was the Jews the spelling would be better. But this is Harry Bennett making threatening noises, either on his own or on the Old Man's orders, and one has to draw the line somewhere. He stands up from the table.

"I appreciate your concern, Harry, and I will take it under advisement. You listen to my show?"

"Sure," say the Little Man. "Right before *Amos 'n' Andy*."

• • •

"Were you there when they pierced Him in the side?
(Were you there?)"

Mavis likes the hymns where the verse is repeated. Even the little children can catch up and join in—

"Were you there when they pierced Him in the side?
Oh sometimes it causes me to tremble
(Tremble, tremble-)
Were you there when they pierced Him in the side?"

-DeWitt, with a good strong voice, getting deeper all the time now, and Earline can keep up. It's hard to tell with Alvin, only six, who sings some of the words and doesn't always know what they mean-

"Were you there when the sun refused to shine?

(Were you there?)

Were you there when the sun refused to shine?"

"Of course, none of us in this generation," proclaims Reverend Bradby, easing directly from the song to his sermon as he often does, "were present on Calvary Hill that sorrowful day, but you'll agree that every *one* of us has had a moment, had a day when, though not a cloud was to be seen in the sky, we have *felt* the absence of the Lord's healing Light. Bad things, *ter*rible things can happen even to the best people, can befall even our innocent children, and we ask '*Why*, Lord, *why*?' And does He have an answer for us?"

Mavis tries to come all the way in to Second Baptist at least one Sunday a month, even if Zeke thinks the streetcar fare for her and the kids is a waste. Yes, there is a perfectly good church in Inkster, but Reverend Dix doesn't approve workers for the Ford plant or have the down-home whoops in him like Reverend Bradby does.

"Of *course* He has an answer, but unless we are Moses on the mountaintop, or one of the great prophets of Bible days, He does not reveal that answer in clear speech, as I talk to you good people. Consider *Ecclesiastes* 9:11—'Again I saw that under the sun the race is not to the swift, nor the battle to the strong, nor bread to the wise, nor riches to the intelligent, nor favor to those with knowledge—but time and chance happen to them all.'"

In other words *luck*, which has been on her mind lately, Willis being let go at the foundry but Zeke somehow passed over—Zeke says there's no clue as to why, as Willis was just as steady and hard-working as he is. And Mavis agrees with her husband that the Lord had nothing to do with it.

"Now we know that often the race *does* go to the swift—followers of the magnificent Man o' War a decade ago will bear me out on this—"

There is an enthusiastic "Amen" from a man in the congregation, then laughter—"-and strength is certainly no disadvantage in battle. So what is this ancient wise man telling us? Only that these attributes—speed, strength, wisdom, intelligence—are no guaran*tee* of success, that accidents do happen in our world, one may be in the wrong place at the wrong time, the winds of fortune may choose either to blow at our backs or bar our progress head on, and that time— I'm speaking of *Bib*lical time now, e*ter*nal time—puts all of our worldly gains and accomplishments in perspective. For when that Final Trumpet blows, the greatest king, the wealthiest mogul, will stand equal in judgement beside the pauper in rags."

Mavis is pleased to hear that luck that has nothing to do with Satan either. She remembers the Jesus-shouters in Alabama stating that a man whose mule breaks a leg must be a sinner, instead of just another sharecropper given uneven ground to plow.

"Now this is not to advise us to become lazy, to give *up*. No, brothers and sisters, the Lord gave us this life both as a gift and as a *test*. And the test deals with the question of *how* we run the race, *how* we earn our bread, *how* we use our gifts of wisdom and intelligence!"

"That's right."

"Amen."

On the other hand, she hopes that once in a while when His eye is not on the sparrow, the Lord looks down and tosses a bit of luck at the feet of a poor sinner who can sorely use it. When one of her loyal players hits the number, Mavis doesn't wait for them to stumble on the good news, she seeks them out and pays off on the spot. It is her favorite part of the job-

"In my capacity as a leader of this ministry, I do not *wait* for time or chance to improve life for our people—when I see injustice, I call it *out*—"

"Amen—"

"When I see an opportunity for the advancement of our race, I *seize* that opportunity—"

"You tell it!"

"That's right!"

"And when one of our brethren suffers a setback and is in need, I do what I can to al*lev*iate that situation, if only with a sympathetic word."

"That's the way, Reverend."

It's why she feels fine about selling the dream books—what's to stop the Lord from slipping a hint to a striver while they're sleeping?

"We can look about us on the streets of this city," says the Reverend Bradby, changing his tone to something rueful, "and see those men, of all races, who have been dispossessed. The mysteries of an economic system beyond their ken or control have rendered them *jobless*, have made them re*dun*dant to the flow of capital, to the regard of the wealthy and powerful. Time and chance, people, time and *chance*—just as there are fat years there are those of fallow, and diligent, hard-working men and women may be left as flotsam on the bank when the floodwaters recede. So many of you good people have come up from the southern states, like the Israelites fleeing Egypt, searching for opportunity, for a better life for yourselves and your children, and have had the good fortune to achieve some part of that in this great city. To have it suddenly torn from your grasp—it may seem like a *pun*ishment."

Last week's sermon was about how the Lord and Satan got into an argument about the depth of the faith of Job, resulting in a kind of bet—the Lord challenged Satan to vex Job with all manner of afflictions and disasters, allowed, no, *dared* him to make the man's life a waking nightmare, to see if he would keep the faith. Mavis hopes the Lord has got that out of his system. Life is hard enough even with Zeke still working—working, as he tells it, "four feet short of Hell" for what has now fallen back to only six dollars a day—without the Almighty playing tricks on folks to see if they'll stay grateful.

"This present De*press*ion, as they call it, is a trial, is a *test*. Not one sent by the Lord, but by the Midases and Nebuchadnezzars of our modern world, those worshippers of the Golden Calf whose greed and usuary have resulted in a Panic. And of course in this nation whenever there is a plague upon the land, whenever there is a great hardship, it is *our* people who suffer the first and the most—"

"Amen to that, brother."

"Tell the people—"

"What, therefore, can we *do*? What can we share? How can we help? Of course, it is natural that your *fam*ily should come first, but how wide do we cast that net? If you escaped a burning building would you not bring a ladder to save those on the floors above?"

Mavis looks at her children—little Alvin leaning on her, half-asleep despite Bradby's fire, Earline who loves to dress up for any occasion, starched and spotless in white, DeWitt listening, following the logic but a bit restless—and wonders if time and chance will be kind to them. There are days when Zeke comes home so tired he can barely eat, barely speak, and it's hard not to resent Mr. Ford for having such control over their lives, for making her feel like they could all go under if this one handhold should slip away—

"Now I have been told that *pol*itics has no place in the pulpit—"

"Watch out, Rev!" calls the racehorse lover and again the people laugh. Bradby even ran for City Council a few years back-

"-but there is something important that we can do—even you lovely sisters have won the right to throw your effort into it—and that is to *vote*. I imagine you are all aware of the recall campaign that has been organized against Mayor Bowles."

A short chorus of disapproval ripples through the congregation.

"The candidate favored by the nefarious Klux Klan, an evil which has followed us north and always gains strength in times of economic hardship. It has become clear that Bowles, professed to be a *dry* advocate, professed to be a re*for*mer, is in fact in league with the very agents of corruption he promised to put out of business! We have an opportunity, brothers and sisters, to be heard, loud and clear, and as an added incentive, if a new election is called, Bowles's opponent will be none other than Judge Frank Murphy."

This time the ripple is one of approval, the woman in the fox fur across the aisle from Mavis adding a "Thank you, Lord!"

"I don't believe that Judge Murphy if elected mayor, will have the power to turn the economic tide in this city, in this country, but I do believe we will have a man in high office who at least at*tempts* to be fair! This may seem like an insignificant thing in face of the desperate situation many of our people find themselves in, but let me assure you—it is a *step*, and not a small one—in the right direction. Join me in song—"

Reverend Bradby is clever at this, leaving you with his last thought and moving into a hymn-

"If I walk in the pathway of duty
If I work till the close of the day—"

He doesn't have an overwhelming voice, but Deacon Fry, who can make the angels weep, is never far behind with his sweet tenor-

"I shall see the great King in His beauty

When I've walked—the last mile—of the way."

Then Mavis and the congregation and even DeWitt, who loves this song and pitches his voice higher to sing it, join in on the chorus-

"When I've walked—the last mile of the way
I will rest (I will rest) at the close of the day
And I know (and I know) there are joys that await me, Oh Lord
When I've walked—the last mi-yi-yi-el-mile of the way!"

Kaz has never had a day on the line this bad, and he's been down to three days a week since June. It is hot, brutal hot on the streetcar back home, too many people jammed together, so he gets off at Campau and Goodson to walk the rest of the way. Which is why he finds the place right there in front of him and remembers Bud Novak passing him on the overpass coming into work and muttering "Konopka's." It's usually cooler inside, so why not?

Stosh Konopka himself is there, right between the paintings of Kościuszko and Pulaski that flank the Polish flag behind the bar—his place referred to as a 'lunch counter' since the Volstead Act threw a monkey wrench into everything. Stosh gives him a nod-

"Hey, Kaz, long time no see. It's a lot cooler in the back."

The back is where you can get a drink most times of the day, so he goes through the door. There are a half-dozen guys sitting around a pair of card tables, but nobody is playing cards. They give Kaz the nod, but none look too sure about it. Kaz sits alone right by the bigger electric fan, the sweat on his face suddenly chill. A few of the faces look familiar, one guy maybe four positions down the line from him at the Rouge, but with so many workers, so many buildings, it's hard to say.

Nobody is wearing their identification badge.

"Scorcher out there, huh?" observes an older guy with one cloudy blue eye, the other sharp and brown.

"All week now," Kaz agrees. "Those poor guys in the foundry, step outside and it's just as bad as the smelters."

"You ever work in there?"

"Naw. In my father's day it was a lot of Polish and Litvaks, but now it's mostly the colored guys."

Stosh comes in and lays a beer in front of Kaz. Kaz notices that the others aren't drinking.

"What do you think about this recall deal?" asks another of the men.

You could get out on thin ice with this real quick. Bennett's Service Department goons and even some of the straw bosses on the line have been drilling them with the idea that it's good for Ford to keep Bowles in office, and what's good for Ford-

"I'm just glad he's not one of us," Kaz tells him. "Like that character here—Jezewski."

The men laugh. Jezewski is a drug store owner who was mayor of Hamtramck and so obviously working in cahoots with Big Chet LaMare that the Governor and state police came in to take over the city. Word is he's out of prison now and making noises about running again-

"Hey, that much moolah to be made selling tarantula juice, everybody's gonna get into it. Rum runners and bookies are the only bunch still fully employed."

"You mean they're not down to three days a week?"

Kaz notices one of the men glance to the one-eyed guy, who gives a little shake of his head.

"No, they're on weekends too," says Bud Novak, stepping in with a grin on his face. "Poor bastards need a union."

Bud pauses by Kaz, laying a hand on his shoulder. "You all have met Kaz Pilsudski? He's over in B Building at the Rouge."

Kaz can feel the other men relax. You don't wag your tongue freely at the job, never knowing if there's a snitch within earshot.

"We were just getting acquainted."

"Stosh won't let anybody back here he don't know," Bud assures them, "and if somebody tries to blow in without permission—Prohibition bulls, Company ginks—he's got a foot buzzer and this contraption that throws a deadbolt on the door."

"So what's the deal here?" asks Kaz, suddenly uncomfortable. "I know it's not the Klan or the Black Legion, cause they don't take Catholics."

The men laugh again.

"Just some fellas want to shoot the shit without losing their jobs," says the one-eyed man. "Your dad was Prokop?"

"Still is. He just got on over at Briggs, hanging on by his fingernails."

"I remember him from Highland Park. Good guy."

"This is Lester Collins," says Bud. "He's come to spread the word."

"The word about what?"

"First of all," says Lester Collins, "how was work this week?"

Kaz thinks for a moment, then shrugs. "Work was work. But it felt like I was running uphill all day."

"That's cause they stole three seconds from you."

"Three seconds—?"

Bud pulls a stopwatch, the kind they use at track meets, out of his pocket, clicks it a couple times. "I been smuggling this little wonder into the building for a couple of weeks—you can imagine how tough it is to find a gap where the Company eye isn't on you and I can get it out of my pocket long enough to time the belt. This week my task got parked in front of me three whole seconds sooner than last week—all day long. We got a guy in your building says they pulled the same act there."

"How can they do that?"

"They have the mechanic tweak the conveyor, the foremen light a fire under the guys feeding parts to it, 'Let's *move* it, you sonsabitches, go, go, *go!*' You pull that enough times—gradually, so we don't notice right away—and sooner or later you're getting a couple hours a week more out of us without it costs you a dime."

"So it's not just me—"

"Kaz," says Lester Collins, "it's *never* just you. That's what I come here to talk to you fellas about. Cards on the table—I'm in this outfit, it's called the TUUL—the Trade Union Unity League—"

"Reds?" asks one of the others, not unkindly.

"Oh, we got plenty of them, including Party members, which I don't happen to be. What we're trying to get working people to do now is to start *think*ing."

"If that thinking is about pushing a union in," Kaz tells him, "for*get* about it. Henry Ford will take the whole thing apart and throw it into the river before he'll sit still for anybody organizing the Rouge."

Collins smiles. "Time will tell. Right now I just want to put a bee in your bonnets. You're in assembly—you know any of the guys in the rolling mill?"

"Hell no."

"Or in upholstery, scrap metal, or soybeans?"

"I hardly know any guys in my own building, and if I do it's not from work—"

"Know any people work on the railroad? People who cut trees down or sew clothes? Longshoremen?"

"What have they got they got to do with us?"

"One word—*class*."

A moment of silence as the men try to guess where this is going.

"So you *are* a Red," says Bud.

Collins laughs. "I am an American and a Ford production worker. I voted Al Smith for president along with maybe five other people, and hope that someday, God willing, the Tigers will finish the season with a winning record. But from what I've seen from life I know the biggest thing that separates people is not whether you're Polish or Italian or Irish or a Jew or white or colored—it's whether you're one of the many who pro*duce* the goods or one of the few who rake in the profits."

Kaz knows there are craft unions, some even operating in Detroit and Dearborn, but those are guys who have a skill that is hard to learn and vital to their employer—if they sit on their hands, the whole deal gums up. But his job, and he guesses those that the others in this room do at the Rouge—well, in the words of Grimes his foreman, "Jesus Christ, Pilsudski, a fucking *monkey* could take your spot!"

"You've got to start seeing the world in terms of class," says Collins. "Find fellow workers on the job you can trust—I know you got to be careful with that—and when the opportunity comes, grab hold of it."

"Right now I'm trying to grab hold of the rent money," says Bud.

"The capitalists will patch this current craziness up eventually—they'll want to get the money machine rolling again. And they need *you*, all of you, to do it. Tell me, what would happen if the auto workers and the coal miners and the truck drivers and the steel workers and the ladies that sew your underwear all decided to go out on strike at the same time?"

Another moment of silence as they consider this. Kaz thinks of Molly and the kids, of little Sonia with all her problems-

"There'd be guns," says Kaz. "They'd call out the state police, call out the army, there'd be shooting."

Lester Collins is not smiling now. "It may well come to that. Guns on both sides."

A sobering thought. Bud Novak raises his hand.

"Can I shoot Harry Bennett?"

The men laugh.

• • •

When the house Mr. Ford is building for them is finished, João will live there with Beatriz and Flavio. It is any one of a long row of identical boxes the carpenters are putting up, the sounds of saws and hammers audible from the thatched-roof mess hall where he sits eating with the single men. The carpenters will be among those who eat dinner in the smaller second shift, so many people working here now at Fordlandia. Flavio is no longer one of them, with the new *patrao*, who they call *o lenhador*, the wood cutter, saying that Mr. Ford does not approve of hiring children and that as soon as the school building is finished Flavio will have to go there to learn things.

The men sitting around João eating their rice and wheat bread are not happy.

They are on the side of the mess hall for the common laborers, taking up two thirds of the room, with the skilled men in their own section. Yes, they have to stand in separate lines outside while the Company clerks write down the numbers on their badges before they can enter, but both groups have waiters to rush their food to the table and bring more if they want, the same food every day, but always enough. The new ruling is what has them upset-

It is a matter of freedom and dignity, says the one they call Gaúcho because he is from Rio Grande do Sul, even if he claims never to have ridden a horse. What if I wanted to eat dinner at Pau d'Ague?

You would have to pay for it—

I have to pay for this—they take the cost of it out of my wages.

Pau d'Ague is even further from where we're clearing now. You'd have to eat faster—

Yes, but that should be my choice. I'm selling my labor, not my *soul*.

A few of the men laugh. Rio Grande do Sul is always in an uproar, a state that has its own civil wars, and the people there like to argue.

They've done this so we *have* to eat here, so they know where we are every moment of the day until the whistle screams at three o'clock.

The first few weeks the steam whistle made flocks of birds rise into the sky, but now they seem to be used to it, just as the workers and the people living on the margins of Fordlandia or across the river have. A whistle to wake up, one for the start of breakfast, one for the start of the working day, one to begin and end dinner, and a final whistle at three o'clock, or, more accurately, at what is three o'clock in Detroit, Michigan, where Mr. Ford makes automobiles. Fordlandia does not keep the same time as the rest of Brazil, which does not please Gaúcho.

When my father was a young man, he says, there were still slaves in this country. We've let these *gringos* bring back those times—

But after three o' clock—João begins to say-

After three o'clock you will go to the *cabana* they are making to put you in, and you'll wait there until they blow that whistle again.

You can leave any time you want to, Gaúcho.

Leave for what? Where is there work? Before this I was working at a *cafezal*, but now a pound of coffee earns half of what it did a year ago—

Is that the fault of the *gringos*?

No, it's the fault of our government, for giving this land away to them, for selling the riches of our country and putting the money in their own pockets! That gang of *Paulistas* who have stolen the election and put this Prestes into power—

João is aware that there was recently another election, but has never voted in one. The goings on in Rio or São Paulo are so remote, so unconnected to his own life—he has heard that people in the United States have lost their money, just as they have in much of Brazil, but here in Fordlandia it has had no effect. João thinks Gaúcho and the others who complain have forgotten this.

They're going to find out that we won't stand for it any more, says Gaúcho. This time we're going to show them.

Who is going to show them? asks João, who has never lived so well, even able to pay off his debt to Dom Fernando.

The Brazilian people, says Gaúcho. We will act as *one*.

• • •

It's another scorcher, the City Clerk's office with only two puny fans working, half the scribblers in Detroit crammed in waiting for the results while overworked public servants and the occasional councilman poke their heads in to check on the recall numbers. All the ballot boxes are going to a central precinct to be counted for this contest, but the polls close at different times depending on your neighborhood. Typical Chinese fire drill, even without Bowles in charge of it. Smitty is happy that nobody is honoring Reading's injunction not to light up—the killjoys have managed to exile the barleycorn but not the tobacco leaf—and the two fans push the smoke from opposite directions so that it piles up right in front of the clerk's desk, where it is stirred into swirling clouds by reporters flapping their hats. Too many lids and not enough hooks to hang them on. City Clerk Reading seems to be taking it well, leaning back relaxed in a swivel chair and chatting till the next precinct report comes in.

"You got anything down on this?" asks Danny Curtis from the *News*.

"Naw, the odds against Bowles were too steep," says Smitty, "and you always got the possibility it's been fixed—"

"This isn't Chicago."

"That's what this city's motto oughta be. Instead of whatsit—"

"*Speramus Meliora, Resurget Cineribus—*" chimes in Rybicki, here for the *Dziennik Polski*. "We Hope for Better and We Rise From the Ashes."

"Bowles is the *ashes*, and he's only been in six months."

"The say Gillespie's got the real power."

"That fits even better—the Public Works commissioner running the town. He's got near as many jobs to hand out as Henry Ford."

Smitty and Curtis are using the window sill as a partial seat, both smoking, pads and pencils in their pockets waiting for numbers or drama. A young woman, somebody's secretary, hovers at the door considering the sea of perspiring journalists she'd have to squeeze through to get to the city clerk, then hands it to Benton from the Hearst paper.

"Would you please pass this on to Mr. Reading?" she asks and makes a hasty retreat, scribes evaluating her hindquarters as she goes. They pass the slip of paper from one to the other, all taking a glance at the numbers on it, before it lands on Reading's desk.

"Returns from Black Bottom," he announces after a gander. "Overwhelmingly in favor of recall."

Laughter and comment for a while then, Black Bottom almost all colored these days, and therefore no fans of the Klan's favorite mayor. The office boy chalks the numbers up on the board that's been brought in, giving the room the feeling of a horse-betting parlor. A healthy turnout along Hastings Street, easily nullifying the earlier pro-Bowles votes from the couple northwest precincts the white refugees from the sunny south have settled in. Harry Bennett likes to brag that he has these former enemies working side-by-side at the Rouge, keeping them too busy spinning wingnuts to look at each other, much less come to blows.

"Colored people keep coming to the polls like this, they'll be a factor to deal with."

"That's what Frank Murphy is hoping," says Rybicki.

"You think he'll run if the recall goes through?"

"Only if he's asked politely."

"Hey," says Danny Curtis, pointing. "I didn't know Driesson was bald."

Driesson's desk is right in front of Smitty's at the *Free Press*, where he never removes his fedora, but here he is waving it in front of his face as sweat rolls down his forehead.

"You can put that in your lede," says Smitty. "'Two firsts occurred today—a big city mayor was recalled from office, and Dutch Driesson bared his hairless dome in public.'"

"You think Bowles is cooked?"

"Do the math—more than half the precincts in, he's down what—eighteen thousand already. I don't see where he makes up that kind of ground."

Danny Curtis is scoping the smoke-filled room, a frown on his face. "How come this dump is still City Hall?"

It was a grand building in its day back in the last century, the clock tower making it the tallest structure in Detroit at that time, huge windows to let the light in, lots of black walnut, oak, impressive staircases, but far too small for the city it now serves.

"They had plans all drawn up for a new one when the stock market tanked."

"Ah—"

"And Ford puts most of his civic charity into Dearborn."

"I hear the Rouge workers, the ones who are still hanging onto to their jobs out there, got the day off after they were advised how to vote."

"And Harry Bennett's people are out in front of the polling stations in case they have a memory lapse."

Smitty looks for an ashtray, considers Danny's hat, turned over in his lap, then stubs his butt out on the floor. What you deserve, inviting a posse of inkslingers into your office-

Danny shakes his head. "That's a lot of votes for the mayor if the auto workers do what they're told. Plus there's the anti-booze vote—Bowles is still the dry candidate."

"Dry as a rum cake on St. Patrick's Day. Can you imagine firing a police commissioner for raiding juice joints—"

"Emmons didn't consult the payoff list. But Christ, *wait* a month or two before you can the guy. Even the Purples leave a beef sit for a while, let the victim get comfortable—"

"Just like my editor."

Smitty laughs. "Yeah, I heard about the St. Valentine's Day massacre over there."

"Everybody else is getting bounced to the bricks—why not reporters?"

The buzz in the room quiets suddenly, and Smitty stands to peer through the scribblers and the smoke to clock the arrival.

It's Bowles.

Reporters part like the Red Sea before Moses, allowing their stolid lump of a mayor to march straight up to the city clerk's desk, red-faced and shouting even before he arrives.

"You know this whole thing is a gigantic conspiracy and a fraud," it goes, "and you're a party to it!"

It is only half a performance for the press, and Reading fields it nicely.

"I'm sorry, Mr. Mayor," he says, "but I'm just doing my job here. The people have made their will very clear, or we wouldn't be having this vote."

"Half those petition names were forgeries!"

"Please, Mr. Mayor," says Reading with a polite smile. "We're not Chicago."

Danny Curtis digs Smitty in the ribs. "See?"

"*Non sumus Chicago*," says Smitty, who got to study law for a year before his father's haberdashery went under. "It has a ring to it."

Bowles stalks out, pausing to point a stubby finger into the face of Driessen, who has clapped his topper back on his skull. "And *your* outfit had better watch out!"

Bowles being a crook but no Al Capone, the reporters are free to laugh when he's gone.

"Jesus. I mean, you can be on the take and still be good *com*pany," says Driessen. "Look at Jimmy Walker in New York. But *no*body likes this prick."

Radio technicians appear then to set up their equipment, and Smitty joins the print crowd as they're flushed out into the hallway.

"Make way for the artisans of the airwaves," grumbles Danny Curtis. "Here to serve our illiterate citizens."

"They read fine," says the engineer carrying the big WMBC microphone in. "But they prefer their news *cook*ed, and with a little gravy on it."

The runners keep coming with more results and the radio boys keep stretching wires and cables down the hallway and then there is Jerry Buckley, walking toward them wearing a tailored suit and trailing an appetizing young secretary. He flashes his Ipana toothpaste smile-

"Hey, fellas."

"Silver Tonsils," calls Smitty. "Looking sharp."

"Whereas you, Smitty, resemble a deadbeat newshound from the pictures. Who's that actor—Skeets Gallagher—"

"They always make us out to be drunks and cynics."

"Now where'd they get that idea?"

The reporters in the hallway laugh. Buckley is a familiar face around

Detroit, only becoming a radio heartthrob in the last couple years. He was some kind of lawyer before, did legwork for his brother at the prosecutor's office, snooped for Harry Bennett on a couple things, and was a nightclub fixture, chasing skirts and claiming to be a songwriter. A regular guy.

"What's it looking like in there?" Buckley asks, glancing into the clerk's office still full of radio technicians stepping over each other.

"Bowles is taking a beating."

"Really?"

"Don't act surprised—you socked it to him pretty hard this week."

Buckley shrugs his shoulders. "I'm just one voice."

"Climb off of it, Jerry. Anybody with a radio from here to Ypsilanti tunes your show in, got your mug plastered on those billboards—if you grew yourself one of those William Powell mustaches you'd have to beat the dolls away with a stick."

"After my wife finished using it on *me*."

"That's right, you're *mar*ried—" Smitty sees the young secretary giving the boss a look, like this is news to her. He's seen Buckley plenty of nights at the Kit Kat Club, just a block from the LaSalle Hotel where he broadcasts, and never with the missus.

"I'll be happy when this is all over," says the microphone jockey, "and I can get back to more important issues. The biggest crime in this country isn't bootlegging, it's that old folks have to go into the poorhouse at the end of their lives, that folks who work till they're seventy don't get a pension—"

"You been slicing that baloney awful thick," says Danny Curtis.

"You think the way it's set up now is fair?"

"No, but what's going to change it?"

"A third of the population out on the street with nothing in their pockets is what. If this money crunch gets any worse—"

"You sound like a Red."

"I sound like the voice of the common herd."

"You catch any heat for going after the mayor?" asks Rybicki.

"Who says I 'went after' him?"

"'Gillespie is the real mayor of Detroit,' 'Bowles has put handcuffs on the police commissioner,' 'Detroit stinks from the top'—or words to that effect."

"Hey, you've been listening to my show!" Buckley grins. "Sure—I get some threatening notes, phone calls to the station. There's always crackpots."

"Any of them with Italian accents?" asks Smitty.

"I'm more worried about the characters in the white hoods."

The Klan has been torching crosses in Detroit, one out on the grass in front of this building when Bowles lost in '25. One of Smitty's colleagues who lives out far enough to rate a mailbox opened it to find a dead rat with a threatening note pinned to it one day. No stamp, no return address.

"This recall had to happen," says Buckley. "We've had what—ten, eleven gang killings just this month—"

"Two of them right on your doorstep."

A pair of out-of-town hoods were shot in their car parked right in front of the LaSalle Hotel entrance just before Jerry went on the air a few weeks ago, the shooters strolling back through the lobby and out the other side. He could have looked down from his mezzanine window and seen the whole thing.

"Exactly what I'm talking about. And all Bowles can say is 'Let them rub each other out'—like a hail of bullets never hit an innocent bystander."

"Word is Chet LaMare was behind those garlic-eaters getting popped at the fish house-"

Buckley holds up a hand to stop him. "Save it for the next police commissioner."

"Any idea who that's going to be?"

"Fellas," he says, stepping into the Clerk's office, "I don't *make* the news, I just throw my two cents in after it happens."

• • •

The station has him cutting in for three minutes every half hour with the numbers, which continue to build on the recall side. In between, he chats with Reading or goes out to smoke with the newspaper boys. He wasn't so sure about the whole deal at first, but the throw-the-bum-out camp got their signatures and donations so fast and then the calls to the station, most citing Bowles as 'a disgrace to our great city,' convinced him it was okay to say on the air what everybody downtown has known all along. The guy never even made a pretense of being straight once he was in, bootleggers seen strolling into the mayor's office with grins on their faces, every gang in Detroit in on the act except the Purples, and them only excluded because getting cozy with Jews would queer Bowles's appeal to the Klan. And yes, among the calls that Jerry took himself have been a few warning him to shut his trap or pay the price.

Circulate around the nightspots and you're going to meet some rough characters, many of them good company if you stay on their shiny side. The musicians and dancers he knows live in that world—"Sure, Mr. Cellura, I'll come over to your table and say hello after my set." If liquor is illegal, who's going to own the clubs that pay a decent wage? But the hoods he knows, the ones he likes, anyway, make no bones about what business they're in. A creep like Bowles, on the other hand, running as the dry candidate, the whites-only candidate, the 'Christian values' candidate-

It's been a pleasure to help knock him off his high horse.

But hootch peddlers are businessmen, and if Bowles is vital to their enterprise and Jerry Buckley's big mouth is seen as a threat—well. He's never actually *fired* the pistol. But his buddy Stretch urged him to carry it, and Evelyn, sweet kid, is willing to hold it for him it in her handbag here in City Hall. Ruins the line of his suit.

The Mayor sends a flunky up at ten o'clock, throwing in the towel, the newspapermen immediately beating their feet to the nearest telephone to call in the story. It would have been nice to corral Bowles with a microphone in hand, but he's never given newshounds, print or radio, the time of day. Another strike against the guy—

"Mayor Charles Bowles has just conceded, accepting that he has been recalled as mayor of the city of Detroit!" Jerry barks into the microphone, trying to put some oomph into what's been obvious for hours. "There will be a new election within ninety days. With eight hundred and fifty-two precincts reporting, we have 120,770 votes for recall and only 89,907 against. Ladies and gentlemen, you have *spoken*."

He takes a few more minutes to moralize, speculating as to whether Bowles will walk away or try to get reelected, and closes by thanking the folks for their good citizenship. The poll watchers coming in have commented that the female turnout was way down, the suffragette crowd maybe realizing that yes, politics is a dirtier game than they care to be associated with.

If only they'd stayed home for the Prohibition vote.

It's pretty late after the wrap-up, but Gedge wants him back at the studio to tuck the night owls into bed, so he says goodbye to Martin and the technical boys and heads downstairs with Evelyn.

"Do you want this now?" she asks just before they step out of City Hall, holding up her handbag. Sometimes Jerry thinks he's carrying it just to impress the girl, who though a smart cookie in other ways remains pretty innocent. But it's late and half of Detroit knows he's coming out of this building, so yes, hand the thing over.

He puts it in the side pocket of his jacket, where it makes an unsightly lump and weighs a ton. Any self-respecting button man would clock it in a second, and then—what? Decide not to engage with somebody who's heeled? Know an amateur when he sees one and complete his business with a funny story to share with the *paesani*? Luckily, enough cabbies have seen the lights still on so there's a choice, and he has Evelyn wait up on the steps till he finds a trusted face among them, a Greek named Stavros who's a crazy Tigers fan, poor sap.

Once they're in the cab heading up Woodward, Evelyn relaxes a bit.

"You'd feel better if you had the bodyguard Mr. Gedge offered," she says.

"I could ride in a bullet-proof automobile like Capone does, too, but it wouldn't make me feel better. This will blow over in a couple days."

"So why the gun?"

"To defend your honor, if need be."

This gets a chuckle out of Evelyn. Good kid. At first he felt he was putting on airs even having a secretary, but with all the appearances, the charity work, showing up to call raffle winners and bingo numbers, somebody has to keep track, and Jeanette is strictly a stay-at-home mother these days.

"They've been killing each other like crazy lately."

At least a dozen already this month, and it's not because of the heat wave.

"It's called *vendetta*," Jerry explains. "Some of it goes all the way back to Sicily. *Your* great grandfather stole *my* great grandfather's goat. Then here it's about territory—Singing Sam Catalanotte's bunch have got the west side, Tocco and Zerilli are strong on the east, the colored have their own people in Black Bottom and Paradise Valley, and the Little Jewish Navy own the river."

"And the police—?"

"Are easily bought. Or at least rented. There's some hard cases who won't play ball, but they tend to get farmed out to the nether precincts."

Jerry sees out the window that the Fox is showing *Good Intentions* with Edmund Lowe, who played Sergeant Quirt in *What Price Glory?* a couple years ago. Now that it's all talkies you wonder what his voice sounds like. The Rhythm Kings are still listed as the house band and there's a Fanchon and Marco prologue. Jerry knows that a certain young Sunkist Beauty has recently left town for another show-

"What will they do if the liquor law gets changed back?" asks Evelyn. It isn't as dramatic as the recall, but the public, and even some of the more daring and level-headed politicians, are starting to realize what a bonehead idea the Volstead Act was.

"Well, you won't see any bootleggers lined up for free soup and a crust of bread out on Michigan Avenue. They'll still have dope to sell, illegal betting, prostitution, extortion. The independent outlaws will still have banks to rob, they'll have the snatch racket—"

"Would you pay my ransom?"

Serious or flirting? Jerry just laughs. "So far I never heard of secretaries being used as payoff bait. Mistresses yes, but the gals in the typing pool only have to watch out for their bosses."

Jeannette has never met Evelyn and he's sure she'd prefer he hire somebody at least forty years older, but the kid is good for his mood, always on the upbeat. She never shares any dope on her own love life, which is fine with Jerry.

"There's so many people still out on the street," she says, looking out the taxi window. "What are they are doing?"

"Detroit never sleeps."

"Well *I* do. Remember you've got the Women's City Club at two tomorrow."

"I will see you there."

Stavros lets him off at the LaSalle and continues to take Evelyn to her mom's house out past Eight Mile. There are maybe a dozen people in the hotel lobby, Will Janszco still up like always and inviting him to his room for a get-together.

"Are we celebrating or mourning?" asks Jerry.

"Oh, they'll be some from both camps there, but Charley Bowles isn't invited."

Jerry calls Jeanette from the phone booth to tell her he'll be staying the night at the room he keeps here. She sounds upset.

"Somebody already called. They said 'Your husband won't be coming home tonight.'"

"You all right?"

"I wish this was over."

"It is, it is. You heard the results?"

"Rosemary and I listened to you."

"She's up late, then."

"Sleeping now. I worry about you there. The two men who were shot outside—"

"Hey, the house detective is a pal, he's on the lookout for anybody acting fishy. I might as well be sleeping at the police station."

Jerry makes sure there's nobody in the elevator but the operator, a little Irishman named Corrigan who's probably been at the hotel since it was still called the Savoy. The WMBC station manager, Bill Gedge, and a skeleton crew are still open for business when he gets off at the mezzanine.

"Pretty lively night," says Gedge. "We've had so many calls—mostly saying good riddance."

"Any—you know—discouraging words from anonymous sources?"

Bill gives him a stiff smile. "Oh, the usual. Poor bastards will have to find another stooge to put in office."

"When they do, a little subtlety would be welcome. Keep the graft *un*der the table."

Jerry sits into the booth for a late bulletin and a goodnight to the herd, solemn as a judge thanking a jury in a murder trial. Bill is holding the phone up when he signs off.

"For you."

It is a woman, a familiar voice he can't quite peg.

"I got a story that has to get out there, Mr. Buckley. A big story. Only they're watching me during the day."

One out of ten of these 'big stories' ever pans out, but some are good for local color.

"Any chance I can come see you at the station?"

He's definitely too wired to sleep.

"Lobby of the LaSalle Hotel, about an hour from now?"

There are always a few employees and insomniacs down there, and it's well-lit. He's not batty enough to meet a stranger on their own turf-

"I'll be there," says the woman.

Very familiar voice, but he can't get a handle on it. "How will I know you?"

"I'll know *you*. I seen your picture."

It is past midnight when Corrigan takes him up to his room.

"So they've given Mayor Bowles the old heave-ho," says the Irishman. "In my day, you elected a bad character, you held your nose and took your medicine till his term was over."

"There's some value in that. But the man broke every promise he ever made."

"Then good riddance to bad rubbish, I say."

The bed looks inviting but he knows he'll just lie there, so he throws some water on his face, checks his hair in the mirror, ditches the pistol—a .38 is too much of a cannon, he thinks, I'll have to get something smaller—and goes down the hallway to Janszco's room.

There's more than a dozen people still percolating there, smoking, drinking, Rudy Vallée and His Connecticut Yankees, of all things, schmaltzing from the phonograph.

"How you holding up?" asks a woman, almost a looker, who he's sure he's met before.

"Tired," he tells her. "And I think my number might be up."

He doesn't know why he hit the minor key all of sudden, maybe the long day. Or maybe it's the depth of the corruption, the stink of the hypocrisy, the faces of those poor jobless stiffs lined up in front of the soup kitchen who he passes every morning-

"Those greaseballs wouldn't dare hurt you," the woman tells him. "Not somebody who's got their picture on a billboard."

Bill Gedge insisted on the billboard, up at the corner of Woodward and Temple. "I'm a *voice*," Jerry told him, "let them imagine what I look like."

Bill said that would be fine if he was old or porky like some of the station's lineup, but he had the looks to draw the female listeners.

Jerry forces a grin for the woman. "All that picture means is they'll never mistake some other poor slob for me."

In the elevator down to the lobby he asks Corrigan if Roscoe Kearns, the house detective, is up and about.

"There was a domestic altercation on the third floor," the Irishman tells him. "And he had to escort a gentleman to the police station."

Jerry buys today's *Free Press*—already old news and good only for lining the canary's cage—at the desk, and settles into a wing chair facing the Woodward Avenue entrance. The guy reading the *Times* in the next chair places him right away.

"You're Jerry Buckley."

"Guilty."

"Naw—it's good what you do. Somebody's got to tell the sons of bitches off."

"I try to call attention to things—"

"Gillespie and that crowd must be pretty steamed at you. Up there on the mountain, pointing fingers—"

"Like Moses."

The lobby lizard grins. "Sure. Like him."

"Only Moses never saw the Promised Land."

The guy leaves it at that and Jerry scans the front page. A *Free Press* editorial in a box, urging a *yes* vote on recall, the paper throwing their weight behind it in the last few days. An article about Gillespie's rally at the Light Guard Armory, where the lawyer Louis Colombo, introduced as Henry Ford's personal representative, urged support for Bowles. An article about a father and stepmother arrested for keeping their ten-year-old son chained to a pillar in their basement all summer-

It isn't a noise but a feeling that makes him look up over the paper. Two characters in light brown suits, dark shoes, Panama hats pulled low over their eyes, stepping straight toward him.

Those are .38s, just like mine, he thinks, before the first one starts firing-

• • •

After the first whistle that ends breakfast you only have a little while to hurry to the time machine nearest where you're going to work that day. There's a stiff piece of paper with your name on it—João recognizes his—tucked into the rows of them and you have to push it into a slot in the machine and it makes a sharp noise and has another little mark on it when you pull it out.

You slip it back onto the rack and by that time probably the second whistle is blowing and the *capataz* of your work detail yells for you to get moving.

They have cleared and planted so far that if you happen to get up on the ridge and look toward the river there is nothing but rows and rows of growing rubber trees in every direction, many now taller than João with their tops leafing out and about to touch branches. Flavio, who is very good with numbers like his mother, has counted over two thousand of them while doing the weeding jobs the Company sometimes gives him, paying him coins at the end of the day but not making him punch in at a time machine. What Flavio seems to want more than anything these days is to be given a Ford badge with his own identification number stamped on it—João's is B1365—that he can pin on his shirt. Within an hour of starting, heat and hard labor force the men to hang their sodden shirts up on whatever is available and pin the hot metal badges to their belts.

Road building is hard work.

You clear with axes and machetes, pull stumps with crowbars or fill the holes left by the big ones the tractors pull up. You dig up and pile rocks. You move rocks and dirt in wheelbarrows. You drag downed trees and underbrush to piles where it will be burned. There is shade at the sides of the path you are cutting but don't dare get caught lingering in it. Today the *capataz* is the one everybody hopes not to be assigned to, an Argentinian, notorious for making *trabalhadores* cut the pockets off their pants so they won't be tempted to stuff their hands into them. João is hoping for the day, at least three years from now when the first-planted trees will mature, when he can go back to being a collector of rubber sap, something he is better at than almost anybody now in camp.

Today he is moving felled trees, most of them small and scrubby, dragging them to a pile that grows and grows, occasionally joining with another worker to carry a big bole after trimming the branches off. A separate pile is made of the wood *Senhor* Rogan considers valuable, to be milled into boards and made into buildings. There are so many Company buildings down by the shore of the Tapajós now, as well as the separate little *bairro* for the Americans, rows of little white wooden houses that remind João of an orderly cemetery with identical headstones and crosses.

There is one of those, too.

"*Vamos, pessoal!*" calls the *capataz*. If we have to be out here in this fucking sun let's get some work done.

There is a new hospital building where they are taken to get shots for all kinds of diseases and where the wives and children of the married workers are treated for free, a power house and a machine shop, and the new mess hall, finished just last week, that nobody likes. For a while João was having nightmares, terrible nightmares where he and the other men were tied to each other by the ankles and forced to do all their tasks in unison, screamed at or whipped if one of them swung an axe or chopped down with a shovel out of step with the others, but then Gaúcho said it was the quinine pills they are made to swallow at the end of every day when they come to punch their cards in the time machine again, and that he should slip them under his tongue and spit them out when none of the overseers are looking. João hasn't had a nightmare since he started doing this, and hopes that the sweats and shakes, which he has suffered from since he was very young, don't start up again.

When the whistle for dinner sounds there is little satisfaction in looking back at what they've already cleared, only a pathway through trees that will probably be cut down for more rubber planting in a few years.

No truck appears to carry them, so the workers march to the mess hall, nearly a hundred men already stacked up outside under the sun by the time they get there.

Line up and don't shift around, the *capataz* tells them, so the clerks can check you in.

This is how they line the cattle up at the slaughterhouse, says Gaúcho, talking heatedly to some of the skilled workers waiting closer to the entrance. And we give them no more trouble than the cattle do.

If the food were any good it might be worth the wait, says a carpenter from São Luís. That fish they dumped on our plates yesterday—

If you don't eat it the day it's caught, says da Silva, who was in fact a fisherman before he heard about the wages being paid here, it will make you sick.

It is a long wait and then still a line when they get inside, men expected to take a tray and walk past servers ladling out food instead of sitting at the table with waiters coming by like before. The new mess hall is all concrete with a low metal roof and it is hotter in here than outside.

One of the *gringos* who hands them their pay once every two weeks, tall and red-haired and not much liked even by the other *gringos*, also has the duty of supervising the shifts coming in for dinner.

Don't bunch up like that, he calls to the men in his terrible Portuguese that is nearly impossible to understand. Stay in line!

Gaúcho moves out from the rest of them and steps up to stand right in front of the man, so close to his face that João feels nervous in his stomach.

We are not dogs, Gaúcho tells the pay clerk. You can't treat us like this. It doesn't matter how much money you pay—

He doesn't understand you, calls the *capataz*, hurrying up to join them. Leave it be for now—

"*Volte para a fila,*" says the scowling pay clerk. Get back in line.

Gaúcho plucks his Ford badge off, ripping his shirt, and presses it against the surprised *gringo's* chest.

You can stick this up your ass, he says, then turns to the watching crowd of workers, holding his arms out wide. If any of you are men, he says, it's time for you to show it!

A plate spins right past João's ear, barely missing the pay clerk and smashing against the concrete wall. It is like the first pop of a string of firecrackers at the beginning of Carnaval-

-João ducking and covering his head with his hands as suddenly everything that can be lifted and hurled is in the air—food, plates, chairs—and he runs for the exit just behind the pay clerk who joins the *gringo* who was taking their badge numbers in leaping into a pickup truck and roaring away as half the crowd from inside chases after them throwing whatever they can get their hands on and screaming curses.

It's time to fix the clocks! shouts Gaúcho and the men rush off in every direction, João stumbling away from the mess hall where the crashing and shattering noises still ring out, heading for the little married workers' *bairro* and passing a dozen men smashing the pressure gauges on the main water line with chair legs and finally meeting Flavio running toward him-

"*Todo mundo é louco!*" he warns. Let's go find your mother.

Dozens of women have broken off from their grinding of manioc and mending of clothes to hurry toward the sounds of smashing and shouting, Beatriz among them.

Is there a fight? she calls out, gripping a white-painted fence post she's torn up from the ground.

It's us against the *gringos*, João tells her, taking the fence post. We'd better get across the river.

Beatriz scowls. And I just cleaned that whole house!

Ostenfelt and the new steward, Coleman, are the first to arrive with the warning, skidding the utility truck on the gravel road and into a ditch in their hurry. Jim has kept a tug and the *Bellcamp*, a small launch, anchored around the bend upriver from the main dock, and delegates Curt Pringle to gather the American families and lead them down the path he's had cut to them from the management compound. They've left trees to form something like a park around the cluster of identical houses—not so different from those back in Pine Camp—so fortunately the rioters won't see them leaving right away. Jim sends Gomes to contact Belém for help, hopefully before anybody thinks to cut the power at the radio station. This leaves seven of his Michigan crew, mostly lumbermen, to slow the mob if possible, with a truck that can take all of them left running by the road to the back of the plantation.

There are perhaps thirty-five, forty workers, most of them skilled mechanics and drivers who've come from other states for the steady pay, the business disaster that hit back home just as bad or worse here in Brazil. Many of them look and act drunk, shouting in what is not quite unison as they approach the reception office-

"*Brasil para os brasileiros, matem todos os americanos*!"

Brazil for Brazilians, kill all the Americans.

Rogan wishes one of the good translators was with him, his Portuguese improving all the time, but still like what a five-year-old kid would be able to say.

"*Diga-me qual é o problema*," he says.

And they tell him what the problem is, but all at once and so many different problems that he catches only that they don't like the food or how it is given to them or having to work in the heat and the rain when it's *uma estupidez* and having every moment of their workday timed by clocks and *gringos* telling them where and how to live and you know what you can do with your fucking rubber trees. A couple of the men are carrying metal cans of gasoline and all have something to hit you with or throw at you in their hands, while Jim has had Pringle and the other men who went to the boats with him take all the guns. Norma and Kerry should be on the tug now, Pringle instructed to wait until it's no longer safe and then head upriver to what passes for civilization.

Jim can see black smoke in the sky behind the workers now, can hear crashing and shooting. He calmly tells his crewmen to head for the truck and make their way to the launch, and then lets the drunken workers know that they can do what they want, but he's going to call Mr. Ford and pass on their complaints.

"*Senhor Ford não vai ficar feliz*."

Positive that Mr. Ford will not, indeed, be happy, Jim walks purposefully toward the beginning of the escape path while his Michigan men go for the truck. The workers seem mollified, or at least distracted by smashing windows and throwing wads of office records out of the reception building, some sloshing gasoline on every flammable surface in preparation to burning it to the ground. So far they seem to have left the trees alone-

When Jim is out of sight from the rioters he begins to run.

Kerry hugs him when he clambers onto the tug, flocks of birds passing overhead to escape the smoke. Norma just looks at him, as if the whole deal is his fault.

Maybe it is, he thinks. I wasn't trained for this.

They keep telling her to try to get to sleep, but why would you want to? With everybody she knows down here all on the tug boat, just anchored and not making its machine noise, you can hear the soft voices of the families talking with each other, and beyond that pops and bangs and voices shouting, echoing over the water, and a big moon in the sky overhead though it's like seeing it through frosted glass because of all the smoke that has drifted out from the plantation. It was scary for only a few minutes, not knowing where the people going crazy were, but after all, her father is in charge. Just now there is an animal noise, not a bird, because she is starting to recognize the sounds each makes and the names people here call them—*macaíba, tucano, hoatzín, cotinga, oropendola*—but a jumble of rapid barking sounds that might be a bunch—a troop?—of white-cheeked spider monkeys—*macacos-aranha*—getting together to discuss what the humans are doing in their forest now.

That's the kind Kerry wants one of.

There's a pretty reflection of the smoky moon on the water and a red glow over the treetops from downstream. Her father says they've anchored in a spot protected by really thick jungle on both sides, so they can have lights on and not worry about the glow from the little smudge pots they've laid out to keep mosquitos away. Nights and days are always about the same length here, and when the sun comes up and they can see to navigate her dad says they'll chug up to one of the bigger towns, so food and water won't be a problem. There is only one little cabin to do your business in and you have to make your way around all the groups of people sitting or lying on the deck to get there and then there's a line waiting. She's been told that monkeys just let go wherever they are up in the trees, so don't walk underneath them, but so far hasn't had the chance to. Sometimes when her father is in a really good mood he calls her "my little spider monkey" but she's not so little any more.

The only really bad thing is that mom is mad at him for some reason, her jaw all tight and her arms crossed around her chest like she's cold, which it isn't really even though it's night time and almost Christmas. Nobody else probably notices because they have their own worries—leaving their houses behind, what's happened to the few men who aren't aboard here or on the launch anchored just upstream—and because dad is staying away from her, talking with some of the men about plans for tomorrow and checking in with each of the families to be sure they're okay. He did stuff like that back in Pine Camp but nobody there ever tried to burn the village or the sawmill down.

In the book about the Swiss family they are on their way to a new home in Australia when they're wrecked on the island and have to figure out how to survive, and a lot of it seems like fun—they have dogs and adopt a baby monkey named Nip and find an English girl named Jenny who's been marooned there before—the character she would be if she was in the story and was a few years older.

"It's going to be all right," Kerry says to her mother for the third or fourth time since the sun dipped below the treetops.

"You know that, do you?" says her mom, the first time she's bothered to answer.

There's a boy Kerry goes exploring with, named Flavio, who teaches her the names of the birds and animals and some other words and sometimes gets jobs on the plantation. He's not so different from her tree-climbing friend Tim back in Pine Camp, and it's a beautiful language to try to say, like some strange kind of music. She hopes he and his family are safe.

"There will be stores wherever we go tomorrow," says Kerry. "We could go shopping."

• • •

It is illegal, it is unethical, but it is in character.

Edsel tries to think of how else Father could be sniffing out the details of his private life—a life Father does not approve of and is certainly not interested in—without some sort of a spy. Edsel's secretaries, Lepine and Backus, are above reproach and not party to many of the things that have leaked out, so who else could it be?

Harry Bennett is having his telephone tapped.

Law officers know and use the technique, and certainly Harry has a good number of those under his influence, even bragging that he shares his knowledge of underworld activities in Detroit with the Federal Bureau man, Hoover, but how could honest lawmen justify surveilling a citizen as upstanding as Edsel Ford?

The gangsters, perhaps, whom Bennett claims to cultivate in order to keep them under control, might have their own operatives, men now or formerly working for the telephone company who could connect a wire or two-

It is Christmas vacation for the children and he doesn't want Father to know all their travel plans, which include joining up with the Kanzlers in Ormond Beach, an ordinary enough rendezvous considering that Eleanor and Josephine are sisters and he and Ernest best of friends. But Ernest, bent on helping Edsel in the campaign for the New Ford, perhaps overestimated his position in the Company hierarchy, and submitted a rather aggressive memo to Father, leading to his ostracism and eventual banishment while Edsel was off in Europe back in '26. Eleanor is always reminding him that the Company is Father's, but his life is his *own*. It is not so simple as that, he tells her.

Father has a loathing for tobacco and alcohol—he's not alone in that, just ask Representative Volstead—but enjoyed in moderation in the manner Edsel and his friends do-

"Riotous living" is Father's judgement, hobnobbing with "a passel of wastrels and layabouts."

Edsel deals with the accountants, though Father doesn't like to hear them called that, preferring the term 'number jugglers'." Edsel is the liaison to the Ford factories in England and Germany. He organizes, as much is allowed, the flow of automobiles to their dealerships, which now includes getting the older models off the lots and disassembled to feed the smelters. Edsel puts in a long, often taxing day, at the end of which, like any other automobile executive in Detroit-

You can't say 'executive' around Father.

Executives are the enemy, riding their desks up on Mahogany Row, men who couldn't change a tire on a Model A with an instruction book and a wrench in hand. Executives, Father has said, might as well be *bankers*, the vilest word in his vocabulary.

Being on the boat in Florida will be a relief from the strain of trying to keep the Company solvent while the nation is going broke, of dealing with a new wave of layoffs and the disturbing news from Brazil, but it won't be a total escape. Guardian Trust, the financial institution Ernest assured him was foolproof, is reeling as badly as any of the major banks since Black Friday and the subsequent panic, and Edsel is afraid his brother-in-law will be seeking a sizable injection of capital to shore it up.

And there will be no hiding that from Father.

Edsel peeks out of his office door to find Backus sitting there, diligently working on the complicated tax forms that pile up this time of year.

"Jim? I'm hearing some strange noises when I use the telephone here. Could you have somebody come and see if there's anything unusual going on in the system?"

"Of course," says Backus. "Do you want to accept calls before I've done that?"

"Of course, depending on the caller. But at the moment—at the moment, I'm not *in*."

"Let me know when you're back."

"I'll do that."

Edsel closes the door, heads for his washroom. What he'd really like now is a nice relaxing cocktail, but his stomach is acting up again.

"It's probably an ulcer," Eleanor tells him. "That job is eating away at you."

Edsel closes the washroom door, lies back on the leather couch. Quietest spot in the River Rouge complex. The inner sanctum. When he closes his eyes he can picture warm water, seagulls hovering in a bright blue sky-

Quitting would only confirm Father's suspicion that he is a weakling, not fit for the rough-and-tumble of the auto business. And considering the hundreds of thousands of workers—yes, even with the cutbacks and branch closings it is still that many—who depend on the Company for a living, quitting would not only be cowardice, it would be gross irresponsibility.

Maybe if they book a sleeper car to Maine, but change trains in Chicago, it could throw Harry off the scent-

• • •

It is the first day of the new year, 1931, and João stands in a long line by the dock waiting to be paid. Most of the workers are owed up to the end of last week. Men scoop their money off the table and then are escorted by soldiers onto the steamer by the dock, more soldiers waiting on board. This is a surprise to many, who thought the new revolutionary government would come to chase the Ford *estrangeiros* away, not help them dismiss all their workers and bring in new ones. Da Silva, standing in front of him, is angry at the betrayal.

This is *our* land, he says.

But da Silva is not from here, and the land has never belonged to anybody but the handful of *aristocratas*, unless you count the naked Indians who've been pushed into the *savana* upriver. João hopes that Dom Fernando will not be too angry at him for coming to work here, the old man just shaking his head sadly back when João settled his debt with paper money from Fordlandia.

This will come to a bad ending, said Dom Fernando.

And it has, most of the men around João looking a little ashamed though still angry—since the soldiers leveled the outlaw *favela* and spread quicklime where it used to be, lots of them have had to sleep in the open or on the littered floor of the mess hall where it all started, or in the hospital, though many are afraid that is the likeliest place on the plantation to catch a disease. Most of the married workers' housing was spared, and what was left of the little American village was protected by the soldiers who came in the flying boat. Beatriz and Flavio have packed all their belongings and are waiting by the path that used to be on his rubber-tapping rounds, João hoping he can talk the soldiers out of making him get onto the steamer.

Do you know where you'll go? he asks da Silva.

Somewhere far from *gringos*.

The Argentinian *capitaz* comes up the line then, followed by a dozen of the married workers whom João knows pretty well. He points at João-

"*Você—siga-me.*"

João obeys, stepping out of line and joining the group trailing behind the foreman.

What are they going to do with us? he asks Bruno Silviera.

We're staying, says Bruno cautiously, aware that the Argentinian understands Portuguese. They need somebody to clean up.

A MESSAGE
to thousands of women who've said,

'I've always longed to drive a roadster'

Deep in the heart of almost every woman who drives a car is a longing for a roadster . . . a trim and stylish car that she may call her very own.

That dream, long cherished, can now come true. For here, at an unusually low price, is a roadster that is the very answer to your hopes. So alert and reliable that it puts a new joy in motoring. So altogether smart and stylish that it merits an admiring turn of the head on every highway.

The 1931 Ford De Luxe Roadster is beautifully finished in a variety of colors. Blonde or brunette, there is a color to suit your particular taste and type---perhaps even to match your Fall ensemble.

"THESE THINGS ARE COMPLICATED."

Joe Tocco is always packing when he visits Harry's office, the size of the bulge indicating at least a .38, maybe a .45. He's a smiley guy, good company, if not the sharpest of the *amici*.

"What's complicated?" says Harry. "One guy's got something—a territory, a club, a racket—and another wants it, so he kills him and takes it over."

Joe shakes his head. He wears bow ties too, and keeps his hat on his head unless called to the witness stand accused of something, which happens fairly often. "There's personalities involved. Things that go way back—you know, Chet was born on the mainland."

"Mainland—"

"Ittly. Not like Singing Sam, who was the head of the *Unione Siciliano* here, and most of the other main guys. Which was held against him."

"Prejudice." If he can keep it straight, Harry will relay all this to the Chief, who is fascinated with the ins and outs of the local underworld.

Joe shrugs. "It's a factor. Anyhow, Singing Sam gets a cold, big deal, right, only he's kind of like the referee here, and when he dies from the cold you can imagine—any sport, football, boxing—you pull the referee outa there and what've you got?"

"A free-for-all."

"Which nobody wants, so New York and Chicago get involved, they say Gaspare Milazzo should be the acting *capo di tutti* here, which hurts Big Chet's feelings."

"He was a sensitive man."

"Yeah, a lotta pride. And then—hey, you knew Chet pretty good—he can't keep his mouth shut, goes around saying *he* shoulda been picked, and some of his own crowd, Angelo Meli that owns the Whip Café with Leo Cellura—"

"Who's on the lam—"

"A wise decision on his part. So like I said, some of his own people don't like this and start to drift away."

"But not you."

The Beer Baron of Wyandotte grins, showing a space between his front teeth. "I'm just an honest bootlegger, I don't go in for politics. Now it gets around town what he's been saying, gets to Bill Tocco, who's no relation to me, and Joe Zerilli—"

"Tweedledee and Tweedledum." The two are brothers-in-law, Tocco married to Zerilli's sister, with a strong foothold in some legitimate businesses, each man as wide as he is short.

"-and even though Chet was best man at the wedding, their displeasure is relayed back to him. So he calls for a sit-down, to work things out—"

"At the fish house—"

"Right, and it's supposed to be Milazzo, Tocco and Zerilli, Angelo Meli, Tony Ruggieri and maybe some other guys I forget. Only everybody smells a rat except Milazzo and one of his boys—"

"Who get shot to pieces while they're waiting for the meeting to start. I figured Chet was behind that."

"Well he shoulda told his shooters not to go ahead till the big targets make the scene. All it does is kick off that month where everybody's blasting everybody else—"

"Till they perforate Jerry Buckley in the hotel lobby. Who was behind that?"

"Shit if I know, Boss. If it's people in the rackets get taken out, people don't care so much, but you go blowing the brains outa citizens—"

"Don't call me Boss. Chet used to do that."

Another grin. "Hey, you *are* the boss over here. Word is the Old Man don't do a thing less he clears it with you."

"It's convenient to have people think that sometimes, but it's not true."

"And nobody ever shot at you—"

"Except Legs Laman."

The beer baron laughs. "That's right."

"I heard Chet left town first. Louisville?"

"Yeah, he liked to bet on the nags, figured they wouldn't track him there."

Harry sees Joe glancing again at his paintings on the wall. The tigers he can maybe handle, lots of bold colors, which the guineas tend to like, but then the portrait of his daughters, Billie and Trudie, in muted tones. Keep em guessing.

"So why'd he come back?" he asks.

LaMare's wife found him murdered, lying in a pool of blood in their kitchen, despite the German shepherd guard dogs and the arsenal that included hand grenades and a tear gas gun the cops found in the house. Somebody he knew, somebody he let in-

"What's he gonna do, try to start from scratch in somebody else's town? I guess he figured he still had enough of an organization—"

"Being run by his man out there in Hamtramck—"

"Joe Amico. Only Joe maybe figured it was healthier in the long run to associate with the other side—"

"You think *he* did it?"

"Him, maybe, and maybe Elmer Macklin."

"There's somebody wasn't born in Sicily."

"We make exceptions."

"The papers said he had a bodyguard—"

"Chet's wife was driving that guy home when it happened. Which might have been a setup."

"His wife?"

"No, not her. But if you're a bodyguard, arrange for your own fucking transportation, right? He says his car engine was on the fritz—"

"It couldn't have been a Ford."

Joe laughs, then shrugs philosophically. "Loyalty is a wonderful trait, but it can get you dead."

"What about that young guy of yours, the bright boy—"

"Tony."

"Tony D'Anna."

Joe's face shows a flicker of unease. "We have agreed to part ways."

D'Anna has already approached Harry, wanting to take over Chet LaMare's fruit concession at the Rouge, and maybe pick up a Ford dealership-

"I'm sorry to hear that. He seemed smarter than a lot of the characters in your business."

Harry always treats them as fellow businessmen, which they eat up, and is careful not to get in their debt.

"He lost an uncle and his father to *vendetta* back in the Giannola days, had to be the head of his family before he was twenty."

"My father was murdered," says Harry. Hit in the head with a chair in a barroom brawl, and Harry figures that never knowing the guy probably explains some of who he is today.

"It's a tough world," says Joe pleasantly.

Harry looks at his watch. "Listen, I got a delegation of priests in five minutes—I forget what you came in here for, Joe—"

"The fruit concession."

Harry laughs. That was something he handed Chet without being asked for it, like the Chief gives him houses and boats and cars instead of paying him like the other so-called executives at the Rouge. Keep em guessing.

"Beer is not a fruit, Joe. How do you qualify for—"

"Chet didn't know a banana from his daddy's dick," says Joe. "We got people right off the boat handle the warehouse and the peddling part. I figure with Chet gone, you got an opening—"

"An opening for what?"

"For what we just been doing. Keeping you informed of what's going on in the world."

"Like the Movietone News."

"Yeah, the racket report."

"I'll think about it—it might just work out."

"And the car dealership—"

"Let's maybe start with the concession, see how that goes. A dealership needs people who aren't just off the boat." He gets to his feet, signaling that the meeting is over, and Joe Tocco catches the hint, getting up and offering his hand.

"Nice talking with you, Boss."

• • •

The commissary is in what used to serve as a grocery and dance hall, before the village started defaulting on payments, before Edison Power turned the electricity off and the trash people stopped picking up and they had to sell the one police car, the three officers, basically volunteers who have other jobs and hustles going, now trying to cover all of southwest Inkster on foot. Fat chance with that—Zeke knows three people been robbed right on their own unlit streets. Of course there never was more than four or five streetlights in Inkster, even where the white people live, the place more of a post office address and an idea in people's heads than a real village. Mondays the commissary is packed, fresh produce from the farms Ford has made deals with coming in at the end of the week, and the place shuts down on Sunday. He doesn't see Mavis behind a counter anywhere—

"You buying or selling, brother?"

It is Willis from the foundry, coming through with a crate of snap peas over his shoulder. Zeke has to grin.

"Look at you, Willis! Get you some overalls and a straw hat—"

"They lay you off too?"

"Got us on four days a week now, so I'm loose Mondays."

"Three days off is too much time for a man to get in trouble."

"On what? I'm making a dollar a day," Zeke tells him.

"Naw—"

"Company hired me back, right, two weeks after they let me go. Only this is after Mr. Ford took over Inkster—"

"He can have it."

"Well he's *got* it, on his terms. On paper I make six a day like we were doing before, but they only hand me *four* at the end of the week and the rest goes into this general fund racket—"

"Uh-oh."

"Which pays to keep this place going and to fix up houses and build that new school and pay the electric bill and—"

"So you and me taking home the same pay."

"They pay your lazy ass a dollar to stand around looking country?"

Willis laughs. Zeke wonders why his friend wasn't called back when he was—both of them family men, no trouble with the law, passed inspection by Reverend Bradby.

"Uncle Henry just sent some folks over to fix my roof," says Willis. "Couple of Hungarian fellas, talking that goulash."

"Hunkies on the roof—"

"But since I'm not putting in to no general fund, I got to sign an IOU to Uncle Henry's collector man there—"

He nods toward the display of field greens, where Donald Marshall is talking to a big woman in a dress too small to contain all of her. Marshall keeps an eye on the colored workers at the Rouge for the Little Man with the bow tie, Harry Bennett.

"What's he doing over here?"

"Got him in charge of your *cred*it. Marshall don't like you, you best pack up what little you own and get clear of Inkster. Shit, now he seen me—later, Zeke."

Willis heads toward the back with the crate and Marshall locks onto

Zeke, the crowd making way for him like he's still wearing a Detroit police badge and not just a Ford Motor Company special.

"I hardly recognize you without your goggles, Crowder."

"I don't see you up near them smelters much."

Word is Marshall will take you apart if you cross him, and then get you fired.

"I know what goes on."

"I bet you do. My wife's working here today, I got to see her."

"Working the produce or working the numbers?"

Once a cop always a cop.

"Now where'd you hear that rumor? We even get people knocking at the door sometimes, no hello, just 'Gimme a nickel on three-seven-six.'"

"You've got kids in school."

Zeke smiles like this is just a conversation. "Three of em now. Be nice if there was enough *books* so's they didn't have to double up—"

"Mr. Ford is going to take care of that."

"That's good news. You see him, ask if he could send a couple Hungarian plumbers over to my place, unstop the toilet—"

"You know where to make a request."

"I'll think on it."

Marshall, done with him, moves on to his next suspect without a goodbye. There is a bakery and a shoe store and a dry goods section attached to the commissary and Zeke wonders if Mavis might be in one of these, but first runs up on Jarvis Stokes, flashing his two gold canines.

"Zeke! My favorite Ford mule! What happen, they kick you outa the stall?"

"No production on Mondays right now."

"Damn. I knew things was bad, but if Mr. Ford gonna stop making them ugly automobiles—"

"We still make them, just not so many."

Jarvis works for John Roxborough, the numbers man, and is sent to collect from Mavis now and then.

"I'm a Packard man myself."

"Good for you."

Jarvis also runs a couple girls on the street in Black Bottom, and Zeke has never cared for him.

"Yeah, I seen you boys climbing off that streetcar after a shift, too pooped to pop. Can't keep your ladies happy that way—"

"Some are happy enough."

"That's what they *tell* you. But the way it works, you feed em and we fuck em."

The commissary is too crowded to be busting anybody's skull in, but Zeke is sorely tested. Jarvis doesn't look like he weighs near as much as what Zeke lifts on a pole a couple hundred times a day, though they're just about the same height.

"What you doing way out here, Jarvis?"

"Just come out to visit your lady." He nods toward the back room, grinning. "Don't worry now, just a fi*nan*cial transaction."

Roxborough bankrolls a couple fighters, but Jarvis is not one of them. A stiff right hand would put him in the lima beans.

"What kind of Packard you got, Jar?"

"740 Roadster."

"Lemon yellow with a white top?"

He grins. "That's my baby."

"Did it have four tires when you drove it out here?"

Jarvis's face falls. "Fuck, man—"

And he is gone. Zeke saw it parked across the street when he walked over, wondering who was stupid enough to park in Inkster without paying a street punk to watch his ride. But the tires, whitewalls with spoke caps, were all still there.

Mavis is sorting peaches in the back.

"You throw them bruised ones away?"

"They go to the bakery for pies. Something wrong with the children?"

It is always her first worry, though all three have been born with good sense.

"They all in school like they're sposed to be. I just run into Jarvis Stokes."

"That boy vex me something awful. Why Mr. Roxborough use him to collect—"

"Maybe he scares some people."

"Not me."

Zeke smiles. "No, I don't suppose he does. You got anything left after he collected?"

"Three dollars. What you need money for?"

"Lerone Hines got a cousin sposed to be a plumber—"

"They all say that. Half of em never even *seen* indoor plumbing."

"My offer is he takes a whack at it, then if we get three good flushes—*after* somebody's done their business in there—he gets paid."

Mavis thinks this over, her number wheels spinning.

"Neither of us can fix it," says Zeke, "though the Lord knows I've tried."

Mavis digs into her apron and hands him a crumpled dollar bill. Ford has set six dollars a week in goods and services as the limit for a family of five, coming out of the general fund, and they still owe Mr. Rhinehardt, the landlord, for last month's rent. To think there was a point, before all this money crisis started, when Zeke thought they might buy the house-

"You know I got another lecture from Mrs. Davis who runs this for the Company," says Mavis, sorting peaches, "about how we should have one of those gardens."

A couple hundred gardens have been plowed, residents, especially ones with ties to Ford, encouraged to grow some of their own food, with seed provided for free.

"You got time to tend it?"

Mavis looks to see that nobody has come back, then kisses him on the cheek. "You go find that man from Mobile. I don't want to be holding my nose in my own house no more."

Jarvis and his Packard are gone when Zeke steps outside, but Maceo Suggs is there, at the edge of a small crowd gathered around a dark-skinned man standing on a platform made of crates, wearing something like a flag for a shirt, with horizontal red, black and green stripes, one each, on it, and peddling the Garvey goods.

"As you well aweer," he says, turning his head to catch the eye of all present, "world we live in divided into race and nationality. Each of dem endeavor to work out their own *des*tiny."

Maceo gives Zeke a nod as he stands in beside him. Maceo has a photograph of the Jamaican Napoleon hanging over his bar counter, the man wearing an elaborate uniform with a huge feathered hat.

"We 'ear a cry of 'France for Frenchman,' 'Germany for German,' of 'China for Chinaman,' 'Ireland for Irish,' and 'Palestine for Jew.' We of the Universal Negro Improvement Association raising the cry of 'Africa for the Afri*can*,' to the four 'undred million here in United States, in West Indies islands, in countries of Sout' and Central America and Africa wit' Negro blood coursing tru their vein!"

"These people still at it?" says Zeke softly.

"Moses is in exile," says Maceo, attention fixed on the orator, "but his message gathers power."

Garvey was thrown in prison for something to do with the mail, obviously not the real reason, and then deported back to Jamaica by President Coolidge a few years ago.

"If you believe the black mon 'ave a soul, if you believe he was endow wit' the senses given by the Creator, then you must acknowledge that what other men 'ave done, the *black* mon can do!"

It is pretty noise, thinks Zeke, especially when the West Indians lay it out, their erudite, Englishy sense of words and musical rhythm always a pleasure on the ear-

"The Universal Negro Improvement Association believe in and teach the pride and purity of *race*. We believe the white race continue to perpetuate, and the black race must do the same—but *sep*arated. The Creator plan don't approve of mongrel."

Mavis, a quarter white and maybe more than that Muskogee Indian, would be dragging Zeke away by the arm now, muttering how this man's mama has to drink buttermilk so she won't pee ink-

"There is not 'ope," says the Garveyite, changing tone, "for the colored mon in America. We got to go back to where we be*long*. Why should not Africa give the world a black Rockefeller, a black Carnegie, a *black* 'enry Ford?" proposes the orator. "Be not deceived—*wealt* is strength, wealt is power, wealt is justice, wealt is *lib*erty!"

"Don't I know it, brother!" Zeke calls out and there is laughter and applause. The Garveyite smiles a beautiful smile and raises his fist over his head.

"One God! One Aim! One Destiny!"

• • •

A great light has gone out of the world.

Thomas Alva Edison is dead.

Henry sits in the inventor's laboratory, now the most visited attraction at Greenfield, Edison's only caveat when he first walked in the door during the Golden Jubilee being "It's too clean!"

Who knows, if he hadn't met the man during the early struggle, been able to tell him his plans for the gasoline combustion engine, and been rewarded with "You keep working on that, young man!"—would he have lost hope?

Probably not, but the fire would not have burned as brightly.

He often wonders, Henry, if they have been touched by the Divine, not 'mere mortals' but somehow found open-minded and industrious enough to be guided to the path of discovery. Both of them plain men who believe money just a tool and not an end in itself, with only the basics, important though they are, of education. Practical men, not content to absorb facts and make a museum of their minds, but able to take ideas not of their own provenance and see the possibilities, do the gradual, often frustrating toil of trial-and-error to make those possibilities into something solid and useful.

The pile of metal weighing down a table in the center of the room is another of those possibilities. Maybe he sensed Edison's spark beginning to fade when he told the engineers they'd be working here instead of the Dearborn laboratory, maybe he's a superstitious old man hoping that this is a tent of miracles, allowing the Great Tinkerer one last triumph.

"I don't want any damn *ex*perts sticking their fingers into this," he told them. "You've got an idea, tell it to me in plain English, don't go waving blueprints at me."

It's not even a new idea. Cadillac, Viking, Oakland, have all put an eight-cylinder engine on the road, but those are atrocities fit to be melted down into ball bearings or shovel blades. The facts are inescapable—the more cylinders you fit into the same displacement, the shorter the stroke for each, cutting down the required piston speed while speeding up the crankshaft revolution. Eight cylinders will run smoother than four, or, God help us, six. We could *double* the horsepower now available, but the tricky part is to make something compact enough to fit into a Model A. Using the V-shape will help, but a new cylinder block will have to be designed, there is exhaust and overheating to be dealt with-

A trio of the laboratory brains step in, surprised to see him there without the lights turned on.

"Mr. Ford—"

"Good morning, boys," he says, rising from the bench on which the Wizard must have sat thousands of times, "let's get our knuckles dirty."

• • •

The jungle along the Tapajós is an orgy of tumescence and putrescence, thousands of species of plants and animals co-existing or competing with each other for survival, roots intertangled, trees coffled together with creepers and lianas, the few paths through the steaming jumble hidden from eagle-view beneath a thick canopy of green.

And then there is Fordlandia.

The land has been denuded here, then spiked with identical saplings in long, even rows, and at the edges of this vast insult are the roofs of identical dwellings, also in long, even rows, till closer to the river's edge you find larger structures, the wharves, and a huge water tower with *FORD* emblazoned on its side.

Three men stand by a head-high sapling in the open sprawl of the plantation, inspecting its leaves.

Jim doesn't have a name to give it, but he knows it isn't good.

Clusters of little black spots, spreading to join each other, the worst-affected leaves curling black at the edges as if burnt. The trees seem to grow in fits and starts, whorls of leaves coming out and then it's all stem-and-branch growth for a while, then another round of leaves, a dozen of them, give or take, growing in each spiral. There are crawling bugs of various sorts on the leaves of the oldest, tallest saplings, but so far those don't seem to be threatening to kill the whole tree like these black spots are-

It isn't good.

And these are the new plantings, put in after Johnston was sent down from Dearborn to relieve Jim of the supervising job he never wanted, and dug up much of what had been planted by Blakely in the first year. Why didn't they hire some sort of tree expert—botanist? arborist? A grower from here, or an American who'd worked somewhere in the world planting rubber? When Jim first asked, Blakely just said "The Old Man doesn't want any professors in the pudding."

Jim is there with David Riker, the old Confederate, and João, one of the few workers not replaced after the food riot, a steady hand at the mill who seems thrilled that Jim has finally learned how to pronounce his name.

"*Ferrugem*," says the Brazilian, running his thumb over one of the newish leaves already peppered with spots. Jim looks to Riker.

"Rust," translates the old man. "Maybe you'd call it 'blight' up north.

It's a fungus I've seen on rubber trees in the jungle, but it never seems to spread to the other species around."

It shouldn't even be his problem. The Scotsman, Archibald Johnston, has been sent down from the Rouge factory to put things in order, and has done an incredible job in a short while, hiring hundreds of new workers, clearing more and more land for planting, and beginning to build the 'model city' that Mr. Ford has envisioned. There are at least a hundred new adobe houses, each with a quarter-acre garden plot attached, laid out on paved streets with sidewalks and streetlights. The mess hall has been reclaimed, there is a bakery, a barber shop, a shoe store, tailor, butcher, stores for dry goods, groceries, fresh vegetables, and fish—it feels like Pine Camp on an enormous scale.

People back home are out of work.

"Do they always grow alone in the wild?" he asks.

"Most often, yes," says Riker after consideration. "Perhaps four or five in a hectare."

A hectare, Jim has learned, is about two and a half acres, and Johnston's goal for the next year is to have two hundred thousand trees growing, which with the spacing he's ordered will be roughly fifty per acre.

"Has anybody here in Brazil every grown them on a plantation like this?"

Riker doesn't have to think. "No, sir."

"Why not?"

The *confederado* smiles. "We don't have the means to attack a situation that you Yankees do. Think of the resources that have gone into clearing this land."

"But somebody *some*where must have."

"Oh yes," says Riker. "I have seen photographs of plantations nearly this size in South East Asia. Propagated, I am afraid, from seeds my father helped to smuggle from this area."

"And they don't get this blight thing?"

"Not that I've heard of."

"Why not?"

Riker smiles again. Jim gets the feeling he merely tolerates Northerners, but appreciates the chance to speak English.

"If you can solve that, Mr. Rogan, I will nominate you as the next president of Brazil."

Joáo can tell that they are wondering about the spots. All that he knows for sure is that God made some animals, some fishes and birds, who want to live in groups—traveling together, feeding together—and others that prefer to live in pairs, or even all by themselves. Why should this not be so for trees? Maybe if they grew some *castanheiras do pará* in between the rubber trees the disease could not spread so easily, plus there would be valuable nuts to harvest. But it is clearly not João's place to be offering suggestions-

• • •

On Tuesdays Norma plays hearts with Audrey Pringle and Gail Quick and Peggy Myers at the Garden Club. The girls talk about how long it takes to get things—even the ones available from Manaus—to Fordlandia.

"We ordered the refrigerator in February," says Peggy. "It *still* hasn't come. If I want to see an ice cube in a drink I have to come here."

"Tell me about it," says Gail. "I asked for a mirror to hang in the bathroom? Three of them have come, all *late*, and every one of them broken in shipping."

Norma doesn't have much of a hand. She focuses on a bright orange lizard on the wall just behind Audrey's head. They don't move for the longest time, then they do. Somehow they cling to the wall without falling off—something sticky on their little feet-

"Dan says it's now policy at the hospital not to treat prostitutes, even though they might be giving the workers diseases—"

"I thought Johnston got rid of them."

"They stay up in Pau d'Ague, that that local wealthy family owns—"

"The workers have the energy left to paddle a boat up there?"

"The girls paddle *down*."

"Enterprising of them."

"Anyhow, Dan says they *do* have to treat family members who show up, which is now more than half the cases—"

Peggy's Dan is an administrator at the hospital. Norma has thought of volunteering there, but what does she know about medicine?

"Do they ask for, like, a marriage license or something?"

"Are you kidding? Down here?"

On Thursdays they play pinochle, which is a bit more challenging.

"Somebody died there yesterday. Fever—you hope it's nothing contagious."

"I heard a quote that 'the jungle is the graveyard of the white man.'"

"Please."

"Whose turn is it?"

The lizard darts up the wall a foot, then stops.

• • •

The building is longer than it is wide, with open sides, a wooden floor, and a high roof above. They've had dancing there some nights, with music from a record-playing machine, and once in the rainy season his class was allowed to play *futebol* under the roof, boys and girls together. But tonight is the best, *filmes* with sound, shown on the white screen that pulls down at the far end of the building. Flavio comes early to claim a chair on the aisle so nobody too tall can block his view. The first night they did this, so many people, like Flavio, had never seen such a thing before, and they talked in excitement all the way through the story so you couldn't hear what people were saying from the screen. He hopes they'll be quieter tonight.

The children's seats fill up quickly, most, like Flavio, still wearing the school uniforms they've been given, joking and pointing and looking around to see who else comes in. Flavio sees the nice *branca* girl who always asks what things are called, Kerry, and waves to her. Pretty soon the room is full, adults not only sitting on their side but standing in the back, some even watching from the outside where they are allowed to smoke. You can only see the glowing tips of their cigarettes, like fireflies, which is good because that means it's dark enough to begin the showing.

First they show a story with the drawings that move. Bimbo, who is maybe a rabbit but it's hard to say, wearing a sweater and pants that somehow don't cover his *umbigo*, strolls along whistling and every few steps lands on a metal disc that covers a hole in the street so that it flips up a little, till he steps on one with no disc and falls into the hole, rolling down a long winding chute till he lands on his head in a stone room, surrounded by *ogros* or maybe men dressed like *ogros*, all wearing the same suit with no buttons, black hairy hoods with eyes staring out from them and a half-melted candle on top of their heads, each holding a board with a nail through it behind their backs.

The leader starts them all chanting words Flavio can't understand except for the end, where he keeps singing a phrase that must be asking Bimbo if he wants to join their *culto*.

Bimbo says "No."

And keeps saying no though they pull all kinds of mean tricks on him, the room turning upside down and Bimbo tumbling around, then a huge sword trying to stab him in the *bundo*, then falling into a dark room where when he lights a match he sees all the candlehead men sitting in a circle around him asking if he wants to join again, and again he says no.

It must be an evil group, thinks Flavio, involved in *Camdomblé* of some sort, for Bimbo to resist for so long.

He is pushed up to a place with four doors—one with a skull and crossed bones on it, another with the number 13, the next with a big ? mark, and the last with what looks like Bimbo's handprint—he only has three fingers and a thumb and wears gloves. He opens the first door and there's a mirror inside, his reflection telling him to be careful but to open the next door. Behind the next door is a full skeleton standing up talking on the telephone to somebody. In front of the big ? he turns to look at the audience and shakes his head—not even going to look. Behind the last is a boxing glove on a spring that shoots out and punches him hard enough to knock him to the floor, which jolts the ? door open to reveal a bicycle. Bimbo jumps on the bicycle and tries to pedal away, but it's only a machine with belts and gears like at the sawmill attached so he's really turning a wheel with three hands in gloves attached on arms that smack him in the *bundo* one after the other. Finally the bicycle breaks away and he pedals into a room with a little rectangle of a water pool with a fish swimming in it on the floor, riding three circles around it with smoke coming from his *bundo* because of the spanking. He jumps off and you see closer that bugs from his pants are running from the heat and smoke and leaping from his *bundo*, little parachutes opening so they float to the floor. A door opens and it's Betty, who Flavio has seen in one of the cartoons last month and was hoping to see again. Betty has a very big head and a very short dress which barely comes down over her big bump of a *bunda* and wears a garter on one of her big bare legs. She puts a finger to her lips, then says what Flavio thinks is "Come inside, big boy," but he's not sure.

But when Bimbo tries to follow he is sliding down a chute again, this one with ups and downs and axes that try to chop down on him as he runs and then a circle staircase to jump down, then running next to a big stone wall with his shadow huge running beside him till there is a big blade sticking out that cuts the shadow's head off, the rest of it still running next to Bimbo till he starts to dance sideways facing it and it can slip back under his feet and he runs through gates with jagged teeth on them that snap shut just behind him and would cut off his tail if he had one, Bimbo so scared that his heart comes out his mouth and he looks at it beating too fast before swallowing it down again, finally landing in a room with the leader of the *ogros* standing over him.

But this time when he says "No!" the leader throws his disguise off in one motion and it's *Betty*, who starts to wiggle her hips and smack her *bunda* to drums and flute music and wave her arms like they have no bones in them and Bimbo starts to giggle and show his teeth, so that when she sings to ask if he'll join now, he says "Yes!"

Then the walls of the room are pulled up like a curtain and there are all the *ogros* in two long lines and they all throw their disguises off to show they are identical Bettys, everybody dancing to the music and finally the main Betty jumps into Bimbo's arms.

The school children and even many of the adults are clapping and calling out at the end of this. Flavio has learned that in the shows where the drawings move anything can turn into anything and the rules of how things really work don't matter. A flame of fire can jump up and tap you on the shoulder to let you know your *bundo* is burning. Knives and forks and plates can sing and dance. Creatures that look like they're half rabbit and half mouse wear people clothes and get romantic with real people like Betty.

Flavio turns to see Kerry, who smiles and wiggles her eyebrows up and down at him. Many of the other *branco* children who go to the school stay with their parents while they watch, but Kerry always sits with the *brasileiros*.

The real-people *filmes* are usually about gangsters who shoot each other and sell liquor, which must be a crime in Chicago, but this one is set in the past somewhere they had castles and only torches for light. A scientist puts the brain of one dead man into the body of another, which Flavio can tell right away is not a good idea. Lightning brings the man with the new brain alive, and he starts to walk around and kill people, growling rather than talking, and it is really frightening. The people in the village nearby want to kill him, which is natural, and then he comes upon a little girl playing by a pond. Flavio doesn't want to watch this part so he turns around in his seat and sees that Kerry is still watching but has her hands over her ears in case the music tries to scare you. Finally the villagers chase the monster, who is carrying the unconscious scientist, up into a windmill, where he throws the body down, the windmill blade breaking his fall like what would happen in a cartoon, and then they all set the windmill on fire.

A terrible way to die.

Tomorrow is Sunday, so Flavio's father won't have to work and they can sleep late, which is good because Flavio knows he will have nightmares.

Even when there aren't *filmes* to watch he's been having terrible ones, which his father says is the quinine they all have to take.

Nightmares are better than malaria, says his mother, so he never spits it out.

Maybe, if he's lucky, Betty will be in one of the dreams.

• • •

There need to be women.

Women work too, in the home, in the factories, some, like Rosa, in restaurants or hospitals or plugging wires into a switchboard. And a lot of them who should be out working are unemployed now, and, if truly cursed by capitalism, evicted from their dwellings to face this bitter cold.

It is freezing, Rosa and her brother Ira stomping their feet in place, breath huffing out in white puffs as they wait for the show to get on the road, surrounded by hundreds of men and a few women in their heaviest coats with collars turned up, their hats pulled low against the wind, ready to march.

"There's still time to go back," says Ira.

He's not chickening out, just going on about how it might get violent and she'll be unable to protect herself.

"I don't see any weapons," she says.

Almost all the men not wearing gloves have their hands buried deep in their pockets, and the flimsy sticks the placards are hung on won't be much in a fight.

"I'm not talking about *us*. We're going to Dearborn—different rules there."

"I'll be fine," says Rosa. "Look at how many we are."

She was hoping only for a couple hundred, but already there must be over a thousand crowded onto the grass of the park, the Detroit police that Mayor Murphy says will be their escort standing in clusters at the edge of Fort Street. Now and again a streetcar stops at the corner of Downing and several men jump off without paying the fare, maybe one or two cops making half-hearted chase until the chiselers are safe within the cheering crowd. Maybe it was the speech that Foster gave at the Danceland Arena last night, or maybe these are just men with nothing else to do, with no job to report to, more bored and curious than committed to the future. It really doesn't matter—they've come.

The Unemployment Councils are scattered in their neighborhoods and not accustomed to joint actions, the TUUL is a grab bag of philosophies—so it is a lifesaver that Foster and the CP, the only group with a long-range program, have come in to motivate the masses. Rosa started in the YPSL, but her chapter was gradually absorbed when Joe York got involved, and now she is recording secretary for the Young Communists, who even advanced her the money to take a stenography course at night.

It's like another language.

Joe York, tall and thin and intense, is up at the head of the street with Goetz and some of the other organizers. He is a very serious young man, which Rosa likes, but he never really looks at her during meetings. Maybe he's shy too.

A group of the men who say they all worked at Ford until recently are singing the song that's been going around, the one that goes to the tune of *My Bonnie Lies Over the Ocean*-

I'm spending my night at the flop house
I'm spending my days on the street
I'm looking for work and I find none
I wish I had something to eat.

They've only been over from Chicago for a few years, Papa fleeing from a deportation order, but long enough to know that winter here is just as cold, just as windy-

Sooo-oup, sooo-oup, they give me a bowl of soo-woo-woup
Sooo-oup, sooo-oup, they give me a bowl of soup.

Albert Goetz is shouting over a bullhorn now, the Hunger March scheduled to start moving at noon, which passed a while back. People are still arriving.

"Are we ready?!" calls Goetz.

A roar of readiness.

"Remember, this is a peaceful assembly—we march to the gate, present our demands, and disperse. Let's move it out!"

Another cheer and the shivering mass of them shift into Fort Road, the police making way for them, the beefy Irish sergeant nearest Rosa and Ira grinning and shaking his head.

"You people only done this so's we'd have to freeze our nuts off, right? You think Henry Ford is gonna come out and invite you in for tea?"

"If all of us shout together," says one of the recently fired auto workers, "he'll at least hear us over the factory noise."

It takes a while, so many trying to squeeze onto the pavement at once, and when they actually start to move toward the plant Rosa finds she is walking alongside Joe York. She knows that his family is Polish and changed their name as did her own—Schimmelman to Schimmel—but thinks the Yorks are Catholics. Joe, in one of his many direct quotes from Marx, has said that "Religion is the sigh of the oppressed creature, the heart of a heartless world, and the soul of soulless conditions. It is the opium of the people," which seems at once sympathetic and dismissive. Papa still goes to Temple Beth El on Woodward, but only to argue with Rabbi Franklin about what it should mean to be a Jew.

"You Communists are too sure of everything for a good argument," Papa tells her. "But the rabbi knows that life is *mys*tery."

Only a little up the road they encounter the strange sight of Mayor Murphy standing up in an open car, lifting his hat despite the cold and the wind to wish them well.

"I'm with you all the way!" he calls.

Joe York makes a derisive noise. "If he's with us he should be marching."

Ira made Rosa register and vote for Murphy in the election after the recall, and before that he got in to watch the Ossian Sweet trial, coming back with tales of "a judge who's not in the bag."

"He gave us a permit," Ira says to Joe York.

"A permit to march out of the city limits."

"He's done what he can for relief—"

"Electoral politics," says Joe with finality, "is a dead end."

"You don't believe in democracy?"

Rosa has only managed to steer Ira to one CP meeting and he came out complaining that he couldn't breathe for the hot air expelled during the long debates.

"You'll see when we get to the Dearborn line. We've got no permit there, the mayor of Dearborn is King Henry's cousin and owns a Ford dealership, and the chief of police used to work for their Service Department. When we get to Dearborn, you'll see democracy in action."

Rosa, the bickering making her anxious, turns to walk backward and read the placards being held up, the bearers wrestling to keep them aloft in the stiff wind.

We Want Bread, Not Crumbs

Tax the Rich and Feed the Poor

Starve in the Richest Land on Earth?

We Want Jobs!

There are the usual red banners and signs urging support for the Scottsboro boys, but most of the faces she sees aren't political activists, they're the Forgotten Man, out of work, out of a home in many cases, shameful at being desperate, the men she sees peeling scraps of half-rotten food off the ground when the Eastern Market is about to close, the vendors leaving what they can't sell and won't eat.

Rosa was in on the debate over what the demands would be, taking notes, and even got to make a suggestion. A few of these were from delegates still working at the Rouge, men who had to sneak in and out of the hall to avoid company spies. Two fifteen-minute breaks a day instead of one, a seven-hour shift without reduction in pay, end to the speedups, abolition of the graft system of hiring, the right to organize without interference or punishment, and above all the dismissal of Harry Bennett and his Service Department of snoops and thugs. Others were to alleviate the suffering of those Ford considers no longer needed—a lump sum of fifty dollars, free medical care in Henry Ford Hospital, five tons of coal and coke handed out for the winter—and an end to evictions and foreclosures. Rosa was thrilled that her idea, no discrimination against Negroes for all jobs in the plant, was seconded by Joe York and adopted by a narrow margin. There are only a handful of Negroes in the Party in Detroit, and very few, considering how many of them are now jobless, among the throng moving up Fort Street to the Ford plant.

Ira is pointing off at something to the left.

"See that building? That holds a shaft elevator for the salt mines. I'm going back there tomorrow, see if there's any work."

"The salt mines—"

"I can claim family experience. Didn't the Egyptians have us digging salt before Moses showed up?"

They are supposed to be walking eight abreast, but that has quickly broken down, the line ahead and behind now just a jumble of bundled-up marchers filling the road from side to side, a pair of Detroit motorcycle policemen cruising back and forth along on the margins.

Sylvia, who has taken Rosa's shift at the Early American Dining Room in Hudson's, will be nice and warm now, the lunch rush not yet over. Rosa has come to like it, the noise and the bustle, and by half past two the volume slacks off and you can help each other out, talk a little. She can't imagine an entire shift at maximum speed like the Ford men describe, she's tired enough at the end of her eight hours as it is. Rosa wishes they allowed you to share tips, as it is really a team effort, but the supervisor, Mrs. Pritchett, is an advocate of competition.

"The better you are at your job," she tells them, "the more you shall be rewarded."

Ira thinks the answer is syndicalism. "We get a union in at Federal Screw," he was always saying, "we got a shot at a decent living."

Most of his fellow workers agreed with him, but at least one of them went to management saying Ira Schimmel is a Red, Ira Schimmel is trying to organize, and Ira Schimmel was out on the street.

"Chicken sticking neck out," their mother would say to Papa when he'd come home late from a meeting, "is losing head."

The marchers have become a powerful river now, Rosa exhilarated to be a part of it, so many bodies pushing forward from behind that if you stop moving you'll be swept off your feet or crushed under theirs.

"Democracy," announces Joe York suddenly, having had time for analysis of the problem, "will be vital to the workers' republic once we establish it. But for now—Discipline, Clarity, Action."

"I'm all for the action part," says Ira, hunched shuddering in a coat not nearly thick enough for the day. "If we don't keep moving we'll die out here."

"An excellent metaphor for our situation versus the capitalists."

"You really think it'll come to revolution?"

"Inevitable."

"So, like, a labor union is only—"

"'Unions are organized by Jewish financiers, not labor,'" says Joe York with no emotion visible on his face. "'A union is a neat thing for a Jew to have on hand when he comes around to get his clutches on industry.'" A deadpan pause. "I'm quoting Henry Ford."

Ira is a fierce Zionist, claiming that if there ever is a true socialist state it will be in a revived Israel. He turns toward Joe with raised eyebrows. "You agree with him?"

The ghost of a smile on Joe's lips—he's such an intense young man-

"We may not all be Jewish in the labor movement, not even close, but Ford is right about one thing—we *do* want to get our clutches on industry."

The river of men begins to back up and swell out onto the sides of the road then, Goetz standing up on a flatbed truck ahead of them, again on the bullhorn.

"We are approaching the Dearborn line," he calls out. "Now remember, we don't want any violence! All we are going to do is to walk to the Ford employment office." The crowd has gone mute, silence moving from front to rear like a slow wave-

"Though we understand that the Dearborn police are planning to stop us, we will try to get through to complete our mission! But remember, no *trouble*."

"March on!" cries somebody behind Rosa and there is a cheer, Goetz climbing down and the throng beginning to move again.

"You know, if Henry Ford does agree to our demands," Ira says to Rosa as they wait for the people in front to get going, "he'll *own* us. We'll have to take up folk dancing."

The papers are always writing up the dances the auto maker hosts in the ballroom he's created in part of his Dearborn Engineering Building, and his role in having old-fashioned waltzes, schottisches, and square dances taught in the public schools. Ira, who obsessively plays the recordings of a young Negro cornetist and his 'Hot Five' on the Victrola, claims facetiously that this is the real class war, between the Virginia Reel and 'Jewish influenced' hot jazz.

"We could use that coal, though," Rosa answers, stomping her feet as she begins to walk again, trying to get some feeling back into her toes.

There are men in uniforms lined up in front of the bridge going over the Rouge River. She and Ira follow Joe York, who is pushing his way toward the front of the march. The Detroit police and the two motorcyclists are nowhere to be seen now.

"You stay right behind me, Sis, no matter what," Ira tells her. "Grab onto my coat if you have to."

There is a fire engine just behind the Dearborn police, firemen hurrying to link a hose to a hydrant. Ira's coat doesn't have a belt to grab and she loses him, now just trying to keep Joe York in sight, struggling to follow him even though he's moving toward the trouble instead of away from it. The first cannister sizzles past her ears and hits an older marcher square in the chest, knocking him to the ground as the tear gas starts to spread and rise into the wind—

Smitty always carries an oversized handkerchief, good for comforting grieving gun molls, now plastered over his face as he kneels in the field beside Fort Road, eyes only watering a bit as the wind swirls the gas around and, if anything, sends it back upon the fearless public servants who fired it into an unarmed crowd of no-hopers.

Even with scareheads and the usual editorial warning about a Red takeover, the Lindbergh toddler will get all the front page ink—the kidnappers, whoever they are, sending a second ransom note just yesterday to up their demand to seventy thousand Gs. But Smitty is deep in the doghouse again with Fosdick, who spends his evenings at the *Free Press* cooking up the dirtiest, noisiest, freezingest situations to throw him into.

Like this.

Hundreds of the common, unemployed herd around him are picking up or digging up rocks from the field and hurling them with some accuracy at the boys in blue. Smitty was in a similar situation during the Meuse-Argonne campaign, only then he had a gas mask and an Enfield rifle to protect himself with. The thin blue line begins to buckle just as their brothers in the fire department get the hose working, turning it on the closest marchers and knocking more than a few on their keisters. But the hook-and-ladder boys don't like the shower of rocks and frozen dirt clods any better than the cops, and soon the whole official Dearborn contingent are beating a hasty retreat.

A huge cheer. Banners flapping, placards held high, the usual ruckus before the Cossacks ride in with their sabers unsheathed. Instead, a beanpole of a kid wearing a beret waves his arms in front of the agitated masses and poses a rhetorical question-

"Workers! Comrades! What do we do now?"

"MARCH ON!" cry the army of the unemployed, and begin to hightail it for the bridge, some of them thoroughly soaked, with patches of ice forming on their skin and clothing. Smitty holds onto his hat and joins the advance—

There is always, of course, a fallback position for the enemy, and as soon as he turns left up Miller Road with the horde, Smitty can see it—more uniformed coppers plus an equal number of Harry Bennett's plainclothes persuaders, bats, metal pipes and, yes, a few shotguns in hand, standing atop and below the walkover bridge from the parking lot to Gate 4, with the Employment Building just beyond it. And two, count em, *two* fire trucks with their hoses already loaded for action.

This will not end well, thinks Smitty, drifting purposefully out of the line of fire, where he can function better as a professional observer and not get clubbed, doused, or shot by the guardians of private property and the America Way.

There is not much of a conversation when the vanguard of the march come into range of the overpass, more teargas fired, streams of water unleashed, rocks and chunks of concrete flying in the opposite direction, curses shouted, screaming, some of the defenders of the realm charging forward to bust heads, and now the factory gate opening and some idiot driving out into the eye of the shitstorm.

If Smitty's view is not distorted by his stinging, tear-filled eyes, it is no ordinary idiot in the passenger seat, but Harry Bennett—

"You have to look them in the eye," as Clyde Beatty always says. Clyde is a pal, helped Harry pick out the big cats he keeps just down the tunnel from his office, always good for a giggle to bring in on a leash if there's a visitor you want to rattle. "Mastery," Clyde calls it, but to Harry that just means *fear.*

They've ignored the chair and whip, Harry thinks as he steps out of the car—let's see how they like the *pis*tol-

• • •

Rosa can barely see, her eyes hurt so much worse when they're open, her cloche hat long gone and her hair crisp with tiny icicles from the first hosing, but she can hear Joe York and the little man with the bow tie shouting at each other and then rocks come flying overhead, smashing glass and metal on the car and the man with the bowtie is hit on the head and grabs Joe, both of them going down and gunshots now, even a machine gun rattling away like in the movies and somebody pushes her to the ground and she sees Joe York stand up only to go down again and he's bleeding. She crawls to him as people all around her—marchers, police, men with metal pipes—fight and run and shout at each other and random shots now and screams of pain not anger and she is helping a marcher drag Joe away from the fighting, holding him under one arm and backing up, the man doing the same on the other side and it's awful the way Joe's eyes are open but his head lolls sideways like he's drunk or asleep and somebody has come up with a car-

Rosa jumps in next to the driver and helps pull Joe in beside her, hot blood on her cold hands, and there are three badly wounded men in the back seat already and the man who is driving manages to turn the car around without running over anybody, a policeman slamming dents into the roof with his club and then spider-cracking the rear window before they can start back down Miller. The driver keeps jamming his hand on the horn to get marchers out of their way and Rosa rolls her window down to yell "Wounded, wounded, wounded!," taking a hard left on Dix Avenue and then speeding away toward Detroit, then somewhere a hard, squealing right turn and the door must not have been slammed shut because Joe almost falls out the side before Rosa can yank him back in with one of the other wounded men beginning to scream hysterically "Joe's dying! He's dying! You gotta help him, he's dying!" till Rosa has to turn and slap him so he can't make the driver slam into something. The driver keeps the heel of his hand on the horn as they go through stop lights and crossroads without slowing down and there is blood actually squirting, like from a child's water-gun toy, out of Joe's body onto Rosa and the dashboard of the car and she searches for the source, trying to unbutton his blood-drenched coat to find the wound but first they jolt to a stop in front of the hospital.

Henry Ford Hospital.

There are doctors and nurses in white already outside so somebody must have called, but when Rosa, drenched in blood, yells for them to come get the wounded, they just stand gaping, afraid, perhaps, but of what-

"Please!" she cries to them. "Help them! They're so young!"

The wounded boy in the middle of the back seat who hasn't said a thing but just held his stomach with both hands is barely in his teens. Joe is slumped over in Rosa's arms and she can't move.

"Some of you must have children!" she cries. "Please!"

It seems like an eternity, Rosa pleading, the driver out on his feet and demanding that they do their duty, till they finally give in, to the sound of approaching sirens.

"All right, bring them in," scowls a doctor, and Rosa follows as Joe and the others are pulled out of the car, several Detroit policemen appearing beside them as they move through reception, Rosa taking Joe's hand once they have him on a stretcher, and walking alongside back toward the operating rooms.

"Have you been shot?" asks a nurse and Rosa has to think for a second.

"I don't think so."

"Then you'll have to leave us."

Joe's hand is cold and stiff in hers. She has to peel his fingers off to let him go.

She is on her way toward the door, not knowing what to do next, when more wounded, mostly from beatings, are dragged in. Ira is among them, barely conscious, held up by a pair of Dearborn police.

"That's my brother!" she shouts. "What did you do to him?!"

The cops ignore her all the way down the hall to a room with four beds in it, two of them already taken by bloodied marchers. They dump Ira onto an empty bed, throw his feet up onto it, then handcuff him to the sidebar.

"You can't do that! What has he done? None of us had weapons! You can't do this!"

One of the cops wearily pushes her back into the hallway before closing the door behind him.

"Go home, girlie," he says. "We've had enough for one day."

• • •

Edsel is in the dining room with Father and Sorenson when the news comes.

"I suppose we'd better go see this," says Father, as if it is only an annoyance.

As they walk over Sorenson says he knew Bennett would let it get out of hand.

"If Harry let it get ugly," Father says, "it's so everybody sees what their true colors are. Which is *red*."

There is a contingent of Soviet engineers on the premises today, studying time-and labor-saving strategies, and the Company is doing quite a good business with the Russians, every bit welcome during this crazy economic nightmare. Father draws a distinction between the people and the political belief, always a wise policy.

"Harry tends to bite off more than he can chew," says Sorenson.

Father smiles. Bennett is like his favorite naughty child, a status Edsel somehow never got to enjoy.

"I'll wager a few other folks got bitten too," he says.

But Harry is not even on his feet when they arrive just outside Gate 4, looking like a child dressed as a man as they gently lift him onto a stretcher, his head covered with gore.

"My God, is he going to be okay?" asks Father, truly upset. Edsel's eyes water—tear gas still hanging in the air—and he resists the urge to say what he knows is true. If they'd let *him*, president of the Company, come down to the gate, talk to the leaders for a minute, accept their list of demands or manifesto and say "We'll take it under advisement," none of this would have happened. There are dozens of windows smashed on the Employment

Building, police and Service Department men getting first aid, and the chief of the Dearborn police, whom Harry Bennett personally recommended for the job, already extolling his own heroism to Smith from the *Free Press*.

Edsel looks around—if there were photographers or even newsreel men here they have gone, so he doesn't need to drag Father away from the scene. His father seems to be crying as he follows the stretcher toward to the hospital on the second floor of B Building, and it isn't because of tear gas.

"We're going to fix this," says Father. "We'll get our best man working on Harry."

The problem is that between the gas and the water and the part where anybody with a lick of sense gets behind something large and waits till the shooting stops, Smitty didn't actually see much. So for now he jots down the dubious account issuing from the piehole of Chief Brooks. He has permission to quote directly if it's phrased as 'a Dearborn police official states'—insurance in case Harry wakes up and doesn't approve of the tale.

"We knew the Reds were coming," says Brooks, who worked at the Rouge finking on line-workers for a while, "but didn't know there'd be so many or we'd have been better prepared. I reminded the crowd that they had no permit in our jurisdiction, that they were in fact on private property, and asked them to disperse. That's when their specialists began to fire at us."

The rest of it is just more fantasy, but Smitty is sure if he braces any of the hammer-and-sickle crowd for their version it will feature starving babies impaled on the bayonets of Harry's Service Department—it's enough to turn an honest newsman into a cynic. Smitty will ask if he can see the damage in the Employment Building, then try to find a telephone to call the story in. Fosdick will quote Chief Brooks verbatim until he knows which way the wind is going to blow—some of those marchers were shot up bad, and *Free Press* readers are likely to have sympathy for the downtrodden or even have relatives who been cut loose by the Company in the last couple years. If Little Lindy's abductors will cool their heels for a day, this might rate a first-page banner-

• • •

When Harry is finally able to roll out of the hospital bed and stand he is dizzy as hell. His head is bandaged with enough gauze to wrap a mummy, but when he finds the mirror it's the same old mug. He sits back on the edge of the bed, tries to dredge up the chain of events. He thinks he got a few shots off before he went down for the count, and he wasn't hung from the bridge, so the marchers must have been routed. There is a knock-

"Yeah, come on in."

It is the Chief, grinning from ear to ear to see him up and percolating.

"You're back with the living!"

"How long have I been out?"

"Oh, you've been up before, full of beans, but you didn't make a whole lot of sense."

"I didn't talk to any reporters, did I?"

Henry shakes his head. "Strict orders downstairs—shoot em on sight."

"It's not just the Reds, Chief. We got people in the buildings planning to bring the whole thing down. The next time they'll already be past the gate."

"You really think so?"

In a fight, the thing you got to remember is to never let them get back on balance once you've landed a good one. Beat them till they kiss the canvas-

"I know this is a rough patch financially," Harry Bennett tells his employer, "but I think we'd better beef up the Service Department."

• • •

4 DIE IN RIOT AT FORD PLANT

MURDER CHARGES ASKED AFTER RED MOB FIGHTS POLICE

Communists Hurl Stones and Clubs in Pre-arranged Outbreak

Harry Bennett and Others in Hospital Following Battle Started When Agitator Fires Six Shots

Fosdick runs with the Dearborn bulls' version, hook, line, and sinker, which doesn't take long to unravel, making him look bad and somehow landing Smitty deeper in the doghouse.

"All that commotion and you couldn't manage to get hit with one lousy brick?" he said, not really joking, as **FREE PRESS REPORTER WOUNDED** would have given them the moral high ground over the other sheets who covered what is now being called the 'Ford Massacre'.

But no, he had to *duck*.

The weather, at least, is kinder for the funeral march, far too many people collected at the kickoff in Grand Circus Park to walk the coffins to Woodmere. It's Saturday, so they're not all unemployed, notably the men who hold their hats in front of their faces whenever they spot one of Harry Bennett's shutterbugs along the route, as getting caught with this crowd is a sure ticket to the bread lines. The actual facts have come out—four marchers dead and one hanging on by a thread, not a single cop or Service Department thumper hit by a bullet, marchers shackled to hospital beds for hours before their wounds were treated—and even Hearst's *Times* has thrown in with the general consensus, mourning these poor martyred citizens. The banner at the head of the procession—**SMASH THE FORD-MURPHY TERROR**—is obviously the handiwork of the hardline Bolsheviks, jealous of the present mayor's popularity. Frank Murphy has pretty much bankrupted the city trying to keep a substantial percentage of its citizenry from starving, called Harry Bennett "an inhuman brute" and said that chaining people to hospital beds was unwarranted, and neither the he nor King Henry must relish being linked with the other in a Red rallying cry.

The procession has stretched out along Woodward Avenue now, traffic blocked off to the sides by police, the biggest congregation since Hoover came for the Golden Jubilee of Light, but there's no soggy tickertape being thrown into the air. Chants, raised fists, singing—Smitty recognizes *The Battle Hymn of the Republic* with new lyrics—and thousands of red flags and black armbands.

They do love a funeral.

Rosa is not far behind the coffins. She is amazed and thrilled at the turnout and can't wait till she can visit Ira to tell him. The Party is raising money for bail and Maurice Sugar is representing all the marchers who were arrested, stating that none should even come to trial. She's missing the good Saturday tips at Hudson's, telling Mrs. Pritchett she needed to deal with "a death in the family."

Rosa does a complete turn to look at the host of mourners filling the long street behind her. Compared to the day of the Hunger March there are lots of women in the crowd, more Negroes as well. Thirty thousand? Fifty thousand? Who can count them all—she supposes that the newspapers just make a guess and then add or subtract depending on their politics. Let Ira try to play the cynic when faced with this response.

"Suppose we *could* take over the Rouge," he'll say, playing devil's advocate. "How do we rehire all those workers when nobody is buying automobiles?"

"We could make something else. Something people need."

"Cracker Jacks!" he'll say, snapping his fingers. "There can never be too many Cracker Jacks."

"Seriously—"

"And then you employ more peanut farmers and popcorn poppers, there's sugar to harvest in Cuba to make the molasses—"

"You don't have to have every detail worked out."

"But what if there really are more *peo*ple than there are jobs? How do they eat?"

"We tax the rich."

"Show me the mathematics. I want to see real numbers—"

"A lot of the things the people pay for now—we won't have the police—"

"Who will deal with the gangsters, then? The murderers—"

"Crime won't be a problem in a just society."

"The bootleggers are going to make Cracker Jacks?"

"You're impossible!"

"So is the New World you're going on about!"

At which point Papa holds up a hand to silence her brother.

"She's young," he always says. "Let her dream."

Which is infuriating.

Papa has had much of the fire beaten out of him, and his father, Zeyde Pinchas, was a religious zealot, speaking of life as one constant moral battleground, overseen by a rarely-intervening but omnipresent Yahweh who Rosa always pictured as looking just like Rebbe Fischer from their synagogue in Chicago, a grumpy old Jew with a long beard who, though he was barely over five feet tall with shoes on, managed to look down on everyone.

Zeyde, at least, was a Zionist, and a passionate one, holding his hands over his ears and davening whenever Papa suggested a New Israel was not worth the bother if it was not also a socialist paradise. But Zeyde died without seeing the return of the Promised Land, and Papa—Papa has confused his personal setback for the defeat of the proletariat.

But even a fire that has burned out may contain embers-

They turn off Fort Street to enter Woodmere Cemetery, the tall stacks of the Rouge factory visible in the distance. Her mother is buried here, in Section North F with the other worshippers from Temple Beth El. Her mother, nearly deaf from an attack of scarlet fever when she was a girl back in Königsberg, was hit by a streetcar she never heard coming on Vernor Highway not long after they moved from Chicago.

Rosa will visit the grave after the comrades have been interred, sitting or standing by the headstone, trying to imagine what her mother's life was like when *she* was only twenty. Did she dare to dream anything, or was she too cowed by violence against the Jews, by the repression within her own culture, to think past surviving the moment?

When the revolution comes, will it have to be won through killing? Ira was too young to be slaughtered in Europe, a capitalists' war and waste of humanity. But for what is inevitably coming he will have to bear arms if needed, and Rosa-

She has never even held a gun.

It required hundreds of thousands of people in arms to wrest power from the Tsar and his minions, and the plutocrats and their lackeys here are so entrenched. Rosa looks around at the thousands thronged around the coffins now, and tries to imagine all of them with rifles in their hands, tries to imagine the killing, a time when death is too common to be celebrated-

Joe York was twenty. Joe Bussell was only sixteen.

The speakers make much of this, mention others killed in earlier clashes with the ruling class, urge that this sacrifice not be in vain. "Sacrifice" is a word that always brings visions of her mother, lost in this new world, deaf to its music, head always bent over some task in whatever miserable handful of rooms they could afford to rent. Sacrifice is not ennobling, thinks Rosa, it is only another way to say "We've lost."

Arise ye workers from your slumbers
Arise ye prisoners of want

-sing a trio of comrades standing by the coffins, immediately joined by a dozen more voices-

For reason in revolt now thunders
And at last ends the age of cant.
Away with all your superstitions
Servile masses arise, arise

-Rosa joining in, weeping openly-

We'll change henceforth the old tradition
And spurn the dust to win the prize-

Ira dragged her to the ballpark once, where they sing the newly official American anthem, a dreary, meandering slog written by a lawyer who helped plantation owners get their runaway slaves back, a song that ends with *o'er the land of the free and the home of the brave*—patently false at the time it was written, chattel bondage actively practiced in half of the states-

So come brothers and sisters
For the struggle carries on
The Internationale—*unites the world in song*
So comrades, come rally
And the last fight let us face
The International ideal unites the human race!

Whatever else, Rosa thinks, we have the best song.

• • •

Man, freed from his servitude to Nature, will transcend.

And the agent of that transcendence is the Machine.

The Muralist has always loved machines, not only for what they can do, their vital functions, but for the *look* of them, the synchronicity of the many parts, their shapes, their internal and external movements, their strength and density, the sheen of their metallic surfaces. Trains, when he was a boy in Guanajuato, were less a mode of transportation than a wonderful concatenation of fire and water and gears and wheels, great, steam-huffing mechanical dragons that made the idea of *México* a possibility. And now, holding a commission to celebrate a city dedicated to the manufacture of mechanical devices, he'll need to find a way to link the Machine to the natural elements that provide its substance and power, to the social process that now controls its use and meaning, to the lives of the workers who serve or command its functions.

Which brings the Muralist to Greenfield Village.

He is surprised at how few visitors are here, the entry fee minimal

and so many interesting things to explore. There is nostalgia, of course, the Industrialist collecting the boyhood homes of men whose work and lives have formed him, horses pulling carriages with guests or wagon-loads of hay about the property, but as the Muralist moves from building to building he realizes that a *story* is being told, not in words but in objects, in a chronology of inventions. The idea of Vasconcelos to teach the illiterate Mexican *campesino* his own history and culture through paintings on a wall is here mirrored by a genealogical progression of sewing machines or devices for separating the seeds and chaff from cotton bolls, the earliest of them only extensions of human limbs and muscles, evolving to crank-or-treadle-driven contraptions and leading to a succession powered by steam or gasoline or even electricity. Here, in the cacophonous Armington & Sims shop, one long metal shaft driven by a steam generator spins overhead the length of the building, belts snaking down from it every few yards to power a menagerie of machines, gear-wheels altering the direction and speed of the motive-force, more gears and armatures and valves and sprockets weaving or drilling or stamping or punching or polishing—making silk, lathing chair legs, weaving textiles, shaping parts for other machines. The Muralist has already explored another building containing the history of printing from the earliest pattern cylinders and woodblocks to the lead-boiling linotype, a mechanical wonder that requires a virtuoso to operate, pausing to fill half of his notebook with sketches of the various matrices, discs, molds, elevators, levers, and gears.

The village had been described to him as "the Old Man's folly" or "a pile of scrap iron" and stories were told of the elder Ford's obsessive collecting—it had to be the exact model of cream-separator he remembered seeing at a local dairy in his youth or nothing—but the Muralist has been impressed again and again by the artistry of the arrangement of objects and devices in the buildings. There is both display and context, a collage that forms a complex statement—precisely what he is attempting in his own work. Here, enveloped by the buzzing and clanking and whirring of so many apparatuses, he feels a pang of uncertainty—how to capture this dynamism in a painting? A well-planned photograph of a machine—that linotype octopus perhaps—conveys some of its complexity, but the *movement* is lacking, and movement is the power of the process. Maybe a visible form of energy, like a wave-

The Muralist folds his notebook, feeling dizzy, and looks for a clock. Clocks are ubiquitous in the village, Ford clearly obsessed not only with their inner workings but with the nature of Time itself—and realizes he has been here for more than ten hours without eating, which only happens when he is on the scaffolding immersed in a project.

Aided by a mule-driving drayman in turn-of-the-century garb, the Muralist finds his assistant Cliff Wight and their driver both napping in the automobile. Another man waits alongside, very relieved to see him.

"Mr. Rivera?"

"Yes."

The man speaks slowly and louder than necessary, but considering the Muralist's sometimes feeble grasp of English, this seems more helpful than condescending.

"Mr. Ford hopes that you might visit him for lunch on Saturday. He's very impressed with the time you've taken to view the exhibits."

"Mr. Ford—"

"Mr. Henry Ford."

The Muralist has met the son, Edsel, several times, a handsome, modest young man who is financing the project at the new Art Institute, and has been much more deferential than the usual *patrón de los artes*. Confessing to be "something of a painter," he was too shy to show any of his easel work, but did share some of his automobile designs, rendered in his own hand, which were sleek and beautiful.

"His house is just over there," says the functionary, pointing to a large house of dismal gray limestone that seems modest for one of the wealthiest capitalists in the world.

"Could you be there by noon?"

"*Con mucho gusto*," says the Muralist with a short bow. "It will be my pleasure."

When they are on their way, Cliff asks if he found anything useful in the museum.

"*Por supuesto*. Mr. Ford knows that this is a long story, *el hombre y sus máquinas*, always changing, always improving, always looking for—" -he searches for the word in English—"for libe*ra*tion."

It is dark already, the lights of Detroit ahead of them. Frida has recently begun to paint in earnest, sitting at her little easel in the hotel room for much of the day, and by now probably thinks he is out carousing. She hates it here in Gringolandia—hates the food, hates the dirt and the noise of this city, hates the society ladies who invite them to endless boring social functions—even if none of her ailments and ongoing conditions have flared up, she will be in a state.

But first, something to eat-

• • •

They use the old escape path to the river. Daddy has somebody chop away at the sides when they grow in so it's easy to pass through, even if he doesn't keep a boat anchored at the end anymore. Efigênia comes along because she wants to fish for her family. Mother has gotten used to having a maid—most all of the American families here do, even if they don't have children—though she now complains that she has nothing to do. She plays cards and has cocktails with the other Ford wives, she makes dinner sometimes or teaches Efigênia how to cook home food, but Kerry can never get her to come out and explore.

"I see enough lizards and spiders in the house."

The rainy season over and the water beginning to look more like a river than a lake, flooded areas have been left behind as ponds, and Efigênia is going to use a poison sap she makes from tree roots to catch stranded fish, netting them after they float to the surface. She says the poison won't affect people who eat the fish, but Kerry is glad it's only for Efigênia's family to eat. Mother would have a fit.

They leave her by a pool a few yards from the receding river's edge and continue into the jungle. Kerry has been to the spot a couple times before but Flavio is so much better at finding his way. She carries the fruit in a mesh bag, some of it pretty stinky, holding it out from her body because of the flying insects it attracts. Flavio says his family would eat it, spots and bruises and all, but that the other workers here have gotten spoiled.

They move the way Flavio says hunters do, careful not to make noise, counting eight steps then pausing to listen. She hears a macaw and probably a pair of *potoos*, birds that look like a drawing by a four-year-old. The spot is not really a clearing, just a place where a lot of trees have fallen. Like Mr. Pringle says, "You can't *see* the jungle when you're *in* the jungle," but here there is enough clear space to see nearly to the tops of the surrounding trees. They reach up as high as they can to place the fruit on low branches, then work their way back to the big fallen tree they watch from, sitting on *juta* sacks so they won't stain their school uniforms.

Flavio says most of hunting is actually waiting. He has a soft voice, much quieter than hers, and she tries to match it as they wait.

"Do you think they smell it?"

"When they close enough."

Kerry is still shy about correcting his English. The teacher does enough of that-

"So if they're pretty far away now—"

"They find to eat here one time, two time. They come again to look."

She can't tell exactly how old Flavio is, and is embarrassed to ask. In school they group the local kids by how much English they have, not by years, so you can't know by that. All Flavio has told her, a joke of his, is that "I used to be a worker—now I am only a boy."

It is clear that he likes learning new things in school, but also misses being able to help his father and make money. Kerry's mother never even wanted her to go visit Daddy at the mill back in Pine Camp, saying she preferred a daughter with all ten of her fingers. And here Kerry has to lie a little bit about where she goes exploring, safe from exposure because none of the Americans bother with the jungle if they're not cutting it down.

Flavio points to what looks like wet sawdust ringed around a narrow tree they are stationed behind. When Kerry leans closer she sees that huge, reddish-black ants, at least an inch long, are hurrying up and down the tree, some climbing all the way into the leafy canopy above.

"*Ninho*," says Flavio, pointing to the sawdust pile.

"Nest."

He repeats the word in English a few times, then points to the climbing ants.

"*Formigâo-preto.*"

"Big black ant."

Kerry moves to see closer, but he blocks her with a hand. "*Cuidado.*"

He picks up a stick as long as his forearm and manages to get one of the ants to crawl onto it, bringing it close for her to study. It is the longest ant she has ever seen, and stocky, like a wasp with its wings pulled off. Flavio indicates the stinger on its rear.

"Venenoso."

"Poison?"

He makes a pistol of his free hand and mimes shooting it. "Pow!"

"It hurts like a bullet."

Flavio nods. Kerry points to him.

"*Você—bala?*"

Flavio just laughs. No, he has never been shot with a bullet.

They do not come quietly, branches shaking above as they leap from one to the next, twittering, squeaking, chirping. Flavio tosses the bullet ant aside and puts a finger to his lips. The squirrel monkeys know the humans are there, but expect stillness and quiet before they come down.

Kerry holds her breath.

They descend in fits and starts, crouching and wary, cautious with so much open sky above them. There are at least two-dozen, almost identical, wiry gray bodies with greenish fur on their backs and forearms, small round heads with black fuzz on top, a pinkish mask around their narrow-set eyes.

Kerry is enraptured.

They don't grab onto branches with their long gray tails but use them to balance, their feet long but just as clever as their little hands. They have long middle fingers and a very short thumb and the palms of their hands are just bare pink skin. When the first explorers get to the pieces of fruit they pick them up and stare at them for a moment, try a bite, look again, then nibble away like a chipmunk with an acorn. There is a little squabbling, more monkeys than fruit, but no biting.

Fuzzy, thinks Kerry. These are fuzzy monkeys, not hairy ones, quick and sure in the branches, and she has no idea which are the boys and which are the girls. She'll have to ask Flavio later.

They always leave one piece of *maracujá* very close, and so far there has been interest, but no takers. Today one of the littlest, truly squirrel-sized, is creeping toward it when the screaming begins.

The monkeys are gone like a flock of swift birds, exploding into the treetops, and the screaming continues.

It is Efigênia, and Kerry almost loses Flavio several times as she runs after him, spiny brush tearing at her arms and uniform. She has seen a dead jaguar, shot by an American foreman and later skinned, and hopes that the maid's screams have scared it away.

When they reach her, Efigênia is sitting by the flooded pond surrounded by dozens of smallish, twitching fish, holding tight to her right arm.

Which isn't all there anymore.

"*Caimão*," she says, which is what they call the huge black alligators whose heads you see drifting in the river, eyes and snout just above the surface. Blood is pumping out through her fingers as she holds the bitten arm well above her elbow.

"*Eu trarei ajuda*," says Flavio to Efigênia, a hand on the back of her neck, then looks to Kerry.

"You here. I go," he says.

And runs into the trees toward the escape path and the American compound.

Kerry looks into the pond. Not a ripple.

"*Por favor,*" says Efigênia, her voice weak now. "*Por favor.*"

Kerry has read the first aid pamphlet they give new workers at the sawmill back in Pine Camp. She wishes her school uniform came with a belt. Kerry kneels and puts her hands around Efigênia's arm just above where it's been torn off and squeezes as hard as she can.

"*Ajuda vem,*" she says. The hospital is the nicest building in Fordlandia, white and clean, with overhead fans and both Brazilian and American doctors. They'll know what to do if they come on time. Efigênia leans her head against Kerry's, eyes closed, breathing fast and shallow.

"*Minhas filhas,*" she says.

Kerry knows that the maid has two little girls, has seen them once or twice, but doesn't know their names.

"*Quais são os nomes?*"

She thinks that's the way to say it, but Efigênia takes a long time before answering, not opening her eyes.

"*Júlia e Belem.*"

"*Meninas bonitas,*" says Kerry. They *are* pretty girls, brown as berries with big black eyes and frizzy hair. Kerry tries to think of how to say not to worry, that everything will be all right.

"*Nada mal,*" is all she can think of. "*Nada mal.*"

There are ants now, not as big as the bullet ants, that are crawling all over the dead and dying fish. The fish haven't closed their eyes—Kerry realizes she's not sure if they ever do. She looks around and doesn't see the net—it might have been pulled away with Efigênia's arm. Kerry realizes she's kneeling in a puddle of blood and doesn't think the maid is breathing anymore.

She'll hold on tight till somebody comes.

• • •

"People aren't meant to live in this place. Not human beings."

They are lying in bed, never as cool as it should be, Kerry in the next room, out like a light.

"The Mundurucú—"

"They live like animals."

"They live *with* animals," says Jim. "You haven't met them."

"And hope I never will. I hate you having to go there. It's not what you were hired for."

"I was hired to make this place produce rubber."

"And how's *that* going?"

"There's an expert coming in a couple days, some kind of biologist. Professor Weir."

"That crazy old man shipped people off to this hellhole without a clue—"

"It isn't a *hell*hole. What about the school? The hospital? Johnston is even talking about making a golf course."

"I'm not taking up *golf*."

"It would give you something to do—"

This hangs in the air, Norma not dignifying it with a response.

"Honey, I have a job, we have a home—"

"I saw a lizard moving on the floor today."

"The lizards eat bugs."

"No, this was a *dead* lizard and it was being carried off by a platoon of ants. The ants were about to eat the lizard. We're next."

"You're exaggerating—"

"Kerry saw a woman die today."

Jim has felt Norma, always a good sport, growing more resigned to their situation, but the accident has obviously shaken her.

"People at *home* are out of work, Norma. There are bread lines—"

"Your boss says that's to teach us a lesson."

Norma feels Jim, never one to tolerate complaints about the Founder, go stonily silent. She is exhausted, nerves raw from the screaming fight with Kerry—as if a woman having her arm ripped off by a crocodile and dying isn't reason enough to be forbidden to go gallivanting into the jungle—having to explain, at the top of her lungs, that a mother making sure her child survives whole and unsullied till the age of eighteen does not make her a prison matron.

Though after another year in Fordlandia she will no doubt *look* like one.

"We'll have to get a new maid," says Jim.

• • •

A lot gets thrown in the river. It's a game of hide-and-seek, the rules being that you can't just see the rumrunners with a boatload aboard, you have to actually lay hands on them while there's still at least a case on board. DeWitt and Alvin come down some nights and sit with the other guys, watching and listening, the Detroit cops and Federals with their spotlights and the leggers running blind if there's not a moon. Sometimes there's a show, cops on their bullhorns, boat motors roaring, real movie stuff. And sometimes there's no bullhorns, the boats coming together, agreeing on a deal, then going their separate ways.

"Somebody just made a contribution to the Police Fund," DeWitt will tell Alvin then.

With a serious chase there are often wooden crates of liquor being tossed overboard, and maybe the boys can get hold of whatever floats in.

"They throw so much away," Alvin said the first time they got lucky. "But they still keep hauling it."

"Supply and demand," his big brother explained. "You make something illegal, make it scarce, and it's gonna sell for a hell of a lot more than it costs to make it."

Only once was there gunfire, pistols and maybe rifles instead of machine guns like in the movies, and all the boys on the bank cheered when the booze boat ducked behind Belle Isle and the Federals gave up.

"Stick and run, stick and run!" shouted Alvin, who is nutty about the fights, hanging at the Brewster Center to watch the amateurs train, learning language he best forget when he's home.

Tonight they are on a salvage expedition.

There's a spot, about a half mile down from where they watch the boat chases, where things drift in—tree branches, garbage, dead fish, and sometimes, if you're lucky, the good Canadian stuff that some booze boat has had to ditch.

It is their secret, found on a hunch, and they have to sneak around through ofay territory to get there. There is an old, rotting dock, one corner dipping toward the water, that makes for a perfect entry. They keep the rope stashed there, and Alvin has gotten good at tying and untying knots, looking them up in a library book about sailing. It starts tight around DeWitt's hips, but always slides up under his arms before they're through, and is looped once around a solid post for safety. Alvin handles the tote bag, lowering it down whenever DeWitt comes up with anything worth keeping.

The water is always cold, even in the middle of summer, and once he's in DeWitt works quick. When you're under it's near impossible to see, so there's a lot of groping around down in the pilings—now and then you will grab onto something you don't even want to *think* about what it might be.

This is their lucky night.

DeWitt always goes down feet-first, raising his hands over his head to sink faster. He's wearing only his unders, with bare feet to feel the bottom, and they come to rest on what feels an awful lot like a wooden crate. He squats down to grope with his fingers, pushes back up to the surface

"Pry bar!" he calls to Alvin.

Alvin sends the iron pry bar, another thing they keep stashed here, down in the tote bag. DeWitt pulls it out, takes a deep breath, goes under again.

He doesn't land in the same place, but close enough to locate the crate quickly. He finds a crack, wedges the bar, yanks. A slat pulls open enough for him to get three fingers in—he feels the top of a bottle.

"What we got?" calls Alvin, excited, when DeWitt comes up.

"Bottled and bonded."

"Damn." Alvin has that big grin, always a happy-go-lucky kid. "I'm gonna *retire*."

It's his new favorite word, having heard that Jack Dempsey was retired from the ring.

"Get that bag hanging down here where I can reach it."

On the next dive DeWitt gets the crate open enough to pull out a bottle, sending it up to Alvin with the pry bar. Thank you, Hiram Walker & Sons. He's starting to feel achy cold, but it's a full case, too waterlogged to hoist the whole thing up, so it will have to be a few bottles at a time.

The next dive he wiggles two out before he has to come up. While he's slipping them into the bag, not always easy while you're also treading water, something from under the dock bumps him from behind.

"Coming out!" he calls when he figures out what it is.

"What for?"

"Coming out!"

Alvin hauls the bag with the bottles up and DeWitt hauls himself out, wrestling wet rope and pushing his feet off on slimy piling, always his least favorite part of the job.

"Why you coming out?" asks Alvin when his brother crawls up onto the tilted deck and catches his breath.

"That's all there is. The rest is all broken."

"You sure?"

"You want to go down and look?"

Alvin does not swim. There was a decent pond when they lived in Inkster, but he never took to it. DeWitt thinks he's afraid of bumping into a fish.

Alvin arranges all three bottles in the bag, stuffing newspaper in between so they don't clank together, while DeWitt pulls on his clothes.

"How the other ones get broke down in the water?"

"Maybe when the crate hit the dock. Or maybe it was bullets from the Hootch Squad."

"At-at-at-at-at at-at at-at!" goes Alvin, making a machine-gun sound.

"We're lucky we got what we did."

"How come there's never any colored gangsters in the movies? Just some old cotton-picker in overalls, playing his harmonica when they take the white boy to the chair—"

"Who you think makes those stories?"

"White folks."

"There's your answer."

DeWitt starts out ahead of Alvin, needing time to think this over.

"Hey, wait up."

Alvin is a good kid, accepts it like a man when DeWitt tells him no, you can't come on this one. He is scrawny as hell, not like DeWitt or their father, who can lift a ton of liquid metal on a long wooden pole. Maybe Alvin thinks if he watches the fighters long enough he'll grow some muscles.

"What you think they'll pay?"

"Well, that dry law is about over here, but good liquor still hard to *get*."

Even with his clothes back on DeWitt is still cold. And then there's the other, the memory of that bump, turning and seeing-

"Look out."

There are white boys, maybe a bit younger than DeWitt, but three of them, standing in the street they have to go down to catch the streetcar to Black Bottom.

"You lost?" asks the biggest of the three, dark haired with a beak of a nose.

"Just passing through."

"You don't pass through here," says the boy, shaking his head, "without our permission."

"And who might you be?"

In a different situation DeWitt might fight them, lay one out quick and scare the other two away, but he's got Alvin. Alvin gets even a bloody nose, there be hell to pay at home.

"We're the Dixie Gang," says the boy. "This is our river."

"That's a long stretch of water to protect."

"We own a chunk of it," says another of the boys. "What's in the bag?"

"It's ours," blurts Alvin. "We found it."

The first boy snaps his fingers, holds out his hand. "Give it up."

DeWitt holds them with his eyes as he takes the bag from Alvin, pulls out a bottle, holds it up over his head.

"I could give you this," he says, "or I could bust it over your head."

The boys look to their leader, who is calculating. "Any more where that came from?"

"Sure. But you got to get wet to find it."

The boy nods. "Okay. Pay the tax and make yourselfs scarce."

DeWitt tosses the bottle gently and the boy catches it, then steps aside.

"Don't come back."

The boys don't follow them. DeWitt can tell that Alvin feels bad about it.

"If they pulled what we just done in Inkster," he tells his little brother, "I'd of charged them *two* bottles tax."

That gets a laugh. They come to the streetcar stop, and DeWitt can see it coming down the track three blocks away. Streetcars are neutral ground, the brakemen pretty tough customers who won't put up with any scuffling.

The body, what DeWitt got to see of it, was so bloated you couldn't tell if it was man or woman, colored or white, just a floating bag of gas with some rags of clothes stuck to it. Nothing you want to be caught within ten blocks of, especially if you're the wrong color for the neighborhood. It's somebody's job to fish those things out, cut the clothes off, see if they can figure out who they were, but DeWitt doesn't want any part of it. Bad enough he's got that picture in his head, got the feel of it bumping against his naked skin-

If Alvin doesn't *know* he doesn't have to think about it, doesn't have to tell lies. Let him be a kid for a while longer.

A white lady stares at DeWitt some on the streetcar. At first he thinks it's the bag with the bottles in it, but then he realizes his unders have soaked through his pants and it looks like he's wet himself.

A story to tell her friends.

They get off at the Hastings and Adams stop and head for Antoine's, where they've sold their treasures before. They're block away when Alvin stops in his tracks.

"That's him."

"Who?"

"Him."

It is Joe Louis, Alvin's favorite fighter. Alvin has dragged DeWitt to the Golden Gloves around town a few times and with Louis it's not much of a show—first round, boom, a short punch you hardly see and the other guy kisses the canvas. Three of them were in the first round, and the last bout, where he won the light heavyweights at the Olympia, it went for three but the opponent finally went down. Alvin is tugging at DeWitt's arm.

"Let's go say hello."

"He's with a friend."

"That doesn't matter."

Joe looks peaceful, like a lot of fighters when they're out of the ring, light-colored, maybe a bit Indian-looking. He grins when he sees Alvin come up.

"I know you."

"We saw you beat Biskey! He went down like a ton of bricks."

"Yeah, that was a good fight. People got their two bits, worth."

"This is my brother DeWitt."

Louis nods to DeWitt. "You look like you could be in the ring."

"Too much work for me."

The boxer nods. "Don't I know it."

His friend points to the tote bag. "What you got in there, a chicken?"

"We found it in the river," says Alvin, almost hopping with excitement.

"You found a dead *chick*en in the river? Let's see it."

DeWitt lifts a bottle of the whiskey from the bag.

"Fell outa somebody's rowboat, did it?"

"There was a whole case but most was broken," Alvin informs the friend. DeWitt wonders when the floating corpse will be found, or if after a while the body deflates and sinks back to the bottom.

"That's a quart of good liquor you got there, you want to sell it before it gets legal."

"We give you one free," says Alvin to Joe.

The fighter laughs. "Thanks, but I don't drink. Training."

"Oh. That's right—"

"Joe's gonna go pro pretty soon," boasts the friend. "Got to be ready for whoever they throw at you."

"Watch out, world," says Alvin.

"How old are you?"

"Eight," says Alvin, who is only seven. "We had a fight with some white boys but DeWitt scairt em away."

"That right?"

DeWitt shakes his head. "Cost us one bottle to get clear."

Louis gives them an easy smile. "Yeah, maybe you could be a fighter. Got to use your *head*."

Alvin is just about dancing as they continue to Antoine's.

"Joe Louis said he knew me by sight."

"He's just an amateur," says DeWitt. "There was how many, more than a thousand in that tournament—"

"But he's *go*ing places, Dee. You gonna remember this day."

DeWitt thinks it was a bare hand, bloated and purple, that touched him first, that rested on his shoulder for a moment.

"I expect I will."

• • •

Pulaski Park is crowded with little ones at this hour, most even younger than Sonia. And yes, some are toddling only with the help of their mothers, but that is the one- and two-year-olds. Sonia is tall for her age, skinny, and they catch a few stares both when Molly is holding her daughter's hand and when she isn't. Sonia wants to walk on her own, wants to climb the slide and sit on the teeter-totter by herself, but she can't, really. She looks like she's dizzy or drunk when she walks unaided, and Molly tries to stay near. Kaz is strong enough to carry her on his shoulders, and will do that when they're in a hurry, Sonia accepting help for the joy of the ride. But Molly spends most of the day with her, the kindergarten saying they aren't 'equipped' to deal with a child with Sonia's—with Sonia's problems.

The doctors make a big deal about how much worse it could be, how some with the same condition can't stand up at all or see very well or have spasms or can't even *try* to speak. But it's bad enough, the constant shaking, how hard it is for her to do normal things, her frustration now that she wants to talk. Thank God she's not old enough to be embarrassed, no hesitation in public making her noises that Molly is only beginning to understand.

"She's the smart one," Kaz will say out loud when the twins aren't there to hear. "We'd better watch out."

And Sonia beams.

And she *is* smart, pays attention to everything, loves the dramatic radio shows where you have to follow a story, loves picture books even though it's still hard for her to turn the pages. She's figured out a way to eat her cereal without spilling too much, grabbing her left wrist with her right hand and lowering her head close to the bowl.

Someday she'll have to go to school.

Someday she'll worry about what the other kids think.

But right now she is their joy, Molly talking to her softly all day long, and not baby talk but really filling her in on what she needs to know. Kaz is worried about money of course, his days at the Rouge having been cut back, but it gives him more time where he's not exhausted to be with the kids, to read to Sonia from the picture books. And the twins always let their 'different' little sister follow them around, have learned to help her up when she wants to climb something and stand close for when she wants to come down.

She wants to climb up the ladder and go down the slide.

But she is waiting, watching while a couple younger boys clamber up and shoot down—two, three, four times before they get bored and run off to flush a flock of pigeons into the air.

Sonia knows it takes her longer to do things and doesn't want to be in their way.

It might as well be a twenty-foot cliff she's climbing, each jerky grasp of a rung and shaky step up a triumph, and it takes her a long time to get her legs properly pointed downhill once she's seated at the top. Molly has learned how to stand close but directly behind so she can't be seen, arms ready to catch. She hurries around to the foot of the slide, then Sonia gives her the big, lop-sided smile and somehow pushes off, making a happy noise for the two-second ride. She lets Molly give her a hand-up to stand.

Sonia sees something and careens away, still smiling, holding her left elbow too close to her body and moving almost sideways the way she does, and Molly sees that she's heading for a bench at the edge of the park, one always occupied these days by four or five down-and-outers, men with nowhere else to go and nothing else to do. The other mothers don't like it, and a few have even spoken to Hamtramck policemen, who just shrug and say if the men don't hassle anybody or actually lie down to *sleep*-

Sonia is heading for an older man on the end of the bench, hat pulled low over his forehead-

When he spreads his arms wide Molly realizes that it's Kaz's father, Prokop. She hopes he's just on a short week at Briggs and hasn't been fired again.

"*Mój maly!*" he cries as he takes Sonia in his arms. "We both have day off!"

• • •

"The first machine is *sensillo*—simple—you make a wheel of stone and put a stick of wood through the center so you can roll it to crush the maiz. Then some wise man he discovers that a more large, more heavy stone can be used and a—*como se dice esto?*" The Muralist makes a gesture with his hand-

"A crank."

"That a *crank* will turn it more easy, and if a donkey is trained to walk in a circle it can crush not only *maiz*, but the canes of sugar—"

"And if you have a chute to guide the juice directly into the cauldron it's got to boil in—"

"Yes," says the Muralist, "one thing leads to the next. *Es un proceso.* And your museum reveals the process of invention, one leading to the next—"

"Mus*e*ums are where they store old bones," says Henry. "The Village is an edu*ca*tional center. The way they teach history in school—what year somebody slaughtered somebody else on a battlefield—*bunk*. *Doub*le bunk. The way civilization moves forward is by one fella figuring out a better way to do something that needs doing, and then the next saying 'I can top *that*.' Hell, I never in*vent*ed a thing in my life—I just took ideas that had been kicking around for a while and made them *work*, polished em off, adjusted the balances, took one thing from here and another from there—"

The Mexican spreads out his arms. "This is what I do as well! I have study the classical painters, the Impressionists, *los cubistas*, the art of the Nahua and the Maya, and all of these are a part of what I bring to make a poem that even an *analfebetado*—a one who does not read?"

"Illiterate."

"Even *he* can understand the story, the idea of the picture."

He is a huge toad of a man, this Mexican, with eyes that bulge out from an enormous head, and a belly that precedes him like the prow of a tugboat.

"You're going to paint on the walls."

"Is not so simple," smiles the Mexican.

Henry had a bunch of Mexicans at the Rouge, good, solid workers, kept their heads down, but with all the banking problems Hoover has ordered them out of the country, out of the way of the born-and-bred Americans desperate for jobs. When it was time to cut production in half, he told Harry to turn them loose—let the government take the blame for it.

"I paint not on the wall, but on layers of *yeso*—of *plas*ter—that is built up on the wall by my assistants—"

"You have helpers?"

"*Seguro,* no one man could ever do this work. They mix and apply the plaster—each layer is different—they crush the pigments to make the paint, they build the *andamio*—is a platform you are working from—"

"Scaffolding."

"*This*, yes. I plan each one of the panels and then draw them with charcoal and color on a cartoon—is the size of the panel but made of paper—and then my helpers they push a pin along the outline of the drawings to make holes, then this is put up against the plaster on the wall—"

"A template—"

"-and chalk that is ground into a powder is then struck against it, leaving a guide—"

"You came up with this on your own?"

"*Por supuesto no*, it is something very ancient, and each time for the plaster and the paint one must try one thing and then another. I have discover a certain combination of the dust of marble and then lime, and of course the water must first be *destilado*. The first coat must be thicker, stronger—it will be raked with stripes so the next will *pegar*—estick to it—much better. And then, some mixtures of the paint is very beautiful, but will fade quickly, even indoors, or a different class of final coat may be needed if there is gold and silver in the picture that must catch the light—"

"A lot of trial and error."

Again the Mexican smiles. "At times I will work on a panel for one, two, three days, and at the end tell my helps to remove all that I have done—"

"Start from scratch."

"Yes. The scratching comes first."

"I can't tell you, Diego, how many engines and transmission assemblies I've had to toss away—of course, we got a nice little scrap-iron operation at the Rouge plant, melt it down and make it into something else—"

"I fear that my waste is good for nothing—"

"But you *learn* from those foul-ups, don't you?"

"Oh yes, but is a great *esfuerzo*—a great effort—at times one loses the faith. When I am creating a *mural*, I think of nothing else."

"I just got over one of those. It's called the V8 engine."

"I would so much love to see this come together on the line of production! So many things working together inside—"

"We'll fix you up with a pass and you can get a gander at every part of the process."

The Muralist makes a V with his hands. "Is a beautiful shape, this motor."

"It was a son-of-a-gun to keep the size down," says Henry. "You could drop one in a ten-year-old Model A now, and she'll *fly*."

Harry Bennett tells him that the Mexican is a Red, but he seems too good-humored, too open to new ideas—who knows what passes for Communism down there? And Henry doesn't care for bankers and stock market finaglers any more than the Reds do-

"I hope to capture not only the *proceso* of your work," says the Mexican, "but also the es*pir*it." He has polished off his lunch as well as seconds, and made no complaint at the lack of alcohol. Edsel, always consorting with Rockefellers and DuPonts waving their Harvard degrees at you and plastering their names on this or that so-called charity, has chosen well with this fellow.

"Try these," says Henry Ford, reaching for the soybean fritters, "they taste just like chicken."

• • •

They've got Kaz on engine blocks now, no tools required as he steers the heavy load from one conveyor to another. If they choose to move you elsewhere on the line you don't ask why. Less time-pressure than the last spot, but his back is sore at the end of the shift.

"Next time you run into Henry Ford," says Bud Novak whenever they see each other on the streetcar, "just tell him to raise the belt up a few inches. I know he sits up nights worrying about our comfort."

Today is the same routine, pushing blocks, only there is this fat, sloppy, pop-eyed character watching him and the other workers up and down the line, scribbling in a notebook and sometimes coming close to stare at some piece of the process—there are parts crossing overhead on hooks as well—

like he's never seen such a thing before. It's never good when a guy with pen and paper comes around, as there's usually a speedup or two jobs getting combined into one within the week. The fat guy doesn't look like the usual engineer, though, no glasses, no hat, no *tie*, and it is well known that Ford Senior dislikes fat people and will sometimes have them fired on sight.

Quinlan, on a parallel line mounting pistons, says he stepped around the guy on a trip to the bathroom, and saw that he was drawing *pictures*, not writing notes and numbers.

And he didn't have a stopwatch.

• • •

Doctor Weir arrives on the pontoon plane. He looks like a movie professor, tall and somewhat distracted, gruffly demanding to see the plantation before settling in to the quarters they've prepared. Jim and Archibald Johnston and Gomes, the translator, walk out into the rows with him, privy to a succession of disapproving grunts and sighs and shakes of the head as Weir examines the trees.

"Who's been in charge of new plants?"

Johnston nods toward Jim.

"Where have you been getting them?"

"Upriver a day or two," Jim explains. "Then we have a place where we start them just a few miles from here, kind of a mother seed-bed—"

Weir is already making a face-

"We try to get seeds from the healthiest trees. Ones that produce a lot of latex—"

"You understand that only half the genes come from the tree that drops the seeds. The pollination could be from anywhere."

"Uhm—*genes*, right—" Jim has read some about this but it isn't totally clear.

"Like anything in a particular area, there are excellent mixes and those that are disadvantageous." The scientist is looking straight at Gomes, who doesn't react. Jim hopes that Weir is not trying to be insulting. "Have you ever heard of bud-grafting?"

"I've heard of it, but—"

"You *have* worked with trees?"

"Not this kind."

Weir nods his head, winces before he sighs. "I will give you a manual of standard procedures developed for Goodyear's plantations in Sumatra. I'm sure on your automobile assembly line you have *pro*tocols of some sort—"

"Naturally," says Johnston. "Every movement refined and calculated down to the second."

"You'll want to apply that kind of discipline here, once we've corrected the methodology."

Jim is both relieved that the burden is now off his shoulders and resentful that it was ever placed there. "So what are we doing wrong now?"

Weir does not hesitate, gazing out at the rows and rows of scrawny, insect-ridden trees.

"Everything."

• • •

Whatever they needled the beer with is giving Zeke a headache. They say the dry law is going to end with this new president and it can't happen too soon. Stupid idea to begin with, and these days when you lay your two bits on the pine there's no telling what they'll hand you.

DuPree and Deleon Barrow, who lives not far from their new place on Alfred Street, took him to a blind tiger on Hastings Street for a quick one before the fights, a place with no name that had a bar built up from old wooden crates and steam pipes you had to duck your head under, all plastered with signs that said **WATCH YOUR HEAD**. Zeke said the joint should be called the Cellar and they told him there was already a place called that in Black Bottom, plus one called the Basement and one called Denny's Dive just across Gratiot in Paradise Valley. They say he'll come to like the neighborhood because it's so much livelier than Inkster, but so far it just looks like more people crammed into less space.

"Got Italians to the east of us, Jews to the north, but we *own* Hastings Street, Zeke. Anything you buy there, you buying from another colored man."

DuPree has been beating his gums about Black Bottom all night, like he's got real estate to sell, but Deleon is newer to Detroit and not sold on its wonder.

"Don't no colored man own the house *we* live in," he says. "We paying ten dollars a month for two rooms, got to share the bathroom with two other families. You hear the commode flush and there's three, four people out on the stairs want to be next, holding their own toilet paper."

"Didn't *have* no toilet paper where I come up," says DuPree, who has a long and impressive list of what he did without back in Caloosahatchee or wherever it was he escaped from down south.

The Naval Armory is a new building down at the foot of the Belle Isle bridge, lots of painting on the walls of blue ocean, sailors, battleship cannons, and a drill hall that converts easily into a boxing arena with bleachers. The amateur bouts are only a dime to get into and Deleon's brother Joe is in the last bout on the card, light heavyweights. Zeke has met him at the streetcar stop, a shy, light-colored boy who's been pushing truck bodies at Briggs, the outfit that took over the Highland Park plant from Ford. Last Zeke heard they were only paying two dollars a day.

Zeke sees Jarvis Stokes walk past down the aisle next to them, all the way up to the dollar seats at ringside, taking a knee to flash his gold teeth and chat with a well-fed citizen in a porkpie hat and a tailored gray silk suit. Zeke points the man out to DuPree.

"Who's the character in the righteous rags?"

"Jarvis?"

"Naw, the butter-and-egg man he's talking to."

"That's John Roxborough. He'll sell you some insurance, go your bail, steer you to a deal on property—"

"So that's John Roxborough the *num*bers man."

"Yeah, and Jarvis just one of his little collection boys."

It is a raggedy crowd, some here to get out of the rain for a few hours, and then some who come hoping to see a fighter get laid out, maybe killed—usually not a feature of amateur nights. From the names and shades of the boxers the whole city is represented, and there are scattered cheering sections for the Poles and the Irish and the Italians and the Jews and the Spanish-name boys and the colored. There is even a southpaw over from Windsor with a maple leaf sewn on his robe, who outclassed Battling Nicos Stephanopulos in the flyweights.

"Mr. Roxborough got a piece of a couple local boys. Just a sporting man, you know, cause there isn't much money to be made off a colored fighter."

"That's all Jack Johnson fault," says Deleon. "He won the heavyweight belt and commenced to strollin around with white women—"

"He *mar*ried a pair of em!" interrupts DuPree. "Got some money in his pocket, he wouldn't deal in coal no more. Every since then, won't no white champ step in a ring with a colored man."

"There's Kid Chocolate—"

"He's *Cu*ban."

"Gorilla Jones—"

"I'm talking about the *big* men, where the real money is. Take Deleon's brother—he's three porkchops and a side of mashed potatoes away from being a heavyweight. You think that the one who's in now—Sharkey—you think his handlers would let him go toe-to-toe with Joe?"

"But Joe just started—"

"Let him notch a few wins on his belt," says DuPree, "and watch them white fighters run."

At the moment two brownish boys who look like twins, maybe a Mexican and an Italian, are pawing at each without much effect, making the audience restless.

"Hit him, hit him, hit him!" shouts a man even further back from the ring than they are. "Jesus, somebody hit *some*body!"

Zeke is here mostly because Mavis needed him out of the house, having a conference there with one Madame Queenie, who banks the numbers on Alfred and a couple parallel streets, to see if she'll be allowed to operate anywhere in Black Bottom or will have to find a new hustle. When Mr. Rhinehardt told them he was taking down their house in Inkster to build something new, she went on the hunt but couldn't find a thing they could both fit in and afford. The Company is pulling out of the community, something about new federal regulations, but everybody knows it's just a feud between Mr. Ford and this new one in the White House, Roosevelt, who Mavis convinced Zeke was the man to vote for no matter what they told him at work. The new digs are in pretty bad shape, a house meant for one family that has four living in it, half the windowpanes patched with cardboard and a sewer smell coming from out back. And if Mavis doesn't have anything to pitch in, it'll be beans and cornbread for supper from now on.

The bell rings to end the third round and the referee cuts the bout short, declaring a no decision. The fighters, who both clumsily crossed themselves on one knee before the first round, touch gloves politely and climb out through the ropes to a few boos. The next two gladiators are hustled up onto the canvas, and the announcer steps to the middle and begins to shout through a cardboard megaphone. With only near-beer and peanuts available at the concession, there is little stalling between contests.

"Ladies and gentlemen, our final bout tonight, six rounds in the light heavyweight classification. In this corner"—he points with his free hand—"from our great city of Detroit, wearing dark trunks and making his first appearance in the amateur ranks—Joe Louis Barrow!"

Zeke applauds politely as DuPree and Deleon shout and whistle, the only pocket of real enthusiasm for the hometown battler.

"In the opposite corner," croons the announcer, "in the light trunks and recently representing our country in the Summer Olympic games held in Los Angeles—Johnny *Mi*ler!"

The white boy looks at least five years older and a lot less nervous than Deleon's brother, who impassively listens to the referee's instructions. Zeke spent some time in the gym when he first got to Chicago, falling for the line about "a big boy like you could pick up some easy cash" and even having a little talent for the footwork. But finally, the part where you keep getting hit in the face-

Which Deleon's brother proceeds to do, keeping his left way too low, coming in, coming in, just asking to get pasted. Every time young Joe steps into another right hook all Zeke can think of is **WATCH YOUR HEAD.**

"What do you think?" asks DuPree after the first punishment period ends, Joe having hit the canvas twice.

"I think he's not ready for Sharkey."

"No, really."

"At this rate," says Zeke, "he'll be slap-happy before he's twenty."

The brother sighs, disappointed, wincing through the next several knockdowns and excusing himself to go commiserate in the dressing room when the bell rings out the last round. The patrons seem satisfied, having finally seen some real fisticuffs, and start for the exit. Zeke's headache hasn't gone away.

"He got some *pow*er at least," says DuPree as they follow the crowd, crunching peanut shells beneath their feet. "And he's got *heart*. Stood right in there."

"Working at Briggs—"

"'If Poison Doesn't Work, Try Briggs.'"

"Yeah, there's easier ways to turn a dollar. But being a human punching bag—"

"A man's got to *dream*, Zeke."

They'll most likely walk all the way home from the Armory, and the thought of returning to the dump on Alfred Street makes Zeke suddenly weary. Work day tomorrow, sucking in cooked air at the foundry.

"Dream, hell," he mutters. "I'll settle for a good night's sleep."

• • •

The tempera won't absorb if the last thin coat of plaster has dried, so you have to work quickly, confidently, racing the effects of air and heat. The

Muralist sits high up on a plank of scaffolding facing the panel on upper right of the north wall, the section he is calling *Vaccination*, only one of the aspects likely to offend the good people of Detroit, or, more vitally, a member of the Art Institute board of directors. There was a columnist from one of the important local newspapers below for quite some time yesterday, watching him work, examining the cartoon as Cliff and his wife poked holes to trace the principal outlines, a man with thick lenses on his spectacles and a grim demeanor—the Muralist would paint him as an indignant locust. Pornography was hinted at in his jeremiad this morning, the ugly and obscene already despoiling the city's lovely new Institute, which if not nipped in the bud—

And then this Father Coughlin on the radio.

Yes, without much effort or imagination one could misinterpret the grouping he's working on, a cherubic boy held gently by a nurse while being inoculated by a white-coated physician, animals from whose tissue serums are made—a horse, a cow, some sheep—grouped in the foreground, while above the boy three scientists work together in a biochemical plant, formulating some new panacea. Creatures from the manger? The three Magi? The facile imagination will suspect a lampoon, but the idea is much deeper—Science has replaced Superstition, at least among the thoughtful, our inheritors injected with its tenets in their youth-

But there's not a corrupt priest in the entire collage of images, no capitalists dining on gold coins, nary a red flag. The Muralist has been ejected by the Party, personally betrayed by Tina Modotti, and this *mater opus* created in the belly of the beast will do nothing to bolster his petition for readmittance. But he'll keep trying—perhaps when Stalin goes to his grave the Muralist's own thought and that of the *commissars* in Moscow and Mexico City may align once more.

For now, science and machinery, the plastic genius of the brave new world-

The Garden Court is impossible, Italian baroque aimed at Detroit's upper bourgeoisie, everywhere a satyr's head or an ornate molding, a plague of tiny windows—there is no question of his mural coexisting with this *abellimento*, so he has chosen to overwhelm it, convincing Dr. Valentiner of the museum and the principal financial backer, young Edsel, to allow him to cover *all* the walls, twenty-seven panels in all compared to the handful in the original commission. Edsel, ever the gentleman, insisted that the Muralist's fee be increased somewhat proportionately, which will pay the builders of their house down in San Angel. Edsel's father—a gray stick of a man with keen eyes and a farm boy's bluntness—offered a sumptuous Lincoln automobile for his convenience after their lunch together. As the Wardell apartments are directly across from the Art Institute, it was not needed, and one photograph of the Muralist descending into this chariot would bar him from the Party for eternity. So after demurring, Edsel kindly provided a smaller, more tasteful machine to be driven in their few sojourns about the city. Frida walks when she feels up to it, going to the movies with Lucienne Bloch, anything featuring the Three Stooges her current favorite. People stare at her costumes, as they did in San Francisco and New York, as they still do, in fact, in Mexico, except where she is well known.

She is calling to him from below.

Diego, you haven't eaten.

It is true. He has been living like a corpulent bird, eight to twelve feet off the ground, for weeks now, fourteen, eighteen, twenty hours a day, sleeping on the planks sometimes if one of his assistants is there to be sure he doesn't roll off and break something again. The problem of a figure, a plant, a row of machines will pull him in and when he manages to escape from it, triumphant or vowing a further attack, a day and a good part of the night have elapsed without his notice. It is a state he dreads and avoids by doing portraits and easel work, and one he longs to surrender to. What comes between is often pleasurable, fraught with personal drama and not a small bit of debauchery, but he is only waiting for the next wall.

What time is it? he asks.

He notices that both Cliff and Halberstadt are curled up on the rugs they've brought into the Institute, usually taking turns to nap.

It doesn't matter. You have to eat.

Frida holds up a basket covered with a cloth. She has become interested in cooking, even learning a few recipes from his ex-wife Lupe, who more than once and with ample provocation attempted to poison him, but there is no facility for it in their hotel room. The Muralist tosses down a rope that is tied off to one of the scaffolding poles beside him, and she knots the end around the handle of the basket. It feels heavy.

Carnitas, *arroz*, hot *tortillas* and a thermos of coffee.

Where ever did you find this?

Those Mexicans we talked to, the ones you want to help deport.

I offered them some connections back home when they do have to leave. They can't hide from the *yanquis* forever. Besides, you hate it here.

I don't have a job. Or children.

Frida is pregnant, a hope and a menace given the state of her body.

You're painting.

It's only a *pasatiempo*, she says.

Edsel Ford dismissed his own efforts the same way. A shrug of the shoulders, a tight smile, "It's a hobby."

You know that isn't true.

In any case, says Frida, I have to go home. My mother is dying.

The Muralist stops eating.

Something new?

It's a cancer. A spreading cancer.

She is her father's child, cerebral, driven by moods and obsessions. She has told Diego that her mother has no imagination and cares only about money-

When will you go?

Lucienne is arranging it. We'll take the train to El Paso and cross over there. The day after tomorrow, I hope.

He feels dizzy, grabs on to the pole. He sees her very little now that the actual painting has begun, often forgets to meet her when they have plans, but for him to be trapped here with this monster on the wall and her hundreds of miles away in Mexico-

I'm sorry about your mother.

I'll tell her. She likes you now that the *gringos* pay you so much.

Maybe the coffee is too much for his stomach. He puts the basket to one side.

You have saved my life with this, *mi amor*. I'll come over when this detail is finished.

I know.

He listens to her footsteps echoing as she leaves the courtyard, the sound of the door as the sleepy watchman lets her out, then turns to find himself face-to-face with the cherubic little patient. He'll need to add highlights to the blond curls—the local *cristeros* will call it a halo-

And the plaster won't wait.

• • •

There must be at least five hundred of them covering the entrances, hunched up against the freezing wind, one woman clearly having a hard time keeping her PAY US A LIVING WAGE! sign from tearing out of her hands and flying away. Kaz talks his way past both Highland Park police and a couple state troopers and finds his father on the Woodward Avenue side of what is now the Briggs plant, picketing with a bunch of older men and a few women from the sewing department. The old guy looks smaller than he remembers, a bit hunched, but that could just be the weather. Kaz gets in step with the picketers, handing Prokop the egg sandwich folded in a paper bag.

"How long you been out here, Pop?"

His father shrugs, never the owner of a wristwatch. "We chase away scabs," he says. "I got nothing else to do."

One of the smaller plants had a walkout, mostly tool-and-die makers and other guys with skills, and got Briggs to back off on their planned wage reductions, so the workers at Mack Avenue and here at Kaz's old stomping grounds smelled an opening and went out as well.

It's been a month.

"How come you here?"

It is a Wednesday, usually a work day at the Rouge. "The Old Man shut us down. Said without auto bodies we can't operate, but I think he just wants to put the heat on you people. I got pulled in by Harry Bennett."

"Little bastard wearing bowtie."

"You remember the guy—"

Prokop shakes his head. "You step in dogshit on sidewalk, you don't forget where."

"Well, he said I should come over and lean on you, Pop, to say how your bunch is queering it for everybody else."

His father holds up the sandwich bag. "So this is bribe?"

Kaz laughs. "No, this is fried with onions and peppers. Molly cooked it up."

"She is good woman, Molly."

There was nothing in any of the newspapers about the walkout for the longest time, then the people at what they're calling the Auto Workers' Union threatened to picket *them* for not paying attention, which led to the usual editorial squawking about Reds being behind it all. Kaz sees two American flags and zero red banners among the shuffling workers at this entrance.

"What's your committee tell you?"

"First demand is eight-hour day, no dead time."

Briggs doesn't pay for time waiting for materials to arrive, or when the belt goes down, or for your twenty-minute lunch break, and even deducts for 'use of tools'-

"At what rate?"

"Guarantee of twenty-five cents for hour."

"That's *all*?"

"I was making thirteen cents. Women in upholstery getting eight—"

"Shit."

"Yes, is shit. Then they have racket, deduct for health insurance, but nobody is ever getting doctor or medicine from this."

Kaz and his father assembled Model Ts in this building before the

Rouge opened, and then Briggs took it over, supplying bodies to Ford and Chrysler and Hudson for a lot less than they could make them themselves. The Dynamo of Dearborn never mentions that when he brags about still paying the highest wage in the industry.

"Warm enough for you?" calls a striker carrying a sign that says **ORGANIZE, UNITE, FIGHT!** to a nearby member of the Detroit riot squad who is hopping from one foot to the other, hands stuffed into his coat pockets. He laughs.

"Why can't you people pull these things in May or August?"

"It doesn't work that way," calls the striker. "After we win this, come around and we'll help your outfit organize."

"We could sure use it. They've cut our pay nearly a third."

"So where does it sit?" Kaz asks his father.

"Briggs say yes to pay rate, hours, dead time, but refuse to recognize union or promise not to fire organizers."

Kaz has gone with Bud Novak to talk with Lester Collins a few more times, and Lester says this strike was, in fact, supported only by the Communists at first, but now everybody else has jumped on board, the Unemployed Councils getting the jobless not to scab and even having them picket in solidarity on the other side of the street.

And that trying the same thing at the Rouge would be suicide.

"You alright in your place, Pop?"

"So far I can pay rent."

His father is wearing too many layers of clothes to tell if he's lost weight. He'll never wear glasses even if he needs them, and he seems to hear just fine even with the flaps of his fur-lined trapper hat turned down over his ears.

"Like Model T," he used to say in the days when he rubbed elbows with the Old Man on the production line. "Built to last."

Kaz thumps the old guy on the shoulder.

"You do what you have to, Pop," he says. "Dinner at our place Sunday."

She told Mr. Gersh at the delicatessen she had an important test today. Rosa feels bad lying to the man, who is very sweet and gave her the delicatessen job after the Early American Dining Room at Hudson's had to let go a quarter of their staff. He has been teaching her how to keep kosher when she marries, two things she believes to be extremely unlikely. Mr. Gersh only reads the *Jewish Chronicle*, so if there should be trouble and her photograph or name make the main papers he'll never know. Her shift behind the counter, just four hours, pays a dollar a day and she's allowed to bring home leftover scraps of corned beef.

Certified kosher.

The Party asked for volunteers to fill out the ranks of the strikers here, but to deny membership if arrested or interviewed. Rosa has tried to make inroads with the female Briggs employees, exploited even worse than the men, but it is clear they don't trust her, shy of her political affiliation or thinking her a company spy. So she has joined up with the City College students, 'respectable young intellectuals,' according to one Detroit newspaper.

She's walking in step behind an American flag.

Hershel, the most intense of the City College cadre, argues that this is fine, that the people can seize any symbol and alter its meaning, but Rosa can only think of her father's tormentors calling him "a goddam immigrant kike" as they kicked him on the ground.

"Briggs's conditions still outrageous—"

-chant the students-

"Don't accept starvation wages!"

Hershel is quite adept at placards and phrases, telling Rosa that if he dared cut ties with his father, still his only source of financial support, he would go to New York and write plays guaranteed to inflame the masses.

"Dead-time rackets
Lousy pay
We deserve an eight-hour day!"

But though his argument that virginity is only a construct of bourgeois thinking might be true, his insistence that she should surrender hers to him lacks analysis. He is an acne-scarred mess of a boy, spoiled by his mother, and worse, incapable of listening to anyone else without interrupting.

"To exploiters
We won't kneel
We demand a better deal!"

Ira is so hopeful about this Roosevelt coming in, as if the real rulers of the country will allow the man to do anything truly useful for the working class. Charity is not *change*, it's only the few at the top who possess a conscience desiring to feel better about themselves. The AFL declared this walkout a wildcat strike and won't support it, the company never saw it coming, the newspapers ignored it till it started to scare them—true progress arises from the will of the People.

"Down with wage cuts
Down with spies
Auto workers organize!"

Rosa shivers and chants along with the students, feeling almost like she's one of them, a college girl, instead of an aproned dispenser of *gefilte* and rye bread. She wonders if your ears can turn black from frostbite-

• • •

It says 'Little Harry's Social Club' on the guest card, so Bennett takes a lot of ribbing whenever he pays a call. You can come in by tunnel just like at his office—somebody said it was dug for the church next door way back when, to hide runaway slaves—down a few stairs and either flash your card or say you'd like to become a member. Nothing too swank. Harry still misses the Aniwa Club with its orchestra and dancing, good eats, gambling in the back rooms, but that was too good to last. The Harry who owns this speak is a Jewish loan shark in tight with the Purples, who offers real beer from the wood and unadulterated Canadian Club whiskey, proving that it doesn't all just pass through Detroit on its way to Mr. Capone's successors. Rich mahogany paneling, radio on softly for the music broadcasts, and a Belgian named René behind the counter who knows how to mix one hundred different cocktails.

Harry snuggles up to the altar, orders a whiskey and soda, no ice, and swivels to rate the custom. A number of prosperous-looking chiselers, some with law degrees, warehousemen up from the river just a block away, the overstuffed heir to a local fortune who owns a good chunk of Paradise Valley, currently escorting a pair of Grosse Pointe dollies out for a walk on the wild side—you get a nice blend in here. Harry takes a sip of his drink, then stands as Tony D'Anna comes in from upstairs. René has a drink on the bar before he reaches it, so he must be a regular.

"Mr. D'Anna—pleasure to see you."

"I thought you Ford executives had to take the pledge."

Harry grins. "No 'executives' at Ford. There's the Chief, there's Edsel, there's Sorensen, and the rest of us are just do-it men. The Chief has an idea out loud, points to whichever of us is nearest, and says 'Do it.'"

"You're selling yourself short."

As a matter of fact, he's come up a notch in the last week, Liebold developing a bad case of the nerves and opting for an unannounced rest cure. Harry had him traced to an out-of-town hotel, then put out a story in the *News* that he might have been kidnapped, leaving Ernest a pile of explanation to come up with if and when he does return to the Company. How a guy with so little moxie ever climbed so high remains a mystery, but for now it means Harry is delegated to make this deal.

"The Chief understands by now that the world outside of the Rouge River plant doesn't always play by his rules," he says. "When there's a situation he might not be comfortable in, he sends me."

"You're even willing to force down liquor."

"Anything for the greater good," says Harry, and takes a nip. He spots his man in the corner, gives him a 'hold off' sign down by the hip.

"So to what do I owe the pleasure?"

D'Anna is a smooth one, comfortable talking to corporate heads or charity matrons, while holding his own with the racket boys. Harry's kind of guy.

"Well, we've got a small problem right now—"

"All those line workers taking a hike—"

"The Briggs Body Works is not—"

"Is not much more than a front so your outfit and a couple others can farm out part of the production to penny-pinchers. You've shut your own operation down—"

"Worse than it looks on the surface," says Harry, already impressed by the guy's savvy. "This way we don't put more machines on the street than the public can afford, and our people get an unpaid vacation."

"I bet they're thrilled."

"My pitch to you has got nothing to do with that—not directly. You understand that this Roosevelt is serious about nixing the Prohibition—"

"So?"

This one requires a certain amount of tact—he may know and *you* may know, but there's things you don't call by their actual name.

"So certain lines of income are about to dry *up*, so to speak, and an astute businessman such as yourself has always got a line on what comes next."

Big Chet would have told him to spill it by now, but D'Anna is only listening, calculating-

"Even with production cut in half, we're sending automobiles out in four directions, far enough that it doesn't make sense to hire a thousand drivers to deliver them to all the dealers."

"There's trains, there's trucks that can take—what, four at a time—"

"But who *drives* those trucks?"

D'Anna shrugs. "Your people?"

"At the moment, yes, most of the time. And naturally they expect the same rate of pay the guys on the line in the plant are getting. So it's like with Briggs, right? If we had a company who did that one thing, who we could hire by the load, and it was run by somebody very good at keeping its people under control—"

"Willing to work for less—"

"That would be part of it, sure—"

"Trucks cost money. I mean, to start up—"

"Loans can be arranged, especially if there are serious people backing them up."

D'Anna considers all this for a moment. "Ford trucks."

"At first, yeah, most likely. There's a company called Mack, working on a rig that could haul twice as many cars."

"And this outfit, this hauling company, they wouldn't work with any of the other auto shops except Ford."

Harry grins again. "We'd appreciate that."

He pretends to see his man in the corner, waving him over-

"Hey, look who's here."

The Kid was something of a matinee idol in his youth, even went to Hollywood after he quit the ring, palling around with Charlie Chaplin and jazzing screen starlets, but has put on weight and looks tired and pale.

As might be expected after eight years in San Quentin.

"Kid, I want you to meet a friend of mine, Mr. Anthony D'Anna. Tony, this is Kid McCoy."

The men shake. "You the Real McCoy?"

"That's what they say," says the Kid.

"You were champ for a while in one of the divisions—"

"Middleweight," says Harry. "Back when they might go twenty rounds. Kid fought a bunch of heavyweights too, famous for his corkscrew punch.

Stepped in the professional ring over a hundred times—"

"That's impressive."

"Hell, that's nothing," says the former champ. "I was married ten times and lived to tell the tale."

The men laugh. McCoy was convicted of shooting a lady friend to death, a wealthy married woman whose divorce was taking far too long. In court he explained this caused the depression that caused her suicide, which upset him so badly he robbed her antique store at gunpoint the next day, taking several people hostage.

The jury was more than skeptical.

"So what you been doing since you left the fight game?"

"Lately, I been doing *time*."

D'Anna appreciates this, laughing again, and the Kid keeps his mug a blank slate. He says he's down to a beer a day, his stomach ruined by prison food, and Harry notes that the one left at his table is still half full.

"I just hired the Kid as director of the guards for our thrift gardens."

"Ford has gardens?"

"Thousands of them, all over Dearborn, Detroit, the outskirts—"

"Gotta keep people from stealing the tomatoes," says the Kid. He is a well-read man, a con artist and a performer—you can never really tell when he's on the level.

"The Chief, as you might know, has a predilection for hiring unfortunate men recently out of the jug," Harry continues. "He believes everybody deserves a second chance."

"A man of convictions," says the Kid, still deadpan.

"Which is another thing I wanted to take up with you, Tony. This situation at Briggs—it won't come to anything, but the Reds feed our workers a lot of bull and then they get these wild ideas. We start to gear up production again, I'm going to need more people for my Service Department who can be persuasive—"

"Heavyweights?" asks D'Anna, also with a straight face.

"Size can be helpful, yes, but also if you know of people, let's say they've run afoul of the law once or twice in their youth, got a record—"

"You want I should steer these people to you?"

"They draw a foreman's pay," Harry explains, "without the repetitive nature of much of the work available."

"They had me in the jute mill in San Quentin," says Kid McCoy, staring at Harry's drink. "Enough to drive a man to crime."

• • •

Norma follows the head nurse into the open ward. Twenty beds along each long side of the rectangular room, good ventilation, spotlessly clean, white wooden walls, and overhead fans for the days when there is no breeze. Almost every bed is occupied, men and boys only in this ward. A full house is not unusual according to Nurse Kline, or Esther, as she has asked Norma to address her. A tall woman in her early fifties, starting to gray at the temples with no attempt to hide it, a bit mannish, perhaps, but she's been very welcoming to Norma.

"We can use all the help we can get," she said. "As I'm sure you've noticed, this is not a healthy place. Too many things grow too freely here, including things that make people sick. And then if they really start another plantation—"

The tree expert the Company sent down, Weir, says that everything they've planted here is diseased and has to be destroyed, and they're going to trade land here for a flatter, higher spot seventy miles downriver, called Belterra. The name means 'Beautiful Land' according to Jim, and he'll be in charge of clearing it for planting if the deal goes through.

"Can I catch whatever these people have got?"

"Not the burns or the cuts or the broken arms," Esther tells her. "But some of these patients will have malaria for the rest of their lives, and there are a few recovering from yellow fever—we bring them out here when they're no longer infectious. And we keep the lepers in a separate room."

"*Lep*ers?"

Norma hadn't considered this when she volunteered.

"You won't be dealing with them, not right away. You'll help serve meals to the ones who are bedbound, bring them the water we've filtered and sterilized, take temperatures, do urinals and bedpans—"

"Oh—"

"For the women's ward only. We have a couple young Brazilian fellows in here, very promising."

"I don't really speak any Portuguese."

"Neither do I," says Esther, looking at a chart attached to the foot of a sleeping patient's bed. "We have a few local nurses-in-training, and I get by with only a few phrases. For instance, '*Onde dói?*'"

Norma shakes her head. She's been to the French part of Canada twice but just relied on sign language and speaking in English a bit louder. What they speak here—she can't separate one word from the next.

"'Where does it hurt?'" explains Esther.

"Ah. Ondee dowee."

"Close. And then '*Me dê seu braço.*'"

"Something about the arm?"

"'Give me your arm.'"

"Why would I want their arm?"

"To take blood samples. We won't have you putting anything *in*, but you'll learn to use a syringe. You don't faint at the sight of blood, do you?"

Norma thinks of Kerry coming back soaked with what came out of the maid, how she felt her own pulse race but her mind stay clear. "No," she says. "I'm not squeamish. We had animals where I grew up."

"Pets?"

"Animals. Chickens, pigs, goats for a while. I had to milk the cow."

Esther smiles. "Good training. Nat grew up on a farm—nothing fazed her."

As far as Norma understands, Natalie was Esther's roommate and best friend, a fellow nurse at Henry Ford Hospital, who died last year from some heart problem.

"After Nat was gone I couldn't stay in Detroit," she told Norma, surprising her with a personal story less than an hour after they'd met. "It was either the French Foreign Legion or here."

The idea of volun*teer*ing to work surrounded by jungle at the edge of a river teeming with man-eating lizards is barely comprehensible. They must have been awfully close friends. Or else—

Norma doesn't want to consider the other. At home Kerry never wanted to wear a dress, not convenient for bicycling or climbing trees, and Norma worried that the isolation of Pine Camp and lack of girls her own age was turning her into a tomboy.

"She's just adventurous," Jim would say. "That's a good quality for anyone to have."

They've hired a new maid, a woman named Beatriz whose husband has worked at the plantation since its beginning, who will clean and do some basic cooking and, if she understood their awkward conversation with Jim's assistant Gomes present to interpret, keep an eye on Kerry. No more safaris into the bush.

There is a man sitting up in bed grinning at them who has a gauze patch over one of his eyes.

"*Enfemeira!*" he calls. "*Estou morrendo.*"

"He was clearing small trees for a new road," Esther explains, "and a branch snapped back into his eye. By the time his foremen sent him to us—at least a week later—it was infected so badly it had to come out. He says he's dying."

She steps to the side of the man's bed. "*Do você está morrendo hoje?*"

"*Tédio.*"

"Ah, *bore*dom. I took some measurements, took a photograph of him up close, and sent it off to Detroit. We're waiting for a glass eye."

"And he has to stay in bed till then?"

"No, just till we're sure the infection hasn't spread." Esther reaches into the pocket of her uniform for a worn deck of playing cards, waves it in front of the man's face. "*Joga?*"

The man breaks out into a big smile, several teeth missing. He takes the cards. "*Obrigado.*"

A useful woman to have in your corner, this Nurse Kline.

A quartet of skinny little boys are sitting on the edges of their beds, fussing and giggling with each other. The children are beautiful in their way, as are the puppies of breeds that will grow into ugly or ferocious dogs. Hard not to want to play with them.

"What are these little imps here for?"

"Malnutrition. We do a physical before the workers' children are brought into school—these boys were undersized for their age, some of them anemic—look at their upper arms—"

"Like sticks."

"Not enough variation in their diet, usually. You'll weigh them every two days, take some measurements, take blood once a week—"

"Kids hate needles."

"A*dults* hate needles. Distract them with something, then get in quick—"

"My daughter thinks she wants to be a veterinarian."

Esther smiles. "I went through that phase. But once you learn that humans rarely bite—"

"Can you catch diseases from monkeys?"

This stops Esther in her tracks.

"I imagine so, but I'm only guessing. Monkeys are likely to have fleas and lice—"

"I go over Kerry's hair with a magnifying glass."

"Not a bad idea. This is your daughter?"

"Yes. She's eleven, and is convinced she should have a monkey."

"I don't believe they can be house-trained."

"And I don't think she'll be up for changing some animal's *dia*pers ten times a day. You've got to wash them, hang them up on the line—"

"I always wanted to have children," says Esther, smiling to herself and looking out the window at a stubby palm tree. "But it wasn't in the cards."

Norma notices that except for the little boys, all the patients are staring at them, two white women standing surrounded by native men. Most just seem as bored as the one-eyed man. She has a quick thought of singing for them if a piano could be found, or even just somebody with a guitar, and then is embarrassed. She doesn't know any songs in Portuguese.

"I can give you maybe six hours a day" says Norma, deciding to commit to the work. "I can come over right after Kerry leaves for school. And then volunteer on weekends—I know hospitals don't get a day off."

"If you decide to stay with us, you'll have to drop that 'volunteer' business."

"I don't really need to be—"

Esther stops her with a hand on the shoulder. "Dear, if they don't *pay* you, they don't even *see* you."

• • •

Smitty has never really stood and looked at a painting before. Pin-ups, sure, which are more like cartoons than real women, billboards advertising movies or automobiles where you say "Hey, that looks almost real!," even stained-glass windows in church when he was a kid. But here in the former Garden Court with all the society types, enough pearls hanging off the women to sink a pirate ship, he finds himself planted in front of the north wall, losing touch with the cocktail chatter and violin music and climbing into the mural to figure it out.

On the top there's a long rectangular panel with a sphinx-lady weighing down each side of it, one black with pointy tits and the other red, probably meant to be an Indian, neither of them lookers. The red one has a small pile of what might be iron ore in front of her, holding some of it in one hand, while the colored sphinx is playing with a similar little pile of coal. Between them a sand-colored volcano with giant hands sticking up from it, just hands, all of them gripping some kind of gray rock. Precious minerals, basic elements, something like that. But smack in the middle of the mesa is a rectangular window with a marble frame and an iron grill in front of it, the bars criss-crossing diagonally—and he's reminded what the courtyard looked like before they turned the Mexican loose on it, like a spot for the sandal-and-toga crowd to lay around while servants popped grapes into their mouths, a bunch of little stone pools in the center and lots of bearded heads carved in the stone above the doorways. But now with so much else going on around it the window nearly disappears.

To the left of the sphinxes is a smaller, squarish panel with a bunch of guys kitted out like soldiers, only they've got gas masks over their faces and are working on making some kind of a bomb. A gas bomb. To the right of the sphinxes there's a matching-sized panel that's a real puzzler—a little boy wearing only a loose diaper who's got curly blond hair standing between a nurse and a doctor while the doctor gives him a shot in the arm. The kid doesn't look too happy about this, which Smitty can sympathize with, the pill-pushers having jabbed his arms and even his butt so many times while he was in training and then over in France. And yes, he didn't get the clap or typhoid or the Spanish flu, so maybe it was good for something more than them showing you one more time who was boss. He did get *shot*, though, a million-dollar wound in the meat of his thigh that kept him under the sheets till the Armistice, trying to talk the prettier nuns out of their habits.

In front of the diapered kid's feet are a horse, some sheep, and a cow, which can't be too sanitary, while behind him are some scientist-looking jaspers bent over their work, which involves a big glass ball and some swirly glass tubing like in the *Frankenstein* picture. No scary lightning bolts or electric discharges though, so this picture is probably on the side of the docs—close your eyes, this won't hurt a bit.

Below the sphinxes there's a much narrower panel that's got huge rubies and diamonds that look like they're still stuck down in the earth, and below that you get to the main event. This is clearly the Rouge factory, but the Mexican has somehow crowded the whole deal, a coiled quarter-mile of production in the main assembly building alone, into one big section of wall. Along the bottom of it are the working stiffs on the front line, in overalls and shirts with rolled-up sleeves, intent on their tasks, which on the left is applying power drills to V8 engine blocks as they move along a bench, then on the right muscling something bulky onto a hoist. At the very center a bunch of men strain to push-pull a cart loaded with heavy engine blocks, flanked by two towering steel-milling machines, which lead your gaze back to a worker and a crane silhouetted against the maw of the blast furnace. Overhead belts with different engine parts suspended from them snake throughout the crowded assemblage like intestines, humans and machinery totally interconnected. Nobody has a hand free, nobody is smiling or looking beyond the facet of the operation they are bound to, which is what struck Smitty on his first tour of the actual Rouge. His job was to look around and report on it. Theirs was to complete a tiny facet of the process, again and again and again and again-

There is toil from different buildings shown—foundry work, steel rolling, motor and transmission assembly—but of course the basic commandment of Fordism is that the chain of cause-and-effect never be broken. There's even a little fake bas-relief painted on the west wall, of barefoot men tapping rubber, as if the Old Man's pipe dream of making his own tires has already panned out. Smitty gives Liebold some grief about it whenever he sees him, but the flack just makes noises about "it takes some time to grow a tree."

Smitty likes it how those front-line workers aren't faceless, just regular joes earning their bread, a couple of them colored, one maybe Japanese or Chinese or even Mexican, true enough for the plant as a whole. In the similar tangle of production on the south wall there stands one of Harry Bennett's goons, the muscle-bound snake in the Garden.

The one thing you don't see is a finished automobile—this isn't one of Ford's slick magazine ads. The guys on the floor are, if not the heroes, at least the human protagonists of the story.

Detroit Industry.

Smitty turns to look for Portia von Dusenberg, the young doll who writes for the society page he's tagged along with, and immediately feels the chill.

The little decorative pools in their boxes have been removed, now just an open tile floor under the skylight, with knots of invited swells nervously or angrily eyeing the mural that surrounds them. A line from *Casey at the Bat* sticks in his head—

'A pallor wreathed the features of the patrons of the game.'

The women seem more upset than the men, but of course the women are more frequent visitors, and have perhaps often sat in this spot to reflect with patrician benevolence upon the treasures hung within.

"What has he done to our garden?" he hears.

"Ugly," he hears.

"Inappropriate," he hears.

"Sacrilegious," he hears.

"It's like he's thumbing his nose at us," he hears.

Francis X. Breen, the moral watchdog from the *Times*, has stirred some of this up. The radio priest, Coughlin, has thrown his usual braying two cents in, and the last couple weeks of work on the mural were done with a volunteer squadron of guards in place, most from a delegation of workers who'd had a sneak peek at what the Mexican was up to. All perfect, basically meaningless fodder for tomorrow's fish-wrappers, thinks Smitty, as who wants to read *ad infinitum* about how many formerly-employed citizens have hit the bricks with empty pockets?

He sees Valentiner, the tall, long-nosed director of the Institute, backed up against the south wall trying to explain the Significance of it All to a ring of outraged art lovers, while Edsel flits about the periphery with a cocktail glass in hand and a mischievous smile on his face, looking like the cat that crushed the canary in a drill press. The Woeful Prince is said to have dropped millions when his Guardian Group investment went down the toilet, embarrassing, yes, but he won't be panhandling in Cadillac Square anytime soon. Edsel waves shyly to the Mexican perpetrator and his wife, who have dared to attend despite opinion-column calumny and scandalized matrons—he a towering mound of dough with froggy eyes and she—where has Smitty seen this doll before?

A *doll*, that's the ticket, that long, meandering bender he and Boots Riley went on after the troop ship docked in Hoboken and they, unsung heroes of the Great War, were officially separated from the infantry, boozing their way all the way down to the border and across to the land of cheap tequila and hot tamales. There was a woman on the street selling dolls she might have made with her own two hands, colorfully attired in native costume like the diminutive Mrs. Rivera, and Smitty almost blew a few pesos on one before realizing he had nobody in his life to give it to. A sobering thought, one of the few he can remember from the whole liquor-sodden meander.

In her *Faces and Fashions* column, the delectable Miss von Dusenburg described an interview with the lovely *Señora*, complete with a photo of her intently poking a very fine brush at a very small canvas, and beneath, the caption—*Mrs. Rivera also dabbles in artistic ventures.*

He searches through the overdressed bodies till he locates Portia, looking stately in silk, then makes his way over to her, trying not to step on any toes.

She is by herself, looking up at the west wall, the panels arranged around the doorway—airplane manufacture and use for war depicted up top, and then tall panels on either side. The one on the right is mostly large-scale hydroelectric equipment, an enormous turbine made to look like a human ear, while at the base of it an engineer with a ruler in hand stares out as if facing a window in his office. To Smitty his face looks like what you'd get if you combined Old Henry with Thomas Edison, probably on purpose, as this Mexican doesn't miss a trick. The left side balances this with a mass of steam ducts, a coal-fired oven feeding it from above. At the base is a square-bodied, tired-looking worker with a hammer in one hand and a big red star on the glove of the other.

Portia is pointing at the star.

"I guess he couldn't help himself."

"Keep it on the QT," says Smitty. "We'll have an uprising of the proletariat."

"Not likely in this crowd."

"What do you think?"

"I think an awful lot of noses are out of joint."

"I mean the mural."

Portia turns to take in the four walls, thinking. She is not happy being stuck in the crumpets-for-lunch section of the paper, but gal reporters out chasing racket boys and axe murderers are more common in the pictures than in real life.

"If we're lucky," she says finally, "Edsel can keep the assholes from having the whole thing whitewashed."

• • •

Why whoever scouted for the Company didn't keep looking till they found this makes you wonder, but at this point it doesn't matter. The new acreage, called Belterra, is a hell of a lot flatter than Fordlandia, and Jim is here from the get-go instead of wandering in after they've made a hash of it. He's got a good gang, about forty of the younger, eager-beaver types, twenty to clear trees and twenty to put up housing with the lumber they've rafted seventy miles south down the Tapajós. Birds of all colors and sizes flutter up from the branches, circle and swarm, then choose to relocate further from the action. Jim knows the trees by now, what's worth saving, what's more or less waterproof, when to let the men climb up and strip a tree of nuts before it has to come down.

Brazil nuts, which they call *castanha-do-pará* here.

He'll have a tractor down here next week, and can start them pulling stumps and grading where it's needed. Even if Norma and Kerry won't be here for a bit, it is a relief to be away, to look out over possibility rather than failure. To do the job he was sent here to do. Dr. Weir has taken French leave, off to Asia to gather 'superior stock' that he thinks will thrive here. Jim doesn't see how this makes sense, as the seeds on those plantations came from here to begin with, but any attempt to discuss the planting with Weir ends with a dismissive smile and him saying "Trust me, these matters are complex."

There is a shout from the tree-line and Jim trots toward it, scooping up the first-aid kit the docs at the Fordlandia hospital gave him. The cutters who have stepped out to wave him forward are smiling, thank God—nobody's been hurt badly since they've come here, just the usual cuts and scratches and bouts of diarrhea.

A few yards in from the vast field of stumps they've found a rubber tree, a towering grandfather scarred over with diagonal slashes on both sides of the bole. The men are laughing and pointing, eyes shining, a few of them *seringueiros* from this neck of the woods.

"*Um bom presságio*," says Gomes, arriving just behind him.

Yes, it's a good omen.

"Have the boys cut around it for a while," he tells his *capitaz*. "It can watch over us while we work."

• • •

Back at Fordlandia João swings the *picareta* in rhythm, moving around the base of a tree. The trees in this section are the height of Flavio sitting on his shoulders, and would begin to grow wider if not for the disease in their leaves. There are fallen leaves, deformed and spotted with black, littering the rows. The order is that they will pull all these down, thousands of them, and burn them all so the disease won't spread. After that he and his family will be taken down to Belterra to live in a new *vila modelo* and try to grow rubber there. Fordlandia will feed Belterra its goods and its people, so that one shrinks as the other increases. Beatriz is still working for the family of the *grande chefe* Rogan while he is gone, washing their clothes, cleaning their house, even working in their garden, and he hopes she will keep this job when they are all moved to Belterra. João's dream is that Flavio will be able remain in school beyond what the Company requires, that he'll learn a skill that will make him more than a simple worker. He seems to be good at learning the gringo language, even teaching his mother and father words, and has always been an intelligent boy, eager to learn. The Company says they will keep the money João makes safe for him, but promises on paper are like butterflies in the air—one strong wind and who knows where they will finally land? So if their son needs money to go forward, there it is, buried where only he and Beatriz can find it.

João lays the mattock down and puts his hands around the bole of the tree, giving it a hard yank, exposing the beginning of its roots. He moves on to the next tree in the row. Later they'll come with the tractor, set a hook under the roots, and pull the tree out of the ground. João watched his father have a molar tooth pulled out with pliers once, a lot of blood and cursing, and imagines the tree and the earth might feel a similar pain.

But that is superstitious.

Flavio comes back from the school and talks about science, how science, not magic or superstition, is the way the world really works. João's father would talk to the trees when they collected rubber, ask their pardon for the blade, thank them for their beautiful white blood-

It is a shame to pull all these trees out from the earth, and was a bigger shame to have cut down the trees that were here before for nothing, not even using most of the wood to build houses. It is something like a sin. He hopes the *capataz* will wait for a cool evening with no wind to burn what they have wasted here, so the smoke will rise straight up.

Like an offering.

• • •

They have to go separately and meet in the jungle. Even when Mom is only doing a half day at the hospital, there are now events after school and even a tennis court to use if Kerry needs an excuse. She has sworn not to go anywhere near the water, and has been able to be true to her word so far. She has marked a path with little bits of red yarn hung as high as she can reach on branches, one visible from another, so she is sure to find their spot at any time of day.

This afternoon Kerry gets there first.

She has learned to stand absolutely still, to just listen and keep her eyes open. Sometimes nothing comes, sometimes the jungle life just fills in around her—bugs and birds and lizards and things that move overhead from tree to tree.

Today it is something big, partly knotted around a low branch, something orange with dark brown circles on its side and a sheen like the rainbow colors on the surface of spilt oil.

"*Boa arco-íris*" whispers Flavio, coming up softly behind her. He steps close enough to touch it, but doesn't. "*Não é venenoso.*"

"What's the matter here," Kerry asks, putting her hands around her neck.

The snake has a bulge the size of a small coconut just back from its long, striped head.

"*Uma festa*," smiles Flavio. "It eats something."

"'Ate,'" says Kerry. He's now asked her to correct his English, and she's said the same for her Portuguese. "It *ate* something. I wonder what."

"*Talvez* the mother of this one," Flavio says. She looks away from the rainbow boa and sees that he has something hidden in his two hands. He opens them to reveal a tiny squirrel monkey.

Tiny and scared. You can see its little heart beating under the fuzz on its chest.

"Where was it?"

"On the land," he says, nodding toward his feet.

"The ground."

"Yes."

"All alone?"

"Yes. Is—no mama, no papa—?"

"We call that an orphan."

"*Sim. Un orfão.*"

Kerry holds her hand out and Flavio tries to put the baby monkey into it, but it quickly wraps its arms around her wrist, hugging tight. Kerry raises it up till they are looking eye to eye. It is the most adorable thing she has ever seen.

"We go way, something eat him."

Kerry doesn't want to think about the lump in the neck of the snake on the branch. She begins to plan the case she'll put before her mother. Daddy isn't home to take her part, but if her mother understands that it will starve or something will eat it-

"You're sure it's a boy?"

"Yes, I look. Is *menino.*"

Kerry nods.

"His name is Jocko," she says.

• • •

Sweet corn is yellow, money is green
Stop by and boogie till the sun makes the scene

A SOCIAL PARTY
Given By
ETTA MAE

-at-

625 Eliot St. Apartment 3
Saturday evening, June 24, 1933
From 9 P. M. until ???

LATEST ON WAX — REFRESHMENTS
35 Cents With Ticket (Pay at Door) 50 Cents Without

DuPree handed him the ticket on the way out of work. There are always a couple rent parties on Saturday, some with live music, some just records, but Zeke is usually too tired for that much noise and people. But with Mavis so down after the move and Madame Queenie shutting her out of the numbers, he reconsidered.

"Do you know this Etta Mae, Du?"

"She's Bernice best friend, and she'll be cooking."

"This the kind of party I can bring my wife to?"

"Why not?"

"You know why not."

DuPree laughed. "Just be sure you leave before midnight."

They are coming up the inside stairs, music and voices above, a few people already sitting on steps with plates of red beans and rice on their laps.

"I wonder if Keechie be here." Mavis is dressed to the nines, a dress Zeke had forgot she owned, and smiling, which is good to see.

"Why would she be here?"

"Cause she thrown that last no-good off and is looking for a new one."

"I lost track—who was he?"

"Worked at the post office."

"Mailman, that's right. 'Women likes me cause I de*liv*er.'"

Mavis laughs. She has three different laughs and this is a good one.

A man at the door grins and holds his arms over his head.

"Gotta check for heat, brother," he says apologetically.

Zeke raises his arms for a quick pat down.

"My husband *makes* iron," brags Mavis, "but he don't carry none."

They've taken all the furniture out of the common room to make a dance floor, leaving only a credenza heavy enough to lay the record player on without it bouncing with the Lindy-Hoppers. You can see that the other rooms are even more crowded, people near shouting to be heard over the music.

Which is Armstrong and his Hot Five.

Mavis looks the scene over, waves to her friend Keechie, who is hanging onto a long drink of water wearing a purple shirt, then turns to grab Zeke's hand.

"Imonna get some dancing outa you before you take on any of those ribs I smell cooking. They'll put you right to sleep."

"All right, woman, just don't show me up."

Mavis is a natural on the floor, while Zeke still has to think some about the steps. The Black Bottom, the Shag, the Lindy Hop with all the spins and turn-outs—there's not enough room to be throwing women over your shoulder like the show dancers do, but there are few couples who can really shake a leg.

So it's *Muskrat Ramble* and *Willie the Weeper* and *Cornet Chop Suey* and *Heebie Jeebies* that was such a hit, where Armstrong plays with his voice like he does with his horn, making just sounds instead of words. It's been so long that it takes a couple numbers before Zeke's feet remember where they are and what they're meant to do.

They stand aside for one number, right next to the sport in charge of flipping the sides or putting a new one on, which he does with amazing speed, a man who'd be a foreman's pet in the assembly building. Somebody comes by with a bottle of gin and a stack of dixie cups and Zeke asks for two short ones. Mavis says she's not ready to drink, so what is a man to do? It said Gordon's on the label and tastes like the real deal—got to be careful, with every joint in Detroit trying to unload their tiger sweat now that the law is changing.

It hits him quick, the way gin always does, the mellow feeling washing over as he watches the boogie action on the floor. Young men and women dressed sharp, shoes shined, some of the couples showing their practiced moves, others clearly making it up as they go along—*look* at us, he thinks, wolf at the door, for some of them that thirty-five cent admission hard to come by, but strutting it out on the floor like there's not a care in the world. Damn—just *look* at us.

Finally *Lonesome Blues* comes up and they can dance slow and tight, her body so familiar, maybe more of an armful than the last time they got to do this. A lot of the partying he did when young was about *look*ing for a woman, not having one, and even without a drink in his tank Zeke starts feeling sentimental, thinking how good he's got it compared to the men he passes on the street with their paws out for loose change, not all of them stewbums, some that might even have a family they can't knock out the rent for anymore.

The song ends and they just stand and hold for a moment, then the needle-hopper cues up *King of the Zulus* and Mavis says she has to find the bathroom.

Zeke watches her move away through the dancers.

"I always admired them goods, but never seen em packaged so nice before."

It is Jarvis Stokes and he is clearly staring at Mavis's behind. Without thinking, Zeke lifts the numbers man off the floor by the lapels of his jacket.

"You got something to say, little man?"

Jarvis's voice gets higher and squeakier than usual.

"Put me down, Jack! You got no reason to mess with me!"

There is always a couple bloods assigned to keep the peace at these functions, and immediately there is one on each side of Zeke.

"We got a problem?"

"No problem."

"Then put the man down."

"I could put him down the stairway."

"Just right here be fine."

Zeke eases Jarvis back to the floor, makes a show of straightening his lapels.

"You gentlemen want to behave," says one of the guardians, waiting till Jarvis sneers at Zeke and stomps away before they drift. *Butter and Egg Man* is playing when Mavis comes back.

"How you doing, baby?" she asks, knowing he doesn't love a crowd.

"Just fine," he tells her. "Good to get some exercise."

The side-spinner lays on some Fats Waller then, just piano with none of his fooling around, and Zeke and Mavis try to get together on a foxtrot. It's been way too long. About halfway through there's a rush in the middle of the floor, the two guardians and DuPree looking unhappy as they hurry through the crowd to the hallway door. Zeke breaks off to follow them-

"Don't be getting into any fuss, now," calls Mavis, but he gets to the door and sees what the problem is.

Two white cops, big ones, two steps down from the landing and still taller than DuPree, whose voice is getting tighter as he tries to deal with them. Nobody in this stretch of Black Bottom would ever drop a nickel on a rent party for noise, not on a Saturday night, so these bulls are either shaking the money tree or think there's somebody on their pinch-list inside.

"If you need any help," he says to the coat-checker who's blocking his way, "I'm right here."

"DuPree take care of it."

The conversation goes on a bit more, DuPree pleading his case, then the three step down out of sight for a moment before DuPree comes back up alone, looking steamed and embarrassed.

"Everything all right, Du?" Zeke asks him.

"So much for the *rent*," he says, and pushes in to find that bottle.

• • •

Smitty has never been to the Castle before. He's heard the rumors, but the job has never afforded him a pretense to float down the Huron River and take a gander. It is Harry Bennett's private fortress, where he's chosen to take his family after the resentment in Dearborn reached a certain level. So when the invitation came through one of his muscle boys, who could resist?

The afternoon started at the Legion Hall, both Smitty and Portia conveniently assigned to cover the Detroit Victory-Day festivities, old Julius Stroh himself handing out metal mugs of his Bohemian style suds drawn from a shiny metal keg. Michigan, the first to enact a Dry Law because King Henry wanted to keep his workforce sober on and off the job, has become the first to Repeal, and although the rest of the states have to ratify before hootch is officially legal, why let that get in the way of a party? Portia was charming the old brewer into an interview when Moe Snyder, one of Harry's Service Department goons wearing his Legionnaire garrison cap thumped a paw on Smitty's shoulder.

"You're that snoop from the *Free Press*, right?"

"That depends—"

"The Little Man wants you out to the Castle tonight. He's trowin a party."

Finding the place is not difficult, 'between Ann Arbor and Ypsi', a long line of automobiles pulled off the road. But the gorilla with the flashlight and the guest list is unwelcoming.

"It's spelled S-m-i-t-h."

"Not here."

"How bout Smitty."

"With a 'y'?"

"Try it."

A long pause, the man's lips moving as he reads. "All right, I gotcha. Just follow Ernie and watch your step."

Portia remains amused and unruffled through it all.

"What *is* your first name?"

"I only use it for desk clerks."

"Come on, own up."

"Ulysses," he confesses. "After our eighteenth president."

She laughs. Portia has a world-class laugh. "I'll stick with Smitty."

Ernie leads them in through the gate and then it's all lit up—a path winding through an immaculately-kept garden complete with flowered trellis arches to pass under that must require the services of a squadron of elves. Harry always says his salary at Ford is nothing much, but that the Old Man "maintains several properties" that Harry is welcomed, even expected, to make use of. Spotlights planted in the ground beam up along the sides of the towers, newly added, that have given this buff-colored pile of bricks its nickname, and yes, Smitty spots someone standing up on top.

Someone with a weapon in hand.

"Ritzy digs," says Portia as they enter the main room—polished hardwood floor, vaulted ceiling with ornamental plaster figures, a huge pink stone fireplace. "But you can tell no women were consulted."

"I think Harry and the Old Man designed it together."

"Uh-oh. Secret passageways?"

"Through that door," nods a liveried waiter bearing a tray of champagne in fancy glasses as he hurries by.

The room is pretty full, the starting eleven for the U Michigan football team, wider than they are tall, and at least one of their coaches taking up quite a bit of space. Smitty nods to a judge, two currently-indicted city officials, and the owner of WJR as they make their way to the indicated door next to the fireplace.

"Champagne?" Smitty asks.

Portia shakes her head. "I'm still bloated from all that Bohemian. People kept pushing steins in my face—"

"Because you look like a Rhinemaiden."

Portia is blond and still wears her hair long enough to braid. She snorts. Portia is also an excellent snorter.

"You mean I look like the fat lady at the opera."

"I think the word is *zaftig*. It's a good thing."

"If you say so."

Through the doorway disguised as a wall panel there is a steep spiral staircase leading to more noise and music. Portia, wearing heels for the occasion, has to move slowly and grip the handrail.

"The big society people I cover don't bother with all this secret entrance business. You're just invited into the drawing room for drinks."

"What fun is that? Listen, when we meet Harry, try not to be so tall."

Portia is an inch closer to the secret stairway ceiling than Smitty, maybe seven or eight years younger, and full of whatever rich people eat instead of beans. He avoided her for a while because of the Grosse Pointe pedigree, but reconsidered when he heard her call the president of the Women's City Club "a robber baroness too stupid to be ashamed of herself."

Her best lines never make it into her column.

The guests in Harry's play room, modeled after an English pub, are already well-oiled, and there is a four-piece combo of white boys, probably college joes, attempting to invoke the late, lamented Bix Beiderbecke. Quite a crush. Smitty recognizes the bartender, on loan from Cliff Bell's place on Erskine and John R, and holds up two fingers, calling out "Canadian and soda!"

"Are you trying to get me drunker?" Portia asks.

"Just hold one in your hand and nobody will offer you another. Haven't you ever been to a cocktail party?"

"I was *born* at a cocktail party. Hey is that Bucky Harris?"

Smitty scopes the Detroit player-manager, with his back to the mahogany, holding what might be a Coca Cola.

"Yeah, that's the Boy Wonder."

"I'm surprised he'd want to be seen here."

Smitty laughs. "I'm surprised he'd want to be seen *any*where, the way the Tigers are playing. Harry has a box behind first base at Navin, brings the family and two bodyguards."

"He really needs bodyguards?"

"He's been shot at three times that I know of, but they only hit him once. And *that* guy was discovered floating face-down in the river."

"He had him killed?"

"No, I think the word went out, and somebody did him a courtesy. Harry has friends in low places."

"And high ones, don't forget." It is Harry Bennett, with Legs Laman and the oppressed class's favorite mouthpiece, Maurice Sugar, looking uncomfortable, in tow.

"Harry! Thanks for the invite. This is—"

"Portia, right?" says Harry, taking her hand. She towers over him. "We met at the Institute when they pulled the curtain off the mural."

"What did you think of it?" she asks.

"A knockout. He managed to squeeze the whole operation onto four walls and put us amateur daubers to shame." Harry paints pictures and plays several instruments. "My only gripe is that with all of the mugs he put up on the wall, I couldn't find myself."

"That's cause Edsel supplied the paint," says Smitty. The rivalry between the two is no secret, and Smitty has already polished off his whiskey-

Harry laughs. "Newshounds with their wisecracks. I'd like you to meet my associate, Joseph Laman, and this is the eminent attorney, Mr. Maurice Sugar—"

"Mr. Sugar and I know each other," smiles Portia.

"Of course you do. Listen, it's getting to be a tight squeeze in here—constitutional amendments don't get repealed every day. Care to see the dungeon?"

Harry seems to be three sheets to the wind, but you can never tell with him. He's got two reporters, a lawyer for the downtrodden, and a recently-pardoned gangster for an audience—who better to spread the word that Harry's Castle is impregnable?

"Is anybody in it?" asks Portia, always up for an adventure.

"Not yet, but the night is young. Stick with me and watch your step."

"Watch your step" seems to be the theme of the evening. They follow Harry in single file through another wall-panel-turned-doorway, and start down a flight of uneven concrete stairs.

"Every step a different height," says Harry, his voice echoing in the tight concrete chute with dim overhead lights. "Which I can do with my eyes closed at full speed. Someone breeches security and gets on my tail, I hit the secret button—you didn't see it, did you?"

"Nope."

"I hit the button, the lights go out, and whoever's coming after me breaks their neck."

Portia is being a trooper in her heels, a hand pressed to Smitty's back for balance.

"How could anybody get that close?" asks Sugar.

"Good question. I mean, with my fellas up top equipped with tommy guns, you'd need a small army to get within a football field of the house. But betrayal, I'm afraid, is a constant in our world."

Smitty wonders what Laman, bringing up the rear, thinks of this assertion. He was the brains of the snatch squad who kidnapped the Cass boy. Gerson Cass showed up to pay the ransom for his son, but the Detroit bulls had gotten a tip and queered the exchange, pumping several bullets into Legs as he attempted a rapid exit. Betrayal number one. Then his outfit, flush with money from earlier grabs of small-time bootleggers and square-john citizens, goes back on their promise to take care of his wife and kiddies while he does time without mentioning their names to the authorities. Betrayal number two. So Legs gets in touch with Harry, who he almost murdered for snooping around during the Cass job, to arrange to get him in front of the grand jury that was called so public officials could grab headlines after Jerry Buckley was perforated at the LaSalle. Legs named names, dates, capers that weren't even on the docket, and his old gang went to jail or had time added if they were already residents.

Betrayal number three.

Smitty wonders how Laman, a good-looking stringbean who appears very fit for a guy with that much lead still in him, has avoided the fate of so many other courtroom confessors. Maybe adding your menace to Harry's Service Department is a form of life insurance.

"To the right here," says Harry, stomping on something on the floor that triggers overhead lights in a branching concrete tunnel filled with crates of liquor, "is my pipeline to the river. Excellent for discrete deliveries."

"And what does the boss think of that?"

Smitty can't seem to help himself tonight. He has always half-admired the Little Man's ability to walk a tightrope over a pit filled with hoodlums, angry workers, politicians bent and straight, the press, and the founding and *fund*ing father of the Dearborn Dynasty. But something about the little prick—maybe it's the bowties—gets his goat.

"Mr. Ford," says Harry, smiling and stomping again to reveal yet another branching tunnel, "understands that diplomacy does not flourish in sterile surroundings."

"Wow," says Portia, truly impressed.

"You should hear him recite poetry," says Legs Laman. "The guy could be up on stage."

But Harry *is* on stage, making a sweeping gesture to invite them into the new tunnel. "Come this way. No tricky footwork to deal with."

Harry's version of the story is that Laman and pals intercepted his car on the way home from the Rouge, Legs blowing the windshield out with a shotgun blast, Harry ducking just in time, then hopping out to face his assassins, wherein Laman jammed the shotgun barrel into his stomach, informing him of his error in pursuing the Cass business.

In Harry's version, he pled his case honestly, rationally, and Legs spared his life.

In Laman's version, if he hadn't already discharged both barrels, Harry would have had "a hole big enough to stick your foot through" in his middle.

"As you may have noticed," says the Little Man as he leads the way, "the air is *ri*pening. It is not poor sanitation, nor the Count of Monte Cristo moldering in his shackles—"

They come to a pair of large, barred cages recessed into the wall, which contain a trio of lion cubs, who have smelled them coming and pad up to the bars hoping for entertainment.

"My kitties," grins Harry.

"Oh, my God, they're gorgeous!" enthuses Portia, squatting down for a closer look.

"Are you allowed to keep these?" asks Sugar, who apparently hasn't studied the Legend of the Little Man.

"I keep them till they're three years old and starting to get rambunctious. Then I give them back to my pal Clyde Beatty in exchange for some new cubs. These tykes get about knee-high and I'll let them have the run of the tunnel. Keeps the riffraff out."

"What do you feed them?" asks Maurice Sugar.

Harry winks. "Labor agitators."

Smitty wishes he could quote this, but it will have to wait for the obituary. Harry is the best gossip in Detroit, Dearborn, and Hamtramck combined, and will phone Smitty with a hot tidbit if it's printable and Smitty observes the *quid pro quo*. Several sources told him Harry was deeply involved in bringing the Torch Murderers to justice, perhaps a little third degree down here in the bowels of Castle Bennett, but all Smitty wrote in the *Free Press* was about Harry donning diving gear to search for a pistol thrown in the river, then the civic-minded role he and his Service Department lugs played in transporting the convicted murderers to Jackson Prison without them being lynched first. The fact is that Harry is always fun, often good copy, and a useful guy to know.

Unless you get in his way.

As for Harry's 'associate' Legs Laman, his confederates panicked after the cops shot him up, and David Cass was found, badly decomposed, on the banks of the Flint River.

Portia stands with bright eyes and turns to the Little Man. "Any chance I can play with them?"

• • •

You can play on Adelaide if you don't mind a few cars coming through, maybe one an inning. Clifford has a soft rubber ball he brings, made to throw for dogs to fetch. Nobody Alvin knows has a dog, though you see some scruffy-looking ones slinking around the neighborhood, putting their noses into the garbage and whatnot. The ball is so soft it won't go too far or break a window if it hits one, and you only got a broom handle to swing with, not a real bat. But you still got to hit it square, and catch it in the air, no gloves allowed, for an out.

How it works is you stand on the sidewalk with your back to the solid brick wall of the warehouse, so if you don't hit the pitch the ball just bounces back to Stubby Gans who hurls for both sides cause he can't hit to save his life and won't *run* on account of his blubber shaking all over. There's only nine playing today, so this works out good—you got an infielder and a first baseman, then two outfielders in the empty lot across the street. A fire before Alvin's family had to move in from Inkster left a mess of burnt-up wood and broken glass, till the city finally come and hauled it away. They have to clear it some before they play because people toss whatever they don't want in there, and the pile in the right field corner is getting pretty high.

Games are five innings or twenty runs, whichever comes first, and the most important rule is that you can pretend to be any player you want but don't say it out loud, because everybody wants to be Turkey Stearnes and that leads to fights.

Alvin has gotten to be a good hitter, DeWitt throwing him so many practice pitches and teaching him to keep his eye on the ball. You got to *con*centrate, and when he does Alvin mostly hits line drives, less likely to get caught than pop-ups or grounders.

His side is up eleven to seven in the third when the Jew Girl stops to watch for a spell, sitting on a stoop one house down from home plate. Never says anything, just sits back and watches with a little smile on her face. Whenever they get an audience, doesn't matter who, everybody shows off a bit. They take a harder cut at the ball, they chatter louder-

"*Hum* there, Stubby, fire it in there, *this* guy can't hit, *this* guy can't hit—"

Alvin hits a double and then later lines to Clifford for an out while she's watching. The Jew Girl lives in the building right across from him, the Rose Apartments, which he knows from his friend Rayray, who lives there too, are as cramped and crummy as anything in Black Bottom. Mama says there must be something wrong with the family—the Jew Girl, her big tall brother, and an old man—to still be living here.

I wouldn't want to hurry inside on a nice day, thinks Alvin, if I lived in the Rose Apartments.

Alvin is playing left field, knees bent, hands ready, the way DeWitt taught him, when the patrol car parks in the middle of their game.

Officer Pupp and Joe Palooka step out from the car, the ones who roll around the neighborhood, according to them keeping the colored people out of mischief-

"Alla youse line up in front of me, on the double!" shouts Officer Pupp, called that cause he's got a face like the bulldog in the *Krazy Kat* strip.

They know better than to run, leaving Stubby behind to face the music, and as far as Alvin can tell none of them has done anything illegal today. They wander over, taking their time but finally forming a sullen line in front of Joe Palooka, who is as big and blond as the comics character Pa won't let Alvin look at because of how they draw Joe's colored valet Smokey.

"Empty your pockets," orders Pupp.

Alvin points to the little pile just off from the hat box lid that serves for home plate. "Most all of what we got is right there. Don't want nothing in your pocket when you play ball."

Officer Pupp strolls over to tower over Alvin. "Did I ask for any of your lip?"

You're supposed to say "No sir" to the law, or just to any grownup, but Alvin is steamed that their game has been stopped.

"Turn your pockets inside out."

Joe Palooka is pushing their piled-up things around with his foot, looking like next he might stomp on it all, when the Jew Girl comes over.

"Is there a problem Officer?"

Pupp gives her a long look before he talks.

"These little hoodlums just ran through Meyer's drugstore, grabbing whatever they could get their hands on before they run off. That problem enough for you?"

"When did this happen?"

"We just got the call."

The Jew Girl holds her hands out wide. "These boys have been playing here at least a half hour. I've been sitting here watching them."

Pupp makes a bulldog face, does everything but growl.

"And what brings you to this fine neighborhood?"

"I live over on Hastings," she says, looking at him steady. "The Rose Apartments."

Pupp seems like he's wondering if he can arrest her just for that. "A half hour, you say."

It's maybe been fifteen minutes since she showed up, but she doesn't blink. "That's right."

They've all been standing with their pockets turned out, only Clifford with his little penknife on the ground in front of him. Pupp scoops it up, opens it.

"What you carry this for?"

"Clean my fingernails," says Clifford.

Pupp props the open knife against the curb, comes down on it with his heel to snap the blade off.

"You might slip some day and cut somebody's throat," he says, then jerks his head for Joe Palooka to get back in the patrol car. They slam the doors, drive off.

"Asshole," says the Jew Girl, her face angried up and red, then walks away, calling "Take it easy, fellas," back over her shoulder. She's near out of sight around the corner before they all laugh and stuff their pockets back in.

"Jew Girl might be crazy, living here," says Clifford, "but she know a *ass*hole when she see one."

It's a couple hours later, running an errand for Mama, that Alvin sees her through the bakery window. He goes in, stands for a minute while she orders a half-dozen poppyseed rolls, then pokes her arm.

"Thanks for sticking up for us," he says.

She smiles. "You live across the street."

"Yeah. Why you do that?"

"You boys were just playing. He had no right—"

"He got a uniform and a badge—"

"And a pistol on his hip, I know. That doesn't make it *right*. What's your name?"

"Alvin."

"Nice to meet you, Alvin. I'm Rosa."

"You ain't afraid to live here?" He is surprised to just bust out with what he's always wondered, but she doesn't look mad.

"The country where my father is from?" she says. "Men in uniforms are arresting people like me and him and throwing them in prison, maybe worse. We're *luck*y to live here."

"Them Nazis."

"That's right."

"Cause you're Jews."

"That's right. That's our only crime."

Suddenly nervous, Alvin starts out of the shop. "Anyway, thanks," he says.

"If I see you with your friends, Alvin," she calls, "I won't embarrass you by waving hello."

Nice lady. And doesn't seem crazy at all.

HERE'S PROOF THAT THE FORD V-8 CAN "TAKE IT!"

In the few brief hours of road racing a car takes more severe abuse than in the whole life of an ordinary automobile. Chassis, springs, brakes, body, and engine are pounded and racked, tortured and twisted. If the car has a weakness it will not finish or will finish with the "also rans."

Ford V-8s took the first 7 places, Elgin 200-mile Stock Car Race; first 10 places, 150-mile Ascot Speedway Race, and first 6 places, 250-mile Oakland Speedway Stock Car Classic, under A.A.A. supervision. All within one year!

The reason for Ford V-8's superiority is simple. Like a racing car it has positive mechanical brakes, a Torque-Tube Drive, strong radius rods to give you safer, surer steering and to keep the rear axle in perfect alignment. It is a safer car to drive because its safety is constantly being demonstrated at eighty or better!

Before you buy any car
at any price, drive the Ford V-8.

SEE YOUR NEAREST FORD DEALER

FORD V8

"THE CAR WITHOUT A PRICE CLASS"

FORD RADIO PROGRAM—With Fred Waring's Pennsylvanians

Sunday and Thursday Evenings—Columbia Network

IT'S LIKE EVERY THIRD ONE shits the bed. And the orderlies or whoever just wad it up in the sheets and throw it in the rolling hamper, dump the whole load down the chute onto the steel work table where Mavis has got to deal with the stinking mess. And since she's the new girl in the laundry, it's her job to hose off as much of the patients' doo-doo as she can before it moves down the line. She knows they got bedpans upstairs, she's seen them, so what's the deal? They give you rubber gloves for the job, gloves that Mavis must be allergic to because now there's a rash all over her hands and wrists, looks just as nasty as it feels. But with rent and food to look out for, children that keep growing out of their clothes, and the dentist who has got to be the richest man in Paradise Valley, what Zeke gets now is not enough.

The first wave of linens comes during and right after breakfast, the walking patients out of their beds and the worse off ones ready to be changed. Sprayed off, soaked in disinfectant, washed, wrung out, put through the dryers and then ironed in the big presses—there are a lot of women and a few men down here, most of them colored, and though it's not how they run the auto factory, with no talking or sitting down, if you're going to keep up you better keep *hop*ping.

Her friend Keechie works in the laundry under the Book-Cadillac Hotel and complains about the job all the time, but Mavis would bet money the guests don't dukey in their beds. The one saving grace about her spot at the bottom of the chute is being a fair distance away from the big laundry machines, so if somebody does come up to talk they don't have to shout.

She swears this skinny, big-eyed girl looks familiar.

"Mistress," she says. Jamaican.

"I know you?"

"We live Inkster long time, me bet number wit you."

"That's right. You hit once, didn't you? Nickel bet."

"Me weeger double dat now. Me have a dream last night."

Madame Queenie made it clear that Mavis was not welcome to take action anywhere in Black Bottom or Paradise Valley, territories handed out and backed by John Roxborough the real estate man and a few others like him. But Henry Ford Hospital is way north of there.

"And you read about it in the dream book."

"You cyannot trust dem book. No, dis was number said out loud inna dream—mon come to me door, say he look for tree-tirty-five Winter Avenue, it *so* important he find dis."

"Did you tell him how to get there?"

"In dream me know wheer tis. But me tink in real Detroit city dere is no Winter Street."

"335."

The Jamaican girl holds out a dime.

Thousand-to-one odds say she loses. But booking without a safety net, even for ten cents-

She takes the money. "Let's hope that's the right address."

She remembers the girl now, shy, husband had gone back to the island and stuck her with two little ones. Clarice.

Clarice has a beautiful smile.

"Me already tole dem other girl bout you, tell dem orderly too. Before, we got Big Minnie, work inna kitchen, but Loretta who run the steam press she hit for two dollar, handsome payout due, and Big Minnie she disappear."

So many working on this shift, and then there's the nightbirds just coming off when you show up at the rear entrance. Risk it naked for the first couple weeks, then if fortune doesn't fuck with her she'll go to Roxborough, ask for his backing-

"Don't you worry, darlin," Mavis tells her, picking up her sprayer again, "this yere woman is going *no*where."

• • •

They've got good seats, five rows behind the dugout on the right field side, Ira with an eye out for slicing line drives—his sister has come under protest, believing that sport belongs to the People, preferably neighborhood children, and should not be professionalized.

She's seen a hum-dinger.

Schoolboy Rowe and Johnny Welch battling on the mound, the Red Sox scoring three in the early innings, then the Tigers having a big bottom of the fourth, Ira's man Greenberg knocking in one of what would eventually be four runs to go ahead. Greenberg who said he wouldn't play because it was Rosh Hashana.

You'd think he wanted to take off Lenin's birthday.

The baseball scribes from the *News*, from the *Times*, from the *Free Press* all riding the slugger—the Tigers are in a *pen*nant race for crying out loud, how often is that likely to happen? Misspelling Jewish holidays Greenberg might want to honor, reminding Hank that you *play* the game, so he won't start sitting out Saturdays as well. Finally he caved, said he'd thought it over, and thank Jehovah he's already brought one in so it wasn't a waste to suit up today.

"If he's religious," said Rosa, who's maybe stepped into a synagogue three times in her life, "I don't see where it's any of their business."

"Because it *is* a business," Ira explained. "They pay the players, just like Ford pays his workers."

"Do they have a union?"

The guy to Ira's left, listening to their back-and-forth for nine innings, starts to laugh.

"A ballplayers' union, that's a rich one! The batters would be demanding slower pitches, the pitchers would want to throw from closer, and then the *um*pires would be expected to go out and kick butts on the picket line—"

"If they're paid, then they're labor—"

"Up until this year half of em weren't even *ball*players, lady," says the man to Ira's left. "Just a bunch of stiffs taking up space on the diamond. I bet Henry Ford, if he's got any Jews on his assembly line, doesn't let *them* off for anything but Christmas and New Year."

She has made an effort, Rosa, to grasp the rules and customs of the game as Ira has explained them—what constitutes a double play, the ever-controversial balk, the mystery, still not clear to her, of an intentional base on balls, even the infield-fly rule, when she cleverly observed of a pop up "Why didn't he let it bounce and get one of those double things?"

But it is well past four o'clock and the game continues.

"I thought you said nine innings."

"It *is* nine innings, usually, only we're tied four-four and somebody's got to win."

"They can't play in the dark."

"No, if it's still tied and they can't see the ball anymore they stop, then continue the game on another day."

"I suppose that makes sense."

Hoping not to overtry her patience, there are things that Ira does not inform his sister, the principal of these being that Walter Briggs, head of the auto body factory, is a part owner of the Tigers. The Tigers have taken the field for the top of the ninth, and the first Red Sox batter Rowe faces hits a grounder to third, Greenberg making a nice scoop of the low throw to first base.

"What'd you step in, kike?" calls a Sox fan a few rows ahead of them, three or four beers obviously clouding the man's judgment here in Navin Field.

"Duck," says Ira, putting a protective hand over Rosa's head. Hot dogs, halves of hot dogs, a box of Crack Jacks, and a child's shoe, hopefully to be reclaimed after the contest ends, rain down upon the Boston rooter, some hitting their mark, some sailing past him.

"It can get pretty rowdy in the late innings. Even before Repeal, fans brought hip flasks."

"What the gentleman forgot," says the guy to Ira's left, "is that he's *our* kike."

Rowe gets the next batter on a pop fly.

"Atta go, Schoolboy!" calls the guy to the left.

"Why do they call him that?" asks Rosa.

"Probably picked up a book by accident and somebody caught him with it. He's just a regular fella from Texas."

"They all have nicknames—"

"Mostly. Mickey Cochrane is 'Black Mike,' Charlie Gehringer is 'the Mechanical Man,' Ty Cobb was 'the Georgia Peach'—"

"And the Jewish one?"

She keeps calling him that.

"'Hammerin' Hank,'" says Ira.

"'Hankus Pankus,'" says the guy to the left.

"Or sometimes 'the Hebrew Hammer.' Then there's Goose Goslin—"

"He never had a chance, did he? You know all of these? For all the teams?"

"Sure. It's part of—you know—*sports*. Like this young Negro boxer, Louis—"

"Jesus that kid can slug," says the guy to the left.

"And the more people he knocks out, the more names the writers lay on him—"

"'The African Assassin'—"

"'The Sepia Slugger,' 'The Saffron Sandman'—"

"'The Mahogany Mauler,' 'The Brown Bomber'—"

"'The Tawny Titan of Thump.'"

Rosa does not seem impressed. "Do sportswriters get paid, or do they just get free tickets to the games?"

This seems the perfect opening for the news that prompted Ira's invitation.

"I want to be one," he admits.

Rosa turns to stare at him. "A thumper?"

"A sportswriter."

"You're studying to be a *den*tist."

"Lots of money in dentistry," says the guy to the left. "But you spend your day staring down people's yaps. And then there's bad breath to consider—"

"Hali*to*sis. Rosa, just looking at *pho*tographs of people's oral cavities makes me nauseous. With an actual patient—"

"What qualifies you to write about sports—just because you watch them?"

"I've got a knack for the lingo. You got to make it sing—"

"Add some pizazz," says the guy to the left.

"For instance, that bit of anti-Semitism we just witnessed, if I had to describe it in print-"

Ira pauses for a moment to compose—

"'An insult to the Tiger first sacker's heritage was greeted with a shower of pork and peanuts.'"

"Not bad," says the guy to the left. "I like to two 'Ps.'"

"Are there any Jewish sportswriters?"

"Far too few in Detroit, unless they've Gentiled their names up. Look, we've got one of ours knocking the hell out of the ball for the Bengals—it's time for us to get in step with America."

"Bengals is the same as Tigers," the guy on the left informs her.

"We were *born* here, Ira," Rosa reminds her brother just as Rowe retires the Red Sox for the inning and fans stand up to cheer.

"Is it over?"

"No, but if we can score in this stanza we get the W. Look around, Rosa, what do you see?"

"A lot of people with sore backsides—"

"*Ti*ger fans, rooting together. Rich people, poor people, Hoover backers, Roosevelt Democrats, there's Catholics, Jews, Baptists—"

"I bet there's even Moslems," says the guy to the left. "And the other from the Bible, whatsit—Catamites—"

"I don't think that's a religion," says Rosa.

"My point is I'm sick of being the odd man out," says Ira, "getting our heads beat in. I want to be part of something that brings people together."

"Like hating the Yankees," says the guy on the left.

Mickey Cochrane comes up to bat.

"Let's go Black Mike!" calls Rosa, cupping her hands. "We want to go home!"

"Atta girl—"

Cochrane grounds out.

"So it could just keep going on and on?"

"We'll leave if they hit thirteen innings or it gets too dark to play," promises Ira, "whichever comes first."

Charley Gehringer slams a hanging curve past them into right and it one-hops into the stands.

"Home run!" shouts Rosa. "We win it!"

The fans around them laugh.

"It's a ground-rule double."

"But it went into the stands! If he runs fast they won't be able to get it away from whoever grabbed it—"

"He stops at second. It's a rule."

"Pretty stupid rule."

The Sox manager signals to Welch on the mound to issue Goose Goslin a free pass.

"He's throwing it wide on purpose again."

"If Goose is on first they could get a double-play and be out of the inning."

"Why not just tell the umpire to let him go to first?"

"Cause the pitcher might accidentally throw a wild one past the catcher," says the guy on the left. "I seen it happen in the minors."

Billy Rogell is up next. He takes a healthy cut but only lifts a high, easy fly ball to center, Gehringer staying put at second.

The fans start chanting "Hank, Hank, Hank!"

"*Then from five thousand throats and more, there rose a lusty yell,*" Ira intones over the chanting. "*It rumbled through the valley, it rattled in the dell. It pounded on the mountain and recoiled upon the flat—for Casey, mighty Casey, was advancing to the bat!*"

"I thought his name was Hank."

"Casey is the slugger in the famous poem," Ira explains.

"Who *whiffs* in the clutch," says the guy to the left. "For the love of Mike, don't go jinxing our guy."

"Hear that?" grins Ira. "Greenberg is *his* guy too."

Greenberg takes a low strike, waits out a wide one, and then raps a sharp line drive into left center field with Gehringer already on the run. There isn't a play at the plate.

Game over.

Rosa is up on her feet cheering with the rest of them. Ira hasn't seen her smile for weeks, still in mourning for the shortcomings of the Briggs strike and Roosevelt's NRA program. The guy on the left is thumping Ira's back with joy.

"He comes through again! Holy moley, what a hitter! Listen, you people got so many friggin high holy days—what's the next one?"

"The Day of Atonement, Yom Kippur," Ira tells him. "It's in a week and a half."

"Do you think he'll play?"

• • •

He keeps asking for coffee, and it's good here, rich and strong, but Norma has been warned. LaVerne, the main night nurse, caught her coming in just before the wake-up siren.

"Ixnay on the java for Mr. Pringle," she said softly, jerking her head toward a room two doors down from the desk. "He says he can't sleep, then he sits up smoking cigarette after cigarette and ringing for coffee. No wonder he's got the jitters."

Curtis Pringle has been here as long as Jim, he helped build this new hospital, probably the best in all of South America, and seemed like such a get-it-done, easygoing guy when Norma first met him. She heads down to check on him as the siren wakes the rest of Belterra up.

Audrey is in with him, sitting on the edge of the bed as Curtis paces the room, smoking. Patients are supposed to come sit by the desk or just outside the hospital if they're going to smoke, always the worry about beds catching on fire, and it is prohibited in the big common ward. But the sight of Curtis Pringle with a cigarette in his mouth seems so normal-

"How are we doing this morning?"

"He can't sleep," says Audrey. "And if he can't sleep, *I* can't sleep."

The left side of Audrey's jaw is badly swollen but not discolored. A quick thought of the banged-up wives and girlfriends who come in to make sure nothing is broken, but Norma pushes it away. Their houses have always been right next to each other, here and back in Fordlandia, and she would have heard-

"You hear that?" Norma says to Curtis. "You're keeping your wife up at night."

"I close my eyes, but things keep jumping around. Crazy ideas—" Curtis pauses to look out his window, workers hurrying past to punch in for their shift. "Is everything okay with the planting?"

"Jim says it's going fine."

"The top-grafting?"

"He says it can take one or two tries, but there's starting to be lots of good-looking trees."

The plant expert, Weir, doctor or professor or whatever he was, came back with some seeds from Asian plantations and then took a powder without telling anybody—jumped on a river trader's launch before sunrise one morning and departed for who knows where, the only evidence he's still alive the bill for his services received in Dearborn. Mr. Johnston has them following some of his recommendations, and the plantation keeps expanding.

When Curtis pulls the cigarette out of his mouth his hands are trembling.

"You have to check them every day," he says. "There's the leaf blight, the beetles, this time of year you get caterpillars—"

"Mr. Johnston has the school children picking off caterpillars," Norma reassures him. "An hour after classes every day."

"Could you bring some aspirin?" asks Audrey.

"Let me check his med chart. I don't know what the doctor has—"

"It's for me."

"Oh." Norma comes in from the doorway, gives the swollen jaw another look. "Can you say 'ah'?"

"What, you're a dentist now?"

"Let me take a peek."

Audrey throws her head back, makes a long, exaggerated 'ahhhh' sound-

A pair of molars have deep brown pits in them, the gums around them bright red and swollen.

"How long has this been bothering you?"

"A couple weeks maybe."

"She complained about it a month ago," says Curtis.

"No I didn't."

"You said you couldn't concentrate on the movie. What was it—?"

"Soldiers going crazy in the desert—"

"*The Lost Patrol.* That was at least a month and a half ago."

"Well it hurts *now.*"

"I'll get you some aspirin," says Norma.

She is at the desk accounting for the pills when Jim appears in the hallway with Dr. Niles, who has come down from Henry Ford Hospital to supervise.

"Curtis up?"

"He never got to sleep. Audrey's in there with him—there's something wrong with her jaw. You should get a look, doctor."

Dr. Niles nods his head. He's had Norma come in to observe a couple fairly complicated surgeries, "Just in case we need an extra hand some day."

If we ever get out of this green hell, Norma thinks, following them with aspirin and a cup of filtered water in hand, I'm going to take whatever classes are required and get certified. Esther says I have a knack for it, and

Esther does not idly hand out compliments.

Curtis looks relieved to see the men. "You puzzle it out, Doc?" he asks. "I know these tropical bugs are mysterious, but maybe you got a handle on it."

"I'm afraid not," says the doctor. "I'm sending you back to Dearborn, where they can get a better look and you can recover in more familiar surroundings."

"These surrounding *are* familiar. I been here since '27."

"The effort of keeping up with the plantation may be complicating your condition—"

"I'm no quitter."

Jim steps forward to lay a hand on his friend's shoulder. "But what you are, buddy, is a good Ford man. The Doc's in charge here, and orders is orders."

Men are such jerks, thinks Norma, but this will probably work.

"As long as it says on paper I was *told* to."

The Pringles have no children. They had a dog in Fordlandia for a little while but it ran wild and then got shot when the pack it joined became a problem. Norma slips Audrey the pills and water, which she makes quick work of.

"You'll need to make a report, of course," Jim continues. "Tell them what's really going on here. Who knows what that damn Weir said about us."

"I will," says Curtis, sitting down beside Audrey now as if he has suddenly run out of gas.

"We've got the pontoon plane leaving for Santorém tomorrow," says Jim. "Norma can help Audrey pack up what you need."

"I'm scheduling an hour with Dr. Anders at two this afternoon for you, Mrs. Pringle," Niles tells Audrey. "He'll take a look at those teeth."

"I'll be fine—"

"I'm not sending damaged goods back up to Dearborn," he says with an effort at a smile. "My colleagues will think I'm on vacation down here." He looks to Curtis. "And you, sir, are restricted to milk and crackers till you touch down in Detroit. And no coffee to go with that milk."

Curtis holds up his crumpled pack of Camels. "How about these?"

"In moderation," says the doctor, reaching. "Mind if I bum one?"

Norma is the last to leave them, promising to come by when her shift is over and help Audrey get organized for their travel. They sit on the edge of the bed together, Curtis shaking all over now, and Audrey with her head in her hands, obviously in pain.

Another year in lovely Belterra, thinks Norma, and that will be Jim and me.

• • •

The house is not so much bigger than the one she and João have been given, but is full of American things. Things that need to be washed or dusted or picked up and wiped off or even polished with special creams. João says that Senhor Riker the *confederado* told him these American houses are called 'Cape Cod', a place on the ocean named after the kind of fish they catch there.

So in America even the fishermen are wealthy.

There are the *binóculos*, which you put to your eyes to see something far away, that are to be wiped with a special cloth and then put back in their case. There are special small bowls made of different materials for leaving the part of the cigarette you don't finish smoking. João will smoke a cigar when he can get one, but always outside, and cigarettes, even the Brazilian Hollywoods, are too expensive a habit to form. There are little tables on both sides of their bed, and little lamps that use electric bulbs on these. There is a machine with a wire that you plug into the *tomada*, which powers it to make a loud noise and suck up loose dirt from the floor. Flavio tells her that this is named after a man who was once president of America, and may have invented the machine. They have enough knives and forks and spoons to invite many friends over, some that are actually made of silver and must be rubbed with the cream *Senhora* Norma has showed Beatriz how to use. They have small squares of cotton you wipe your mouth with when eating, and several sheets and pillowcases so that there is always a fresh set on the bed when they get into it at night. They are nice people and deserve these things—*Senhor* Jim, who always greets her in Portuguese when he sees her, is the man who saws all the wood now, leaving before the first siren and coming home even later than João, and the *Senhora* is a nurse at the hospital. But there is so much that needs cleaning-

Beatriz washes their clothes and linens every other day, in another electric machine, and then hangs them out on a line to dry. The main line is on the side of the house, then a smaller one behind it where the *Senhora's* brassieres and underthings go. Even the little girl, who clearly does not need one yet, has brassieres to wash and hang where few can see them.

And then there is the monkey.

Flavio says that the little girl, Kerry, saved it after its mother was swallowed by a snake, which is a kind thing to do but monkeys are meant to live with other monkeys. *Senhor* Jim has built a cage of wood and wire mesh out back that it lives in, with a thin, dead tree that goes up through the roof for it to climb on. There is a bench inside the cage, which Beatriz sits on to eat her own lunch, sharing bits of food with the monkey, whose name is Jocko. He is very polite, never stealing but just watching her, and if she gives him a big piece of fruit he will scamper up into the branches of the dead tree to eat it. Compared to before, selling food to people in the shack town next Fordlandia, this is very lonely work, the few other *brasileiras* working in the American houses too busy to come and socialize, though they meet and are driven to work in the bed of a truck every morning. One has a toucan to clean up after, a few have to deal with dogs, but the Rogan's have the only pet monkey in Belterra.

When her legs get tired from all the washing and cleaning, Beatriz likes to sit down on the long *sofa* and look at a painting they have hung on the opposite wall. The painting shows an opening in a forest of tall, identical trees with knobby bark, all of their branches weighed down by clumps of white, which Beatriz knows is snow, though she has never seen any in person. There is snow covering the ground as well, and little bits of snow falling from above, and what you see through the trees is either a very flat field or a pond that has frozen and been covered by snow, and on this stands a deer with very big horns, its head held up as if it's listening, wary that something or somebody might be stalking it. Beatriz has lived that moment, walking through trees in the evening and hearing something like a cough and stopping, head held high, to listen for what might be a jaguar.

Beatriz worries at night, worries when she hears the rubber trees have suffered another *moléstia*, worries that *Senhor* Ford, who she knows is an old man, will die and his children will forget about their people in the jungle, worries that perhaps this Rogan family is cursed—who else has had a maid lose her arm to a *caimão*? The world may seem so beautiful—cool and clean and bits of fluffy white falling from the heavens—but something could be stalking you-

• • •

The caterpillars are long and green with black dots on the back and try to cling to the leaves so you can't just tear them off. Kerry and Flavio, even though they are in different classes, usually manage to share a bucket, as Miss Bishop does not overexert herself supervising the harvest. The pairs are to work for an hour or fill their bucket with caterpillars, whichever comes first. At the end you bring the bucket to be dumped into a barrel that is then loaded on a truck and taken to the incinerator they've built for waste wood.

Once Flavio kept a handful of them back and they snuck down to the river together, Flavio throwing them into the current and then walking along with it to watch as they floated squirming on the surface till nipped away by fish coming up from below. And once Kerry rushed home and came back with Jocko on her shoulder. He had a fine time jumping up into the young rubber trees and eating caterpillars, but seemed afraid to even look into the bucket once it started to fill up—too much creepy-crawly. But the other kids all gathered around to watch him, so Miss Bishop said he was a distraction and couldn't come help again.

Today they head off down a row in the opposite direction from the others, Miss Bishop planted on her folding chair reading a book, and soon

are all alone with the birds and the caterpillars. When the birds manage to snatch one they don't eat it there, but fly away with it wriggling in their beaks. Kerry wonders if they have baby birds to feed.

"What did they teach you today?" she asks Flavio.

"We learn the war of your states," Flavio tells her. "When they fight over owning black ones."

"Did they have that here? Slavery?"

Flavio nods. "In the day of my *avô*—the father of my father."

"Your grandfather. That's not so long ago."

"I don't know the year it is ended. I know your seventeen seventy-six, and four of July, and eighteen hundred and twenty-two, when we become free of the Kingdom of Portugal."

"Do you know what these turn into?" Kerry asks, holding up a caterpillar that is curling into itself.

"*Mariposa falcão*," Flavio tells her. "But is not so much color as the butterfly."

"Butterfly" is Flavio's favorite English word, the image of such a thing making him happy.

"A moth, then. A 'hawk moth.'"

"Is a good name, no?"

Most of the other kinds of caterpillars that have attacked the planted rubber trees have stinging hairs, and each student has been given a pair of thick cloth gloves to use when picking these off. The trees are sprayed as well, for mites and ants and cutworms and white flies and other bugs, but the spray doesn't kill everything.

"The insect eat the leaf, the bird eat the insect, maybe we eat the bird," Flavio tells her. "Is how the life goes."

"But nobody can eat rubber."

"No, this that we do with the *borracha* is not natural."

Kerry's father has taken her to watch the little bit of latex they've gotten out of young trees turned into sheets of rubber, a chemical she can't remember the name of used to speed the process. There is a kind of magic to it, but not nearly as much fun as the time they made syrup from birch trees back in Michigan.

Nobody can see them now, far down the row with an almost-full bucket of caterpillars. She has been thinking about this for a long time, and today—today there's something about the way the strands of his black hair stick out from the uniform cap the boys have to wear, the sound of his voice-

There is an adjusting of noses, hers longer than his, to get to the kiss. She steps away, then looks for another caterpillar on a branch she can reach.

Flavio is surprised but it isn't a bad thing. A little scary, maybe, but not bad. He has stopped thinking so much at night about Betty from the cartoons and started picturing Miss Dove, who lectures all the classes about hygiene and health as well as teaching numbers. She has normal ones that you can't ignore instead of little bumps like Kerry, and has nice legs even if her skirts cover her knees. Miss Dove treats him like a boy, but a boy who she likes. Now he'll have to think some about Kerry. This changes them being together—anything could happen.

"They're starting to crawl out of the bucket," she says. "We'd better go back."

BY EVERY MODERN STANDARD THE FORD IS A BIG CAR

"Gee, Pop, I bet there's room for my bicycle too!"

UP-TO-DATE buyers don't judge cars by the length of their hoods. They have learned that it is the usable space inside the body—the room it gives them—that counts.

Because of skillful design and a compact V-8 engine, the 1937 Ford V-8 has inches more body room than many higher priced cars. More room for you—more room for your luggage—because the V-type engine requires less. (Two banks of four cylinders each, instead of one long line.)

Extra space means extra comfort. This big-car comfort and big-car performance make the Ford V-8 a really BIG car—with smaller car ecomony. It's THE QUALITY CAR IN THE LOW-PRICE FIELD.

Ford V-8 for 1937!

THE FUNERAL PARLOR CHARGED AN extra five dollars to get the paint off his father's body. Prokop was found lying in a puddle of it in the spraying room, Zephyr Blue that day, already gone from some kind of stroke. He'd been having trouble breathing lately, and when you're spraying, not dipping, it hangs in the air.

The line had to shut down for nearly ten minutes.

It's raining lightly at Mount Olivet, the undertaker having passed out umbrellas to the few who have come. Mostly Pop's old cronies, guys he worked with at Highland Park when it was only Ts rolling out of the shop. Molly and the kids are here with Kaz, of course, but his few friends from work only offered their condolences before begging off. Prokop got quoted by the *Free Press* while he was picketing during the Briggs strike, and they took a photo of him, so coming here if you're not a relative might get you on a list. Briggs had to take him back, part of the agreement to call off the walkout, but they stuck him in spray paint hoping he'd quit.

Pop never quit anything.

Kaz looks around but doesn't see anybody taking photographs or names. Father Jan from St. Albertus handles the Latin, and the little headstone is right next to his mother's. It's a beautiful cemetery even in the rain, big oaks and maples scattered around, a stone mausoleum, benches. He and Pop saw a deer in here once when they came to visit his mother's grave.

Burying somebody turns out to be pretty steep, even just the bare minimum ceremony he could afford. Pop's hidden cash didn't amount to much and Kaz's own savings got wiped out with the bank failures, and with the Rouge still only operating at four days a week it's been a tight squeeze. Molly keeps saying she could go to work, but the twins just turned thirteen and little Sonia still has the braces on her legs—they need somebody at home.

Kaz listens to the rain on his umbrella and the drone of the Latin and tries to work up a picture in his head, his father in better times. The one that comes is of himself in short pants waiting on the front steps, and then down the street walks his father with two or three other Ford men, tired and dirty and telling jokes in Polish. Or sometimes he'd run to meet him at the trolley stop and get to wait while Pop downed a cold stein of beer at Matusek's, where no English was spoken and the red-and-white flag with the eagle wearing a crown covered the entire back wall.

Whenever Kaz asked about the old country, Pop would lean down to him and say "Do you know what is *wieśniak*?"

This was a bit of a problem at first because cousins on his mother's side were Wozniaks, but eventually he could tell the two apart.

"Sure, Pop—a peasant."

"A *wieśniak* does not own land, he works land that is owned by wealthy man. And to that wealthy man he is *srać na piętę*—shit on the bootheel."

In the Highland Park days Pop thought he had it made, bringing home that five dollars, unheard of for a laboring man, making the automobile that you saw everywhere on the streets, eventually owning the house that Kaz will now sell for peanuts and split the money with Leon and their sister in Toledo whose husband hasn't worked since the Crash-

"Here, I am my own man," he would say. "Here laborer has dignity of his trade."

This was something they'd told him at the Ford night school when he was learning English, and the idea stuck. Stuck until the layoffs and the rollbacks and then being bounced over to Briggs, which was just a front for all the big companies to have their bodies assembled on the cheap. The last few times Kaz visited Pop at the house he barely talked, depressed and disappointed.

"Part of machine is worn out, they put a new one," he said just last week, shrugging his shoulders in resignation. "Is no big deal."

The Black Legion, men in pointy hoods who are death on Jews, Catholics, unions and the colored, are in the news all the time now, members on trial, and Kaz hopes the ones who murdered George Marchuk from the AWU in Forest Park, and the AFL organizer at the Hudson plant are going to jail. Bud Novak says the prosecuting attorney is secretly a Legion member, so there's not much hope the big shots behind the outfit will be bothered.

It's going to be a war.

Psacharopulous, now supervisor on Kaz's stretch of the line, has it in for him and wants to make him quit. He would, too, even without another job lined up, but when the showdown finally comes at Ford, it will have to be men *in*side the plant who shut it down, not castaways—of which there are thousands and thousands now on relief or living in Hoovervilles and hobo camps. Until that day he'll have to soldier through, handle the speedups and the daily harrassment as best he can, and remember just what he is to the Company.

Shit on a bootheel.

• • •

"My dear friends, amongst other things, we in the National Union for Social Justice are Christians, insofar as we believe in Christ's principle of love thy neighbor as yourself," says the Radio Priest, apparently in front of a large and appreciative audience. "And with that principle I challenge every Jew in this nation to tell me he does not believe in it!"

A huge cheer of approval is heard from the radio.

"Sis, he's talking about you again," calls Ira as Rosa hurries from the bathroom to the room that doubles as her bedroom and storage. Papa is in his chair, Ira on the couch with his legs dangling over the arm, and Rosa crowded in with whatever can't be fit anywhere else. Because they are perverse, because they say they "want to understand the great unwashed masses," and principally because they are both out of work with nothing better to do, both her father and her brother are kibbitzing a radio message of Christianity and Americanism from the shrine of the Little Flower in Royal Oak, Michigan-

"You'll get a cancer listening to that show," she calls back, hurrying out of the dress she wore to work. "It's poison."

"I am not talking about the many good and religious Jews," Father Coughlin continues, *"but the communistic and atheistic Jews, those who believe that a Federal Reserve Bank has the right to coin and regulate the value of money—they're not even American!"*

"Watch out Papa," says Ira, "he's going to hang the financial crisis on us again."

"Who cares? We're all cousins to the Rothschilds."

It is like a vaudeville routine, the two of them, with Papa laid up and Ira unable to pay for another semester of dental school-

"And so, Mr. Roosevelt, so loquacious in 1933 about driving the money lenders out of the temple, is now bent upon another policy, which I believe is driving the workman out of decent annual wages!"

"Is Roosevelt a cousin too?"

"No, but the Jews have him in their pocket," says Papa.

"Ah."

His are wonderful children, good human beings, and very clever, thinks Asher Schimmel. He fears for them. They—Rosa especially—continue to put themselves on the front line of the struggle, which will always turn violent. Asher was not a leader in the packing house in Chicago, committed, yes, but only a laborer with animal blood on his apron and a willingness to open the eyes of his fellow man.

"My English is good," he said to the leader of their cell when the Company brought up a legion of scabs, colored men from the south. "I'll talk to them."

And talk he did, for a while, the colored men, sharp knives for gutting swine in their hands, never turning to look at him, rarely saying a word. Afraid, resentful, victims of at least two centuries' worth of the worst oppression. He explained how they were being used. He explained, honestly, what they would face if they joined the walkout when it came. He told them his own story, the persecution he knew as a boy, told them the only way to change such things was to resist. To unite and resist.

He never learned if it was getting through.

The foreman told him to stay late, he'd earn overtime, a word Asher had never heard uttered out loud on the killing floor. Some breakdown for an esteemed client, he was told, who was hosting a barbecue. He knew the cuts to make, wrapped them neatly in butcher paper.

"You'll see the extra money on Friday," said the foreman when he was done.

It was winter, already dark for hours when he climbed up onto the elevated train platform. The two from the Red Squad were waiting there.

They had his name. They had the names of his wife and children. They spoke of jail time, of deportation.

Subversive, they said.

Communist, they said.

Kike, they said.

They offered a deal while the train rolled up and the other people got on and off. Stay in your group, keep your ears open, and when something big is planned, you tell us about it.

He should have known to play along till the platform had filled with riders again. Instead he called them Cossacks and held his hands out to be cuffed. They threw him down the stairs. Down one flight, following, picking him up and throwing him down the next to the sidewalk.

"Oh, look," said the first person to find him, a little girl. "The man slipped."

Asher fears for his children. It isn't the physical violence—it is their choice to brave that or not. What he fears is what he's learned parked here by the radio, day after day, useless for work, useless to the struggle, a useless by-product of the System. In Chicago he was certain that the battle was the People against the Bosses.

Here in Detroit, he has learned, sadly, that it is the People against each other.

"I, therefore, am choosing right instead of might, choosing to be on the side of justice instead of the side of modern capitalism, with its intermingling of socialism and communism."

"Hey Sis, I think he just accused you of being a modern capitalist."

There is not even a cold water shower for Rosa in their excuse for a bathroom. Their landlord is a very modern capitalist who understands he can easily find renters, colored people, even more desperate than the Schimmels to take the lease in a minute, and therefore can ignore the plumbing situation.

"I stand here my friends to warn you, to tell you what the future holds—that this Relief that fails to relieve, by pumping up taxation, by doubling its effect on the payrolls of the nation—is due to tumble and fall before one year this April!"

"Now he's Nostradamus."

When her father brought home his first relief check he laid it on the table and wept. But they needed to pay the rent, to pay the butcher and the grocer and the electric bill, to try to keep Ira in school—

"You think you know what Depression is—you people living on the WPA envelope, the WPA envelope filled, partly, by the money taken from industry and commerce, and from the pay envelopes of those who are working. How long can that last?"

Typical divide-and-conquer tactics, Rosa thinks as she pulls on her cleanest dress. Make the employed workers think those who have been let go are lazy, sponges who'd just as soon stay on relief, or worse, some kind of foreign menace trying to ruin the country from within. And it works on some of them—

"You WPA workers and those who are living on the dole system, how long can it last for the Federal Reserve Bank to invent and coin and issue its own bogus money, against the debt of a nation? And when the bond market drops as it's dropping now, print even more fresh five-dollar bills?"

"Papa, what's the last time you saw a five-dollar bill?"

"At the picture show. I think some sharpie had one in his roll."

"You haven't been to the pictures for years, Papa," calls Rosa.

Her father laughs. It's at least good to hear him laugh. "The one where they shot the monkey from airplanes."

"It was a go*ril*la, Papa. A giant gorilla."

"Whatever it was, it should know you don't climb on a building. Hide be*hind* one maybe, but climb to the top and you're a sitting *duck*."

"View the New Deal of 1933 and '34—did it revere the Bill of Rights for which men have bled and died? Oh no, it took the Bill of Rights as it's taking our Constitution today, and tore it to shreds and handed the spending power over from the people, from the Congress, to the President of the United States, one step backwards, one step towards dictatorship!"

"You're the expert, Sis. Is Roosevelt a dictator?"

"He's a necessary way-station," she says, hurrying back past them to the bathroom, "on our journey to social justice."

Both men laugh. She shuts the door to the bathroom, as much as it will shut, but can still hear the Catholic orator stirring up his believers.

"Since that black day, since the chief executive of the nation has won the full power of spending billions of our hard-earned dollars, Congress must grovel on bended knee before him, and we who once loved Patriotism, we who once loved Democracy, we who once favored Justice, lie with a heel upon our backs, waiting to be crushed!"

Another rousing cheer can be heard. Rosa takes a quick peek at herself in the warped mirror—Ira says it's perfectly fine and that *they* are gradually becoming distorted—and decides against lipstick. It's a syndicalist meeting, not a tea social.

"*I wish to leave this thought with you*—" shouts Father Coughlin as Rosa hurries out the door without a goodbye, picking his voice up from someone's apartment on the second landing, "*form your battalions! Take up the shield of your defense, unsheathe the sword of your truth, and carry on so the communists on one hand cannot scourge us, and that the modern capitalists on the other hand cannot enslave us!*"

We could use a speaker like him, she thinks. Too bad he's a Fascist-

• • •

Kaz sees her on the streetcar, nice-looking, Italian or Greek, dark hair, wearing a beret and looking out the window as if she's not sure where to get off. When it reaches the stop she does a dance with the brakeman.

"I'm so sorry, I—I left my change purse in the dress I wear at work. It has a pocket—"

"I'll bet it does," says the brakeman, who looks like he's had a bad morning and is blocking her exit. "And you were in such a hurry to visit your sick grandmother."

"No, really, I'm sorry—"

"Here," says Kaz, tapping her shoulder and offering her two dimes.

"Oh—that's too much—"

"You got to get back home from wherever you're going, right? And this gentleman doesn't want to hear that story again."

"Thank you. That's very kind."

She gives the brakeman a dime and steps down, Kaz doing the same. She starts down Junction Avenue, Kaz trying to stay a few feet back. He sees her tense up.

"I'm not following you," he calls softly.

"No?"

She has turned to stare at him, intense, more ready to fight, he thinks, than to run.

"Look, let me walk ahead, and you can go anywhere you want to."

"Okay—"

He hurries a bit, trying to look casual, happy that nobody else got off and there's nobody hanging on the street corners looking nosy. Mickey Donlan was fired a month ago, just a "You know why" when they handed him his last pay envelope. With the GM plants allowing the UAW in, it has gotten even more tense at the Rouge, workers afraid to chat as they come over the walkway from the parking lot and transit stop to the gates, afraid even to talk together on the streetcars for fear a company spy will report them. 'Ford stomach' is no joke, and Kaz's jaws are sore from grinding his teeth at night.

It's full a block before Kaz realizes she's turned to look at something. It is a billboard the union people have put up, the third one he's seen-

Fordism is Fascism!
Unionism is Americanism!

He noticed it out of the corner of his eye, but so many years working under the glare of the Service Department has trained him not to focus on anything 'suspicious.' The girl has a little smile on her face as she looks it over, hands on her hips. Kaz keeps walking. They're feeling their oats, the union people, had a big rally in front of City Hall, waving a huge American flag and singing *The Star-Spangled Banner*, shops having nothing to do with the auto industry pulling walk-outs and then asking to join the UAW.

But everybody knows these are just prelims, that the real fight, if they can ever get Ford into the ring, is yet to happen.

Kaz stops by the Dom Polski, the west side center just as nice as the east but in money trouble now, and therefore happy to rent office space to anybody who can scare up a few bucks. The girl is slowing to look the building over. He reads the saying chiseled on the cornerstone-

"'*Jedność i zgoda to siła nasza*.' You know what that means?"

"No, I—" She's a bit flustered, maybe embarrassed for thinking he's a moll-buzzer and just looking for action—

"'Unity and Harmony Are Our Strength.'"

"That's nice—"

"Or less poetic—'Either us Polacks hang together, or we hang separately.'"

She laughs. Terrific laugh.

"We're German—German-*Jew*ish," she says. "But my father wouldn't let us learn anything but English."

"You don't work for Harry Bennett, do you?"

Another laugh. There were Jewish girls in school when he was a kid, but back then there were lines you didn't cross.

Still are.

"You going in?"

She looks again at the building, a big pile of light-colored brick with fancy columns and another saying etched over the doorway.

"I think so."

"The office spaces are in the back. We'd better get off the street."

• • •

It isn't a very big room, but there's only two dozen of them standing and sitting around. Rosa recognizes Bill McKie, who comes straight at her.

"Schimmel?"

"That's right." She is thrilled that he knows her name, McKie a Scots mechanic and open CP member who has managed to convince a surprising number of Rouge laborers that union is a possibility, even at Ford.

"Any ideas ye hope to put forward are welcome," he says, "but keep the Party oot of it."

"We're not *spy*ing are we?"

McKie grins. "We're meant to be in the vanguard of the fight fer justice. Right noo, that's in the auto shops."

It has been an amazing turnaround since Lewis led the break from the CIO, backing the strikes in Flint and here on the west side. Militant actions—a sit-in and surviving a police siege at Fisher Number Two in Flint, creating a diversion to occupy Chevy Engine Number Four, getting an agreement at Kelsey-Hayes and other local suppliers beneath Ford's long shadow. Ira says it's only because Roosevelt and Governor Murphy have refused to call out troops to support the companies, but workers have been joining Local 174 in droves.

"Mrs. Gelles asked me to represent the Ladies Auxiliary. She's back in Flint."

McKie nods. "Glad you're here, young lady. We'll need ye."

Most of the women in the Auxiliary and the Emergency Brigade are wives or sisters of men who work for or were fired from the plants, but any volunteers, if vouched for by the right people, are welcomed. Rosa knew several of the members from the Hunger March, and her ability to type and willingness to knock on doors has been useful-

Victor Reuther walks into the room.

He and his brothers were in the thick of it in Flint, Victor driving a sound truck that circled the plant when the police attacked with tear gas, talking over a loud speaker to keep up the morale of the occupiers and to warn them of enemy movements, until he was charged with inciting a riot and had to leave the state, his brother Roy taking over only to be dragged out of the car by goons and beaten.

So many fights. So many, for a change, *vic*tories, and Rosa has missed them all.

If you don't count Papa's occasional relief money, Rosa is the only breadwinner in the house now, up at the delicatessen counter dealing with people all day long, while Lenny who keeps the trays filled in the back hums along with the radio all day, his interaction limited to nodding when she calls for more brisket. There has been so little time for politics—

"Okay, people, I thank you for coming today," says Victor Reuther. He looks more like a young college professor than an auto worker, though he was in the same machine shop with his brother Walter when they went to investigate the Soviet system. Rosa listened to them speak about it when they came back—glowing words for the spirit of the proletariat, embarrassed disdain for the inefficiency and mismanagement within the factory.

"I'll try to make this brief, and I advise you to not all leave at the same time, and to be discreet with what we talk about. Nobody knows I'm back in the Detroit, and it would be good to keep it that way."

Rosa notices the man from the streetcar standing in a corner with his arms folded, wondering if she's dealt with him before. Too old to be a YPSL, an out-of-towner if he's CP—maybe somebody in the Local she's never seen.

"As you're aware, we've made great inroads with the companies here in Detroit, in Flint, in Toledo, our membership is growing, and we have a good deal of public support. But we all know whose music we have to dance to in this city. Henry Ford has stated that he will never, *ev*er recognize the UAW or any other union, and he has assembled a small army of thugs at the Rouge River plant to back up that claim. This is not a situation where a small cadre of our people can take over a building and hold it till management agrees to negotiate. Ford owns the Dearborn police, he owns *Dear*born—we'll have no protection there."

"Ford will only go union," interjects Bill McKie, "when the workers, the vast majority of them, choose to shut it *doon*."

"Exactly. So how do we reach them? How do we win their hearts and minds? Bill here has been organizing, quietly, for years, and he's only gotten a relative handful of men and women, secretly, to commit. If we try to track people down in their homes—well, that could easily get them fired—"

"Men I know and respect see me on the street," says McKie, "see me and cross to the other side."

"There are a few places on the edges of the factory complex that are on public land," says Victor Reuther, "places that thousands of workers pass through every day, arriving for and leaving their shifts."

Rosa's stomach tightens. He's talking about the overpass, where they killed Joe York.

"We propose to sponsor a massive leafletting campaign, handing out—"

"Excuse me—" says the man from the streetcar, raising his hand.

"Brother Pilsudski," says Bill McKie.

"You know the place is like a fort."

"Yes—"

"There's no neighborhood, just railroads tracks and roads that belong to the Rouge—"

"We'd be on public land—"

"Surrounded by Harry Bennet's outfit."

"We intend to invite reporters, photographers, some clergymen, a few representatives from Senator LaFollette's committee, and we'll be asking our

Ladies Auxiliary to do the actual leafletting," says McKie, looking at Rosa.

"We'd be honored," says Rosa, and the men laugh. She has no right to volunteer for the group, but can't imagine Mrs. Gelles or any of the other members saying anything different.

"Fine," says the man from the streetcar. "But with the Service Department looking on, guys are just going to toss your paper on the ground."

"So be it," says Reuther. "But how is he going to feel when he does that? These women risking—I'm not denying that there will be a risk, even with all the witnesses we'll have—and them such cowards they won't even glance at a flyer they're handed? How would you feel?"

"Worried I might lose my job."

"Is that a new feeling?"

The streetcar man, Pilsudski, holds his hands out in defeat. "You got me there."

"I think we can get a permit to leaflet in Dearborn," says Reuther, "if we bring the press in on it early, make Bennett look like a coward if he pulls strings to block us. We hit gates Four and Five right at the shift change when we'll reach the most employees, and we'll paper the streetcars coming in and out with the literature, tack it up on the streetlights and telephone poles they have to walk by, let them know we're *here*, and we're just waiting to support them when they do what they've always wanted to."

"And you're putting the women right up front," says Pilsudski, still mulling the idea over.

"We'd use orphans," grins Bill McKie, "but it's scheduled for a school day."

• • •

The call is from Dearborn City Hall, somebody he doesn't think he's met on Mayor Carey's staff. Harry is taking target practice with his pistol, putting more holes in the map of fucking Brazil, a situation he could clear up in less than five minutes if the Chief would let him.

"They want a permit to hand out leaflets?"

You give these people an inch, he knows, and they'll take a mile, but the idiots in the White House and the Governor's mansion have let things get out of hand-

"Why would the press be interested in that?"

They shut the whole city of Detroit down for half a day, Walter Reuther on a flatbed truck under the Stars and Stripes, making noises like he's the working man's savior. Giving people ideas they don't have the brainpower to handle-

"If they ask, say this is America, and the Ford Motor Company believes in free speech. What is it for a permit now, five bucks? Tell them I offer to pay it."

What his people have found out is that the rabble-rousers intend to get near the gates, buttonhole workers coming and going, hand them their propaganda. What they pulled in Flint and at the Chevy plant—occupying a building with a handful of radicals and whipping up a frenzy among the rest of the workers—has no chance here. Too big, too much security, the colored won't go for it, and here they're dealing with Harry Herbert Bennett. It's one thing for the union to step into the ring when the Feds and that fucking Governor Murphy have their opponent's arms tied behind his back, but here—you play with fire, you get *burnt*.

"No, no, I appreciate the call," says Harry to the Dearborn mayor's flunky. "You've got to grant the permit, it's only fair, but gee, I don't know what our men will do about it. I got thousands of people to keep track of over here, and some of them—you know—might take of*fense*. Say hi to the mayor for me."

Harry hangs up and blam! hits the red X drawn over the new plantation site dead center.

"Mildred," he says to his secretary, pushing the button, "get Sam over here."

Walter Reuther actually worked here for a couple years, good tool-and-die man, never made any trouble, no sign that he was a Red. Then he quits and goes off to hobnob with the commissars in Russia, he and one of the little brothers actually teaching the commies how to use Ford equipment they bought by the carload hoping to drag their sorry-ass country into the twentieth century, making dies to stamp out cars that nobody in the factory could afford to own. The brothers come back with a mission—Harry is sure of it—to spread chaos throughout American industry.

Harry stands, does some deep knee bends. It's a relief, in a way, to know they're through dinking around and want to start the main event. Such a pain stomping out all the little brush fires—at one point he had a squad ready to stroll past the police lines, bust into Kelsey-Hayes, kick the shit out of the occupiers and bring back whatever equipment was needed to make the damn brake shoes here at the Rouge. He finally got on the phone and told the weak sisters over there to settle on the wages, but if they agreed to recognize the union Ford would never buy another part from them.

And the UAW claimed that as a victory.

Mildred buzzes and says Sam is there, should she send him in.

Sam Taylor is as thick in the head as he is in the body, but loyal, and afraid of nobody as long as he's got a dozen or more pals to back him up.

"We're going to have visitors, Sam."

Sam is a roving foreman within the Service Department, and head of the Dearborn Knights, a 'fraternal and protective association' that Harry set up. He never takes his hat off.

"Who's coming?"

"Bunch of agitators from the UAW, fronting like they're a civic organization."

"Trying to get inside?"

"Inside the heads of our people, yes. Passing out lies, causing discontent—"

Sam frowns. "They can't do that."

"That's the spirit. Would you let somebody come and shit on your front lawn?"

Confusion. "We don't have a lawn."

Harry smiles. "How about your doorstep?"

"Hell no."

"What it is, they'll come with some do-gooder types, and they'll come with shutterbugs from the papers. Kid gloves with the do-gooders. And the camera boys—well, bring some of your widest Service men, have them park themselves in front of the lenses—"

"I get it—"

"There are certain gentlemen I'm sure will be in attendance, who don't want to miss an opportunity to look like heroes. Let them get a *taste*, a good one, and then we'll see if they come back for more."

"How do we tell them from the do-gooders?"

"I've got plenty of photographs for you and the boys to study—these characters aren't camera-shy. But they've had it pretty easy up to now, a night or two in jail, a whiff of tear gas. We need them to understand just who they've decided to fuck with."

"The Chief is on board with this?"

There's this idea, maybe even promoted by the Chief himself, that Harry is running his own game here at the Rouge. What did the magazine call it? His *Gestapo*. It's usually an advantage, a little bit of fear being a powerful motivator, but at times it slows the process.

"I told the Chief what the story is, the whole situation. All he said to me was "Harry—*deal* with it."

• • •

The wags at the paper handed Smitty a silver football helmet—must be from the Lions team George Richards at WJR has brought into town—when they heard he was being sent out to the overpass again. No joke.

He's down on Miller Road razzing with the usual bunch—writers on the labor beat, the camera boys with their Speed Graphics bragging about shots they've made—when the union contingent pulls up in a car. The oldest of the Reuther brothers, Walter, then Frankensteen, who's the organizational director, J. J. Kennedy and Bob Kanter. Word is they've invited some of the local Holy Joes, all faiths included, and some good-government types to witness this exercise in free speech. They'd be better off, thinks Smitty, behind the Beef Trust of the U Michigan gridiron eleven, in full gear.

Reuther is a real live wire, a red-headed ball of energy, dressed today with vest and watchchain like a prosperous banker as he comes out of the automobile grinning and glad-handing the scribes, thanking them for coming out to see democracy in action.

"What do you expect, Walter?"

Smitty got to interview him a couple times during the Kelsey-Hayes siege, and knows the regular guy routine only goes so far—every word he says is part of the gambit.

"What I expect to happen, what I *hope* will happen, is our Ladies Auxiliary will arrive in a few minutes and station themselves down here to pass out flyers to the Ford workers as they enter and leave the plant."

"So I should have gone to cover the bingo at Saint Mary's."

Reuther grins. "This is one occasion, Smitty, where I hope to disappoint you boys."

"I take a gander at the reading material?"

The union leader pulls a handbill from his pocket, forks it over. "I passed packets of these out to our women just an hour ago. There'll be a couple streetcars full of them coming."

It is a single sheet, just a pitch to join the UAW, citing some of their recent successes. Unlike the Bolshie firebrands of Smitty's youth, Reuther tries to keep it from getting personal, hoping to "sit down with the Fords and work things out."

> **FORD WORKERS**
> **UNIONISM NOT FORDISM**
> **Now is the time to Organize!**
> **The Wagner Bill is behind yourselves!**
> **Now get behind yourselves!**

The *Free Press* camera jockey, Snaps Wiley, comes over then, squinting at the sky.

"Where are you gentlemen going to be during all of this?"

Reuther points up to the footbridge over Miller Road, connecting the parking lot and streetcar platform to Gate Four. "We'll be up there."

"That's in your permit?"

"Ford built it, but it's leased to the railroad—public property."

"There's a terrific shot up there where you all could be standing on the footbridge with the Ford Motor Company sign on the building right behind you—"

Reuther grins. "Let's do it while we've got the time." He calls to his companions. "Hey fellas—they want a few photos up on the bridge!"

Smitty troops up with them, Reuther dropping quotables as he climbs. "The time has clearly come for the Ford Motor Company to get in line with the rest of the auto industry. The right to unionize is protected by federal law now, and our union is inviting the thousands of workers in this plant to join us in shaping the future."

"You just used 'Ford' and 'get in line' in the same sentence," says Smitty. "My editor would call that a *non sequitur*."

"America was under a *king* once," says Reuther. "That changed too."

The Local 174 officials are all smiles as the photographers click away, lots of "over here, over here" trying to get them all to look in the same lens at the same time, Smitty scribbling on his pad earning his thirty simoleons a week and thus unaware as both sides of the footbridge suddenly fill with Harry Bennett's strongarm boys, led by Sam Taylor, strolling forward with mayhem on their minds.

"This is private property! You get out of here!" shouts Taylor.

"We have a permit," says Reuther, reaching into his jacket, but they are all over him, slugging and kicking and cursing while their fellow apes move to block the photographers, Snaps Wiley collared and having to surrender the plates he's exposed as Smitty is shouldered up against the safety fence by a couple bruisers.

"I got a press card!" he calls out, hoping not to be mistaken for a UAW minion.

"Shove it up your ass!" suggests the nearest Service Department stooge.

They have Reuther down, dragging him by the legs toward the west stairway, while Frankensteen, a hefty piece of work who played tackle for the University of Dayton, struggles to fight back till one of the mugs yanks his jacket over his head to pin his arms, his pals slamming the man with kidney busters till he goes down.

"That's enough, that's enough! Pick him up," shouts Taylor, but once they've hoisted Frankensteen up on wobbly legs, Taylor pastes him on the button and he goes down again.

"Off the bridge! Everybody off the fucking bridge!" comes the word and Smitty is swept before a flying wedge of Service Department men to the stairs, where their colleagues are ungently tossing Reuther, thump, thump, thump, down the concrete steps. Smitty has seen one man, maybe Kantor, flipped over the fence, a drop of some thirty feet, and grabs tight to the rail on his way down, Frankensteen soon kicked and prodded past him, the man's bulk providing a bit of padding as he holds his elbows up by his ears to protect his bloodied skull. Taylor has his goons prop the man up again when they're on the road, and they lay into him once more, shoving, yanking, knocking him down and grabbing his legs to pull them apart and kick him in the balls, Taylor standing on Frankensteen's stomach and grinding his heels in-

"Beat it, snoop, or you'll get the same!" shouts a torpedo in a yellow fedora, giving Smitty a push, and he backs toward the parking lot, seeing one colored man among the attackers, pushing newsmen away but with a terrified look on his face, as if worried that the rope and the tree are only a step away. A streetcar pulls into the stop then and there's another bullrush of Servicemen to push the passengers, mostly Auxiliary Brigade women with sheafs of handbills in their mitts, back into the cars.

Fordocracy in action-

-as Rosa ducks under the arm of the first thug and squirms past another pair, more afraid of being trapped in the streetcar with them than whatever might be happening on Miller Road. She runs away from the footbridge, seeing other women doing the same, seeing two Dearborn mounted police

sitting placidly on their mounts watching the show, and there are screams and shouts, but, so far, no gunshots.

There are islands of grass in the middle of Miller Road and Rosa plants herself on one of these, keeping an eye on the battles at the bottom of the footbridge and on the streetcar platform. Cars are coming in both directions, windows rolled down on this warm spring day—I volunteered to hand out flyers, she thinks, and they'll have to arrest me or kill me to-

"You okay, honey?"

Incoming, a couple men in a battered Model A.

"Don't stand alone, join the union!" she says as she drops a couple handbills into the driver's lap.

"Jeez, you want to get us fired?"

"Throw one out the window when you pass the goons and stick the other in the glove box," she tells them. "You can read it later."

The man in the passenger seat laughs. "Gutsy broad," he says as they speed away.

There is nothing *broad* about me, thinks Rosa, but I'll take it as a compliment. The fighting and shouting seem to have moved over to the parking lot now. A trio of her fellow volunteers hurry up, breathing hard.

"They went after Mr. Reuther and the others," says the first of these. "It looked really bad."

Rosa points south on the road. "Spread yourselves down that way," she says. "Stay on the islands and they can't touch you."

"They can't touch us *le*gally."

She shrugs. "We're here to challenge the Company. Let's do it."

It took the Supreme Court to clinch the Wagner Act as law, and though most employers still ignore the fact, it's on the books. Electoral politics in this country might be a sham, but you can't hesitate to use their rules if they're in your favor. Another car stops, this one leaving the fray behind. The driver leans out of his window-

"If you want to jump in, sister, I can get you out of here."

She tries to give him a handbill, which he pushes away, looking back toward the bridge. "You see what they're doing to your friends—"

"They're *your* friends too, if you work at the Rouge. Those hoods would do the same to you, and for no good reason."

"Tell me about it—" he calls as he pulls away-

"UAW!" she calls after him as the shift buzzer sounds-

-and Kaz sees blood on the pavement as he crosses the footbridge. Ace Spangler catches up with him.

"The Service Department unloaded on some union people," says Spangler, whom everybody agrees is a Company snitch. "Gonna be a mess on those streetcars."

"I guess—"

"I can give you a lift if you want."

Turning it down might get him reported. "Uh, sure. Thanks."

More blood on the stairs to the parking lot, and a lot of shouting over there.

"Think they can come in here and cram their union down people's throats," says Ace. "Oughta see a bug doctor—"

"It does seem pretty crazy," says Kaz. "I mean after what happened with that march—"

"Maybe this time they'll learn their lesson."

Ace's car, last year's 48 Series with the grille Kaz thinks looks awful, is easy to get to. Ace helps put rear seats in all day and is a real gum beater, always a suspicious activity at the Rouge where humming on the line can bring the foreman down on you.

"Once they get their claws in," Ace says, pulling the car out onto Miller Road, "the front men will fade and the real people behind it will crawl out from where they been hiding. We'll be taking orders from *Mos*cow."

There is a girl standing on an island in the middle of the road, waving handbills at cars rolling by in both directions.

"Look at her! They say these Red babes got no compunctions—they'll give it up for free."

It is the Jewish girl Kaz met on the streetcar.

"Keep driving," Kaz says, rolling up his window.

• • •

Smitty has done his good deed for the day, helping to hustle Reuther and Frankensteen, what was left of them after the working over, into Snaps Wiley's bucket-of-bolts Dodge, the big man checking for loose teeth while Reuther muttered the address of a union-friendly doctor.

No Henry Ford Hospital for those two.

Smitty sees a trio of Service Department men huddled around the car Scotty Kilpatrick, the *Detroit News* lenser, drove up in. They stomp away looking proud of themselves and Smitty legs it over before Kilpatrick can make tracks.

"Got room for a fellow crusader?"

Scotty nods him in.

"Some clambake, huh? You get hit?"

"Nope."

They pull onto Miller, head west. There's a young woman in a beret, cute trick, peddling the UAW sheets from an island in the middle of the road. Smitty waves the flyer Reuther gave him at her.

"They grab your camera?"

"Left thumbprints on the lens, but I kept hold of it. Do gorillas have thumbs?"

"But they got your plates, huh."

Scotty smiles. "They got the *blank* ones yeah, I kept them out on the seat where they could see them."

"But the shots you took—?"

"Under your feet."

Smitty bends and lifts a corner of the floormat. A half-dozen plates. He whistles.

"Good stuff?"

"Four or five beauties—got em while they were rolling up for the scrimmage, got em while they were whaling away on the big guy—"

"Frankensteen. So you think you got some clear shots, faces that can be identified—?"

"If they gave a Pulitzer for photography I'd be a shoo-in."

"Ooh, baby! Let's see Harry get out of this one."

Smitty has a twinge, just a little one, knowing it will be a better story if one of the union men dies, or is at least paralyzed—

"Where can I drop you?"

"If you're headed for the dark room, I'd love to tag along."

• • •

Harry has Sam on the carpet, the big man sweating, hair wet when he finally pulls his hat off. He says nothing to the man till Mildred steps in and hands him the statement he just dictated. He glances at it-

"We done what you said to, Harry—" Sam starts, but Harry puts up a hand to silence him. He looks to Mildred.

"Who have we got?"

"Smith from the *Free Press*, then the *Times* and the *News* and the colored paper, I forget the name—"

"Put me on with Smitty."

She exits. Sam has his hat in his hands, nervously twisting the brim. "You told me to step easy with the newsies," he says.

A buzz, and Harry picks up the phone.

"Smitty," he says, "this is all you're going to get, and I'm sending a printed copy over to your sheet to make sure there's no misquotes." He reads from the statement—*"The affair at the Miller Road footbridge was deliberately provoked by union officials. They feel, with or without justification, that the La Follette Civil Liberties Committee sympathizes with their aims and they want to trump up a charge of Ford brutality to take down to Washington and flaunt before the Senatorial committee."*

Harry notices that Sam's knuckles are swollen on both hands.

"I know beyond a doubt that no Ford Service men or plant police were involved in any way with the fight. As a matter of fact, the Service men were issued instructions that the union men could come and distribute their pamphlets at the gates as long as they didn't interfere with the employees at work. The union men were beaten by regular Ford employees who were on their way to work on the afternoon shift."

The Hearst paper is likely to buy this, making no bones in their editorials of their distaste for the UAW. As for the others, the trick is to ignore any outrage and remember that the public has the attentive capacity of a hummingbird, easily distracted by the next hot headline—

"The union men called them scabs and cursed and taunted them. A Negro—that's a capital 'N'—who works in the foundry was goaded and cursed so viciously by one union organizer that he turned and struck him. That was the first blow, and then the union men milled around for a few minutes, punching at each other, before they withdrew. I would be glad to testify before any official investigating committee and I will have no trouble convincing them that the union cold-bloodedly framed and planned today's disturbance."

Sam looks puzzled, as if trying to recall the dust-up as Harry just described it.

"What's that you news boys say on the phone when the copy is finished? *Thirty.*"

He hangs up, looks to Sam.

"You didn't let them get any fucking *pic*tures, did you?"

• • •

They stand looking at the powerhouse, Johnston and Jim Rogan and Gomes, with a few of the cutters and a half-dozen of the security men behind them.

"How many do you think went in?"

Gomes asks João, who says it was nearly all the unmarried men, the new ones.

"Sixty of them, maybe seventy," Gomes tells his *patrãos*. "The ones who come late, without women."

"Do you know what they want?"

"I believe it is only more money for their work. Because of the rumors."

Surrounded by trees, it makes sense to keep burning them to fuel the steam turbine in the powerhouse, and the woodcutters have taken over that building and say they won't leave until they are satisfied.

"There are always so many rumors," says Jim. "What's this one?"

Gomes seems reluctant to tell. "A saying of Mr. Ford was printed in the newspaper. He said that this plantation was not here to grow rubber, but a model of how people should live."

"So?"

"They believe only a man ready to quit would say such a thing, and wish to make more money before their jobs are gone."

They've never been able to keep as many laborers as they need here at Belterra, some men disliking the work or the nature of the community, some leaving the moment they have a certain amount in their pockets, some laid up with malaria, typhoid, worms, syphilis-

Johnston nods toward João-

"Ask him how prepared they are for a siege."

What did they bring in? Gomes asks João.

They brought their tools—axes and saws, he answers.

No food and water?

They don't plan to be inside for long. White people cannot live without electricity.

This is relayed to Johnston, who scowls. "It's the damn *Estado Novo*," he says. "Putting ideas in people's heads."

The Vargas government have enacted their own version of Roosevelt's New Deal, which at least on paper gives the working classes many new rights and possibilities. Here on the Tapajós, however, it remains more of a rumor, São Paulo as distant an idea to these people as Dearborn, Michigan.

"We'll keep the place surrounded around the clock. Nobody comes out, nothing comes in." Johnston turns to Jim. "How many generators do we have?"

"Seven including the backup at the mill."

"Gas them all up and put them where they're needed most." He points to Gomes-

"And you," he says, "are to inform the gentlemen inside that we can survive a lot longer without electricity than they can survive without food or water. When they're willing to come out, empty-handed, I'll be willing to discuss whether they have a future here."

João, watching *o chefão* walk away, is very glad that he refused to join the men inside. He has a house here now, and a family to think of, and the idea that you could sit inside one of Mr. Ford's buildings and demand more money for your work has never occurred to him. *Senhor* Rogan has made João something like a *capataz* of a dozen wood cutters, and although he is not paid more than they are, it is an honor. The furnace in the powerhouse must always be fed, and maybe a few days of it lying idle will allow them to get ahead of its appetite.

But who now will do the cutting?

• • •

Afterward, Zeke can't remember what came before the spill. He knows all the movements, does them in his sleep most nights, knows what they should have been. They've got him sand-casting engine blocks now, the molds advancing on a knee-high conveyor, stop-and-start, so you have to stay in rhythm. The big crucible with the hot stuff is hung by chains from an overhead sliding rail, and you don't want to be moving sideways while you pour. They measure the load so you can fill a half-dozen molds with it, the metal staying between 2500 and 2300 degrees, which as Flournoy says is "ten times hotter than hell." The top has been skimmed before you get it, so you just line the lip up with the mold, then use the handwheel on the side to tilt the crucible till it pours. There are four on his section of the line, poured till empty then pushed on down to be relined and refilled while your next load is rolled up.

Maybe it's the heat.

Zeke has had a hard time concentrating lately, feeling weary, and it's like he suddenly wakes up in the middle of an action not knowing how long he's been missing—one thing if you're brushing your teeth at night, another if you're pouring molten steel with other men around you. It was the first pour from a crucible he'd just received, he knows that, not so much of a tilt before it starts to come out, steady, steady, give gravity time to do its work, let the hot stuff sink into all the nooks and crannies in the mold, it's a *feel*ing as much as watching the top, and Zeke doesn't know if his mind went soft again or he just didn't read the pour right—sometimes there's flames you got to look through—but it ran over bad and he spun the handwheel too fast maybe and there was more of a splashback than a spill just when Otis Gamble was hurrying back from the one trip to take a whiz he does every afternoon and it burnt through the damn boots they wear for protection like they were made of paper. DeLuca, the foreman, somehow got Otis carried out and the floor cleaned up without having to stop the conveyor.

"Pour it while it's hot," he said to Zeke. "I'll take care of Otis."

Maybe ten minutes later he came by again. "He's on his way over to Henry Ford. We left the boot on for them to deal with. Is the equipment okay?"

"Seems to be."

"Then keep at it."

Zeke didn't go home when the shift ended, taking the streetcar straight to the hospital, and has been sitting in a waiting room trying not to fall asleep for nearly an hour now. A white man with some gray in his hair comes to sit across from him, noticing the Ford identification badge pinned to his shirt.

"I used to wear one of those." He talks loud, like there's traffic noise in the room.

"You and a lot of other folks."

"You in the foundry?"

"Yep."

"I was over there for three years. Shake-out. Sucking down all that crap that goes in the air when you knock the molds apart."

"I'm a pourer."

"Finally I slipped the straw boss a little something, maybe he shared it with somebody in Employment, and they moved me over to stamp out fenders."

"How was that?"

"Wham, wham, wham all day long—my hearing's totally shot."

"Work is work. You on the line now?"

"Naw, they sent me a valentine when they switched over to the Model A. 'Services no longer required.' What they done is farm out all that body work to Briggs."

"You try there?"

"Wouldn't take me—or the other thousand stiffs lined up with me outside. So I been sitting back on Easy Street, collecting relief, while my wife scrapes gum off the floor of a couple movie houses, gets paid under the table. But I'm hoping to get a night watchman job here. Don't do enough in the day to sleep, so I figure give me a uniform, I can haunt this place."

A woman comes in then, looks around till she sees Zeke, the only dark face in the room.

"You're here for Otis Gamble."

"Yeah—"

"You can see him now. Come with me."

He follows the woman down a hallway and up some stairs. Mavis will be done with her shift now—she always says just picture her in the basement standing on a pile of wet sheets.

"He okay?" Zeke asks the woman.

"Okay enough to talk to you."

In a room with five other beds, four of them occupied, Otis lays back with his foot wrapped in bandages and held up by a sling. Zeke grabs a chair and sits at the head of his bed.

"How you doing, brother?"

Otis turns his head, holds up three fingers. The pupils of his eyes are huge, like you could fall into them.

"Lost some toes."

"Damn."

"There's worst things it could of burnt off."

Zeke forces a smile. "Did you see what happened?"

Otis shakes his head. "I *felt* it though. Put me in a world of pain, Zeke. That ride over here, I hurt enough for two lifetimes."

"How's it now?"

Otis smiles with his whole face. "Now, they got me *flying*. I see what them dopey boys all about. If you could stay this way all day—" He trails off.

"I'm damn sorry, man."

"Oh, it weren't you, Zeke. They shouldn't ought to make us speed up like they do to that assembly line."

"I wasn't rushing it, I just—you ever be up there and you forget whether it's morning or afternoon?"

"Hell, yeah. I forget my *name*."

Otis works hard like everybody in the foundry, no slackers there except for the Service Department heavies who drift through giving you the fisheye, but O has always got a hustle on the side. He's confessed to Zeke that his job insurance is owning a Ford car he bought on time from the Old Man's cousin, got a dealership on West Fort Street.

"They aint gonna fire anybody still owes a bundle on that automobile. That or I run up a big bill at his hospital. You just need to stretch those payments *out*."

"Wife been by yet?"

"Naw—she's got the little ones to mind. Maybe her sister come by to deal with them, she'll take the streetcar."

"They get you here quick enough?"

"Hell, yeah. The Rouge got a couple ambulances at the ready, don't a day go by without they haul somebody over here they can't deal with upstairs in B Building."

"You'll be back on your feet in no time."

"Sure. Maybe they put me on one of those jobs they give the cripples and the blind folks. Sit at a table and sort the nuts from the bolts." Otis laughs. "Hey—they didn't shut the conveyor down, did they?"

"Man, who you think you are," says Zeke, "Henry Ford?"

• • •

It is a warm night and Zeke takes a long walk down to the river. If Otis can stand up without those toes he'll be back pouring hot metal soon enough. Zeke remembers when he first scored the job at Ford, how it felt like all his troubles were over. "You made for *life*, buddy," said a man on the streetcar, looking at the badge, on his very first ride to the old foundry. Life seemed to be getting bigger, especially next to what he could see ahead if he stayed down south, where colored men who worked shares were always slipping backward, backward. Zeke finds a piling without tar on the top and sits on it, watching boats pass by on the river.

There isn't nearly as much traffic back and forth with Windsor as there was during the dry law. It was a good show while it lasted, cops and robbers on the water, and nobody he knew ever rooted for the cops. Off to the left of the disused pier he's on is where there was a good-sized Hooverville, shacks made out of old packing crates, always a fire or two going in the winter. At some point they moved everybody out, and you can bet it wasn't to go live in any government housing. So there's lots of people still worse off.

But tomorrow he's going to have to get up and walk into Hell again, and the day after, and the day after, and feel lucky they're almost back to five days a week. How many more years, if it doesn't kill him first? He thinks about those boys about to put up the bridge over to Canada—be up high over the water every day, breathe in the open air, and when you walk away it's *there*, it's *done*, and it won't be junk in ten, twelve years. Zeke has seen the old Fords torn apart for metal, thrown back into the smelter to get turned into new ones—like a snake eating its own tail.

A snake that will swallow him whole.

Zeke sits and thinks for a long time, the sun going down late in July, and it's dark by the time he starts to walk home again, not feeling like a streetcar ride, skirting around the neighborhoods where he knows he isn't welcome, and by the time he gets to Vernor Highway he can tell something is up. There are shouts coming out of the bars, shouts coming out from the open windows of the falling-down apartment houses, and he's nearly home, hoping Mavis isn't too worried, when a bunch of young bloods bust out of the Brown Bomber's Chicken Shack whooping and laughing like Lincoln just freed the slaves.

"We done it! We done it!" shouts the one closest to Zeke.

"What we done?" he asks.

"Laid that mick out on the canvas! I bet he aint got up yet—Joe is the *champ*!"

The accident with Otis has made Zeke totally forget about the fight, forget he promised DeWitt and Alvin he'd take them somewhere with a radio and the right crowd to listen in-

"Knockout?"

"Eighth round."

"Joe went down once in the first," says another of the young men. "Must of tripped or something."

The street is filling up, black folks stepping out laughing and smiling and whacking each other on the back, somebody blowing a cavalry charge with a trumpet from a second-floor window.

"We'd done it! We got the belt!"

"And you think they'll let him *keep* it?" he says.

"Why not? He won it."

"He got whipped by that German."

Joe had been knocked out by the German, Schmeling, after a terrible performance, and it had been like all of Black Bottom took the beating. Zeke saw people weeping in the streets-

"Send that Heinie back over! Joe take care of him, too, less they fix it somehow."

"Colored man won the *belt*!" says the first young blood, dancing in the middle of the street, crowded enough now for a block party. "That changes *ev*erything!"

Zeke is a half block closer to home before the grins and the cheering all around begin to get to him. Joe Louis Barrow, who used to work out two blocks from where he lives, is heavyweight champion of the world.

Damn.

• • •

The rubber planter is a hard man, snarling orders and insults at his native workers, dismissive of his alcoholic white overseer, unhappy with the yield of the trees he's planted. When the supply boat chugs up the river and a very blonde young woman gets off, it's clear that she's a prostitute hiding out from the authorities in Saigon, and Norma wonders if Kerry should be watching this. But it's that Clark Gable and Jean Harlow and they're kidding each other a lot more than they're sweatily making love, and it's so close to Norma's own personal nightmare, her crazy fear of what was going on here when Jim was in Fordlandia and they were stuck back in Pine Camp, that she has to see how it ends. When the clueless young engineer arrives with his society wife it's clear there's going to be trouble, and only a prostitute would tolerate what Gable puts her through, sending the engineer off on a surveying mission so he can work on the wife, a lot of laughing from the audience in the folding chairs and benches during the scene where he shows her how they process the latex, and of course he ends up acting noble and Mary Astor is such a bad shot she only wounds him from four feet away and it ends with him and the prostitute kidding around, together again.

Jim is no Clark Gable. He buttons his shirt up clear to the neck, doesn't drink gin out of the bottle, and wouldn't ever try to seduce somebody else's wife.

He also can't dance, a characteristic he shares with most of the white men here, glaringly apparent when they clear the seats from the floor and start to put on records. Mr. Johnston says that at the dances hosted by Mr. Ford back in Detroit they only play old-timey songs, but a couple of the doctors who've arrived recently have volunteered their own collections, and so the social part of the evening begins with *Sweet Leilani*, a lot of swoony Hawaiian guitar and a man singing in a near-falsetto voice with a chorus under him, then Bing Crosby coming in to croon the song in a relaxed, lower register, almost as if he's there to explain it to white people. She wonders what they grow on plantations in Hawaii besides pineapples. She dances with Dr. Niles, who can actually stay in time, as that Billie Holiday whose voice is so intriguing and sad sings *I've Got My Love to Keep Me Warm*, thinking during it that if the Company hadn't sent Jim here they'd be in some other little sawmill town in the UP for what—the rest of their lives? The people back home who write to her are still just getting by, especially in Detroit which used to seem so exciting. And here—here even the workers' houses are nicer, certainly cleaner, than the leaky shack Gable has in *Red Dust*, and he owns the plantation. If you get shot here you don't have to give instructions to a prostitute to get the wound clean.

Then they play that song the little girl with the incredible voice sang in the movie they showed last year, singing while she's staring at a publicity photo of Gable the movie star, *you made me love you but I didn't want to do it*, and Norma drifts over to the side windows with the rattan louvers pulled up, mosquitos not so bad tonight, and sees a very young couple standing together talking, then the girl kissing the boy, very briefly, having to go up on her toes.

It isn't till the record ends and they move away from each other that she can see that the girl is Kerry.

"She's not a tomboy," Jim always says when Norma slips into one of her worrying jags, "She's just not a girly girl."

I suppose I should be relieved. They put on Tommy Dorsey's version of *Marie* then, and Jim taps her on the shoulder.

"Want to take a spin?"

In the movie they call the rubber workers "coolies" and they all wear those conical hats that are so big that you can't see faces, so they could be anybody. The workers here have been asking for more money lately, and some other things, and Mr. Johnston has had to fire a few of the ones he says are radicals. It isn't so much the money, says Jim, as being afraid of what the people in Dearborn will say if you give in to a union. After all, the Brazilians have been given housing and a hospital with free care and a nursery and a school for their children to go to-

"I'd like to know how they got all those trees to grow side by side," says Jim as they dance.

"Hollywood," says Norma. "They can make anything look like it works."

Jim's foxtrot is passable until they have to change direction, which requires Norma to do a lot of steering while moving backward, always backward, but they cover some ground on the floor, all their fellow Americans dressed in white and tan with a few colors here and there, occasionally hearing, over the sound of the generator powering the lights and record player, snatches of guitars and drumming from where the Brazilians live. Norma sees Gomes, who does most of the translating for Jim, is one of the few natives out on the floor, dressed tastefully but putting a lot more hip and rear end into his foxtrotting, as is the luscious creature pressed up tight to him. Who is—yes, who is definitely the mess cook they call Connie who Jim admitted was working as a prostitute when he found her among the Indians. If any of the Ford people are upset by this, they're hiding it well-

"At least we don't have tigers," says Jim suddenly.

Of course Gable has to shoot a tiger during the story, sitting in a tree next to the man whose wife he has stolen and using a rifle with a flashlight attached to the barrel. There are still jaguars in the jungle here, but in Belterra the white people live up on a plateau surrounded by acres and acres of cleared land, and only the insects and the birds that feed on them venture out from the edge of the jungle. Jim still worries about the planting, but Johnston tells him Mr. Ford now considers the whole place 'a social experiment', the community and its operations more important than how many tons of rubber are ever produced.

It's an expensive hobby.

The song ends and Busby, an orderly who came down here from a hospital in Grand Rapids, lays on *Song of India*, which starts out very mellow and then begins to swing. One dance is Jim's limit, so they stand holding hands and watch the others move to it. There are many days when Norma forgets why they are here, caught up in the small dramas of the nurses and doctors, and the more serious ones of the critical patients. She feels needed.

"We have to talk," she says.

She knows Jim always hates the sound of that, preferring that she just jump into whatever it is without any buildup.

"About what?"

"About Kerry and the maid's boy."

• • •

"They make a huge deal out of the stupidest things."

Kerry knows he doesn't understand English, but he does read her moods, so now he's come down to cuddle in her lap and be petted while she sits on the bench in the enclosure and complains about her parents. Jocko likes to be rubbed on the head, likes her to pull his tail through her hand.

"Like I'm going to run away with him or something. I mean, where are we going to *run*? Steal a boat and go up the river?"

Jocko has never bitten her, and if it wasn't for the pooping problem, she'd have him spend the night in her room.

"And then Daddy, saying how he might be a nice boy, but they're so emotional and they carry knives—"

She kissed Flavio, not the other way around, and he probably got yelled at or worse at home and hates her now.

"There aren't even any white boys my age here!"

There is one, Dr. Niles's son Spencer fourteen just like she is. But Spencer has those oozy spots on his face and only mumbles and calls the local kids Brazil nuts, or worse, nigger toes, and probably has stinky breath if you got up close. Even her mother wouldn't wish Spencer on her.

"When you're old enough," she tells Jocko, holding him up so they can look eye to eye, "I'm taking you out near where we found you, taking the leash off, and then we'll watch what happens when the whole troop comes down to eat fruit. I bet they'll be happy to see you."

When they take walks around the plantation he is half fascinated and half scared of the jungle, scurrying up trees as high as the long leash will allow, playing around, then running back to leap into her arms, terrified by something or at least pretending to be. He's not ready to go wild yet. Her hope is that when the day arrives he'll join up with a bunch that lives nearby and still come to visit her, the way she would with her parents if she got married.

"He probably just likes Miss Dove like all the boys do," she says. "So I'm just practice."

He seemed surprised the first time, maybe a little scared, but the other night he kissed her back. He really did.

"If they think I'm not even going to look at him or say hello, they're crazy."

It won't be Romeo and Juliet like in the play, she knows that much. There are no balconies in Belterra, first off, and a Brazilian boy, a *seringueiro*, can't go wandering around the white people's complex, not unless he's pushing a wheelbarrow full of gardening tools. And she knows the teachers will be told to snitch on them, so it will take some planning.

Jocko climbs up to hug her tight around the neck, which she loves.

"You and I will have to take some long walks," Kerry tells the monkey. "You never know who you'll run into."

• • •

"Flavio, meu filho," his mother said, I don't wish to lose my job, so please stay away from the *meninas brancas.*

Flavio tells himself that it's not like he went after her—she started it. But now that it did happen, it's something more to think about. Now, when he's lying in bed waiting for sleep to fall upon him, he has a choice of three to imagine stories about. Miss Dove, Betty Boop, and Kerry Rogan-

• • •

The sun isn't up yet when they get to the Castle. Winter ice on the pavement so Smitty has to be careful steering his rustbucket, a couple deer, nuzzling through the snow in hope of something to eat, lifting their heads to stare indignantly.

What are you doing on my road?

Which is pretty much the treatment they get from the Praetorian guards when they pull up and beg for an audience. Portia spent the night, a welcome and frequent occurrence lately, and has insisted on coming along, wasting her feminine charm on Harry's lunks till one finally acts on Smitty's repeated pleas to "Just let the boss know who it is."

When Harry walks out past the state police cars in the driveway he's already wearing the damn bowtie. The squirt doesn't have far to bend down to talk through the driver-side window.

"I didn't know buzzards got up this early."

"Harry, you had the county and city police radio-flashing every officer in the field, and who knows but what the Army, the Navy, and the Marines are in it too. I promise you, every paper including the *Dziennik Polski* will be out here within the hour."

Harry sighs, maybe a real one. He looks like he hasn't slept. "Ten minutes and you vanish." He points in at Portia. "You're a society scribbler—"

"She could talk to the ladies," Smitty offers. "I'm sure they're devastated by this."

Harry sniffs and jerks his head to follow him in. The driveway is dry as a bone, Harry's elves ever industrious, but the elaborate garden has taken the winter off, making the Castle seem more a menacing fortress than a charming anachronism. The lord of the manor starts his tale as he walks, not turning to look at them-

"Trudie and Billie—that's her older sister—leave home after breakfast yesterday, going down to the Normal College where Billie is getting her degree. I got Billie a car—beautiful Tudor Sedan—" he points to a shiny turquoise job with a V-shaped grille—"only the engine was frozen stiff at that hour, so they come in to call this boyfriend—I guess you could call him a boyfriend—of Trudie's, this kid Russ, and he comes over in his heap to give them a lift."

They enter the room with the giant fireplace, state troopers with coffee cups in their mitts eyeing them warily, as Bennett continues-

"Billie's got classes, and Trudie's got things to do in Ypsi which Russ is willing to drop her off for. So not long after noon somebody from the office at the school hands Billie a note from her sister. It's in her handwriting, saying she's got these sporting events—she's a hell of an athlete Trudie—and then an awards dinner she forgot about and will call us at home when it's over so I can send a driver in. Only she never called."

"We believe this note was written under duress," says Dan Leonard, a state police captain Smitty has crossed paths with a few times on stories. "We've found no evidence of an awards dinner in Ypsilanti last evening."

Harry points to the next room, looks to Portia. "My wife and daughter are in there," he says. "Tell them I said it was okay to talk."

With Portia out of earshot, Harry, red-eyed, lowers his voice and fixes Smitty with a look.

"Strictly off the record—I got connections with every serious gang in Detroit. The Purples are in the toilet, and none of the others would dare fuck with me, they got too much to lose. And the Reds in that joke of a union, they don't have the balls. My real fear is that this is some fucking amateur with big ideas got themselves in this far and now they're terrified. Scared people do crazy things, like what happened to the Cass boy—"

"I expect you have your own people on this," says Smitty.

"They're out there beating the bushes. And my pal John Bugas, who's the FBI head in Detroit, has his people waiting to jump in the minute there's a ransom note."

"Anything I can do to help?"

Smitty means it. Whatever else Harry is, you can tell he loves his kids.

"When you write how you talked to me here, call it 'Mr. Bennett's home,' not 'the Castle.' People, especially whoever this creep is, get the wrong idea."

Harry excuses himself then to greet the competition, Curtis from the *News* and Breen from the *Times* clearly pissed to see Smitty already on the story.

"Off the record," says Captain Leonard, "and I *mean* that, my money is on the commies. This Federal Screw situation is heating up, and even if Ford doesn't own that outfit—"

"Harry's man Gillespie is in the thick of it," says Smitty.

None of the parts suppliers can survive without Ford, so they march to Harry's orders. Federal Screw hires a lot of Polish women, who might not be expected to wave the red banner, but the hours are long and the pay is meager-

"Of course, sometimes with a girl it's a romantic angle," says Leonard. "Do *not* quote me on that."

"My pen is at your service, captain."

Harry jerks a thumb as he passes with the other reporters, indicating that the ten minutes are up. Smitty gets some earnest, no-stone-unturned comments from Leonard and collects Portia. Even though the sun has peeped over the horizon it's freezing in his car.

"So Mrs. B is a stepmother," she begins, breath fogging the windshield as Smitty drives.

"Bingo."

"What about the girls' real mother?"

"We are forbidden to refer to the first Mrs. B."

"Is there a restraining order?"

"No, just Harry calling the owners of every sheet in town—some of them his very good friends—and laying down the ground rules."

"They're afraid of him."

"Detroit, all of us, are passengers on a storm-tossed vessel. Write anything that might threaten the auto industry, especially Ford, and editors act like you're drilling holes in the hull—"

"They might be right." Portia shows him a slip of paper with an address in Ypsilanti written on it. "Here's where we're going."

"Your favorite hash house?"

"Russell Hughes, the alleged boyfriend."

"You think—?"

"The stepmother and sister are sure she's been abducted, but when I asked about Russell, their backs went up."

"Trudie is how old?"

"Seventeen. Russell plays with some dance bands here and in Ann Arbor. Drummer."

"Uh-oh."

"At any rate he's the last friendly person to see her."

Portia has him wait in the car, idling the engine to so it won't freeze up, and spends a few minutes talking at the door of the modest Hughes house. She returns shivering and excited.

"He willing to talk?"

"He's not there. Came back around ten o'clock yesterday, grabbed some things, and said he was going to stay overnight with a friend."

"Aha—"

"One of the things he grabbed was his drum set."

Smitty whistles. "They're all hopheads, you know—drummers."

"I know. Like all newshounds are lushes."

Smitty has eased back on the sauce since he started making time with Portia, which hasn't done his liver any harm. And the juniper juice has lost some of its charm since it's become legal-

"So what now, Sherlock?" he asks her.

"Well, having been an impetuous young girl myself, I'd give them an hour's drive, maybe two hours, before they just can't wait any longer. If I'm not totally wrong about this—"

"Worth following up on."

"Back to the *Press* then, and we get on the telephone to all the county registrars—the Trudie they described is going to want a license in hand before facing any hotel desk clerks."

Bennett is newsworthy enough for the story to be rammed into the early editions, a kidnapping, even without a ransom note yet, always a hot item on the street. While Portia dogs the county paper-pushers on the phone, Smitty pumps his police contacts, mostly desk donkeys he's done a favor or two for over the years. Things begin to percolate-

The Ypsi city police discover that Trudie withdrew fifty bucks from her account at about eleven that day.

A pump jockey at a gas station filled the tank of Hughes's jalopy while Trudie used the facilities around half past three. He saw a suitcase and some drums in the back seat.

None of the boy's local musician friends know of a dance gig—he would have bragged about it to them.

It's nearly quitting time for public employees when Portia gets a call-back from Bay County, a justice of the peace named Miles Baxter reporting that yes, he had a Gertrude Bennett who said she was nineteen and her father worked at Detroit Electric, hitch herself in sickness and in health, in fat times and lean, to one Russell Hughes in his Auburn parlor yesterday evening. As the JP obviously hasn't read the papers or listened to the radio today, Portia chooses not to inform him of the former Miss Bennett's background or sudden disappearance.

"Give me a half hour start and then give Captain Leonard a ring," says Smitty when she tells him. "I'll get to Harry before the riffraff show up."

"Got it."

Smitty checks the room to be sure none of his fellow wage slaves are looking before kissing her on the cheek.

"You're wasted on that tea-party beat."

"Tell the boss."

Once clear from the lights of Detroit, the drive to the Castle is even more perilous than it was in the morning, Smitty keeping it under thirty on the worst of the roads. Reporters with his track record are still at only thirty-five bucks a week, no overtime, but if the story is worth it you're never off the job. By now a good deal of the work is just maintaining contacts, slapping a little balm on bad feelings when something he's filed hits a sore spot, pumping up egos, standing some desk officer to a snort or listening to their tales of woe about the department even when none of it is printable. Something, on a small scale, like what Harry Bennett does with his day when he's not worried about abducted daughters.

Portia couldn't wait and called ahead, so there's no rigamarole with the gatekeepers.

Harry's bowtie is on crooked and he hasn't shaved today.

"I look like an asshole from this."

"You look like a concerned father," says Smitty, "and it'll blow over quick. Can you give me a reaction when you got the call?"

"All I got to say—and I mean it—is I hope the guy has a job and can support her," he snarls. "They're on their own now."

Smitty pats Mr. Ford's man on the arm. "It's terrific news, Harry, congratulations. Get some sleep."

• • •

`My father is Kaz.`

Sonia has waited till everybody is gone to really try it. Something special for her thirteenth birthday, her father said, and lifting the present you could tell it wasn't clothes—way too heavy. Then a plain box inside to keep the surprise going, and when that was opened-

A shiny new Underwood Champion typewriter.

Maybe not so new, but her father had spent time buffing it up and putting in a fresh ribbon. Sonia got teary then, and said "This is the *best*," which everybody in her family can understand, even the way she drags it out.

`My father is Kazimir, but everybody calls him Kaz.`

They are a little disappointed she hasn't used it more in front of them, mostly just practicing rolling sheets of paper in straight, waving away any of them who want to show her. She's seen it in the movies and in the secretaries' room at school when she used to have to wait there for her mother to walk her home. She can walk to school by herself now, not straight enough that nobody stares at her, but she gets there on time if she leaves early enough.

If Sonia holds her left wrist with her right hand to steady it, she can steer it over the proper key and then jab down with her index or pointer finger, sometimes one right after the other if the letters are close.

Such a beautiful, satisfying sound.

You have to be careful not to hit between keys or the shafts might stick together. Miss Aubuchon told her that the layout of the keys—qwertyuiop—was originally to slow typists down so there wouldn't keep being a jam, and that a linotype machine at the newspaper, with no shafts, has a much more sensible arrangement.

She'll never be fast, but she's getting steady.

`My mother is Molly.`

She asked and her mother said that isn't short for anything, she was just named Molly.

At first if Sonia made a mistake she'd pull the paper out, frustrated, but paper costs money and she's gone through half the pile they gave her already. She hates spelling anything wrong. Early on in school, when she should have been in fifth grade but they had her in Special Class with kids of all ages, they'd be stuck in the very back of the auditorium for the yearly spelling bee and Sonia could reel off every word, even the ones for the older classes. You just have to read a lot, which she does, all the time. Special Class was not represented in the competition, and knowing the answer is no use if you can't say it so the teachers understand.

'Liaison' has at extra 'l' in it.

`Liaison.`

It looks funny, even typed out, but so do a lot of other words in English. Sonia has read all the *Nancy Drew Mystery Stories* her mother gets from a friend and that Sasha handed down to her, and the newspaper on Sunday, which is the only day they get it, and pretty much anything in the school library when they let her go there during physical education. Miss Aubuchon has made almost all their tests the kind where you just circle a letter or fill in boxes, which Sonia can handle, but she's still out of luck if it's an essay or anything you have to write. Stan once joked that her handwriting looks like she drew it with her eyes closed, which is pretty true no matter how long she toils at it.

But that will change, now that she's got her Champion.

`My mother works at home and my father works at Ford.`

Capital letters are really tough still, twisting her hand and using her thumb to push the Shift key down seems to be the best option for some, while for others hitting the Caps Lock on and off is the only way. She tried just writing everything in capitals once but it looked like a Western Union telegram in a movie.

`My brother and sister are twins but not the kind that look alike.`

There are still some kids at school who make fun of the way she walks, the way she tries to talk when she bothers to try. They never do it if Stan is around, who will pound them, or Sasha, who will kick them in the shins with no warning. All of them in the family have learned to be really patient, not finishing sentences for her when she wants to be heard, looking at her and even having a conversation if they've got the time. Her father likes to sit with her after work and listen to the radio—whatever show she picks is fine with him—but of course she's too big to sit in his lap anymore.

I am Sonia and I have palsy.

She is getting faster, but even if she was like those secretaries and could make the typewriter rattle like a machine gun, it will never be as fast as people can talk, and they'll have to stand and watch over her shoulder unless they have one of those setups like the police in the movies do, where someone in Chicago types to look out for a killer with a scar over his right eye on the run and it spits out in station houses all over the country. Gangster stories are Sonia's favorite kind of picture, lots of shooting and tough dames with terrific slinky outfits to lounge around in. They're her favorite stories to read, too, now that she's discovered Stan's secret stash of magazines—*True Detective* and *Black Mask* and *G-Men* and even the sleazier ones where it's clear what the hoods and molls are up to when they're alone together. She used to always feel like the girl on the cover—hands bound behind her back, gag over her mouth, struggling desperately to be free—but someday soon, when her typing catches up with her mind, she'll be the one to write the stories, maybe even better ones.

The man in the trench coat looked like trouble.

Her <u>kind</u> of trouble-

• • •

If you aim straight at the headpin it's hard to go wrong.

Kaz doesn't bowl enough to be good at it, but if he sends his first ball hard and straight at the headpin it fades just enough to either make a strike or only leave one or two pins standing, and it's never the seven-ten split. It's the dinky stuff, hitting one pin over by the gutter to make a spare, that gets him.

Garden Recreation is crowded tonight, most all of the lanes busy, which is good to see after the ghost town days during the worst of the bank scare. Kaz worked as a pin setter here as a kid, scared of the flophouse rummies who shared the job, back when there were shops out front and a big poolroom setup on the second floor with a gallery for spectators at the high-stakes matches. The shops went when they widened Woodward Avenue in the mid-'20s, and the pocket billiards action has moved elsewhere. But this is still the place where working stiffs come to let off steam and swap stories, the guy who rents you your bowling shoes willing to polish the ones you come in wearing for a nickel. And with the pins crashing all night long, the people in the next lane can't hear what you're saying.

It's Kaz and Bud Novak against Sewermouth Donati and Fritz Friehoffer from the Rouge, both of them pretty fair keglers, with Bud filling out the score sheet. But the real game is to feel the two out about the you-know-what.

"You got a brother works at Kelsey-Hayes, right?" Kaz opens when he and Donati, hung with the moniker Sewermouth due to his colorful vocabulary, are sitting down together. "What's it like over there?"

"Compared to us, it's a fuckin paradise," says Donati. "They're organized, right, got the union in there, so if management tries to sneak a speedup by without a negotiation, things come to a standstill pretty fuckin quick. And then my brother Rick, he's on one of these UAW flying squads, so if one of the other plants goes out, sits in, whatever, he comes over before or after his shift to bulk up the picket line, put a scare into the fuckin scabs when they show up. Right now he's in the middle of the deal at Federal Screw."

Fritz makes a tough five-seven split.

"Atta boy, Fritzy!" Donati calls out.

"They get any *work* done over there at Kelsey?"

"Look, the whole business has slowed down again, everybody's talking rollbacks, so it's not like the outfit can get be*hind* on sending out parts. But you know management, whenever they can fuckin nickel-and-dime you, they'll do it."

Fritz comes back and Sewermouth gets up to roll. They're only using one lane like most of the bowlers here, money still tight and you pay by the game, not how long it takes you.

"You been practicing," Bud accuses Fritz as he passes. Fritz is a tool-and-die maker, Rouge royalty, who takes the train all the way down from Flint on Monday morning, shares a room at the Strathmore Hotel just across Woodward all week, takes the streetcar back and forth to the Rouge, and eats breakfast and dinner here at the Rec. He's in his living room.

"I get a few games in most nights," he says.

If there's ever a walkout at Ford the big question is whether the skilled workers will support it. They make more money, work at a human pace, and consider themselves craftsmen, like the AFL characters-

"Somebody told me," Kaz says to him, fishing, "that Reuther, the union guy, used to work in your department."

"Oh, yeah, Walter." Fritz sits and wipes his forehead with a handkerchief. He is a big man in his late fifties, and bowling makes him sweat. "He was there a couple years. Good head for the trade, taught a lot of the new fellas when they come in. Never made a peep about organizing, so maybe that idea come from going to Russia."

Bud throws a strike.

The Company mouthpieces and the newspapers have been making a lot of noise about the Reuther brothers' trip to Russia, working at a factory there, like it makes them dyed-in-the-wool Reds. But the actual Party members Kaz has talked to think the brothers are just FDR Democrats who put up a radical front, and will fade when the inevitable workers' revolt really gets going.

None of which is worth caring about while a man on the Ford line can't cut a fart without getting reported by the Service Department.

Donati makes the wood fly but somehow leaves the kingpin, which he curses in both English and Italian.

"So things are copacetic up there now?" Kaz asks the tool-and-die man.

'Up there' is how the assembly line guys refer to any of the skilled operations, no matter what building they're in. Fritz takes a long moment to consider this, the thunder of balls smashing pins filling the pause. "We have our problems," he says finally.

All the tip-toeing around the point you got to do makes Kaz *feel* like some kind of subversive, but there's no avoiding it. Guys are still getting let go just on suspicion, or because a foreman or Service asshole just doesn't like them and makes up a story.

Donati misses the kingpin, sitting smack in the middle of the lane.

"Fuckin son of a bitch goddam five pin, how can you fuckin miss *that*?!" he says as he stomps back, smacking his forehead with an open hand. "I ought to cut my fuckin fingers off."

"Tough to pull the trigger on that power drill without your fingers."

"One of these days, that foreman keeps riding me, Imonna drill a hole in his fuckin skull."

"They ever give you any grief about your brother," asks Bud as he pencils in the open frame, "him being out there with the pickets?"

"Oh, sure, they brung me in on the carpet. I told them sorry, the kid has a screw loose, but I'll try to give him a talking to. The usual bullshit you gotta throw at em."

Kaz works his fingers into the holes, gets his feet set. He looks at the little arrows on the lane near the foul line, not the pins. Stan is working here now, picking up some change. The player finishes his first ball, you set the pegs with the foot pedal so you don't knock down anything standing, clear out the deadwood, hit the other pedal to pull the pegs out, then yank the chain to raise the gate and step out of the way. If you're smart you got wax in your ears. Stan isn't working their lane, which is too bad, because the guys would give him a healthy tip.

Kaz's ball fades at the last second, hits solid between the headpin and the three, pins flying, but somehow the four is left wobbling, wobbling—and never falls.

Someday they'll invent a machine to spot the pins and all these kids and wine guzzlers will be out of a job. Someday the whole damn assembly line will be machines and we'll all be out on our asses—including the goons in the Service Department.

Molly worries every time Kaz leaves the house for organizing, kids growing out of their clothes, Sonia in and out of the doctor's office, but what's ahead for them if it doesn't change? I can tough it out like Pop did if that's what it takes, but the idea of young Stan being sentenced to the Rouge the way it is now—

He manages to nick the four pin just enough to bring it down.

"Lucky fuck," says Donati when he walks back.

"Skill and precision," Kaz says, "like our V-8 engine." He nods toward the scoresheet. "How're we doing?"

"We don't have to look at the score sheet to know that Bud is the strike leader," says Fritz, turning his head to avoid their eyes.

It just sits there for a moment, nobody laughing, then Sewermouth Donati weighs in.

"Yeah," he says. "That's clear as shit."

• • •

Half the office is going over to fill the ranks, and even if Rosa is the only woman among them, you have to put yourself where the need is greatest. So many of the workers at Federal Screw are women, and it was almost all women who went out at the cigar factory down the block just a year ago, so if you want the benefits, she thinks, you have to take the risks. She does make a quick stop home to put on as many layers as she can manage, more for the padding than for the cold, as the couple people she's talked to who were out yesterday said it was getting pretty rough.

"You look like a stuffed sausage," says Ira from the couch. He's been in another funk since the people recruiting for the Lincoln Brigade turned him down, explaining that to get to the fight in Spain you had to climb over the mountains from France—no asthmatics needed. Papa, who used to hate all war, says this is the beginning of another that will sweep the world, working people everywhere standing up to Fascism-

And he's quietly glad that Ira isn't going.

"I wish I could wear a man's hat and stick something solid underneath it."

"You're planning on getting whacked on the head?"

"It's a possibility."

"If you land in the hospital, have them call Gersh at the deli," says Papa. "He'll send somebody over to tell us."

Mr. Gersh has remained sympathetic even though he had to let Rosa go, missing too much time with her organizing work. She's one of the switchboard girls on the telephone company graveyard shift now, plugging and pulling, and volunteers at the UAW office. She sleeps when she can.

"I'll be fine," she reassures them. "We're coming out in numbers today."

And what numbers! On the streetcar to the west side she can recognize more and more union members as they pack in, some carrying placards, all of them as jazzed as Ira gets when the Tigers are in town for a big game. Then the short walk to the factory, more and more bodies, hundreds, no, *thou*sands of workers and sympathizers joining together to completely surround the Federal Screw complex, shouting slogans and visiting with each other, enough to keep one line going clockwise and the other in the opposite direction, the cops on foot droning out "Keep moving, keep moving," as they pass, and the UAW speaker car also circling, a different voice almost every trip, first Victor Reuther, then Stanley Nowak, head organizer here who has a Polish-language radio show, and yes, here's the giant American flag they always display at the rallies in Cadillac Square-

It is thrilling.

Thrilling and a little frightening each time Rosa walks on the side of the factory along the railroad yard, where dozens of mounted police and three times that many on foot are congregating, all holding the long billy clubs she's seen in action before, and one cop who just stands grinning at the picketers, hefting a shotgun-like thing with a dozen shells in a circle beneath the barrel.

"Manville gun," says a man walking behind her with a **SOLIDARITY!** sign. "Tear gas."

She makes two more complete circuits of the screw works, everyone's breath puffing out in the cold air, before the sound car rolls by with the word, Victor Reuther's voice blasting from the two loudspeakers fixed on top.

"*Shift change is in three minutes*," he advises. "*Coming out the main entrance.*"

Rosa is swept along with the throng heading for the east side of the main building, and sees that the mounted police are now moving parallel to them, horses' hooves making sharp sounds as they head down John Kronk Street. It gets tight when they turn left onto Martin, the street narrower, picketers too many and too jammed together to keep moving and there is a mounted cop right next to her, enormous horse, and she wonders again who can these men be? They're not paid any better than a Ford worker, and they can't all be Klan or Black Legion members—is it the uniform? Getting to carry a stick and a gun? They go after criminals, sometimes, and there are stories where they help pregnant woman birth their babies or find lost children, but don't they understand who they're working for here?

As if in response to her thoughts the mounted men form a phalanx, three horses wide, and head into the crowd, prodding with their long clubs, moving to the front entrance of the plant. Once there they begin to push outward, making a kind of chute from the door to the street, as something like a paddy wagon with blackened side and rear windows backs into position to receive scabbing workers.

A roar from the picketers as perhaps two-dozen scabs, almost all of them men, step out between the mounted police, trying to look at nobody. The walkout started Monday when management announced a ten-cent-an-hour rollback of wages for everybody in the plant—people barely getting by as it was. It's been a tough year already, almost as bad as '29, but the company refuses to open their books to back up their claim that it's either pay workers less or go out of business.

"Who *are* those people?" she shouts over the booing crowd, and the man with the sign shouts back into her ear-

"Some of em are the guys who keep the machines running, they get skills pay. Maybe some guys that aint had a job forever. I wouldn't want to be one of them today."

She thinks of Ira, stuck on the couch, feeling like a failure-

Then a bottle sails through the air and hits a horse on the flank, making it rear, and the mounted cops and the cops on foot start swinging and it is a free-for-all, the picketers and the men in blue too mixed in with each other for there to be sides to the battle, just clubs and bricks and rocks and clubs and *Bam!* tear gas now, the cops as likely to breathe it as anybody and somebody yelling something from the sound truck but Rosa too busy trying not to get knocked off her feet in the melee to make sense of it as she sees a young worker in a brown leather jacket and no hat grab on to the back of a mounted policeman's gun belt, strapped outside his jacket, and yank him off his horse and then a half dozen of the horsemen are chasing her and dozens of others down Martin and then off onto Otis Street, even narrower, women out on the front steps jeering at the cops and Rosa stumbles, almost goes down and it's the young guy in the leather jacket who grabs her arm and they run on the tiny lawns, parallel to the houses, a mounted cop breaking off to gallop after them till a woman throws a coffee pot's worth of boiling water down from her porch and his horse quits the chase.

They cut down a pathway between the backs of houses till they get to Dennis Street, and suddenly there are no more cops, no more picketers, the shouts and whistles and the booming from the sound car still audible, but suddenly seeming far away. They stop running.

He's a nice-looking boy, probably Italian, with a terrific smile.

"You okay?"

"I'm fine."

"Some rumpus, huh?"

"I've been to worse."

"You work at Screw?"

"I'm—I'm with the union."

"Me too. I work over at Kelsey, already done my shift, but I'm in the flying squad."

"Must be lively these days."

They walk side by side.

"Yeah, it's really hopping over here on the west side. I'm starting to recognize some of the bulls."

Rosa shoots a look back toward the riot. "What do you think we should do now?"

The Italian boy shrugs his shoulders. "The scabs are either packed off by now or they been beat to hell, so the point has been made. I say we get off the street—cops'll be looking for heads to bust, make some collars. They'll be at the streetcar stops—"

"Right—"

"And my place is just over on Livernois. C'mon—"

Rosa has no idea where Livernois is, but follows the young man.

His name is Riccardo—Rick. Rick Donati. The little house is not far, like he said, a ground floor apartment he shares and Polish people in the one upstairs.

"They cook cabbage," he says as they step into the small living room, a rumpled sheet and blanket still on the couch. "It takes some getting used to."

"Is your roommate—?"

"Still on his shift at Kelsey. We don't see that much of each other. This is kind of his bedroom," says Rick, rolling the sheet and blanket into a wad and tossing them onto a chair. Rosa thinks of her brother, still in his pajamas when she left-

"It's good to share the rent," she says.

"But not the bathroom. Hey, take some of that off, the radiators will cook you in here."

Rosa sheds coats and sweaters. Jean Harlow is just as flat as me, she thinks, but she's blonde and wears that slinky stuff that barely covers them. She can smell the cabbage, and thinks of it floating in her mother's *borscht*-

"So you get paid, working for the union?" asks Rick Donati.

"No, I—I volunteer. I work nights at the telephone exchange."

"Switchboard—"

"Right."

He smiles. "You ever listen in on the calls?" A really nice smile.

"We're not supposed to, but around three o'clock when there's not much action—"

"*Who knows what evil lurks in the hearts of men*?" says Rick, using the voice from the *Shadow* radio show. "The switchboard operator knows!"

"It's only the people who have telephones, the ones who work or stay up late—"

"And probably guys calling women who aren't their wives."

"Those I never listen to, it's too embarrassing. Uhm, may I use your bathroom?"

The little mirror hung over the sink is warped just like at home, making one of her eyes look a lot bigger than the other. She takes her beret off, fluffs her mop of hair, the little curls always with a mind of their own. It has to happen sometime. Only totally bourgeois girls wait till they're married, and marriage as an institution probably won't last long after the revolution-

She can tell that her underpants are sweaty from the running.

Rosa pees and closes the lid before flushing the toilet. It still makes a racket, just like the one in their apartment, Papa going three or four times a night lately, using two canes to get there. Here there's a little tub, big enough for a five-year-old to lie in, with a shower head above it and a curtain that looks moldy. When she sees the society ladies in the movies—Mary Astor, Myrna Loy—they have rooms that are just for sitting in front of a mirror and doing your makeup while a man in a tuxedo looks over your bare shoulder. Rooms bigger than her whole apartment. And rather than being resentful she always thinks maybe they've earned that, with the stupid men they have to put up with-

It has to happen sometime, and if she was totally disgusting he wouldn't have invited her in.

"You see what I mean about sharing the bathroom," says Rick when she comes out, beret in hand.

"Do you two cook?"

"I can make a pot of spaghetti, and Carlo knows how to heat it back up." He shrugs. "There's a hot dog joint up by the streetcar stop, we hit that pretty often."

"Your flying squad—is there a leader?"

"We got shop stewards at Kelsey now, so if there's an action, they'll spread the word. Going out to picket like today is like—ap*pre*ciated, but not expected."

He seems too easy-going to be in any of the progressive parties, maybe didn't even finish high school before going into factory work. Which doesn't mean you're stupid.

"Do the shop stewards do only that?"

"Someday they might, but now they're just guys on the line who get twenty minutes a day to move around the floor and check with us, see that everything is jake. You girls on the switchboard organized?"

"I wish."

Rosa sits on the couch, nicer than the one Ira gets to sleep on, trying to act casual. She tries to avoid looking at her shoes, a pair of old clodhoppers which she hates but are good for running away. Rick has taken his leather jacket off and just stands there, not sure where he should park himself.

I am twenty-six years old and not anybody's idea of a good girl, Rosa thinks. Enough already-

"So," she says, looking him straight in the eye, "when does this Carlo come home?"

• • •

It turns out that keeping tabs on the guy is no Sunday picnic, even though they've rented an apartment just down the street from his place on LaSalle. The guy is never fucking home, and it turns out neither is the wife, always off at the union hall or making a speech or throwing a monkey wrench into the works at one of the parts outfits that Gillespie handles for Harry Bennett. The plan has been gone over enough times, so maybe because Federal Screw rolled over and signed with the fucking Local this morning, Bud gets the call.

"It's on," somebody tells him. "They're home now."

So he goes by Percelli's place, and Eddie's got the heaters stashed behind his icebox, which Bud almost gets a hernia helping him move out of the way.

"Do these things still shoot?"

"I don't know, I never used them."

Terrific. Even if the idea is only to scare the shit out of the little prick, you want to know the hardware is in working order.

Whatever they pay this guy at the Local, he's not spending it on rent. A couple beater cars out front, nobody on the street, sun just about to drop below the roofline—perfect.

"I do the talking, if there is any," he tells Percelli as they get out of his car. Eddie used to move hootch for Chet LaMare in the bad old days, and is not known as being trigger-happy or too jumpy to trust. Just a guy picking up a few dollars.

They tug their hats down low and climb to the second floor, Bud having cased the spot enough times to know which door, and knock. With as many shit lists as this guy is on, you'd think he'd at least have a peephole to scan the visitors with, but no, some broad not the wife opens the door with a big grin on her kisser and there they stand, .45s drawn and ready to do business, and it's a fucking *party*. There must be at least ten people inside, men and women, with a birthday cake on the table, not cut into yet, all looking like "Who invited these two?"

Bud senses Percelli ready to scarper, so he pushes past the broad and points his pistol at Walter, whom he's seen a couple times back when he worked as John Gillespie's bodyguard and there were negotiations up in Flint, and yeah, he's the red-headed brother-

"Okay, Red, you're coming with us!" he shouts, hoping for at least some screams from the ladies, but nothing, just the skinny brother and a couple of the other guys holding up their hands and drifting into his line of fire-

No way he leaves, they say.

Shoot if you want, but he stays, they say.

You can't kill us all, they say.

Actually, we *could* kill you all, Bud thinks, but it would be a fucking mess and not the point he's been sent to make, so he grabs the floor lamp standing next to him, the cord popping from the wall socket when he attacks Reuther with it, the thing not weighted right to be much of a weapon so he tosses it and pulls out the sap he was going to work him over with later and starts flailing with that, the union bastard catching most of it on his arms as he backs up, practiced by now at taking a beating, and Bud finds himself yelling to Percelli "Shoot him! Shoot the Red bastard!" hoping he'll have sense enough to point but not to fire and something whizzes by his head and smashes against the wall.

A pickle jar. The broad who opened the door threw a fucking pickle jar at him, and now one of the guys must have gone out the window because there's somebody on the street yelling "Help! They're killing him upstairs! Call the police!"

"Out!" says Bud, pointing to the door, and Eddie beats him to it, running down the stairs like a couple of pansies got their fannies slapped, the guy on the street still yelling bloody murder but backing away when he sees them. Bud is glad he put on a bogus plate before they started over, the least you can do if you're out to kidnap somebody, and Percelli doesn't even have his door shut when Bud flattens the gas pedal and they blow the scene.

"Fucking dimwit sonsabitches!" he observes as they drive, "Tell me they're home and forget to mention they got half the communist fucking party over for cocktails! I mean how fucking stupid can you be?"

He pulls into an empty lot on Linwood, kills the engine. The .45, in his jacket pocket now, is digging into his side so he yanks it out and tosses it into Percelli's lap. "And what have you got to say for yourself?"

Eddie, who hasn't opened his trap since they left for the job, thinks for a moment before he answers.

"That cake looked good."

• • •

"Tell me they weren't recognized."

They never met Percelli before, says Gillespie on the other end of the phone, and though Bud Holt was with him up in Flint, he stayed in the background-

"You'd make a lousy gangster," says Harry.

Harry has to put up with Gillespie because when Gillespie was Water Commissioner he fixed it so Dearborn ran its own water system and basically served the Rouge. He lived next door to Liebold and had his fingers in a lot of dirty business, then got wiped out in the Crash. So the Chief, who likes to have people who owe him big on the payroll, hands him to Harry to use as a cat's paw with the supplier outfits, and also to spy on what Harry's up to, only the guy is dumb as a doorstop. Kidnapping fucking Walter Reuther at his apartment-

"What you're going to do now, John, is to bring those two dimwits over to Colombo and work out some alibis that will hold up in court. And if you ever pull another bonehead stunt like this again, I'll personally feed you to my cats for breakfast."

Harry hangs up before Gillespie can put the whine on him again. The guy calls himself an 'investigator' when they send him into a situation, but he's there to make sure the parts keep flowing to the Rouge and the union doesn't look like too much of a winner, all while keeping the Ford name out of the papers. It saves Harry a trip to Flint or Kansas City.

When he gets back to the private room the *linguini vongole* has come and Joe Adonis has had a second glass of wine. Snappy dresser, not too much grease in the hair, good table manners, and Harry doesn't trust him as far as he could throw him. It never ends with these people—you bring in cats to take care of the mice, then you've got a cat problem—

"Troubles?"

Harry shrugs as he sits. "Union stuff."

"They're giving you a run for your money."

"Not us, not Ford. There's this guy, Homer Martin, president of the whole UAW outfit? I got him in my pocket."

"Expensive?"

"You just got to *flatter* the guy. I got box seats at the ballpark, tickets to swank events, took him out hunting a couple times—"

"I wouldn't go out in the woods with nobody carrying a rifle, I don't care who he is."

They laugh. Harry is hoping that Martin and Frankensteen and Reuther, none of whom likes the others, will start to battle among themselves like the Purple Gang Jews did, and pull the union down with them.

"So I hear you've got a car dealership in Jersey."

The gangster grins. "Not your make."

"You know we've got an assembly plant in Edgewater—"

"Yeah, my house is just up the hill in Fort Lee."

"Mr. Ford is looking for somebody reliable to ship the output from there."

Adonis stops eating, interested now. "Reliable."

"The cars get delivered on time, the drivers are kept under control—"

"This is an offer?"

"It could be."

"And I do what to deserve this?"

"A while back I hired Pete Licavoli—"

"I heard of the guy—"

"I hired Pete to put together what we call our Fire Squad. Only they don't operate a hook and ladder, they put out a different kind of fire—"

"Labor stuff."

"That was the agreement. Half of his guys have done time in the pokey, all of them deserved it. They were good for a couple years, set the tone for my Service Department at the Rouge, only now Pete says they want double the pay, or else—"

"Or else what?"

"He and his boys already took a shot at me. I came out of my car ready to shoot back, but—well, we haven't come to an agreement yet."

"And you want him off your back." Adonis sits back, wipes his mouth with his napkin, thinking. "You got a guy here, they call him Tony Cars now—D'Anna. Why don't he put out the word for you?"

Harry is ready for this. "Here—Detroit—we're like the minor leagues, right? But your connections in New York, they go across the country."

With Luciano and Genovese stuck back in Italy, Joe Adonis is right next to Frank Costello in charge of the New York rackets, and they carry weight in every city east of the Mississippi.

"When *you* put the word out, people know it *means* something."

Adonis only considers this for a moment. "All right," he says, leaning back to the table. "Let's talk numbers."

Something can always be worked out. You just have to flatter the guy-

• • •

Lester doesn't take bets in his shop, but there's always a couple characters in there, never take their hats off, handling the action. Lester's got enough seats that it's just part of the atmosphere. He straightens hair too, only in the back room because the congolene smells so strong, and during the dry law you could always buy a quart of decent whiskey here. Some of the other barbers have been on for years, but Zeke always waits till Lester is free to cut his head.

The books and the players are all talking about the Louis fight.

"I think the fix is *in*," says Cootie. "They don't want no colored man to have that belt."

The same old song.

Joe comes back to Detroit a lot to hang with his friends, you see him out on Hastings dressed sharp and leaking money, people don't even have to lay a story on him. You hope he stashes some of it away and gets out of the game before his brains get scrambled-

"You think Joe gonna lose tonight, put some jack on it," says one of the books. "You don't have to call the round and I'll give you three-to-one."

"Joe has fought three white men already," says Lester, quietly snipping. "Why didn't they fix one of them matches?" Zeke likes to keeps his hair short because at work it feels like it could catch fire any minute, so he's here twice a month.

"Don't need no fix with this Smelly," says DuPree, who comes in to shoot the shit and learn where the fun is. "He already knocked Joe out once."

"But the Jew fighter knocked Schmeling out," says Lester. "And Joe knocked *him* out."

"No telling with these big heavyweights," says Zeke. "One lucky punch and the other man hits the deck."

"Yeah," says the book. "So why nobody will bet against Joe at the odds I'm giving?"

"Because it's dis*loy*al," says Lester.

There is a moment of silent agreement with this in the shop.

"I bet there is plenty white folks out there betting on the German against the American," says Cootie. "That aint loyal."

Lester is back in Zeke's kitchen now, finishing up. Cutting colored hair, you never know what will get thrown at you, but Lester is an artist. Takes his time, too, and more than once Zeke has fallen asleep while under the scissors.

"Maybe some," says Zeke. "But when I was leaving work just now, my foreman, Italian guy, sticks his thumb up and says 'Hey, I hope it goes good for us tonight.'"

"Us."

"That's what he said."

A moment's quiet, except for snipping, while they ponder this.

"If Joe was in the ring with that Primo Carnera," says Cootie finally, "your foreman be singing a different opera."

Walking home, Zeke's scalp feels good in the air, the witch hazel maybe, but he still has a bad feeling about the fight. No skin off his ass if Louis goes down again, those are the breaks, but the boys, and even Mavis and Earline now, are so caught up in it. Like it's a token of something, like all those good and bad luck signs the old cottonheads believed in down south.

If Joe wins, Zeke is not getting a raise, and his folks back home won't suddenly be allowed to vote.

There's already a houseful when he gets home, Mavis putting the radio DeWitt fixed up in the center of the common room and inviting neighbors over. More talk about whether it will be on the level or not, and even some world politics like how Primo Carnera was behind that Mussolini killing black folks in Africa, and now it's Schmeling standing in for the Führer who just strolled into Austria and seems bent on taking over all of Europe.

"They get a real war going over there," DeLuca has told the metal pourers, "we'll be making tanks and planes at the Rouge to feed it. This joint will *jump*."

Mavis's brother Whitley is making too much noise by the radio and somebody has brought cold beer, so Zeke grabs a bottle and sits in the kitchen with Hiram and Hughie Gaines who deliver coal and haul trash in their own truck and are so wide it's a wonder they can both fit in the front seat. They have bet money on what round Joe will knock out the German, will bet on anything that runs, walks or crawls, and now have a buck riding on which of them poured a bigger head into the glass from his bottle.

"You call it, Zeke, you're the man of the house."

Zeke goes to find a ruler from Earline's pencil box and comes back to measure.

"I think Hiram got it by a sixteenth of an inch."

"You shook your bottle up!"

"Did not. It would of sprayed all over the kitchen!"

"Alright, a buck on who can drink it fastest."

"No bet. You don't even *swal*low."

All the ceremony and announcements they do before a big fight comes on the radio now, Mavis with the box cranked up loud in the living room, people still talking some but you can tell they're nervous, not sure how this is going to turn out. When he gets to go to a movie, Zeke always knows how it's going to end about halfway through, which cowboy or gangster is bound to bite the dust and which one will get the girl. But with sports there's always the chance you'll be disappointed, like life. Where you *know* you're going to be disappointed.

The ringside bell goes off then and the fight announcer comes on, talking a mile a minute like it's a horse race, calling Joe "Louis" and Schmeling "Max," a lot of back and forth in the first minute, somebody gives the other one "the old one-two," and Zeke can see through the door to where Alvin is sitting. His son has got his eyes closed and fingers crossed on both hands, not shouting encouragement like the others, and if he could Zeke would jump in that ring and flatten the Kraut for him, but it sounds like Joe is doing pretty well, the left, the left—Schmeling is hanging onto the ropes to stay up and then he's down, up again, and down, up again and *down*, the ref counting, seven, eight, nine and it's over, a technical knockout, which means they were afraid for the German's life if he stood up again, the Gaines brothers on their feet and whooping because they both bet first round with good odds, the floor shaking as they hold each other and hop up and down and Alvin has tears in his eyes as the crowd in the apartment streams out the door to holler, Zeke able to hear the mob on Hastings already, all of Black Bottom pouring into the streets to celebrate their Joe, their victory.

Zeke gets up to follow them and feels a smile spreading on his face. Two beers in his belly, a new haircut, and Detroit's very own fighter, a colored man—

"We *done* it, Papa!" shouts Alvin, throwing a skinny arm around his father. "They can't take this one away!"

• • •

They send a man up from the Photo Department to record the honor.

Ernest Liebold will make certain the picture is seen by the right people, as the Detroit papers, which he doesn't trust, have not been invited.

He suggested to Mr. Ford that he wear a light-colored suit, knowing that the sash the cross is hung on is red and will show up dark in a black-and-white news photograph. The medal hung on it is a beauty, a white Maltese cross with golden eagles in the crook of each arm, a golden swastika in a white disc in their claws. The star pinned on his breast pocket is similar and even more dazzling.

There has been so much misunderstanding in the American press of the German position, and Liebold hopes that Mr. Ford's acceptance of the award on his seventy-fifth birthday, and the Führer's lauding of his 'humanitarian ideals' and 'contributions to peace' will help the people open their minds. Heller, the German consul here in Detroit and in charge of this ceremony in Mr. Ford's office, has told him that Charles Lindbergh is expected to receive the honor sometime soon. There will be some naysayers, of course, Bennett bleating his usual noise from the sidelines, but if America's peaceful relations with the Reich are to be maintained, and the Company's sales and manufacturing interests there best served, this is a proud moment, and one that Ernest Liebold can take a good deal of credit for.

Mr. Ford has gotten so much better at accepting the honors due to him, though he asked that there not be "too much fuss." The run for US Senate back in '18 hurt him terribly, of course, falling short by a mere eight thousand votes to that scoundrel Newberry. Electing senators by popular vote was very new then, and the Company had so many fewer employees-

He has, deservingly, been celebrated often over the years, and people understand that attaching the Ford name to their charity or cause has an enormous benefit, to the point where Liebold must turn down at least one or two offers a week. But a First Class Grand Cross Order of the German Eagle in Gold with Star does not materialize every day-

SOME FORD ADVANTAGES FOR 1941:

NEW ROOMINESS. Bodies are longer and wider this year, adding as much as seven inches to seating width.

SOFT, QUIET RIDE. A new Ford ride, with new frame and stabilizer, softer springs, improved shock absorbers.

POWER WITH ECONOMY. The Ford engine leads the low-price field in horsepower; holds many records for economy as well as for performance.

BIG WINDOWS. Windshield and windows increased all around to give nearly four square feet of added vision area in each '41 Ford Sedan.

LARGEST HYDRAULIC BRAKES in the Ford price field, give added safety, longer brake-lining wear.

GET THE FACTS

YOU'LL GET A FORD

THE PRESIDENT, WHO MOM AND Daddy call "their president," meaning the Brazilians', is in an airplane with floats on it. It circles slowly overhead a few times, and Kerry can hear Flavio saying that it's so he can see all the rubber trees, which makes her proud. Her father cleared that land, and helped figure out how to make it so the trees don't get sick and die. Most of them.

Or at least many of them.

The plane lands then, and Mrs. Aranha talks to the students, raising her voice as it taxis to the dock, reminding them that this is a great honor and to smile while they are singing. Kerry can see that her father is among the men who greet the president as he steps out of the plane, standing just back from the Ford man from Rio who's come to represent the Company. There is a lot of handshaking and then the president, a very short man, is brought to stand before them, all the classes in their school uniforms arranged by age as the musicians play the little introduction notes and they begin to sing the national anthem.

Their national anthem.

Ouviram do Ipiranga as margen plácidas
de um povo heroic o brado retumbante-

At first they were just sounds when she sang it, Mom saying "she's inherited my voice," which is a lucky thing because Daddy can't sing even a radio jingle like *Pepsi Cola hits the spot*. But now Kerry knows the words, 'placid banks' and 'heroic people' being lauded, and she can pick Flavio's voice out from the others behind her, boys and girls in alternating rows for this ceremony. They even worked on the second verse, which starts with her favorite lyric-

Brasil, um sonho intense

-and her dreams really have been more intense since she's been here—brighter, strange creatures, crazy stories that she and sometimes Flavio are mixed up in. The only ones she hates are when Daddy is in trouble somewhere-

O Pátria amada
Idolatrada,
Salve! Salve!

After the *Hail! Hail!* the little president smiles and thanks them and says how nice they all look. Lots of cheering from the workers and some jump on bicycles to ride along with the president and the important men as they're driven up to where Belterra really starts. Mrs. Aranha and the other teachers hurry them into the buses so they can be back in class before he visits the school. Boys go on one bus and girls on another. On the way back they sing Carmen Miranda *sambas* they hear on the radio from Manaus—

Jim Rogan, riding behind the big Lincoln carrying the president and Braunstein, who runs the Ford assembly plant in Rio, is amazed to see how many of his workers have come out to line both sides of the road up to the village, cheering and waving Brazilian flags that some smart river merchant sold them earlier in the week. Vargas has made unions legal in the country, of course, but being a champion of factory workers in a country that's still about agriculture doesn't make a whole lot of sense, and after a few coup attempts he's suspended elections and proceeded from state-of-siege to state-of-siege as a dictator.

The people here seem to love him.

"So he's really popular?"

Gomes, next to Jim in the back seat, smiles. "He tells us it is a proud thing to be *brasileiro*."

Archie Johnston is in the States on vacation, so Braunstein has stepped in for the day, asking Jim to stay close and quickly brief him on the wonders of Belterra so he can pass them on to President Vargas and his interpreter. Henry and Edsel Ford were invited, of course, but were otherwise occupied, and the Company sent autographed photos in their stead. The operation here is so costly, and with Mr. Ford legendary, in the Model T days at Highland Park, for jumping into a position on the assembly line to demonstrate how it should be done, Jim is puzzled as to why he's never come down to straighten things out or decided to abandon it all as a bad idea.

He never came to Pine Camp either.

There is a union at Belterra now, though so far it seems to be only a forum for the workers to air their complaints to the government inspectors who keep showing up, listening sympathetically and then doing nothing. Braunstein says the point of the invitation is to get President Vargas to pull Belterra from the clutches of the Brazilian Department of Labor and into the less regulatory Department of Agriculture. Luckily, thinks Jim, this is not his responsibility.

The Brazilian flag—a blue orb with white dots representing stars inside it, inside of a bright yellow rhombus against a rectangular, bright green field—is as colorful as the jungle birds you see almost daily here, and the cheering people waving them on either side of the road are thrilled to view their distant leader in the flesh. Or just happy to have a day off with pay.

Norma has spent the morning changing bandages and helping patients with limited mobility struggle into their best clothes. They have put a banner up over the beds on one side of the common ward, *Ordem e Progresso!*, the motto on the flag, and the hospital is certainly the most orderly and progressive thing about Belterra. The doctors brag that it deals out the best medical care in all of Brazil, probably true if you remember the patients are mostly poor and uneducated laborers and their incredibly fertile wives.

Norma stands in a receiving line with the other nurses, and when Vargas is brought in, her first thought is "What a little man for such a big country." But her own president back home can't even stand *up*, though in the newsreels the Company sends down they almost never show the wheelchair.

"*Obrigado por ter vindo, senhor,*" she manages to say, thanking him for his trip as he quickly takes her hand going down the line. Kerry teaches her these things and sometimes she uses them to tell Beatriz what to do or at work, but she's never been good at languages. She loves their music, though, what you hear on the radio and what you hear played in the Brazilian part of the village. So emotional, even if she can't make out any of the words—

Old Lázaro, who, fittingly, has been brought back from the dead three times by the doctors here, has been chosen to represent the patients in the ward as a speaker, and from what she can understand and from the laughter it provokes, tells the president that Belterra is the best place in the world to have a heart attack.

A couple of the Brazilian nurses, wonderful girls, have tears in their eyes, and Norma recalls the day she and Kerry drove into Detroit in the wet and were a block away from the parade carrying Hoover to City Hall, the closest she's ever come to seeing an American president in person. Jim says he'd like to shake the hand of Henry Ford before he dies. If that day ever comes, thinks Norma, it won't be on a failed rubber plantation in the Amazon jungle.

Jim follows with the entourage to visit the spick-and-span dentist's office, the dance hall, the new tennis courts, for a short tour of the rows of little Cape Cod style houses the married workers live in, muttering to Braunstein to be sure to point out that they are virtually mosquito-free, unlike the open huts the people here seem to prefer. It helps to have a relatively mild day, as the metal roofs that Dearborn insisted on can make the little boxes into ovens in the summer months. They go to the school, all the students in each classroom they look in on rising to again greet the president, Jim able to sneak a wave to Kerry when they reach hers. Kerry would be graduating next year if they were in the States, not a little girl anymore, and she is more and more of a mystery every day. She plays tennis with the girls' team, the players almost all white, but doesn't seem to socialize with them much. She has uttered vague noises about wanting to study to be a veterinarian, and Jim can only think of old Doc Drysdale where he grew up, who dealt with the local livestock and spat tobacco juice on the barn floor. He's heard there are a few women licensed to do that job now, but hopes it is only the passing whim of a girl who likes to pick up snakes.

There is a special lunch for their party at the obsessively-cleaned mess hall, Jim putting in a word with the kitchen that no, this isn't the occasion for one of Mr. Ford's special soybean recipes, and then they head to the new park Johnston has had him create by pulling out one of every three trees and anything with prickers on it. Vargas will make a speech there, so reporters from Santorém and Manaus have come to witness local history in the making. Jim catches up with Schick, who is here to handle publicity for the Company.

"This is exhausting."

"Wait till tonight," grins Schick.

"Did you really ask the Fords to come down?"

Schick shrugs, smiles. "Twice a year since you started in the first spot. I figure they've got their hands full back home. We got a couple interesting visitors lined up though—you know Disney?"

"The cartoon guy? Mickey Mouse?"

"That's right. He says he wants to look at your all-American village."

The Brazilians love cartoons when they show them at the dance hall, especially Donald Duck, who Gomes says speaks English exactly the way the workers hear it—angry and unintelligible.

"Give us a warning when he's going to show up," Jim says to the publicity man. "My daughter's got a monkey who should be in one of his pictures."

They're calling it a 'musical soirée' in the president's honor, held in the dance hall, all the usual people invited, mostly white but with some of the Brazilians who give orders or work at the hospital. Lights have been set up in the open yards around the hall for the workers and their families to come listen and dance if they want. It is Kerry's first time wearing the outfit Mom ordered from the Montgomery Ward catalogue two years ago and took six months to arrive on a riverboat to Belterra. After constant wrangling Kerry just gave in and Mom chose a dirndl ensemble, the skirt a yellow floral print on percale, whatever that is, extra tight waistband, wide straps over the shoulders, two rows of something called ric-rac, and then a starchy white cotton blouse with a square cut neck and 'eyelet embroidery trim.' Add that to the little yellow ribbons on her pigtails Mom insisted on, and Kerry is convinced she looks like *Heidi* in the Shirley Temple movie they saw a few years back, which would be fine if she was an eight-year-old Swiss orphan girl.

"Awww, you look a*dor*able!" say too many of Mom's white lady friends and fellow nurses, and some of the men her father's age just stare at her in a creepy way. But it's clear when they squeeze into the dance hall before the speeches that she will be able to disappear without too much trouble.

"You go have fun," says her mother with a peck on the cheek.

She can hear the Ford man from Rio making his welcome talk on the loudspeaker as she slips through the crowd of Brazilians surrounding the dance hall, two or three sentences and then a translation into Portuguese, Kerry smiling, graciously she hopes, at the workers' wives who point to the outfit and say "*Táo bonito.*"

She has ridden her bicycle past the little house that Flavio lives in but never been inside. There are streetlights here, on until what her mother calls "a decent hour," but a little further apart than the ones in the white people section, and she is relieved that everybody seems to have gone to the soirée and will not report a little Swiss orphan lost in their neighborhood. Flavio has put only the one light on to signal that his parents have gone out like everybody else, and her heart is racing when she goes to the side door and knocks three times.

"*Tão bonito*," he says as he lets her in to the tiny kitchen.

"I look like a little girl."

"Pretty little girl."

He has dressed up as if going to the party as well, almost the oldest Brazilian boy still at school. After President Vargas came to their class this afternoon Flavio told her that the three men who never took their sunglasses off were bodyguards, probably soldiers but wearing nice city clothes so as not to attract attention. Flavio has a new-looking white shirt on that makes his arms look really tanned, though they're the same shade during the rainy season with no sun for weeks.

The house is only one-story, four rooms—the kitchen where they also sit to eat meals, a bathroom, his parents' bedroom, and his room. No couch, no radio, no pictures on the walls, only a painted statue of the Virgin Mary on a small table. Mary stands with arms spread at her sides, palms of her hands out, her bare foot crushing the head of a colorful snake Kerry has never seen before.

There are no soft chairs, so they sit on Flavio's bed, side by side but not too close at first.

"School is done for me in July," says Flavio.

They mostly speak English together, Flavio with the idea that if his is good enough he could get work for an American company in Brazil, or a Brazilian company that trades with America.

"What do you think you'll do then?"

Flavio shrugs his shoulders. It is a habit he has picked up from her.

"I work. With my father."

"But you're *ed*ucated now."

"That means what?"

She can't think of anything to tell him. "Maybe I could ask my father to get you a job doing more than just cutting trees down."

"Perhaps."

She is not supposed to be seeing him, but Daddy is a softer touch than Mom—

"And where will they send you?" he asks.

"Why do they have to send me?"

"Is what they do with all the white ones after school is done. Send them home to America."

Daddy had a letter from his best friend back home saying he shot a deer right on the main street of Pine Camp, which you can hardly see any more from all that's grown up around it. There's not a 'home' to send her back to-

"You will be marry, then."

"Lord, I hope not."

He pulls on one of her pigtails and she giggles and then they start into what they've started into a few times before, but this time they're sitting on a bed instead of standing up out in the bush and they end up half lying down on it, Flavio sort of on top of her, the dirndl shirt and blouse—'crisp-finished fine Cotton Batiste' if she remembers correctly from the catalogue—making crackly noises and her heart racing again till Flavio is the one to break off and sit up.

"*Meus pais esperam que eu esteja lá.*"

"Mine too," says Kerry, sitting up beside him, arms touching. The older Brazilian girls in school talk about a woman in Belterra who makes something you drink if you get into trouble that fixes it as long as you go to her right away. And she's heard Mom talk about a doctor at a hospital taking a baby out before it really gets started if the mother might die from having it. If it weren't for that risk-

Francine Post at school made a big deal of what she called "my romance" with Bruno Baeza, but that was just flirting and Francine acting tragic to get attention. Kerry doesn't feel romantic as they are up and straightening their clothes—she feels miserable.

They walk back toward the *festa* without talking, holding hands till there start to be people and Flavio lets her go and drifts into the crowd of Brazilians. She wants to cry. Flavio didn't tell her that one of her pigtail ribbons is missing, and she hopes his mother doesn't find it in his bedroom. Somebody is singing as she comes close to the dance hall, a familiar voice, sort of like Connee Boswell of the Boswell Sisters on the radio, but no, no—

It's her mother.

Daddy always says that Mom could have been a singer, and people hear her in church and want her to do solos but she usually puts them off and says "you should have heard me when I was young." The only young photograph Kerry can think of is Mom on their wedding day, and in that she just looks like all the brides, too much makeup and white lace-

You made me love you
I didn't want to do it
I didn't want to do it

She wonders if Mom ever had a boyfriend before she met Daddy, if she kissed him, did any of the other things-

You made me want you
And all the time you knew it.
I guess you always knew it.

Her mother is standing on a little stage they've made, with men playing instruments behind her, singing into a microphone like the women in the movies, only you can tell it's really her voice, echoing a little bit from the speakers set up just outside the big openings in the sides of the dance hall-

You made me happy sometimes
You made me glad
But there were times, dear
You made me feel so bad.

When she finishes, the people inside and many of them outside applaud and she looks a little embarrassed, sort of curtseying toward where the president and his party are sitting. She steps off the bandstand and moves through the people congratulating her with a funny smile on her face, then sees Kerry and comes to her-

"You sounded great, Mom."

Norma cocks her head, frowns. "What happened to your hair?"

• • •

They've had Kaz on mufflers for two weeks now, frame assembly work with a lot of bending. Bud Novak, whom they let go months ago, says it's because they know he has a bad back, and because Schultz, now overseeing his section of the line, is the worst slave-driver in the entire plant. Kaz comes home and lays on the floor with his knees up to his chest and listens to Sonia tell him, in her strenuous way, about what she's been reading. Lots of vamps and hard-boiled detectives. Molly has to help him to his feet when dinner is ready. Molly had a couple months of secretary school before they were married and has been out looking for something now that the kids can mostly take care of themselves, but nothing so far.

"Yo! Get your Polack ass in gear!" calls Schultz as Kaz has to walk out of position to get the last fastener tightened. They've been shifting him every couple weeks, never a good sign, and not good for his ongoing case of Forditis—the first couple days on any new task are rough, trying to get up to speed doing something the guys next to you have been at for years.

"Let's *go*, people, move, move, *move!*"

He's had this crazy idea in his dreams lately, that he runs a shop that does nothing but replace mufflers—Ford, GM, Hudson, Dodge, it doesn't matter—just a two-bay garage with a couple pits. Mufflers wear out or rust out pretty quick, and the all-purpose repair shops always manage to find two or three other things that weren't problems before you took your heap in. In the dream, Kaz is standing in front of the shop on Livernois Avenue with traffic streaming by, standing next to a sign that says **ALL MODELS—ONE PRICE** and there are cars lining up to get their mufflers switched out.

He hasn't had the dream about who is going to *finance* this business yet, but it beats the ones where he's on the line again and can't keep up, or has the wrong tool, or has somehow fucked up so bad they've stopped the conveyor and are screaming at him from all sides-

"Pilsudski, get the lead out, this isn't your lunch break!"

Kaz has found a spot under a sorting table where so far they'll let him leave his lunch, in a metal container with a thermos of cold coffee and whatever Molly has made for him. He can sit on the floor with his back against the wall and eat and pull his legs in when the forklifts pass by. You don't escape the noise, of course, there's nowhere in the entire Rouge complex where there isn't banging or rattling or stamping or rumbling, except, maybe, the executive offices, where Kaz nor anybody he knows has never set foot. From his spot Kaz can also watch these three deaf guys who get their break at the same time, hands and fingers flying, no worry about thugs or spies repeating anything they say. It is like a not-so-secret club, and makes him think of Sonia.

No club for her.

You have to turn to look at a clock, but Kaz has been in assembly long enough to just *feel* the time, about two hours left to this shift, so it's a surprise when Schultz waves him off of the line.

"Go down to payroll."

Kaz looks at him mutely, mind racing-

"You know where payroll is, don't you?"

The urge to smash the guy's teeth in is quickly overcome by the knowledge of what the Service Department, bored out of their skulls wandering around the plant, would love to do to him. He grabs his lunch bucket on the way out.

The payroll clerk looks down a list of names, then hands him an envelope. In it is pay for the two days he's worked this week.

"And I don't come back tomorrow?"

"That's the idea."

Coming home early will only upset Molly, so Kaz takes the streetcar, half-empty this much before the shift change, all the way to the UAW office. Bud Novak, sitting at a table playing cards with a couple other guys, sees him, takes a look at the wall clock, and knows.

"Any explanation?"

"Naw," says Kaz. "Not even a kick in the rear as I went out the door."

"Well, come on, I'll get you on our list."

"What list?"

"When it happens, we'll have a list of people we want reinstated."

All the planning to go after Ford that Kaz has heard about starts with that phrase—"When it happens"—like they are waiting for a smoldering volcano to erupt. But some volcanos never do blow their tops, they just keep smoldering, and when Kaz can get coworkers to talk about the possibility of a strike most just sniff and say "Dream on, pal."

"Is there anything available here?"

Bud gives him a look. "You mean that *pays*? You know how many guys like you that used to work at the Rouge are knocking around Detroit?"

"So you volunteer."

"Helen don't want me home, the mood I'm in, so yeah, I come down here, make phone calls, run errands, go talk to people if they'll listen."

The Old Man has said that he'll shut down the Ford Motor Company before he'll sign it up with a union, and it's *his* to do what he wants with it. The son has a lot of stock, but he's just a design guy who gets in the society pages and is generally liked—the Old Man and Harry Bennett run the store.

"You're in the neighborhood, drop in any time," says Lester Collins, pulling out a sheet of paper covered with names from a metal file cabinet. "We always got coffee, you can check the board to see if there's actions coming up that need bodies. Okay—Kazimir with an 's' or a 'z'?"

Kaz needs to lie on the floor, so he does get home before the shift change and there's nobody there. Bud told him that the Service Department sends your name around to all the parts suppliers in town, so forget about finding work there, and at the GM plants they figure you got fired because you're either a jack-off or a shit-stirrer. Bud tried at Hudson and Packard with no dice, but maybe they got openings for experienced hands this week—you can always try.

He lays down on the rug next to the radio, not turning it on because the silence is so nice, a cushion from the sofa under his head. Stan is finishing basketball season, Sasha has band practice, and Sonia has a regular after school baby-sitting job for a dentist and his wife, two toddlers she describes as being possessed by demons. But Molly is usually here to make up an ice pack or hot water bottle, depending on which of his aches and pains is worse.

With one price, already fixed, for all models, the customers will know they're not getting gypped, and the parts are pretty standard—tail pipe, connector, muffler, exhaust pipe—and lots of times it's only one section needs replacing, so you can cut them a deal. Be his own boss, work at his own pace. He'd start out working in the pit, of course, but eventually just hire guys and work in the front with Molly-

Molly comes in too quiet and screams when she almost steps on him.

"Jeez, sorry—"

"At least put on a light."

"The sun was on the floor when I got here."

Molly has a watch he gave her for her birthday, looks at it, realizes. "Oh no."

"Yeah."

"What did they say?"

"Nothing. Just don't come in no more."

She sits on the ottoman so she's not towering over him. "I'm so sorry."

"I can't say I'll miss it. The pay for this week is on the table."

"I got a job today."

This is news. Kaz struggles to sit up. "Office work?"

"For the Willow Run factory? The one they're building?"

"That's way out by Ypsilanti."

"I'll be working in Dearborn at first, just typing. There's a Mr. Sorenson?"

Cast-Iron Charlie Sorenson has always been the main guy running production at the Rouge, and is supposed to have come up with the conveyor idea by pulling an auto frame across the shop floor with a rope as workers added parts to it. He's also famous for his temper-

"Him personally?"

"I don't think so. There will be a bunch of us. It's a whole new factory—"

"To make airplane parts, yeah. You gave them your name when you applied?"

"Of course I did."

"Pilsudski?"

"I filled out a form, had an interview, they didn't say anything about it. I did fib and say the kids weren't living at home anymore."

"And you're sure you've got it?"

"I just have to go down to the post office and get that social security number thing? And then I report on Monday."

Kaz tries to think around this. They must have been planning to can him for a while, his name on some list, but maybe they didn't share it with the people hiring for this new plant. He imagines Molly on the same streetcar he's been taking for years-

"Is that okay?" she asks tentatively.

"Hey, it's terrific, we're gonna need the money till I get something."

"I won't make as much as you did—"

"Geez, I hope not," he says, grinning. "The kids'll have to pull their weight."

"They already do a lot. And it's only a couple more years—"

"Not for Sonia. What's she gonna do?"

"She's smart."

"She also can't talk so other people understand her, she has trouble climbing stairs—"

"Doesn't Ford hire a lot of people with handicaps? You said there are blind people, deaf people—"

Kaz tries to imagine his daughter punching in at the Rouge. It would break his heart.

"You want something for your back?"

"Naw, you already took a load off it. Listen, when you get there on Monday, and they put you in the harness—"

"Yeah?"

"Don't type too fast at first. Believe me, there's gonna be a guy with a stopwatch, and you want to leave yourself some breathing room."

• • •

Zeke Crowder wears his Sunday-going-to-church clothes to the banquet. Most Sundays he just lays back, listens to some radio—a Tigers' game if there is one—maybe goes out and throws down a couple beers. So wouldn't you know they put him at the same table as Reverend Bradby.

"Ezekial, so nice to see you." When he does go, Zeke tags along with Mavis and the kids at Reverend Dix's, but Bradby has church ladies from all over Detroit in his ear, he knows when you been sleeping, knows when you're awake-

"Reverend."

"How is Mavis doing over at the hospital?"

Mavis is not thrilled about handling sick people's bedding all day, but they can use the weekly pay and what she makes on the side.

"It's a job," says Zeke, "and we're grateful for that."

"Yes, we must be grateful." Bradby never makes you squirm, always friendly, but it's uncomfortable being next to all that goodness and light. "That will be the essence of what I have to add this evening. And perhaps Mr. Marshall is going to call on you to bear witness as well?"

"Lord no. They said to send somebody from the foundry to listen up, and I got picked."

"That's quite an honor."

DeLuca gave them one minute to choose somebody, orders from headquarters, and Otis Gamble, back from the hospital, said "Zeke, you been here the longest, you got to go."

Not yet forty and the newer ones on the job are calling him Uncle Zeke. There's a couple older than him in the building, like the one they call Possum who's sixty if he's a year, but they've been moved back from the heat. Most all the men he started out with have been fired or got too wore out to take it anymore and quit. Or died.

"Mr. Ford the one who shelled out for this do," he tells the reverend, "and I work for Mr. Ford."

Donald Marshall was at the door greeting him and everybody else with that hard handshake and steady stare, giving him a 'now I've got you' grin.

"Zeke Crowder from the foundry," he said. "Glad to see you here. I hear Mavis collecting a lot of nickels over at the Henry Ford."

Once a cop always a cop,

"She's washing a lot of dirty sheets is what she's doing."

You'll see Marshall drift into the watering holes in Black Bottom, glad-handing but never buying a round, just there to remind you that Ford mules got the eye on them even when they're out of the stall. He can get you hired and he can get you fired, and there's a rumor he'll take money on the side to help you get in the door. Zeke can hear him now, standing by the next table, working his business-

"My employer was disappointed to see the election returns from the Negro districts—twenty-to-one Democratic!"

Marshall is all "my employer" and "Mr. Ford" like they go out and play croquet together, when really he's just got his head up Harry Bennett's ass-

Reverend Bradby interrupts the thought. "I see where your oldest boy there—"

"DeWitt."

"He's in the apprentice program—"

"Doing well, too."

DeWitt says there are two other colored boys in the Ford training program, and so far he hasn't caught any static from the instructors or the white boys. He's got a gift, DeWitt, come home one day with three junkyard radios, different brands, started swapping parts between them, and now they got one that sounds terrific and has a dial that lights up in the dark. Alvin calls it Frankenstein.

"That's good, that's good," says Reverend Bradby. "The Company takes care of their own."

There's maybe three hundred sitting at the tables, mostly men, what Maceo Suggs calls the 'Eminent Africans'—Hastings Street businessmen, a reverend or two at every table, men and women with city jobs. Mavis could make better chicken than this with her eyes closed, but maybe not for this many people. The talk at the table during the eating part of the banquet is all Joe Louis, who fought here at the Olympia just a few nights ago and didn't have an easy time with Abe Simon.

"The man had fifty pounds on Joe. That is a lot of lumber to chop down."

"Didn't know Hebrews come in that size."

"Buddy Baer, Max Baer's brother? Wears that Star of David on his trunks, and he's six foot *six*."

"That give you a long reach."

"Joe about wore himself out beating on that Simon. Knocked him down what—four, five times—"

"But he kept getting back *up*."

"Joe Louis knock me down, I *stay* down. I was way up in the high seats, and you could still hear them punches smack the man's head, like busting a watermelon with a baseball bat."

"Joe ought to take some time off. Three fights this year and it's only March—"

"Joe fights so much because the white folks won't stand for a colored man sitting on that title. Some of them white boys back when, they won the belt and then went on va*ca*tion. Got paid to shake hands or dance around for three rounds, call it an exhibition—"

"So they keep wheeling these overgrown punching bags up—"

"You watch boxing?" Zeke asks Reverend Bradby.

"Just the young ones coming up, the Golden Gloves and whatnot," says Bradby. "These professionals—people *die* in that ring."

"They make the choice to climb in there—"

"*You* choose to work in an inferno day after day," says Bradby softly. "And I expect it's for the same reason."

Though Bradby still sends young men he's checked out to the employment office at the Rouge, and Ford still deals out a lot of green to support the Second Baptist, the Rev is not quite on the payroll the way Don Marshall is. He's on good terms with the race men in the city, all those outfits with a lot of initials, speaks at the Lodge meetings, and seems tight with almost everybody but the Garveyites.

"That Billy Conn coming up is quicker than Joe. Boy can move his feet."

"Brother," declares the owner of the funeral parlor the siddity folks use, "step inside those ropes with Joe Louis, and you can run, but you can't *hide*."

And then Willis Ward, who *used* to be the most famous colored athlete in Detroit, comes over to pay his respects. "Reverend Bradby, so good to see you here!"

"How you doing, young man?"

Ward starred in football and track at Northwestern High, and was the first colored player allowed to step on the gridiron for the University of Michigan, Coach Kipke stealing him away from a fancy Eastern college at the last moment. He outshined the competition at both the offensive and defensive end, kicked field goals and fielded punts, and was on the Wolverines' two national championship teams—smooth sailing till his senior year when they were scheduled to play against Georgia Tech. Though the game was in Ann Arbor, the University chose to honor a gentlemen's agreement not to 'embarrass' the visiting team by fielding a Negro player.

"Doing fine, Reverend, real busy over there at the plant," he smiles.

"And how is your father?"

"Oh, cranky as ever."

Bradby laughs. Ward first announced he would quit the team in protest, and then some radical student outfit and the usual Detroit race men—John Dancy, Snow Grigsby, that crowd—got involved and made a big deal of it. Got a lot of ink in the *Chicago Defender* and the other colored papers, but Ward finally just swallowed his medicine, holed up back at the Alpha Phi Alpha house and listened to his team win on the radio.

"Look like you rounded up every colored preacher and politician in Detroit," says Zeke.

Willis Ward grins. He's good-looking, well-dressed, started out at law school before Mr. Ford himself asked that he come over to work at the employment office's Negro Department under Marshall. Word is that it was Harry Bennett who talked him into quietly sitting that game out, telling him "You know who your *real* friends are."

"Oh, with a few exceptions," says Ward. "I don't see Reverend Hill from Hartford Street, or State Senator Diggs—"

From what Zeke can tell, Ward's job is to put a friendly face on the deal at employment, balance out Marshall's hard-nose approach, both of them fronting for the Little Man-

"Perhaps those gentlemen had other commitments," says Bradby. Reverend Hill was his assistant at Second Baptist for some time, and the men are still colleagues in the salvation business.

Ward turns his attention to Zeke, whom he's never met. "And you're here representing?"

"I pour metal at the foundry."

"Ah—then you know about all the labor agitation around town these past couple years. We haven't gotten too involved, because, quite honestly, those other companies don't hire *us* unless it's for clean-up work. But now that it's coming to Ford—"

"You think so?"

"If I'm lying I'm dying." Ward lays a hand on Bradby's shoulder. "I'm eager to hear you speak tonight, Reverend," he says, then drifts off to sprinkle some sugar on another table.

"I married his daddy and his stepmother in my church," says the reverend fondly. "Fine young man. We could do with more like him."

The microphone squawks as Don Marshall looms up behind the podium and the lights dim.

"Good evening—and thank you all for being here tonight."

This is a different Marshall than the Black Bottom cop—smooth, performing for an audience he considers his equals. Looking around as the Ford man greets them, Zeke sees colored men who wear suits and ties, nice ones, to work every day, many the owners of a restaurant or a business, and pastors of churches where nobody ever speaks in tongues or rolls on the floor—smoke rising from their cigarettes now that plates have been pushed away.

"Besides the opportunity to see old friends, and, I hope, some new ones," says Marshall, "you know me too well not to suspect that there is a *pur*pose to this gathering."

Something is cooking at the plant, that much is clear even up in the foundry, some government decision that has the union people crawling out from where they been hiding. But union is white people's business, and the foundry now has only a handful of white workers-

"That purpose, good people, is to discuss a *threat* to our community. As you are well aware, the Ford Motor Company is the largest employer of colored workers in the city—in fact, the largest in the entire state of Michigan. One out of every eight workers at the River Rouge plant is one of *us*, but if certain organizations have their way, that won't last for long."

Mavis says at the hospital they talk all through their shift, loud, because of the machine noise, but as long as they don't run out of linens upstairs nobody is on your back. He's heard some noise out of B Building, where most of the final assembly happens and the cars roll out, how they've been speeding it up, speeding it up, like it's an experiment to see when the men will break. Zeke always thinks of the John Henry song, where John Henry beats the steel-driving machine, but it kills him-

"The American Federation of Labor has a long and sorrowful history of excluding our people from the shops that they control, while their new competitor, the United Automobile Workers, has begun to talk a good game, though only a tiny fraction of their signed membership is not *white*. Oh, they've got plenty of foreigners on their rolls—in fact they are little more than a *front* organization for communist Russia! When is the last time anybody from Russia did something for you? These foreign elements have their own game plan, and taking over the Ford Motor Company is next on their list!"

Lonnie Gibson, who used to work in the rolling mill before he got his colored ass fired for going to hear A. Philip Randolph speak at the Bethel AME, is in one of those communist outfits, said so himself, always bending your ear about the inevitable collapse of the capitalist system, but it always seemed to Zeke like a lot of noise, like Maceo peddling his Garvey line-

"Mr. Henry Ford has done more for our people than any politician in Washington. Lincoln may have freed the slaves, but he never gave them a steady *job* to feed their families with! I'm sure many of you owe your presence here tonight to Mr. Ford, his five-dollar-day when all others were paying half that, and if they hired a black man, it was to hand him a broom and a bucket! And now these unions want to call the shots, put the power in the hands of the same ones who don't want us to live in their neighborhoods, or walk down their streets, or even *work* alongside them on a production line!"

Zeke has always felt that Ford hires colored because he run out of Hunkies willing to deal with foundry work, but since they let DeWitt into the trade school maybe there's something else behind it—Ford always in photographs planting soybeans with George Washington Carver, and then coming in to prop up Inkster when it was falling apart. Of course, if you take the man's money, you get his lecture about how to run your life along with it—

"There are some of our colored elite, if I may use that word, including some men of God who have been aiding and encouraging these invaders—asking us to read their literature, listen to their lies, join their cause. But their cause is most definitely not *our* cause, we do not abandon a true and proven friend for promises of pie in the sky or world revolutionism, we do not serve foreign powers or put the lives of our precious children in jeopardy to follow a red flag down the road of folly! I'm asking you, all of you, to warn your loved ones, your neighbors, of this threat, to ask for their vigilance in protecting the precarious little we have gained thus far, so that we might hope for more in the future!"

Zeke watches Willis Ward, sitting now as he listens to his boss. The Georgia Tech game was at the end of the season in his senior year, so he wasn't missing anything if he did quit the team. Zeke wonders if the man really worships at the church of Ford or if he's just learned when to shout Amen! and keep that fat payday coming.

You get over as best you can.

Reverend Bradby has been introduced now, speaking calmly, believing every word he says-

"If Henry Ford continues to hire one colored man for every eight whites, I am for him first, last, and *al*ways."

• • •

The steel mill at the Rouge is in itself a huge operation, eight newly-elected shop stewards needed to cover all the facets of it. All eight meet at the agreed shop, approaching the shift boss.

"We've got a long list of grievances," says their leader. "We need to see the supervisor."

The man shrugs. "You know where to find him."

The supervisor has his own office down beyond the enormous rollers. Line workers glance nervously as they pass, moving in a tight group.

"He didn't kick," says one of the stewards, a bit surprised.

"He's not supposed to. The courts say we got a right."

"The courts didn't send anybody here to explain that."

"He knows. They spent a bundle on lawyers fighting the thing."

The supervisor looks up from his desk as if he's been expecting them.

"We've got grievances."

"Take them over to Employment."

"Why would we go there?"

"To pick up what we owe you. You left your positions—you're fired."

"Crandall said we could—"

"You left your positions to see *him*, didn't you? You walk away from the job, you're gone."

The men stare at him, smelling a set-up.

"You leaving peaceably or do I call the Service Department?"

• • •

Edsel tries to focus on the conversation and not his stomach.

He skipped lunch today, just having some crackers and milk in his office. His own milk, not Father's, which is unpasteurized and might be part of the problem-

"Our outfit down there can put up houses wherever we move," says Father. "That much they've been able to handle."

Father doesn't like to talk about the rubber plantation, the returns so meager and slow in coming thus far, while here his soybeans here grow like crazy. John Pehle, who is head of the government's Refugee Board, is here, with Alfred Kahn, who built most of Father's factories, apparently representing the Jews, Harry Bennett who sticks his nose in wherever he can, and Archie Johnston, who, if anyone does, knows what is and isn't possible in the Amazon-

"We understand that your operation in Brazil finds it difficult to maintain a workforce," says Pehle. "Bringing in great numbers of these people—let's call them religious refugees—might help to alleviate that situation."

"Anybody fit to work and *will*ing to work is welcome to a job," says Father. "But if these folks are just so desperate they got to pack up and skedaddle—"

One of Father's worst gaffes was the time he claimed he'd never heard of a Jewish farmer, intimating that as a people they avoided physical labor. Jewish farmers from all over the state were heard from-

"I'm afraid many have had no time to gather their belongings, or had them taken away before they were allowed to leave—"

"Just how many are we talking about?" asks Johnston.

The government man seems nervous, as if warned of Father's flights of whimsy or pique-

"A few thousand are already aboard ships at sea, seeking asylum. There will be more—"

"And no room in *your* back yard, eh?" asks Father.

Pehle ignores the dig. "We've seen film from your photo department of your communities in Fordlandia and Belterra. Very impressive. We thought if there was anybody with the experience to take hold of a situation, to organize people on a massive scale—"

"Jews in the jungle," muses Father. "That'd be a new one."

• • •

The union said they'd put Kaz on the list to be reinstated if the labor board decision held, and here he is, back bolting mufflers but on the second shift, which means he and Molly only see each other really early or really late. A lot must have happened in the three weeks he was gone, because there were both AFL and UAW organizers passing out leaflets at the foot of the overpass when he came in, and he's seen guys today wearing UAW garrison caps and buttons right on the line. Schultz has had nothing to say to him all day. The conveyor is maybe even a bit faster than when he left, though, and his back muscles are starting to complain. His head was in the mufflers all morning, trying to keep up after being away, but after his fifteen-minute break he sees guys on the line easing close to each other to pass the word when Schultz is at the other end of his run.

Something is up.

Bill McKie is walking toward him along the conveyer, staring at it intently as if something is wrong. Bill is in the maintenance department, a skilled mechanic likely to be called to check out any machine in B Building. He stands close to Kaz, pointing to the belt as if they are discussing its performance.

"Gotta be ready for anything in here, Kaz."

"I just got back."

"Good—we'll need you."

"Need me for what?"

Big Otto, the Service Department goon in this section, is twenty feet away, staring bullets at them, but Bill doesn't seem to care. "They just bounced some of our people in the rolling mill, clearly a planned retaliation, so there's going to be an action."

"This coming from the West Side?"

"Strictly 600."

The Rouge has its own local now, and Tommy Thompson, its top man, doesn't wait for Reuther and that crowd to tell him what to do. The higher-up union stuff has gotten more complicated than Kaz wants to think about, former overall president Homer Martin being forced out as too tight with Bennett—the Little Man bought him a *house* for crying out loud—and now Martin is trying to open a second front for the old AFL, which never wanted anything to do with line workers.

"Do you have a car?" McKie asks.

"No. I take the streetcar."

"Too bad. We can use as many cars as we can get."

"For *what*?"

The Party-member guys are usually the smartest, they think things out, and so far Kaz has never felt like they're sacrificing workers for some other cause. They're the ones filling you in on the wars being fought in Spain or Poland or France in case you don't read the papers or follow the news on radio, the ones who call people Fascists and are happy to explain what that means. They're the ones who got murdered by the Black Legion when it was going strong-

"We don't know exactly what yet, Kaz," says Bill McKie. "But you're not going to want to *miss* it."

• • •

It's almost four o'clock when Rosa gets on the Jefferson Beach bus, two stops after Rick. He's not a hand-holder, not really touchy in public except when there are guys he knows from work around, holding the back of her neck then as they talk, which she can't tell if it's affectionate or just possessive. When they cross the Belle Isle Bridge it's like entering another world.

"My old man sold ices out here in the summer when he first got here," says Rick.

"Ice?"

"Shaved ice? You pour syrup on it, there's different flavors—"

"I've seen that."

"You never had one?"

"No. I've never had cotton candy either."

"Not Kosher?"

He never makes a big deal about her being Jewish, just joshes a little.

"As kids we knew better than to point and say 'I want that.' Money was tight."

"Sounds like your old *man* was tight. Ices don't cost so much."

"Once a week we got bagels."

"Boiled bread."

"That's how you make it, yes, but—"

Rick shrugs. "Our house, they stuffed you with so much bread before the main deal you could never say you were hungry. People got their different ways."

The park is not too crowded, late afternoon on a week day, and they go first to the aquarium building. Inside, it has a vaulted ceiling painted bluish green and most of the light comes from the tanks, giving the place kind of an eerie, underwater feeling. There are a half-dozen kids without parents inside, playing on the guiderails and making noises to hear the echo. They move away from these and Rick kisses her some, and when she opens her eyes there are fish swimming back and forth behind his head.

"They look like they're picketing," she says.

"Yeah. They either want a bigger tank or to go back in the river."

There are two long rows of windows, freshwater fish along one long wall and saltwater on the other. Rosa, who has never learned to swim, is fascinated by Rick's stories of swimming in the river, amazed that none of them feature somebody drowning. A church group, nuns in the front and rear, enters then, so they head for the exit, Rick doing the father-son-and-Holy Ghost gesture as they pass.

"Is that like a secret handshake?"

"They walk by you, nuns, and you don't cross yourself, it's bad luck. Like a black cat."

They pass up the domed conservatory right next door, Rick dismissing the plants as uninteresting because "they don't *do* nothing," and head for the zoo. Rosa is a bit surprised that he wants to keep seeing her, him never interested in her explanation of the root causes of the labor situation, and her such a lox on the dance floor. Sex, though, is getting better, both of them figuring things out, and he thinks she's smart and funny and doesn't seem to mind that at all.

They start at the seals, Rosa's favorite, the beautiful, big-eyed creatures racing around after each other just under the pond's surface and sometimes flopping out onto the grassy bank to get a fish treat from one of the zoo attendants.

"I wonder if when a fish croaks in the aquarium, it ends up here."

"Of course not," says Rosa. "It might have died of a disease."

"Or boredom. Can you imagine looking out all day long, people gawping in at you?"

"You do the same thing over and over at work."

"That's not boring, it's terrifying. If I bring the stamper down too quick, I take some guy's fingers off. If I wait too long, I get fired. These zoo animals got it easy. These seals, they get to play around, go swimming, free fish every day—where do I sign up?"

The Monkey Mound is next, Rick saying he could watch for hours.

The mound is a kind of huge, stone-and-cement pyramid with a waterfall tucked into the middle of it and rope ladders and trapeze things hung overhead. A couple dozen of what they say are rhesus monkeys, buff-colored, pink-faced, long-tailed acrobats who seem to spend most of their time fighting and making up. Rick says it's like a big Italian family, but for Rosa it's a *Three Stooges* movie with way too many stooges.

"They got food, water, stuff to swing around on, nice high view of the park," says Rick. "The only thing they're missing is another gang of monkeys to have a war with."

"There has to be conflict?"

"*Io e mio fratello contro mio cugino, io e mio cugino contro il mondo.*"

"Translation?"

"'Me and my brother against my cousin, me and my cousin against the world.' Old Sicilian proverb."

"That's awful."

"Hey, that's *peo*ple, that's life."

"So what are we fighting for now, if it's not for a *bet*ter life?"

"In the old country the *padroni* owned the land—here they own factories. You fight so they don't bury you before you're dead."

"The union is about getting everybody to work together—"

"Sure, the Irish and the Italians and the Jews and the niggers—"

"Negroes."

"Right, sorry. But we come together because we got a common enemy. There wouldn't be an Italy if it wasn't for the friggin Austrians. That's why my father come over, they were gonna rope him into one of their stupid wars."

"And the one that's going on now?"

She's been cautious about bringing this up, knowing that Italians might have family reasons to distrust the United Front-

"You mean Mussolini? That friggin gorilla ought be locked up in a cage here."

"He's popular—"

"He's popular with the idiots who think they're gonna get another Roman Empire. And the rest come out and shout '*Duce, Duce!*' cause if you don't they put your ass in a sling."

"Friggin" seems to be Rick's favorite word, but he says it's what you say in polite company—and that you should hear his friggin brother's mouth.

They stop to sit on the low wall around the huge Scott fountain for a bit, a mother nearby holding onto the belt of her toddler as he dips his fingers into the water. It is as grand as the ones she's seen in photographs from Rome and Paris, stairs leading up to the circular basin, stone lions staring out at you through the arcing water, a layer-cake effect up to the highest, thickest spume of water. Henry Ford, she thinks, will probably have one of these dedicated to him after he dies.

"You know who this guy they named it after was?" Rick asks her.

"A pioneer?"

"No, a son of a *bitch*. A rich, rich son of a bitch, who nobody could stand, only when he was about to kick off he promised to foot the bill for this thing as long as they stuck his name on it and put up a statue of him."

"I don't see one—"

"It was sposed to go on top, but they hid it over on the other side. You figure this Mussolini, he's building gigantic shit all over Italy, just to remind the *populi* what a big swinging dick he is—what you got to hope is after he's gone, nobody will remember the guy."

"That depends on how much damage he does."

"Yeah," says Rick. "They named a pastry after Napoleon, didn't they?"

On the way to the canoes they run into an old organ grinder with a little squirrel monkey on his shoulder, cranking out *Lady of Spain* on the box.

"Qual è il suo nome?" Rick asks, pointing to the monkey.

"Giacomo."

"It's like Jackie," he tells Rosa. *"É un piccolo stronzo carino,"* he says to the old man as they move on.

"I wonder where that monkey came from."

"The pet store, where do you think?"

"Not what I mean," says Rosa. "We don't have monkeys in this country—not in the wild. I mean like—what *count*ry do they live in?"

"So he's an immigrant, like his master."

"Maybe. Maybe he was born in Africa."

"I think it was a she, even with that name. I didn't see any nuts hanging down."

There are a couple fallow deer, semi-wild, grazing under some wide-spaced trees along the path to the boats, one of them almost completely white.

"There's a whatsit—albino—"

"No—it's eyes aren't pink."

Rick takes a closer look. "Yeah, you're right. I wonder if they lord it over the other deer, like white people do over the colored."

"Race prejudice isn't a natural thing—"

"If it's not natural, it's sure as shit *com*mon."

There is a beautiful loop canal for the canoes, only four or five in ahead of them. There have been weekends when it's more like Dodgem cars at the fairground than a quiet paddle. Rick takes the oar, as he always does, Rosa happy enough not to worry about tipping them into the drink.

"My people were fishermen, back in Sicily," he says as they glide along. "Generations of them."

"From what town?"

"Sicily is an island, right, so there's a lot of coastline, a lot of little ports. Both my mother's and my father's people come from Trapani—it's in the west. Them and a boatload of gangsters, too, sons of bitches. You work hard, get a loaf of bread, they want half of it."

"The bootlegging—"

"That was just the obvious stuff, what gets in the papers. You think my old man got to sell his ices without kicking back to some friggin goombah?"

"Out *here*?"

"'Out here,' she says. All through Prohibition there was a speakeasy in the basement of that aquarium. My brother Nunzio used to go there."

"So they prey on their own people."

"There must be Jews done the same when your people come over. These gangs go way back to the Old Country, they started out to fight the landowners, but then they turned into a friggin plague. It happens to every outfit after a while. Religions, countries—"

"You think the union could go bad?"

Rick lets them drift as he considers this. "Nah," he decides, "we got too many types just in our own local, even got ni—even got some colored. And we'll just have to see which way the bunch of them go tomorrow."

"What's tomorrow?"

Rick grins, puts a finger to his lips. "If I told you, I'd have to drown you. Here we are."

She hates it when he does that, acts like he has some secret source of knowledge that all her hours volunteering at the Local can never equal. Some exclusive guy thing-

They have come opposite the band shell, the lights just turned on, beautiful, and they ease into a spot where you can tie up and listen. The little orchestra is already playing, what Rick calls old fogey music but Rosa recognizes as Handel. It is a warm night, no mosquitos yet, the moon just rising to reflect on the water, and the canoe rocks gently as they listen. She feels good here, with him, even if it's not a match made in the workers' paradise. Ira refers to Rick as "Garibaldi," as if he can't remember his name, and Papa just keeps saying "as long as he treats you right," not knowing what that usually means in the jazz songs.

He's really good-looking and on the right side and he wants to be with her.

The Handel is in a peaceful mode right now. Papa listens to the Ford show on the radio, liking the symphonies but turning it off for the homilies at the end.

"Rick?"

"Yeah?"

"You better friggin tell me what's supposed to happen tomorrow."

• • •

Early in the shift there is an argument, then a fist fight between a machine operator and a Service Department informer in the rolling mill. A man named Sullivan decides this is it, and leaves his post. There is a big red button on the wall, which he pushes to stop the works. The whole works. Men look up from their stations, puzzled, then see a foreman named Barberey rushing over-

"What the hell do you think you're doing?!"

Sullivan does not have time to answer-

"Strike!" shouts one of his coworkers.

"Strike!" shouts another steel man.

"Strike! Strike! Strike! Strike!" they shout, the ones with metal tools in their hands clanging them on the nearest hard surface. Hot, pliable steel lies motionless on the conveyors, cooling. Sullivan marches away from the stunned foreman, waving his arms for the others to follow-

"After me, fellas! This is a walkout, not a sit in!"

Another man runs to the end of the floor and out onto the service road, waving with the red shirt he's tucked under his coveralls to lookouts posted in the windows of the Pressed Steel and Spring and Upset Buildings. The word is passed quickly, and runners, ignoring the shouted threats from their minders, are sent across the vast acreage to the Glass Plant and B Building-

-where the belts have only stopped moving twice since Kaz started assembling for the Company. A couple years back a guy had a heart attack and fell across the conveyor, and then last month an engine block broke off an overhead rail and did a bunch of damage when it hit. And now the whole deal just *stops*. Guys up and down the line are looking at each other, blinking like moles just flushed out of their hole, and then the flying squad is there, Bill McKie at the head of it-

"Listen up, everybody! We're going *out*!"

"B Building?"

"The whole plant. Grab what you came in with and hit the gate—you'll get the details outside."

At first it is like being herded, some of the flying squad guys with metal bars in hand, driving them toward the main exit, but quickly the guys get into the swing of it, shouting to each other and laughing, Kaz swept up with the mass of them. They look giddy, he thinks, like schoolkids told to go home halfway through a summer day.

"Hey, it's a jailbreak!" shouts a man still lugging his long-handled wrench.

Seven or eight befuddled Service Department lunks stand by the exit door, not looking so tough as they face the first couple hundred line-workers heading out.

"Yo, what's the fuckin story?" shouts the boldest of them.

"Vacating the premises," says Bill. "Don't touch anything while we're gone—you might hurt yourselves."

Outnumbered several hundred to one, the flunkies part quickly as the men stream out past them into the night, Kaz grinning at the sudden guilty twinge when he realizes he's leaving and hasn't punched out on the time clock.

No more pencils, no more books, no more teacher's dirty looks-

When they hit the service road, he sees that workers are also pouring out from the Job Foundry and Motor Assembly, bunching up to squeeze through wide-open Gate Four, no security guards visible, and leave the factory. Somehow a stream of automobiles with their headlights on, mostly Fords, is rolling in both directions on Miller Road, Kaz joining those who climb the overpass to reach the parking lot or get a better look. Just-appointed strike captains begin to shout out instructions, and Bill McKie taps his arm-

"C'mon with me, Kaz. We got work to do."

Kaz points to the cars below. "Are those all ours?"

Bill nods. "We can't block all the entrances to the fortress with just bodies. We'll park them till the Dearborn cops get it in gear to tow, then we'll put them into motion—*slow* motion—all around the perimeter. Plenty of reinforcements from the other shops in Detroit are coming, plus our army of Rouge workers."

"This is UAW?"

Bill grins. "Like I said, just 600. But the Reuthers and the other big muckty-mucks won't dare to withhold authorization. Just *look* at us all."

"Yeah," says Kaz, trying not to think about how much this might cost him. "A real stampede."

Much later, when the sun rises over the Rouge, the roads surrounding it are still full of automobiles, the sidewalks full of men walking. It is not business as usual-

-not even in the foundry. The foundry is crowded with Service Department men. Most are white, recently joined by four or five colored loafers, ex-pugs who fought as middleweights and have let themselves fill out to something more substantial. They were at the gate this morning to escort Zeke and the other workers on his shift into the building, the strikers, hundreds of them, stepping aside but booing them or calling to come join their brothers. Zeke didn't recognize a one of them.

Big rumpus last night, B Building shut down, but Zeke has liquid metal to pour, and you got to keep your head in the job—

"All right, you people, listen up!"

The tone of it gets Zeke and the others beside him to turn, the conveyor still rolling. Some of the molds will reach shake-out unfilled-

"There's been this bullshit walkout in some of the other buildings," says the fattest of the Service Department men. "But the foundry don't stop. And when the shift change comes around this afternoon, nobody goes *any*where."

Zeke can see that the leader and one of the other Service men are strapped with pistols, which he hasn't seen since that crazy fight on the overpass.

"Anybody decides to leave," the man says, "they never come *back*."

Harry is in the tunnel. Any good fortress has at least two of these, access in and out that only a handful of the right people know exist. He's run this scenario in his head dozens of times, but can't believe the enemy have made the most basic mistake—they haven't shut themselves *in*, like in Flint and at Kansas City, they've just taken a powder and think that's going to shake the Chief enough to negotiate with their commissars. They've ceded him the high ground.

Sam Taylor, looking panicked, falls into step with him as he enters the basement.

"Most of the day shift wouldn't come in, Harry! There's too many of them out there to-"

"I want machine gunners on every roof on the periphery," Harry tells him.

"Ready to rattle?"

"On my order, yeah. Where's all that tear gas Gillespie had squirreled away?"

"Still in the vault in the photo department—"

"Break it out and spread it around with people who know how to handle it at all the gates."

"There's so many gates—"

"And I want every one of them covered! You've got enough people, let them earn their keep for a change. Are there employees who came in?"

"Close to a thousand, maybe, from what we can tell. Most of the colored in the foundry."

"Give me two bodyguards, I'll go over there to talk to them. Any vandalism, theft?"

"Hell, I don't know. It's so big—"

"If they haven't shut the railroad tracks down we can bring in boxcars full of people who want to work. If that's not open, there's always barges up the river and into the canal slip. Get Marshall on the phone, tell him he's got to do some damn quick recruiting."

"Okay—"

"I had some patches made up—from now on the ID badge alone won't cut it. Pass them out, and then if you see somebody wandering around without a patch, assume it's an anarchist come to blow something up."

"Dearborn cops doing anything?" asks Sam.

"They're still getting off their fat asses. I called the governor, and he's too chickenshit to send in the National Guard—we're going to have to hold the fort on our own for the first couple days."

"It'll be that long?"

Harry sighs. For the Service Department you need to be a certain kind of tough, not easily bored, with a mean streak that can be kept under control. But the smarts to deal with a free-for-all like this-

"It's a *siege*, Sam. You ever hear of the Trojan wars?"

The office of the westside Local is buzzing when Rosa gets there. People shouting on the telephones, people asking for rides, people saying they can't believe it-

"Those hotheads in 600 stampeded everybody out of the Rouge," says Vic Reuther, not happy. "Now we've got to clean up after them."

"Isn't that what we wanted? A mass action?"

He looks at her like she just crawled out from a sewer. "We were still preparing our position. It's not the *time*."

Dave Leary, over to help from the Mine Workers, is less upset. "Their noses are out of joint because the workers beat them to it," he says. "Now they have to jump aboard quick before the ship sails without them."

"What can we do from here?"

"Head for where the fight is. You can squeeze into my car."

On the way across town Rosa listens to the men talk. Rick had heard at least one of the buildings was going out, probably the rolling mill, but didn't know the time or any other details. The conversation in the car centers on what concessions should be demanded.

"Don't call them concessions," says Leary. "Call them *rights*. And don't base it on any of the other shops in the area—Ford prides itself on being one of a kind. We want a one-of-a-kind contract."

The traffic slows as they approach the Dearborn line, even police cars stuck in the squeeze.

"Have you seen a streetcar pass us the whole way?" he asks Rosa.

"No—now that I think of it—"

"They might have lifted the contact pole on the one in the Rouge station, shut the main line down."

"That's good, isn't it?"

Dave is the only man smiling in the car. "It's great. Somebody did some planning."

They slow almost to a stop when the Gate 4 overpass comes into sight, then pull over and get out. The turn-off to the gate is blocked by parked cars, and most of what keeps crawling along in both directions seem to be cars full of supporters, blasting their horns and waving union banners out their windows. A double line of workers, some still carrying their lunch pails, are already walking back and forth in front of all five of the Miller Road gates.

"Look at them all!" cries Rosa.

It is the uniformed officials who seem disorganized—the usual handful of Dearborn cavalry, others on foot, talking among themselves but not trying to engage with the picketers, overwhelmed for the moment by the size of the walkout. Dave Leary takes her arm, shouts into her ear over the honking horns-

"Nothing much will happen here till they try to bring scabs in or out, and I figure that won't happen till the usual shift change. Get yourself to 600 headquarters, tell them we'll be sending urns of coffee and sandwich makings over, which they can distribute as they see fit. Then get on the phone to our place and make it happen."

Rosa starts back down the islands in the middle of Miller Road, remembering how hard it was to get these same workers to accept a union flyer from her hand. She looks up to the famous eight stacks that tower over the powerhouse building, the ones you can see from miles away.

Only one anemic puff of smoke-

• • •

Zeke has only seen the Little Man in here once before, leading some big shots on a tour.

He remembers Otis Gamble murmuring "Welcome to the zoo" and overhearing Bennett say how many degrees the furnaces were kept at, a number that didn't seem possible. He's got the bow tie on, red today, a couple hundred foundry workers mustered in front of him in rows like an army movie.

"In addition to your Ford badges, you will be given an identification patch to wear," says the Little Man, feet wide apart, hands clasped behind his back. Parade rest, that's what it's called, how you stand if you don't have your rifle up and ready. But the Little Man's got a pistol in his pocket, a big one from the way it hangs-

"Subversive elements have driven a good number of your coworkers from their stations and into the street," he says, "and will at some point attempt to return and take command of the rest of the factory. These are *not* your people. I am gratified to see that here in the foundry, among Mr. Ford's most loyal employees, common sense rules the day. Our enemy has successfully kidnapped several smaller manufacturing concerns in Detroit with similar tactics, and I'm afraid that, given their misguided political bent, we can expect no help from either the federal or state authorities."

Most of the white foremen talk to them like they're a bunch of ignorant field hands, but the Little Man is looking them dead in the eye like they're partners in something. Zeke has heard Bennett was a boxer, and has taken a poke at more than one Company manager-

"I am therefore authorized to make you this offer—any man who chooses to stay will be paid one dollar an *hour* from this moment on, twenty-four hours a day, for as many days as it takes to defend our livelihoods. Cots will be brought over from the infirmary, you will be fed regularly, and perhaps more importantly, you will be *armed*, provided with some extra persuasion in the unlikely case our outer perimeter should be compromised, *or*—" and here he pauses to look up and down at their ranks—"if we should choose to go on the o*ffen*sive. Any of you who do *not* wish to stay may—in fact *must*—leave the complex now."

The Little Man scans their faces.

"But I must warn you that we have no control over what transpires off of Company property, and while battling my way in here I observed a multitude of ignorant, hopped-up Hunkies who think of you as *scabs* who take their jobs and ignore their call for riot."

Through the windows in the machine shop they hear honking and shouting on Miller Road. Zeke tried to get up on the roof to take a look, but there was a squash-nosed Service redneck waving a Tommy gun on the stairs, telling him to get back where he belonged.

"We are counting on you gentlemen," says Bennett, "and I'm certain if it comes to actual fighting, you will acquit yourselves honorably."

The Little Man hurries away then, a couple Service flunkies left with the foreman DeLuca to hand out the new patches. Zeke and the other men who work at the edge of the melting heat keep their metal Ford badges in their back pockets, one less thing to burn yourself on, and are told to wear the patches where they can be seen.

Otis steps over to pass a word. Since they sent Zeke to Marshall's dinner, men have been acting like he's some kind of shop steward—

"Sounds like we prisoners in here," he says.

"Yeah—but *whose* prisoners aint so clear."

They are each handed a new patch. It is a paper circle, with sticky stuff on one side. On the other it says **100% FOR FORD**.

• • •

Smitty has been taking a poll back at the paper—fifteen rounds, Harry Bennett versus Benito Mussolini, bantamweights—who do you like? The Italian might have a few pounds on Mr. Ford's Little Man, but Harry's fancy footwork, able to move backward and forward at the same time, would give him trouble.

And both of them fight dirty.

"I'm going to share with you a wire I have just sent to the President of the United States," Harry announces with one of his tiger paintings as a backdrop, then reads off a sheet of paper.

"Dear Mr. President, I regret to inform you of a crisis situation now facing us in Dearborn, Michigan. An unlawful walk-out strike, followed by the criminal seizure of highway approaches and entrances to the River Rouge plant in a Communistic demonstration of violence and terrorism have prevented the vast majority of our 85,000 employees from continuing their vital work. It is clear that the union's main object is not an election, but rather to tie up a large American industry and cripple the national defense program."

Red Menace talk doesn't seem to carry the weight with Roosevelt that it did with Hoover or Coolidge, so maybe this gambit is tailored more to convince the old King to let Harry wage full-scale war before Prince Edsel can fly back from his vacation to dump water on the flames.

Harry continues. "*Non-striking employees attempting to return to work have been brutally assaulted, women employees have been mauled and cursed, and even a fifteen-year-old boy has been viciously attacked while attempting to attend classes at the trade school. The unions seized our factory like burglars, and if Mr. Ford were to condone such actions by negotiating with them it would be tantamount to an abandonment of our free-market system.*"

The Little Man looks up from his manifesto, an Il Duce thrust to his chin.

"Did you ask Roosevelt to send troops?" asks Smitty.

"That has been strongly suggested, yes."

"You think he will?"

"If he doesn't, we are fully prepared to defend our business and employees on our own."

"How many of your workers are still inside?" asks Danny Curtis of the *News*.

"Over two thousand, most of them in the foundry."

"Most of them colored?"

Harry shakes his head at the perfidy of it all. "That is the most despicable aspect of these subversives' actions. Attempting to exploit racial prejudice and inflame hatred for their own sinister purpose—"

One of the great counter-punchers, Harry, able to turn any fact on its head. The Rouge is the only one of Ford's factories in the States or overseas to hire a significant percentage of colored workers, a combination, perhaps, of strike insurance and the difficulty of finding anybody else to do the hardest and most dangerous jobs.

"The union claims *you're* the ones trying to sabotage the defense program, given Mr. Ford's Nazi connections," says Smitty.

"Typical Red propaganda. I don't recall that our nation is at war with anybody—"

"And your boss has joined Charles Lindbergh in the America First Committee."

"Mr. Ford has always been an advocate of peaceful solutions to the world's problems. Whereas President Roosevelt's lend-lease deal with Britain—"

"Voted into law by our Congress—"

"-puts us in the line of fire in what should be solely European business. American lives will be lost if our ships continue to supply—"

"You're gearing up this aircraft plant out at Willow Run," Smitty interrupts. "Do you think the present government will award defense contracts to a company that continues to defy the Wagner Act?"

Harry gives him the hard eyes and a sneer. Mussolini would definitely have his mitts full-

"Manufacturing armaments for the British to wage war with is not de*fense*. I'm not sure Mr. Ford would accept such a contract."

Harry dismisses the news pests and takes a moment to collect his thoughts. He asks Mildred to get him Sam Taylor at the foundry.

"What's happening there? "

"We haven't been able to get any food in," Sam tells him. "The strikers stripped the commissary and the trucks when they left. And they're throwing rocks over the fence—it's a pretty good heave, but they've knocked out some windows in the machine shop."

"Any encroachment?"

"There's Dearborn cops between us and them, spread pretty thin, but so far they're just pacing around out there. Got their signs, got their American flags—"

"Morale in the foundry?"

"I gotta tell you, Harry, the natives are getting restless."

"Here's what you're going to do—get about a hundred or more of the colored guys, the ones who look like they'd like to tear into some white meat, and give them crowbars, knives, whatever you can throw together, and tell them this is life or death—they can turn the tide and save their jobs from being handed over to the Polacks. Then set them loose."

"That could be a slaughter, Harry. There's thousands out there, and they're organized—"

"So be it," says the Little Man. "Let the other side get crucified in the papers for a change."

• • •

Kaz is stationed just in front of the overpass, clipboard in hand, getting names of picketers who can stay the night, taking messages and telephone numbers so they can contact their people. Bud Novak came by to tell him that Molly got home all right, and that Sorenson is moving the Willow Run team away from the Rouge because of the streetcar line being disabled.

The picketers are still walking on air, but Kaz knows if the Company holds out for long it will be tough for them to cover all the gates, and there are so many desperate unemployed, especially in Black Bottom and Paradise Valley, that Employment won't have trouble scaring up a small army of scabs. He recognizes the leaflet girl, walking down the picket line handing out sandwiches from a cardboard box strapped over her shoulders.

"Hey, do you live here, or what?"

It takes her a moment to recognize him.

"Mr. Polonsky—"

"Pilsudsky."

She nods at the milling throng of workers. "Isn't it great to see them with their heads up?"

The signs have come out of storage-

WHY DID
FORD
GET A
NAZI
MEDAL?

-and-

Let's make
DEARBORN
Part of
AMERICA
Again!

-and his favorite-

★KING★
HENRY
V-8

-while others are chanting and singing-

"When they tie the can to a union man,
Walk on! Walk on!
When they give him the sack, make them take the guy back!
Walk on! Walk on!
When the speed-up comes, don't twiddle your thumbs!
Walk on! Walk on!

When the boss won't talk, just take a long walk!
Walk on! Walk on!"

The young woman, who reminds him that her name is Rosa, offers him a sandwich.

"What've you got?"

"Either peanut butter or baloney."

"I'll take peanut butter—I get enough baloney on the radio."

The union has its own little radio station now, in the Maccabee building in Detroit, and for a while before the Service Department caught onto it somebody near the end of the line was setting the radios to that station before the cars rolled off to be sold. It is mostly pep-talk kind of stuff, but also some news about what's going on in Europe, trying to explain how the German *blitzkrieg* attack could have rolled over France and Belgium so quick, and to not kid yourself that America can stay out of it.

While Kaz unwraps the sandwich she holds his clipboard, glancing at what he's written.

"You're taking names?"

"We got guys signing up left and right, guys who need to go home for a while, guys with friends they can call in to fill the ranks—"

"You know a Rick Donati?"

"No, but I think I know his brother—"

"He'd be on one of the flying squads."

"That what got you into this deal?"

"It wasn't a *boy*friend, if that's what you mean."

He cocks his head at her. It was his old man's worst prejudice from the old country, and Kaz himself never really dealt with any before the union-

"You're Jewish, if I remember right—"

"Guilty."

"The ones that the Old Man's newspaper used to say control all the money—"

He is teasing but she isn't smiling. "Then they didn't share any of it with *us*. We still live in Black Bottom."

"You don't work for the Company, your family neither, so I'm wondering—"

"Solidarity with the people. *All* the people."

"That's a tall order."

"It's our job, here on earth."

Kaz laughs. "Jeez, you sound like Father Janusz—"

At that moment there is a roar, and they look over to the gate and see men fighting-

When the orders were handed down, Otis was desperate to go.

"There's some nasty shit waiting for us outside," Zeke told him. "You think we can fight our way through all that and get clear?"

"There's some nasty shit running through my *brain*," said Otis. "I need my medicine."

"They got the infirmary open—"

"They aint handing out what I *need*."

They haven't talked about it, but it's been clear for some time that Otis is some kind of snowbird, never getting loose from what the hospital was giving him after he lost the toes. All Zeke knows about that stuff is from Cab Calloway singing about kicking the gong around, but he can tell when a man is in a cold sweat.

"There's some police officers out there," the Service Department bulldog told the group they revved up to go fight, maybe seventy or eighty men, all colored. "They'll have your backs."

Don't want a Dearborn cop having *noth*ing to do with my back, thought Zeke, hoping to drop his weapon and alibi his way through the picketers. And all he sees now is white men with clubs torn from the signs they carry, trying to knock his head off his shoulders, Zeke parrying with an iron bar ground down on both sides to make something like a sword.

I'm going to die playing fucking Robin Hood.

"Back inside, back inside!" he hollers, swinging the heavy weapon, backing up steadily trying to make sure none of the whites get behind him. He sees Otis, head soaked with blood, pulled away by a pair of cops, sees men, black and white, go down and disappear into the muddle, then jams his body in the metal gate before the Service Department asshole can shut them out.

"Open it up," he shouts, "or I split your damn head in two!"

The man runs back toward the foundry building.

Some mounted cops finally do appear to herd most of the picketers back onto the road, and when most of the attack squad are safe behind the fence, foot patrolmen hurry up to wave their long billies and threaten to make arrests. Zeke sees blood on his shirt, discovers that it's dripping down from his split lip.

"What we do now?" asks one of the men, one of his eyes already swollen up to a slit.

"Go back in and earn that round-the-clock pay," Zeke tells him. "Less you want another round with these white motherfuckers."

• • •

Smitty sees it from the overpass. What the colored workers were thinking—if *think*ing had anything to do with it—remains a mystery, and he sure as hell isn't going to fight his way inside to interview them. But he'll get something in for the next edition—

> Negro workers loyal to the Ford Motor Company were set upon by hordes of enraged strikers as they attempted to leave the Rouge River facility this evening, a violent clash that left many wounded on both sides. "We just want to do our jobs," claimed one of the battered loyalists as he was evacuated on a stretcher to Henry Ford Hospital, "and to feed our families."

Fosdick at the *Free Press* has never been too fussy about 'verifying the source,' as long it isn't a public figure with easy access to legal retribution, especially if what you've made up sounds like something your anonymous character might say. The *News* and *Times* lay the dialect on pretty thick—"We jus' needs to feed our babies"—and at this point they'll will be wagging their fingers at the union's boldness, hoping to influence public opinion but staying poised to change direction if it turns against Ford. Outrage is outrage, and sells papers in Detroit, as does the race-hatred angle, a tornado always just on the horizon. More colored keep coming up from the south or over from Toledo and Chicago every year, their neighborhoods here busting at the seams, and the white folks' fear that some new Dr. Sweet with his armed friends and relatives will move in next door to them just gets worse. Here in Dearborn, of course, they are covenanted from residence, colored workers at the Rouge allowed a narrow pathway from the streetcar to their post in the factory and back, like a Jamaican maid on her daily odyssey from Black Bottom to Grosse Pointe Shores.

> Animosity between the races has long been an issue at
> the Dearborn plant, claimed by some to be encouraged,
> even exploited, by management.

Smitty will throw that into his copy, though destined for Fosdick's red pencil even if he doesn't mention Harry Bennett specifically. Editors need to be confronted with the truth now and then, if only to make them trot out their speech about public responsibility and leaving opinion to the editorial boys. Fosdick has an ulcer, and Smitty is determined to keep it burning.

He took Portia on a tour of Black Bottom and Paradise Valley a few weeks back, even getting out of the car at a few spots and talking to some of his more colorful informants. Born and raised in Detroit and she'd never set foot there.

"How can they bear living in these horrible, crowded buildings?" she wanted to know.

"Because they don't have any choice. Ever read the lease for your apartment?"

"They don't mention—"

"'*The neighborhood will maintain its traditional racial character.*' And they don't mean the Potawatomis are moving back in."

"The people here all work at Ford?"

"Most of the ones who *get* to work. The others—well, you don't need a social security number to go into business on these streets. What are the last three numbers of yours?"

"Six-eight-three. Why?"

"You're going to make a wager on it."

He took her to Blind Benny, who holds down the news kiosk at the corner of St. Antoine and Beacon, and juggles policy bets in his head. "Why would I write down numbers," he likes to remind you, "when I can't *read* them no more?"

Back in the day Benny's handlers sent him off on a bus to Traverse City for a fight, a set-up as it turned out, the referee allowing his opponent's corner to keep dusting their man's gloves with resin during the round breaks, and permanently damaging both of his eyes.

"I can see light and dark, see shapes," Benny told Portia at the news stand, "even see my colors. But it's all just a *blur*."

"So you know we're white?" teased Smitty.

"Hell, man, you don't need *eyes* to know that."

Smitty had Portia lay a fin on her last three Social Security numbers.

"Any chance I'll win?" she asked as they walked away.

"I never even check. I just throw a little support Benny's way now and then. He's always happy to repeat the latest noise from the street for me."

"He just took the bill and trusted it was a five—"

"That's right."

"But what if—?"

"Never happen. The same way nobody ever lifts a newspaper from his stand without paying. Benny's been to the *wars*, he's a respected member of the community."

"He trusts people."

"He trusts *col*ored people."

Hastings Street was its usual free-for-all, Smitty explaining that the Hebrew writing on the shop fronts was left from when the area was mostly Jewish, but they only held onto a few of the businesses—pawn shops and second-hand stores—and collected rent from the others.

"They've set up a second front on Oakland Avenue," he told her. "Still a long way from your old bailiwick."

"They'll get there."

"Over your Daddy's dead body."

He took her by the Busy Bee and Miss Fat's Goodtime House, showed her Jap Sneed's black-and-tan Three Sixes club on East Adams.

"I saw Earl Hines and Snakehips Tucker in there with seven hundred of our beige brethren," he told her. "Jap has a bar made out of glass bricks, and the best mixologists in all of Detroit."

"You've taken a survey?"

"Oh yes."

He explained that the main streets are even livelier at night, the jukes playing their music loud to draw people inside, some of them open till six in the morning.

"I don't see any police."

"Oh, they'll come through when they feel like it, in pairs and in squadrons. The Department recruits a lot of rednecks from down south, because they know how to handle Negroes."

She gave him her look.

"That's a quote—the Chief even let me stick his name behind it."

"They try to keep order—"

"They'll lean against a parked car and watch a razor fight, betting on which man bleeds to death first. And they take donations from the local merchants—not like they did during Prohibition, but enough to keep the wheels greased."

"You're such a cynic."

"If I had to live here, doll," he told her, "I'd be homicidal."

It was getting dark at the end of their visit, Portia distracted by a pair of young lovelies sitting up behind a bay window, both wearing something sheer and slinky and tapping on the panes with chopsticks to get their attention.

"Oh," said Portia, unable to maintain her characteristic poise, "those are—"

"You know what they are," he told her. "And they're not offering Chinese food."

She thanked him for the tour. Ballsy gal, Portia, and not one to give you the high hat-

Smitty sees Snaps Wiley climb up onto the overpass, lugging his Speed Graphic.

"You get any of that scuffle?"

"I'm worried about the light—you might not be able to tell they were different colors."

"I could give Harry a call, tell him to stage the next one at high noon."

"You think that was planned?"

"You think the gladiators wrestled lions for the fun of it?"

Below them the picketers not wounded badly enough to be shepherded off to the DeSoto local for repairs are full of beans and bravado, reliving their heroics. A pair of mounted cops steer their glue-factory rejects through the crowd to dampen the celebration.

"You got to keep *moving*, fellas," shouts Dearborn's Finest. "Otherwise you're an obstruction."

"*You're* the obstruction," announces one of the combatants. "When we get our contract, your days are numbered."

"We don't work for Ford."

"You don't think so? Bet you ten-to-one he pays for the oats that nag of yours scarfs down every morning."

"Shuffle those feet, Mack," snorts the other centaur. "You aint won this thing yet."

Smitty gives Snaps a big grin, flipping his notepad open. "I love it when I don't have to make up the dialogue."

• • •

Mavis is upstairs, her shift just over, when the paddy wagon comes in to the rear entrance with the wounded. All of them colored men, Ford workers, and she picks out Otis Gamble right away. He is looking bad, scalp open and blood drying all over his face.

"Was Zeke with you?"

"Yeah, he kind of led us out," says Otis, who is shaking like a whipped dog. "But I think he got back inside the gate with the others."

DeWitt sent word over that he'd left the Trade School with no problem, but she's been fretting about Zeke since they heard on the radio about the walkout. That many white folks get their blood up, there's no telling what it will lead to-

"Can you get me something?" Otis asks her. "I'm coming apart here."

One look in his eyes and Mavis can tell what he's talking about, laid up in the burn ward not so long ago, and you *know* what they give out in the shots there-

"Honey, I don't get near any of that. You got to ask one of the nurses."

"But you'll let Ruby know where I am?"

Ruby still barely talks to her, blaming Zeke for those missing toes.

"I'll stop by on my way home. Have they all gone crazy at that factory?"

"It were always cooking, cooking, cooking every day," says Otis, hugging himself like he's freezing. "Only today that pot done boilt *over*."

• • •

Governor Van Wagoner acts like he's being kidnapped, constantly asking if they're almost there. Harry keeps an eye on him in the rear-view mirror. Van Wagoner was Highway Commissioner for years, competent, and should have left it at that.

"I don't think we came this way that other time."

"That might be."

The Governor has been out to the Residence once before, some social function, and is looking for familiar sights. It's clear he doesn't want to do this, but Harry would rather it be him than the woman who obviously put him up to it. Madame Perkins, Roosevelt's Secretary of Labor, unloaded on Al Sloan at GM during the Flint strike, publicly calling him out as scoundrel and a skunk and saying he didn't deserve to be counted among decent men. It's the only thing the Chief agrees with her about.

"You sure he's expecting me?"

"Oh, he'll be there, all right. Mr. Ford always shows if he's promised he will. That's no guarantee he'll *stay* very long if he doesn't buy what you're peddling, but he'll be there."

They near the river, Frank giving Van Wagoner the scenic tour on Harry's orders. Build up a little tension-

"That's not it—"

"No, that's the powerhouse. Mr. Ford generates his own heat and electricity, as well as selling some, at a very reasonable rate, to the city of Dearborn."

It's good to remind them just who they're dealing with. The Chief has been through how many—twelve, thirteen governors since he founded the Company? They come and go, but he's still *here*. Frank turns the Lincoln past the garden, stunning at this time of year, and stops in front of the mansion.

"I'm sure he'll be glad to see you," says Harry reassuringly as they climb out. "He hasn't eaten a politician all day."

Pat Van Wagoner does not laugh.

Harry leads him through the house, skipping the usual commentary on the design and furnishings, and back to the sun porch where the Chief, though he considers it best employed as lining for bird cages, is reading the *Free Press*. You can see the sun sparkling off the river through the big screen panels—Harry always feels his heartbeat slowing down out here, no matter what the crisis of the day at the plant might be.

"Mr. Ford, Governor Van Wagoner has come to see you."

The Chief takes his reading glasses off, doesn't rise to shake the man's offered hand.

"Well—you've got yourself a motorcar factory," he states. "What are you going to do with it?"

Van Wagoner is at a loss for words.

"I believe the governor has a message from Washington."

"He can keep that too."

"This has to be settled," Van Wagoner manages to say.

"Go to it."

"But you've got to—"

"*I* don't *have* to do *any*thing, Mr. Governor. You're the one with an uprising on your hands."

The Chief puts his glasses back on, goes back to the newspaper. Van Wagoner looks to Harry.

"Now you can tell the folks in the White House you've seen him. We'll give you a ride back."

You see most visitors cataloguing what they ogle as they leave, eager to describe the palace of King Henry to their friends. In Harry's opinion it manages to be grand and homey at the same time, like its creator. But the Governor has a stunned, unseeing look on his face as he follows Harry out. A long ride for such a brief audience.

"They're not going to be pleased with this in Washington," he observes.

"I'm sure Mr. Ford is aware of that."

Harry can already hear the Chief summing up the meeting when he makes his evening call.

"Governor of Michigan, huh?" he'll say. "I'd give him six dollars a day."

It was up to eight for a while, but sales have been down, and the Ford Motor Company is not in the welfare business.

• • •

There is a colored man, well-dressed, conferring with the two men Rosa doesn't know who are manning the sound truck when she delivers the two big thermoses of coffee, warm to the touch, extra cups, and a bag of doughnuts.

"If you give me a chance," says the man, bending down to talk through the open window of the car, "I believe I can talk some sense into them."

"They all go to your church?"

"Not so many, no. Attendance there is likely to get you on a Service Department list. They take down the license numbers of the automobiles parked outside."

Rosa notices he's wearing a reverend's collar. Rick says that if you can be married and have kids, you're a preacher, not a priest, and Rosa has only a vague idea of what all the Christian sects are. But if you're colored, it's probably Baptist—

"Are you Reverend Hill?" she asks.

The man turns to smile at her. "That's right," he says. "I don't believe we've met."

"Reverend Hill runs the church on Hartford Avenue," she tells the men in the car. "The Local meets there all the time."

"Hey, take a crack at it if you want," says the union man in the driver's seat. "But them ones who come out to fight seemed pretty worked up."

He hands the preacher the microphone, the cord stretching just enough.

Hill, obviously no newcomer to the task, flicks the microphone on and holds it close to his mouth, looking over the fence toward the huge foundry building.

"Good afternoon," he says, voice blasting out from the speaker on top of the automobile. Rosa puts the tips of her little fingers into her ears. Picketers turn to look toward him but keep walking.

"This is the Reverend Charles Hill of the Hartford Avenue Baptist Church, and I'd like to speak to you fellows still holed up inside the factory."

Rosa sees that some of the windows close to the fence have been shattered. No faces appear-

"Though I know for a fact that as I speak, men in our community are being promised the moon if they will allow themselves to be used, I do not believe that any of you think of yourselves as scab labor. You are *work*ing men."

There are a dozen of the Service Department minders in the foundry now, standing with DeLuca as they listen. The windows on the Miller Road side have been mostly busted open, the reverend's voice coming in loud and clear, with that special echo you get from a loudspeaker.

"*I understand why you have chosen, for the time being, to remain inside the factory. We all know of the Ford company's hiring practices at this facility, and the various charitable acts its founder has performed for people of our race in this area. Charity that comes at a cost.*"

Zeke imagines that when white people use the words 'we' or 'us,' they have only people of their own color in mind, just like the reverend. But Mavis says that when Roosevelt opens with "My friends" on his radio talks, he means colored folks as well. Maybe so, but if he wants the white folks to elect him again he best not make too big of a deal of it-

"*If we, all of us, are to move forward, there has to be an honest dialogue between those who own our industries and those who do the unrewarding toil within them. This dialogue will not be possible within the current structure of management and labor at the Ford Motor Company! It is currently the one-way discourse of a master to his servants.*"

He didn't say "slaves." Zeke remembers enough of life in Arkansas to know it could be worse, having to take your hat off to address a white man, any white man, putting up with lying ledgers and crooked scales, having to sneak past the sheriff and his men if you got sick of it and wanted to leave the county. Just doing the work up here, keeping your mouth shut and your nose clean and collecting your pay, seemed like such a change, such a *priv*ilege when he started out-

"This walkout is meant only to get the Fords to agree that if their employees vote to have a union—and you will be participants in that vote—they will recognize it and accept it as your bargaining agent in the future. I have spoken at length with UAW organizers, including several of our race, who have assured me that among the agreements that management must sign off on before work resumes is that there will be no retribution allowed against any Ford worker after the strike ends, no matter which way they vote or what the color of their skin."

Two days inside now and the food that's been sent up has been late, cold, and not nearly enough to counter the boredom. They're sleeping on cots built for people shorter than Zeke, and they all need to take a bath-

"With this in mind, I strongly urge you to come out now from the plant, and if you do not wish, at present or in the future, to sign on with the union, at least demonstrate your preference when the vote is held. Certain parties—and I'm certain you are aware who they are—are attempting to make this conflict a racial one—"

The furnaces are still going but they've shut the conveyor down for now, no more hot metal trucked over on the giant ladles, no more Motor Assembly to receive the engine blocks. One process feeds the next at the Rouge, and if any one of them stops moving-

"Please show the company, show the nation, that we will not be used as strikebreakers, we will not be used as hostages, and if the union does establish itself at Rouge River, we have the fortitude and the willpower to see that it deals with its own exclusionary policies. I thank you for your attention."

Hill is not a rip-roarer like a lot of the Black Bottom preachers, he won't make your eyes roll back in your head or get you to speak in tongues, but you always feel like you've been addressed as a man, and one with some sense in his head. The foundry workers look at each other, between a rock and a hard place here, and a bunch of them turn to Zeke.

"What you thinkin, brother?"

His friend DuPree was in the Army for a spell, and says it was one place you always knew where you stood. Somebody open their yap and you just look to what he's wearing on his shoulder—anything less than three stripes and you can take it or leave it. It's been that way here since Zeke started pouring metal, go where you're told and no backtalk accepted. This deal of asking questions, of asking *him* what to do-

"Well, one thing we got to think about is whether that Little Man is gonna be good on his word about paying a dollar-an-hour for whatever time we stay here. Have we got to last till the bitter end to earn it, or can we collect on what we already done right now and walk out free?"

They look over to DeLuca.

"I'm just stuck here like you, fellas," says the foreman, one of the better ones. "I got no idea what Bennett will pull."

"Then the next thing we got to wonder is," says Zeke, "if we stay *put*, and that union get *in*, how long you think we be able to hold onto these jobs? And if they can't get us fired, what's it going to be like every shift change, walking past ten thousand white men who hate your guts?"

"Lots of them already do."

"And always will. I'm talking about the most of them, the ones who barely *see* us, we just those niggers up in the foundry, glad *they* don't have to do this work—"

"Mr. Ford will protect us."

"With these characters?" He nods to the Service Department men. He's glad the machine gunners are all on the roof. "Now we know they got some other people they snuck in locked away somewhere, probably half of Mississippi hauled up on an ore barge—"

A young one named Johnsie, who they brought over with a bunch from duco where the paint fumes will kill you quicker than the foundry heat, told him Don Marshall has a pile of new recruits holed up in one of the other buildings.

"Maybe those country boys will stay on the leash and maybe they won't, but *we're* the ones put in the time making all them Ford automobiles, *we're* the ones took the jobs nobody else wants to do, and the main thing we got to consider is whether we can *trust* those union people. Here in the Rouge, we're a good-sized chunk of the work-force, but we're still always going to be out*num*bered. We get into a union, we got to speak *up*. If we hadn't come out to vote for them, we wouldn't have had Murphy at mayor and then governor till he moved on and we wouldn't have Roosevelt at president—we aint dancing anymore unless we're invited to the *party*."

Some of the men laugh.

"Me personally, I'm going home and take these shoes off before my feet start to rot."

There isn't a vote, just a lot of back and forth, and finally old Possum, hair gone white, who in all his time at the plant has never said a mumbling word, shouts out and points—"Them leaving get on *this* side, them staying get on *that*!"

Possum is leaving.

As are about two thirds of the foundry men they've gathered together here, the rest mostly new hires who like the idea of that dollar-an-hour and others who either think Henry Ford is the second Messiah or that they'll be lynched the minute they poke their noses outside the gate, and have decided to stick it out inside.

"All that's leaving," calls out Possum, "follow Zeke Crowder."

But the Service Department men are blocking the way. "Nobody goes anywhere," says the one with the pistol, out in his hand now.

They look to DeLuca.

"Beat it, for all I care," says the foreman. "I just got to check your names off the pay list. What time is it, two-thirty?"

"You don't take orders from him," says the Service thug, waggling the heater, "you take them from *this*."

Possum holds up a double-edge sword, ground from a steel rod, his skinny arms shaking. "Y'all give out these weapons," he says. "You think you get off more than one shot before the rest of us take your Hunkie ass apart?"

There are several hundred of them, all armed, thinks Zeke. And the last thing in the world you want to step in front of is an old Negro who has finally had his *fill* of bullshit.

The Service man jams his pistol back in its holster and steps aside, spitting on the shop floor.

The first fifty of so of them are already outside the building, looking at the throngs of picketers on the other side of the gate, before they collar Zeke again.

"You good at talking, man. Fix it so it's safe."

"Give him a white flag."

"This aint a sur*ren*der," says Possum. "This is a demon*stra*tion."

Zeke walks, reluctantly, up to the gate. There's a white state trooper standing with his back to it. Not so many hand-picked crackers in the trooper outfit-

"Officer?"

The man turns around, his eyes going past Zeke to see the bulk of the men waiting behind.

"Uh-oh."

"See if you can get one of these union guys, one that pulls some weight, to come talk with me. We want to come out and it can't be like that first day."

"Larry!" he calls to another trooper. "Take my spot here. I got to go find somebody."

While the trooper winds through the picketers, lines walking in both directions, Zeke holds up a hand to keep the foundry men back by the building. He had them dump all the weapons before they came out, not a unanimously popular decision-

Two white men in their thirties come back with the trooper, one in a suit and the other still in work coveralls.

"What's the deal?" asks this one, smiling.

"We want to come out."

"Come out and what?"

"Come out and stop being used by Ford to hold your deal up."

"Sounds good—"

"Which means we don't get attacked, not here, not on the streetcar—"

"We put the streetcar out of commission."

"Then how we supposed to get home? We can't walk through no Dearborn—"

"We'll have a bus waiting for you," says the one in the suit. "Tell your people to give us ten minutes, we'll have the bus pull up and send a couple of our flying squads to give you an escort."

"Flying squad—"

"Probably the same guys you butted heads with the other day."

Zeke sighs, looks back as more and more foundry men spill out from the building.

"You're going to need more than one bus."

• • •

So much for the vacation. Edsel sits across from his father, Charlie Sorenson and Harry Bennett on either side of him, with the new lawyer, Capizzi, lurking back against the wall. Sorenson is a hothead and certainly no New Dealer, but he is a practical man and sees the writing on the wall—unions are here to stay, and to move forward they have to be dealt with in some equitable manner.

Bennett, on the other hand, is just a thug looking for a fistfight.

"So you want to give away the store," says Father. It isn't a question.

"I don't want to *give* anything," Edsel tells him. "We should be making cars, not battling each other, and if we could sit down together and work out some reasonable ground rules—"

"Sit down with Communists—"

"Nobody on their side has suggested they take over the factory, and they don't pretend to have the skill to keep the manufacturing process orderly—"

Sorenson snorts at this. "Leave them alone for five minutes and you'd have chaos."

"But within the context of what they *do* put their hands to, they want some concessions. We hear them out, take a look at how it affects profitability, and then say yes or no—"

"Give them an inch—"

"And they may ask for an inch and a half, I'm aware of that, but why go to war before we've tried that approach?"

Bennett is holding his tongue for the moment, most likely biting it. He usually waits till he's alone with Father to spill his poison.

"Where were they when Charlie and I were building this company?" says Father.

"Most of them weren't born yet, so perhaps they take the work for granted. And I have no doubt, Father, that you can still do every job in the plant—but you can't do all of them at the same time."

"We could build machines to do most of those jobs," says Sorenson.

"We've already done quite a bit of that, and you know how much time and money it takes. We'd have to shut down for five years—"

"I'm ready to shut down tomorrow," snaps Father.

"And if the union leadership are really Soviet agents, that's exactly what they want. We live in a democracy, people respect the right to vote—"

"So you say let the lunatics vote to run the asylum."

Usually by now Father would have walked away or told Edsel to just shut up, so he must be considering the idea.

"Between their fight with the AFL and people within their own leadership jockeying for power, they've got more of a mess going than Europe," Edsel offers, knowing Father's dim view of the foreign conflict. "Do you honestly think a rabble like that can sit down and out-bargain Henry Ford?"

Later, when it is just him and the Chief, Harry learns why he let his weak-kneed son win the round.

"As long as it's a secret vote, Labor Board rules, nobody standing over their shoulder with a club in hand," says the old man, "I trust my boys to come through. Some will vote CIO, some will vote AFL, and most will vote no damn union at *all*. You'll see, Harry."

• • •

It is the rainy season, but Norma and Kerry are each toting a big red *guarda-chuva* to open whenever the showers dump again. Manaus might be the Paris of the Amazon, but Norma is certain it never rains in such fickle spurts in the great French city, and that French umbrellas are properly black and somber. If they carry red ones, she'd have seen it in one of those famous paintings.

With the sky not pelting them at the moment, they stand in the San Sebastián Plaza gazing at the Teatro Amazonas, something like an elaborate, multi-tiered pink-and-white birthday cake wearing a dome of glazed tile the colors of Brazil's garish flag. The man at the hotel desk said "*Disculpe, está fechado,*"—closed, like half of what they want to see here, which is a shame because Norma has never seen an opera in person, and with those you don't really have to understand the language because the stories are just royalty and gypsies stabbing each other and you get the drift.

"*A relic of both the Belle Epoque and the great Amazonian rubber boom of the late nineteenth century,*" reads Kerry from the English-language guidebook they found in the hotel lobby, "*the theater boasts roofing tiles imported from Alsace, steel walls forged in Glasgow, stairs of Carrara marble, and inside, one hundred ninety-eight chandeliers imported from Italy, thirty-two of them of Murano glass.*"

"Whatever all that stuff is," Norma observes, "you won't find it in Detroit."

She turns in a circle. The wet cobblestones at their feet are laid in alternate, wavy black and white bands, the plaza's center dominated by an elaborate monument on a stone platform that Kerry says is about the opening of the Port of Manaus to the ships of the world. The bow of an old sailing ship juts out from each of the four sides of the base—representing Asia, Africa, America, and Europa—while a huge woman towers above, looking heroic despite her toga or whatever you call it in Portuguese slipping off one shoulder-

"*Some*body got rich growing rubber," says Kerry, staring at the San Sebastián Church that faces the Theater across the plaza. "And they weren't afraid to show it."

"I bet the Fords are richer than these people ever were," says Norma. "But their taste just isn't as loud."

"You mean 'grand.'"

Kerry has taken to correcting her a lot, which Norma could tolerate if it was just her paltry Portuguese.

"That's another word for it, I suppose," says Norma. "People who get rich quick want the world to know it. Mr. Ford struggled for years before he got his factory going."

"You don't think the people who built all this had to work?"

"I don't think they were out in the jungle scraping sap off the trees."

Kerry reads out loud about the most famous of the mansions they pass as they make their way to Eduardo Ribeiro Avenue, the rain holding off and an eager *garçom* running out with dry-seated chairs so they can sit at a café and watch the world go by. The streetcars and automobile traffic amazed Norma when they first arrived so many years ago on a slow boat from New Orleans to Belém—it has been nothing but Fordlandia and Belterra since then, a bit like if you never left Pine Camp back home. Most of the men here wear white, whether attractive linen suits or street hawkers' rags, with the traffic police trying to sort out the midday snarl in white uniforms with white pith helmets, looking like the hunters in a *Tarzan* picture. The women are more colorful, and seemingly the darker their skin the more able to look lovely in colors Norma wouldn't dare go out in.

They order coffee, which Kerry has been drinking for a couple years now, and some of the crispy fried cod balls that people have been offering from carts on the street corners and Norma promised they could have if they found a sit-down place that served them.

"Just because it comes from a cart doesn't mean it's dirty," Kerry admonishes her. "And just because it comes out of a kitchen doesn't mean it's clean."

Norma mostly ignores the constant admonishment, recalling that at the same age she knew pretty much everything.

"Not many girls get to travel while they're so young," she tells her daughter. "I'm glad you're getting to see all of this before you leave."

"I'm sure they have an opera house in Kalamazoo."

Again with the sarcasm.

"I believe there is a concert hall."

Getting Kerry to accept the idea of the Teachers' College has been a long and arduous campaign, Norma stressing the idea that a profession is a must for a modern woman, Kerry maintaining that there are excellent schools in both Rio and São Paulo, and Jim attempting to duck out of the crossfire.

"You've got a knack for picking up languages. While you're at Western Michigan you can study a few more and then travel wherever you want, teaching English."

Though she's still selling the idea, Norma's stomach tightens at the thought of Kerry living with an ocean between them. Even staying down here with Jim while her daughter is up in Michigan-

"Sure," says Kerry, staring at something down the street. "Maybe I'll learn Chinese."

The something down the street is a parade. The desk clerk said they'd have a safe and spectacular view of *Carnaval* from the hotel roof once it got dark, but apparently the festivities can't wait. Three drummers lead the procession, pounding a lively, complicated rhythm, somebody is blowing a whistle, and behind them four hefty men with their shirts off, faces and chests painted with bright red stripes, carry a platform holding a statue that looks to be at least twelve feet tall—a smiling, jet-black woman wearing a gorgeous white lace dress and a headdress of colorful fruits and flowers.

"It's Kamélia!" exclaims Kerry, already rocking her body to the beat of the drums.

"Be still," says her mother, embarrassed. "And who's Camelia?"

Kerry keeps bouncing on her chair. "Nobody's looking at *us*, Mom."

It is true. The street suddenly fills with onlookers, people lean out of windows, waiters and cooks step out from the café to watch as the drummers, the statue bearers, and finally the whirling revelers behind them, masked and painted and feathered and beaded, move down Avenida Ribeiro in a winding paroxysm—a word Norma learned from Dr. Niles—of joyous movement.

Norma puts her fingers in her ears as they pass by, some of the dancers spreading out to engage the watching crowd, and suddenly there is Kerry up on her feet moving in a surprisingly graceful and provocative way opposite a young man who is nearly as dark as grinning, bobbing Kamélia, a young man dressed in bright yellow from head to toe.

Norma forces an indulgent smile onto her face, sits back to let it all flow by. She is pretty certain that there is no *Carnaval* in Kalamazoo.

• • •

Rosa has never seen so many people in one place in her life, and certainly not such a mix of black and white. Cadillac Square is more than full, onlookers jammed between the great hotels and towers, facing a hastily erected stage with Congress Street behind it. She and Ira and Papa came early, Ira clowning around by sitting in the giant redstone Cadillac Chair at the western end of the square by the Campus Martius, perched on the throne so often occupied by drunks and vagrants. The stone has begun to stain and chip, and the papers say that the monument to the Frenchman who claimed the area for his country and founded the fort that became Detroit will soon be demolished as an eyesore.

"*Apres moi*," said Ira, dwarfed by the eight-foot-tall back of the chair, "*le deluge*."

It is a thrill to be here in solidarity with the workers, of course, many of the what—fifty-thousand, sixty thousand?—men around them wearing their Ford badges and UAW caps with dues buttons on them. But there are legions present who just want to see and hear Paul Robeson. It's what got Ira and Papa out of the apartment, riding the streetcar with all the colored people, Papa moving fairly well with the cane that he says makes him look like Uncle Wiggily.

"You look fine, Papa."

"I look like an old Jewish rabbit."

Ira had become an admirer when Robeson went to sing for the soldiers fighting Fascists in Spain, and Papa likes the spirituals and even *Ole Man River*. Rosa was both thrilled and repulsed by him in the *Emperor Jones* movie—yes, amazing to see a whole film starring a colored man, but the character was so conceited and cruel, like what Edward G. Robinson usually plays, though they always make him Italian instead of a Jew. The other speakers are very clear about the importance of the upcoming vote and not letting the Company divide them by race, and are cheered by the gathered masses. But it all seems a bit distant, even with loudspeakers blaring. A huge space to fill. And when Robeson is introduced and cheered he seems so small a figure, Rosa up on her toes to see above the sea of men's and women's hats to the podium. Then he begins to speak.

It's like the voice of God.

It is a warm, vibrant *basso profundo* that seems not directional but all around you, strong yet intimate. He's talking to me, thinks Rosa, and everybody in this army of dreamers feels the same. Yes, he is taller and sturdier than the others on the stage, Ira says he even played professional football, but it is more than that. In the *Emperor Jones* movie other actors had the camera point at them, but none filled the screen, filled the movie theater the way he did. She saw it at the Orpheum, where the audience is almost all colored and she always wears boots after the time a rat ran over her feet. They cheered when he did some of the worst things, maybe because seeing one of their own as a ruler instead of a goggle-eyed Pullman porter for a change was so novel, they shouted back "That's right!" and "You tell'im, Jonesy!" when he lorded it over the sleazy white trader who bought him earlier. But now the voice is cultured, erudite, almost British-

"The only way to move forward is to strive to*geth*er for a better workplace, a better city, a better world," he says. Rosa was at the meeting where Reverend Hill suggested that Robeson was the one figure, known and popular with both races, who might reach those colored workers still resisting the union or fooled by that disgrace Homer Martin and the AFL faction. "Hundreds of thousands of people listen to Charles Lindbergh's crazy ideas," the reverend quipped, "and that man can't *sing*."

"The best way my race can win justice," Robeson declaims, "is by sticking with progressive labor unions. And the unions will not, *can*not, progress without the black worker!"

The cheers and applause echo off the massive face of the Pontchartrain Hotel, and she sees Papa grinning from ear to ear, a rare sight these days. When Robeson sings it is the incredible, familiar voice, but it isn't one of his favorites, no stealing away to Jesus, or Moses and the Pharoah, or tragic, martyred Joe Hill, but something called *I Will Vote for UAW-CIO*.

Ira, always the weisenheimer, leans close to yell into her ear. "I don't think Bing Crosby will be tempted to steal this one."

Zeke has never liked to hear a spiritual outside of a church building, and is glad the man is sticking to the subject. His favorite singers are Fats Waller and Mildred Bailey, but he doesn't think either of them could grab the attention of this many people standing packed on a street, like you took every fan from the stands at Navin Field for those World Series games and packed them into a couple narrow blocks. Robeson has made it clear he's sold on this UAW deal, but then *he* doesn't have to go back to the Rouge and live with all that mess. Zeke's worry is that he'll end up with *two* bosses telling him what to do, when all he really needs is show me the damn job and leave me alone.

He ought to been a preacher, though, Robeson, have those women falling down in the aisles and the men giving up sin till the next Saturday night, and in some ways he is, only his sermon doesn't draw from the Old Testament. Word is he speaks a half-dozen languages, including one from Africa, that he studied law and got the highest grades at the white college he went to. Usually that kind of brain power in a colored man makes the white folks jumpy, but the ones all around him here are eating it up. Yes, he's a movie star without bugging his eyes and shuffling his feet, but it's more than that. Joe Louis is one thing, but they put the muzzle on that boy, Roxborough himself saying in the colored papers how they taught him never to have his picture taken with a white woman or pop off about race business. This man just shoots from the hip, like it or not, and you can follow his line of thought a hell of a lot better than you could with Marcus Garvey, who Zeke always felt was talking about some fairy-land he'd built up in his head. And so far Robeson seems to be getting away with it.

Zeke went to the AFL's do at the Forest Club, Donald Marshall introducing this Homer Martin character who can do some preaching himself, not bad for a white man. They called it a 'back to work' rally, and there were a couple thousand colored workers crammed into Sunnie Wilson's big place, more than when they had Cab Calloway and his band there, and there was supposed to be trouble from the UAW boys. So Zeke, like half the other men there, listened to the pitch with a metal club in his hand, compliments of the Little Man and the rolling mill. But with all the Detroit cops ringed around outside, nobody even showed up to holler. DuPree says the AFL and Homer Martin are in the Little Man's pocket, that Ford would still be calling the shots even with a union, but who knows? The whole deal smells like politics, which haven't done colored folks any good since they shot Lincoln.

Zeke figures he'll vote, though, which you get to do up here, but doesn't know which way he'll go till he's got the ballot in his hand. And if either of the union outfits do get in, he's got a list of conditions at the plant that got to be *fixed*.

Tawny Troubadour?

No, the man is *black*, thinks Smitty, and pretty damn proud of it.

The Ebony Elucidator?

Fosdick crosses out anything with more than four syllables.

The Sepia Socialist?

Or is he actually, as rumor has it, a Communist? He did send his son to school in Russia-

Smitty will ask one of the Reuthers how many people are here for the rally, and then knock off ten thousand from that for the article, but Robeson is the headliner here, readers weary of the verbal bombshells lobbed by each side during the cooling off period mandated by the NLRB, workers grudgingly back on the job for weeks before the vote, the CIO trying to win the colored over, the AFL, backed by Harry Bennett, trying to muddy the water by running their own campaign, and only minor skirmishes inside the plant. For years the movie theaters have been running newsreel stories of that lunatic with the mustache shouting and flipping his hair around like a Teutonic Cab Calloway, thousands and thousands of Krauts *seig heil*ing him and thrusting their arms in the air, but Smitty hasn't seen anything like this in Detroit since that miserable rainy day Hoover came to town to have dinner with Ford and old Tom Edison. Thousands cheer when Hank Greenberg or Mickey Cochrane come up to the plate, but you wouldn't want to park one of them behind a live microphone at anything bigger than a sports dinner, and that only after several stiff drinks.

The Colored Caruso?

Smitty's favorite is *Let My People Go*, not just the singing, which is enough to make Rudy Vallée want to go hang himself, but the way when you listen to it you stop seeing guys in robes and long beards and start to imagine some field hand busting out of his overalls putting it to Senator Bilbo—*If not I'll strike your first-born dead*. Nothing finer than to see a public bigot cold-cocked with his own Bible.

There's the angle-

A Black Moses spoke forth in Detroit today, not from a mountaintop, but from a wooden platform in Cadillac Square, promising to lead the oppressed multitude out from industrial bondage to the Promised Land of collective bargaining-

I might even get a byline.

• • •

The vote to accept the Labor Board solution had been a free-for-all, two thousand representatives crammed into the meeting hall, AFL and CIO organizers accusing each other of all kinds of treason, while most all the guys from 600 who started the deal said they didn't trust either Ford or the government not to go behind their backs, so why go back in to work a whole month before the vote was scheduled? Lots of yelling, and damn close in the final count but finally they agreed to it. The factory has been on the edge every day since, lots of fistfights just in B Building, though none of them there have been colored versus white. The guys at the Local say it's in the bag, but everyone Kaz knows would like to be in the room when the ballots are counted.

This today is more like payday, guys lined up still in their aprons and coveralls, Kaz's shift voting on their way out, the incoming shift on their way in. The ballot is simple, three boxes on the slip of paper they hand him-

AFL-UAW
CIO-UAW
No Union

He takes the stub of pencil and puts his X by CIO, then moves on to the long desk where the Labor Board people check your identification against the stacks of employment files the Company gave them and the unions went over. There are Michigan State Police standing around to keep order—they must have a height requirement because it's like a forest of them in their black uniforms with the blue crescent patches on the shoulders, hats on indoors. Kaz goes to the J to P table, they check him off and he continues to the taped-shut cardboard box sitting tall-wise on a wooden chair, a slot cut in it, and handwritten on the side-

Deposit
Ballot
Here

He slips his vote into the slot, and, already having visited the time-punch, continues out to the overpass at Gate 4. They've stretched a rope down the middle of it to keep the incoming and outgoing from muddling up, a Labor

Board employee at each end calling out "Keep moving! Keep moving! No campaigning, please."

Kaz sees Bud Novak coming toward him. When Ford had to bring all the strikers and almost everybody they'd fired in the last year back as part of the agreement to drop all the lawsuits, they scrambled everybody's shifts from before up, hoping to keep what they called 'cabals' from forming, and everybody on the line around Kaz is unfamiliar.

"*Jak leci?*" Bud asks.

"*Nie jest sly,*" says Kaz. "Not bad at all."

They say it will be some hours before the Board will be finished counting the vote, but Kaz is too wired up to go home. If it was just him who stuck his neck out, hey, you pay the carny and you take your chances, but the way Bill McKie worked it in the beginning was you approached people till you had ten guys in, and then each of *them* was supposed to go get ten guys. So if this goes sour there's lots of people Kaz feels responsible for.

Once he got his citizen papers way back when, Pop put his Sunday clothes on to go vote.

"This country, they ask you what you think," he used to say. "So is your duty to let them know."

The beer hall is just three blocks down from the Local headquarters, and packed to the gills today. Three deep at the bar, so they have to pass his mug of Oldbru back over their heads and the dime in to slap on the counter. It's too crowded for anybody to play pool, so Kaz sits against one of the tables and soaks up the excitement.

"I still say we should of held out for a contract before we went back in."

"And not work for how long? Couple more months?"

"They had to give us back pay—"

"Be*cause* we agreed to bury the hatchet till the vote."

"So let's say we got the union and they sit down with Ford, and he tells us to go fuck ourselves."

"No, that's Bennett's job."

"He's gonna be their guy?"

“Maybe not in the room, but you know he’s got the Old Man under his thumb.”

“It’s a negotiation, right? So our side demands that they tie a couple cylinder blocks to the Little Man’s ankles and throw him in the friggin river, and their side says no, cylinder blocks are *val*uable—”

“What if we work up this contract and the Old Man won’t sign?”

“The government will take over the plant.”

“You’re shittin me.”

“You heard what they’re building out at Willow Run—”

“That’s airplanes—bombers and fighter planes for the British—”

“For *us*, so the Japs and the Krauts don’t get any ideas. You think the government is going to let that new plant stand empty?”

“They can’t just take over—”

“They said there couldn’t be a Labor Board—now we got one. They said that the social security was against the Constitution, and now we got it—”

“They said the Tigers would never win a World Series.”

“That’s what I’m saying.”

“Remember, if the union and Ford agree on a contract,” Kaz reminds them, “we still get to vote whether we ratify it or not. So we can’t be totally sold out.”

“So you think we’re gonna win this?”

“This vote? Yeah. But that only gets us to the table—”

• • •

Smitty stands with the usual crowd around the Labor Board guy with the calculator, who has asked them not to smoke, but good luck with that. Smitty put two bucks into the pool at the *Free Press*, betting the CIO would get between seventy and seventy-five percent of the vote, but knows the AFL has been telling the colored workers they’ll all lose their jobs if that happens. He brought Jimmy the copy boy with him to run to the phone booth in the drug store down the street and call in the numbers when they’re official, while he tries to hunt up Harry Bennett or maybe the Company lawyer, Capizzi, for a reaction. The Old Man and the Woeful Prince have gotten a lot more cautious about what they blab in public over the years, though it seemed like Edsel kind of enjoyed the flap over the murals at the Art Institute. The results will headline the paper today, unless the Germans invade downtown Saginaw, but it's really only one round in the contest. The Ford Motor Company is not publicly owned, it sits in Old Henry's pocket, and he is a man famous for possessing a whim of iron-

"Okay, I've triple-checked," says the functionary at the adding machine. "CIO-UAW, seventy percent, AFL-UAW, twenty-seven percent, no union, two-point-five percent. And thirty-four people didn't mark any of the boxes."

Zeke is one of those. He is in the parlor at home listening to the radio when they announce the numbers. Alonzo DuPree comes by a few minutes later.

"What you think, Zeke?"

"Don't matter what I think. I'm just a Ford mule trying to knock out the rent every month."

"But the men look up to you—"

"That's their problem. We'll be having shop stewards now, and I won't be *one* of them."

"Really?"

"I'm juggling enough things without adding that to my load. You ought to put in for it, Du."

"You think so?"

"You like to argue, and shop steward is an arguing man's *job*."

"You think they'll turn against us? I bet more of us went for the AFL, and if they find that out—"

"They'll find it out."

"Think we could lose our spots at the plant?"

"No. But now that the Company knows we can't protect them from the union, they won't be sending any more recruiters down to Dixie, will they?"

The Company sends I. A. Capizzi, a bespectacled man in a pinstripe suit, out to deal with the press. Capizzi who claimed the Labor Board had no jurisdiction over Ford because the Company "did not engage in interstate commerce," and helped push the challenge to the Labor Board's existence to the Supreme Court. He will be the chief negotiator for the Company in the pending face-off, and chooses to focus on the federal government rather than the union.

"This is not a groundswell of popular sentiment among our workers, but the end result of an insidious campaign by the current administration in Washington," he says. "The National Labor Relations Board is an exact replica of the so-called courts by which the Communist, Nazi, and Fascist partners purge the men who resist their tyrannies. It is a dictatorial concept imported from Europe."

"But you will negotiate with the CIO?" asks Smitty.

"The law provides that we must speak with them. and the Ford Motor Company always obeys the law."

Or *makes* it, thinks Smitty, the Dearborn City Council outlawing all leafletting around the Rouge plant at the end of '37 and arresting hundreds of organizers till a local judge with brass balls and no close relatives working for the Company declared their edict unconstitutional. Roosevelt's decision to stay on for a third term in the White House must have derailed the Company's hopes of a return to their unrestricted power over their 'own business'.

"Do you think your willingness to honor this vote will lead to more defense contracts being awarded to Ford?"

The way the overhead light hits Capizzi's glasses makes it impossible for Smitty to see his eyes.

"Should we be dragged into those overseas conflicts, there is no company better able to provide what will be needed to defend democracy," says the lawyer. "And we stand ready."

Capizzi doesn't want to be the one to put it front of the Chief, so of course it falls to Harry. The old man, still addicted to the element of surprise, walks into Harry's office from the garage. Harry has the document laid out on his desk and knows better than to ask if he would like to sit down.

"I can go over the main points for you," he says. "They kept hammering away—"

"Just let me see it."

Henry Ford stands and looks at the couple pages for perhaps two minutes, tosses them back on Harry's desk, and steps out the way he came in.

"I'll shut the plant down first," he tells his son.

When Father digs in like this it's not really an argument, more like trying to calm a child who refuses to open his mouth in the dentist's office.

"You *know* we're going to end up in this war," says Edsel. "Roosevelt and Churchill are making all kinds of agreements, he's dangling our merchant ships in front of the German U-boats, gearing up the production of armaments way past what the British will ever be able to use—"

"That's his business."

"If war is declared it will come back to *our* business. And without a union contract—"

"I'm not signing the damn thing. There's no law that says I've got to."

"Our sales are way down. Besides the union boycott, there's this perception—I know it's misguided, but it's out there in the public—that you're a Nazi sympathizer."

"Just shut up Edsel," Father says, and walks out of the room.

It is, as always, like a kick in the stomach. Dinner had been civil, Father avoiding the subject, talking about some new findings at his soybean lab, Edsel drinking half a glass of the offered unpasteurized milk. When Edsel was little and Father had the whole world cheering him on, there would be these things, ideas he'd grab onto and refuse to let go of, certain that to give in was not only irresponsibility but cowardice.

And Father is no coward.

Eleanor brings a glass of buttermilk out to Edsel, who is lying on the couch. He usually likes to look out at the lake, but lately his thoughts have been inward. It's so different, so quiet with the younger boys away at school and Henry Junior off in the Navy, but it's always been good with just the two of them. At one point he was so fed up with the personalities at the Company that he considered walking away, just living comfortably in one of their houses, sailing, visiting friends, but Father brought him up in those factories, it's what is expected, and he's always been so desperate to please him-

"Do you think he listened at all?"

"Oh, he can *lis*ten. Sometimes he'll let engineers go on forever, spill all their grand plans out till they run out of steam, then he'll just say 'Nope' and walk away."

"That's just cruel."

"It keeps people on their toes."

"It makes people miserable, and I can't believe that miserable people do a better job. And all this union business is making your ulcers flare up."

"This feels worse than just ulcers."

"You should have the doctors take a closer look—"

"To do that they have to open you up."

"So? If they're good doctors—"

"It's time in the hospital. Every time I go away, I come back and Bennett has fired somebody else I depend on—"

"I don't understand the hold he has on your father. It can't be blackmail—"

"Harry likes to fight. Father admires a fighter."

"You've put your life into that company, you own half of it—"

"It's Father's company, to do whatever he wants with it. And now he says he'll give it away before he'll sign that union contract."

"I half wish that he does it," says Eleanor. "Life would be peaceful."

Edsel takes his wife's hand. "And I'd be a very happy failure."

• • •

Harry gets the call in the dead of night. Only one person has the private number.

"They didn't ask for a check-off," says the Chief without a hello.

"Sure they did, but Capizzi said it was a deal-breaker. All of the other companies that gave in and signed—Dodge, GM, DeSoto—the union still has to track their members down every month, sweat their dues out of them—"

"The workers want a union, let them *pay* for it."

"You're saying to give them the—"

"If Ford agrees to a check-off, if we take dues out of their paychecks and hand them to the union, how long before the union demands the other outfits do the same?"

"Okay, but it makes us like *part*ners with them."

"Give em everything they asked for, plus the check-off. Let em choke on it."

"That won't be the end, you know," says Harry, wide awake now. "Those radicals in 600 will be pulling wildcat stuff-"

"But that'll be the UAW's problem, won't it? They signed a *contract*."

Harry closes his eyes, trying to think this through. All his plans for a counter-offensive-

"What happened? You told me you'd never sign."

"Oh, Edsel must have gotten to Clara, and Clara went on about how there'd be more fighting in the streets, that people would be killed, and if I didn't sign she'd leave me. What can I do?"

The Chief doesn't sound too broken up about it. Harry has several ideas, but knows this is not the time to bring them up.

"That one clause, though," he says, hoping to salvage something, "where it says my Service Department guys have to wear uniforms now so you know who they are—"

"Right," says the owner of the Ford Motor Company. "Make sure they're snappy-looking."

• • •

It is early Sunday afternoon, Jim and Norma playing pinochle with the Gallaghers and listening to *sambas* on Rádio Nacional when the music is interrupted by a news report.

"Pedimos desculpas pela interrupção, mas temos um novo boletim importante. Pouco antes das oito horas desta manhã, na ilha havaiana de Oahu, houve um ataque das forças aéreas e navais japonesas à base naval da Sétima Frota dos Estados Unidos, em Pearl Harbor. Vários milhares de pessoas foram mortas ou feridas. Iremos informá-lo quando recebermos mais informações."

They have all laid their cards down on the table, straining to understand.

"It sounds like we've been attacked," says Jim, not so sure.

"At Pearl Harbor, on Oahu, which is in Hawaii," says Kerry, who was lying on the sofa reading *Caddie Woodlawn*. "Japanese bombers."

A moment of silence as it sinks in.

"So we're at war," says Helen Gallagher, looking stunned.

"I guess so," says Jim. "But I don't think we have anything to worry about here. The Japs have already taken over a lot of the plantations in Asia, but this is an awful long way to go—"

"Of course," says Norma. "Who'd be crazy enough to traipse out into the middle of the Brazilian jungle looking for rubber?"

When you ride
ALONE
you ride with
Hitler!

Join a
Car-Sharing Club
TODAY!

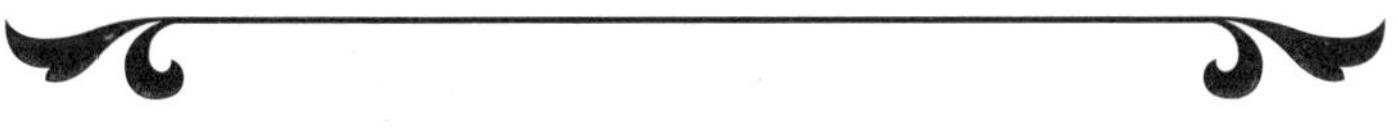

-it says above a picture drawn of a man at the wheel of a nice convertible, possibly a Lincoln. Sitting next to him in the passenger seat, outlined in white but see-through, is the Fuehrer, wearing a military uniform with an Iron Cross pinned on the breast pocket-

THIS WEEK MOLLY IS FASTENING the round Plexiglas window onto the shell of the ventral ball turret.

It's what the gunner looks through to search for enemy planes coming up from below. Eighteen holes to fill, eighteen pulls of the rivet-gun trigger, Hazel crammed inside the turret mirroring her with the bucking bar to spread the metal of the rivet end into a second head. Hazel pushes from the inside as Molly hammers from out, then gives a thumbs-up when it's in solid.

Though they work right on top of each other, there's not much talking in the Willow Run sub-assembly. Molly's team are late in the process, fitting out the turrets before they are taken to the big line to be installed. The main building covers something like eighty acres and has no windows, just lights on all day and all night, pretty much everything under one roof, with manufacturing and assembly on a ground floor surrounded by a mezzanine that holds the offices and the plant's own hospital. Molly's friend Rhonda who works up there as a nurse says with so much turnover, new people coming on every day, they average three amputated fingers a week. In some ways it is a holy mess on the floor, but what Mr. Sorenson has done here is a miracle—putting up a structure so massive in scale so quickly and then making all the more-than-a-million parts right here before putting them together and, once they actually start finishing Liberators, testing them just outside on the airfield.

Molly's typing skills proving to be so clearly shy of adequate, she made sure her name was near the top of the list when they realized they'd need women to replace all the men being sent off in uniform, and handling a rivet gun has steadily become second nature. They put you through a training school that is attached to the plant, a couple weeks of instruction before you're assigned to a specific task. The B-24 Lib is a heavy bomber, meant for long-distance missions, that has superchargers they make at the Lincoln plant downtown to force air into the four engines, allowing it to fly up where there's not much oxygen. The wings are extra-long and thin, which helps them lift off while carrying tons of explosives. Molly often sees midgets—or maybe dwarves, she can never remember the difference—in the cafeteria, who apparently climb up inside the stubs of the wings in the center assembly when it's time to attach the long tips. After the first couple sightings they have become normal to her, just more of the thousands of fellow workers here day and night, seven days a week.

Kaz has been moved over from the Rouge, working in another part of the building nearly a half-mile away operating a giant hydraulic press to stamp out aluminum fuselage parts and helping to change the dies when necessary. She and Kaz have bought a much-used Ford on installment, and because they cram three other workers into it are allowed by the Ration Board to make the thirty-mile drive from Detroit out to the factory together.

As Molly and Hazel move to the next turret, the last one is swarmed by workers installing all kinds of systems, one after the other, till there is so little room left inside that the gunner will have to squeeze into a fetal position, feet on pedals on either side of the round window, breathing through an oxygen hose at higher altitudes, freezing cold and so cramped that he can't wear a parachute.

Molly prays every night that it's over before Stan is old enough to fight.

Mr. Sorenson, despite his bad temper, must be some kind of genius to have planned all this, and she knows how hard he worked putting it together, once seeing him faint from exhaustion—actually fall to the floor—while they were still at the Rouge plant. Kaz says it's not such a different world over here—still the Service Department on your back and lots of tension between the colored workers and the white, many newly arrived from the same southern and hillbilly states where they already didn't mix too well. Nine-hour shifts, eighty-five cents an hour for women beginners like Molly, and the *noise*-

The foreman pokes Molly on the shoulder, taps his watch to indicate that it's lunch break for her and Hazel. Breaks are staggered, always enough people left doing your job so the flow is not interrupted, and every day a different mix of workers in the enormous cafeteria. The food isn't bad, sold at cost on the line, Molly going for a ham sandwich and a slice of pie. She and Hazel sit at a table with some of the girls who mold Plexiglas.

"We're deep in the doghouse," says Doreen. Nobody who knows Doreen has to read the newspapers. "The *Times* says Ford is so far behind it's fouling up the war effort."

"We're still working out the wrinkles," says Hazel, who has a crush on Edsel Ford, who comes through the plant a couple times a week with Mr. Sorenson. He is thin and handsome, always very well-dressed, and never scowls like Sorenson does. "Once we hit our stride we'll be pushing out a Liberator every hour."

"That's what they promised a year ago—"

"The Army keeps changing the design."

"Then it must not be very *good*. They test these planes in the air, and if they don't work right—"

"That metal they wrap around the fuselage," says Maria Mastrofranco, whom everybody likes even if she was born in Italy, "it's so *thin*. I could poke a screwdriver through it. So bullets-"

"It needs to be aluminum to be light enough for the plane to take off. Let's face it, the point of the thing is to deliver bombs to drop on the enemy, not to keep the guys inside it alive."

A thought to ponder as they eat. Stan has pictures of Liberators and other Allied planes tacked up on the wall next to his bed, and reads everything he can about the war's progress, making marks on a map he bought.

"I believe that our main problem," says Sue Ann, who came up from Arkansas with her husband who's in the warehouse, and lives in a trailer camp on the other side of the airfield, "is we've got too many fuck-ups on the assembly line."

Kaz said when he came over they gave him a lecture about watching his language because there were now so many ladies present, nearly half of assembly, but Molly has heard the worst language coming out of the mouths of her sister riveters. After their shift one day she and Kaz drove around the trailer camps and shanty towns that have sprung up—little toddlers running around barefoot, garbage uncollected, worse than anything you'd see in Black Bottom. The Company built the factory out here and didn't figure on the ration people saying you couldn't drive alone from Detroit—

"These people don't know shit from Shinola and they got em working on a machine our boys' lives depend on."

"These people" with Sue Ann always means the colored workers, who she resents having to share the cafeteria with.

"It takes everybody a while to get into the rhythm of it," says Molly. "Even after all the training."

"Our job here is to make bombers faster than the enemy can shoot them down. And so far we haven't produced doodly-squat."

The Liberators haven't seen much action yet, not under American command, and the war isn't going well. It seems like every day Doreen tells them about another place in the world that Molly has never heard of taken over by the Nazis or the Japanese.

Stan says that the ventral ball turret gets mechanically hoisted up out of the way for take-off and landing, but if the landing gear jams and the hoist mechanism won't work the gunner is just stuck down there when they slide in on their bellies-

"They say this is chicken à la king," says Hazel, hoping to change the subject, "but I'm still looking for the *chick*en."

"We're on a meat ration, darlin," says Sue Ann. "And you just been *clucked*."

Molly packed sandwiches the first couple days in the plant, but the food here is fine and you don't have to bolt it down quite as fast as Kaz says they did at the Rouge—one thing to thank the union for. The pay is okay, especially with both of them working, and even if the shift is long and the job the same operation over and over, she feels good about helping to win the peace. And you sure meet all kinds of people here.

"They're almost the same size, you know."

Now they're talking about movies.

"What do you mean?"

"They're both like really short."

"Well they do that so when they kiss one doesn't have to bend down too much—"

"The guy always has to be taller. It's like a *rule*."

"Well, he's maybe a *lit*tle taller than her—"

Priscilla is small and blonde and gaga over the new movie girl, Veronica Lake, wearing the peekaboo hairstyle just like her when she doesn't have it up in a bandanna for work. She maintains that Lake and Alan Ladd aren't actually married, but should be. Sonia has seen *This Gun For Hire* twice, always up for a movie with women in trouble and lots of shadows.

"A girl our size, you don't want to be staring into some guy's armpit."

"So he's what—?"

"I think like five and a half feet."

"That's like *half* of John Wayne," says Hazel.

"He's lucky it's the pictures. On stage you could really see him up next to everybody."

"He's lucky," says Molly, "he's not a ball-turret gunner."

Kaz is worried about his hearing. There are five rows of the huge presses, rarely three seconds when one of them isn't slamming down to bend metal, and the earplugs can only do so much. You feel the impact of each thunderous stamping in your spine—at the end of a shift Kaz feels like he's survived an artillery barrage, and in the car back to Detroit everybody's voice sounds like they're half a block away. Sasha is starting to cook, not bad at it, which is good because Molly comes home as beat as he does. The Service Department, mostly uniformed now, though Bennett must have some hidden squealers on the floor, still give you a hard time, and seem to have taken over the betting pools and black market dodges at the plant. Then last week they had to step back as the Secret Service people hurried through, looking in workers' pockets and lunch pails, and without warning there is a big shiny Lincoln convertible driving down past Kaz's row, with Edsel Ford and Sorenson up front with the driver and Old Henry stuck in the back seat between President Roosevelt and Eleanor—the old man didn't look too happy about it. Their mouths were all moving but of course you couldn't hear a word for the slamming of the machines, and Kaz just had time to wave and be waved back at by Mrs. R before he had to feed the beast again. The metal never stops coming and you don't dare get behind.

It gave Kaz a charge to see the President, smiling, even if he was here to see what the hold-up is—a great big landing field just outside with no bombers parked in it. The man is in a wheelchair, taking trains all over the country to look in on the war production and keep everybody pulling together. Sonia says Roosevelt is her hero, even if he wasn't born with his affliction like she was.

There's no bending over on this stamping job, and the fuselage pieces, whatever their shape, are aluminum and not too heavy. But Kaz finds himself having to turn the radio dial all the way up at home in order to hear, which means it's too loud for the rest of his family.

And whenever a Service Department asshole talks to him, he just points to his ears and shakes his head.

• • •

DeWitt stands, in his underwear, in front of two men sitting at desks. One has light green eyes, the other light blue. He thinks he has passed his physical, but is not sure. He has been eighteen for two weeks now, and doesn't need his parent's permission to enlist.

"We are now in this war," President Roosevelt said on the radio. "We are *all* in it—all the way."

"It says here you're a high school graduate," says the green-eyed one.

"Yes sir. And I went through the Ford Trade School."

"What did you learn there?"

"Principally mechanics—"

"And you are presently employed?" asks the blue-eyed one.

"Yes sir, at the Highland Park plant. We make anti-aircraft guns."

"You're a mechanic there?"

"No, they just needed men on the line. Assembly—"

"So we can assume you're not doing anything unique that is vital to the war effort."

DeWitt knows he shouldn't laugh, though it strikes him as funny. He's not in the army yet but they've been acting like it since he came in with the group of twenty who they put through the scales and the measurements and the looking at your teeth. Sizing you up and writing things down.

"My foreman says any monkey can do my job. Several times a week."

He thinks the green-eyed one almost smiles.

"But you have some mechanical ability—"

"I can make things."

"Such as?"

"I made a radio that works, from salvaged parts. I put a flathead V-8 engine into a friend's Model A and it runs fine. I fix things." He doesn't mention that he fixed the WC after the landlord never took care of it. He isn't enlisting to pick up shit-

"Do you know what a tank is?"

"Yes sir. At the moment we have the Stuart M3 Light Tank," he tells them, "and the Germans have something called a Panzer. That means 'panther' in German."

He immediately regrets this. They don't usually like it if you're too smart.

The blue-eyed one exchanges a look with the green-eyed one. "Go put your clothes on," he says, "and then come back here."

• • •

They keep voting for Zeke to be shop steward for his section of the foundry and he keeps turning it down. DuPree is one now, collecting grievances for the bunch who work outside on cranes and truck-loading scrap metal for the furnace and whatnot, and Du says they've barely hired a new colored worker here at the Rouge since the union got in. There is a batch of them now out at Willow Run, almost all men, still got burrs in their hair and call white men "Boss," jungled-up in shacks thrown up by the big factory making the rednecks that come up with them nervous. They're still putting out iron and steel here in the foundry, metal that the other buildings will make into tanks instead of automobiles. With the Rouge running day and night there hasn't been so much money on the streets of Black Bottom since Prohibition, newcomers at Willow Run coming in to Detroit on their days off determined to throw their pay to the wind, all the clubs and knock shops hopping, lots of good times, lots of trouble to get into.

This is the Arsenal of Democracy

-say the government signs on the walls-

Remember Pearl Harbor

-they say, and—

America Never Lost a War

Zeke jabs the bar into the flask and twists, popping it open, then a couple more jabs to knock most of the steaming mold free from the glowing-red casting inside, chunks of smoking-hot pressed sand falling off and through the grated drag, then quickly scraping with the flat edge of the bar to get as much of the rest clear before Tyrone Banks at the station next to him sets the tongs to the heavy engine block so it can be hoisted and swung onto the return drag for cooling, more cleaning, tumbling, and then the final machining. They told Zeke the move to shakeout was not a punishment of any kind, just what had to be done in the shuffle to switch over from cars to weaponry, but he doesn't buy it. He's complained to the union, claimed seniority, the whole deal, but they say hey, we're at war, it's unpatriotic to kick too much. The tractors and aircraft engines and GPW Willys keep rolling out, already bought and paid for by the government, and the whole industry is so desperate for workers you don't have to worry about getting bounced—so what's your problem?

When your arms start to tire, you can always make like that mold is some Nazi sonovabitch with his helmet on, out to kill your oldest son, and bring the iron down *hard*-

You wear goggles in shakeout, smoke and sand always in the air, the molds still so hot even after they ride under the cooling tunnel that Zeke tries to hold his breath each time he busts one open, worried about scorching his lungs, and there's some kind of *gas* it gives off, can't be good for you. Just one of Satan's helpers here, ought to give me a pitchfork.

The young bloods still working here say the colored enlistment must be low, because there's recruiters pestering them the minute they step out of the factory. Zeke counsels them to wait till they're drafted, unlike his dumbass boy, and if you're dying to get shot at just take a walk around Dearborn without your Ford badge on.

"So you want the Germans or Japanese to come over here and start running things?" challenged DeWitt when they had it out after he signed up.

"No, I don't. You *know* whose asses they'd start beating on first."

"Then we've got to do our part."

"You want me to fight for my country," he said to his son, "then *make* it my country."

• • •

The movie people want to shoot everything.

"We're just here for the raw material," says Phillips, who seems to be their leader. "We'll take notes about what gives here, sure, but they'll cook up the story back in Dearborn. It'll be called *The Amazon Awakens* and they want to see trees pumping out rubber and lots of jungly stuff."

Archie Johnston has been called back to Dearborn to work on aircraft, leaving both Belterra and Fordlandia without a head man, so it has fallen on Jim to serve as guide for the more important visitors. Mr. Disney was a nice surprise, less interested in the rubber than in what he called "the model communities," impressed that instead of one big dispensary there are lots of little shops now—shoe stores, barbers, a butcher, a bakery-

"Main Street USA," he called it, and even gave a talk about drawing cartoons at Kerry's school.

Jim takes the crew out to the healthiest section of trees at Belterra, and tries to explain the complicated triple grafting process.

"Some trees have really good root systems," he says, "while others have really fast-growing trunks that are resistant to the insects that bore into the bark. So we graft a bud of the second into the side of the first once it's a certain size, and once it starts to grow out and get strong, we cut away the old trunk above it and you've got a hybrid—"

"We'll need to get some footage of that bud going in."

"No problem. Next, again at a certain height, we repeat the process with a bud from a tree that has proven to have highly resistant leaves—"

"Resistant to what?"

"What have you got? Insects, leaf blight, stuff even the locals don't even have a name for—"

Because of the war there are American government people here now, biologists sent to boost the rubber production who are doing a bit better than Dr. Weir, and Jim's crews have made an airfield where the army is hiding a bunch of fighter planes under jungle camouflage netting.

"That second graft is done up on a pretty tall ladder, and your camera is awful bulky—"

"We might do some animation. I'm sure you've seen some of our manufacturing shorts—"

"A couple every week. The voice is familiar."

"Terrific pipes. He announces the Lions games on the radio now. So show us where you're actually getting rubber out of trees—"

They want João to change his shirt. When they told him he'd be in the movie he put on his best one, but they say he doesn't look right, so he hurries back home and gets the one he wore yesterday, still a little damp. Then they give him a hat that is much more beat-up than his own to wear, and finally tell him just to take the shirt off, which is embarrassing. It's best to make the cuts early in the morning and let them flow all day long, but it is well after noon, the hottest part of the day, when he shows them how the diagonal slices are made. They have him do it to three different trees, ones too young to yield much yet, but Gomes says that people in America won't know that.

Then they want to shoot some *caimãos*.

João knows where a lot of them are at this time of day and they locate three on the river bank. *Senhor* Rogan and *Senhor* Gallagher are wearing clothes that look new, white men in white shirts and pants with polished boots, and the movie people want the *caimão* to look more dangerous but it just stays where it is, staring at them. So they have João stand where the camera can't see him and throw stones at it till it lifts up its long snout and starts to move toward the river. The movie people keep waving *Senhor* Gallagher this way and that till they say he can shoot, and he hits it just as it enters the river, swimming away with only its eyes showing above the water.

Maybe it will die later.

With the second one they decide to just kill it where it is, and *Senhor* Rogan manages to fire his rifle standing not too far away. Sometimes they will charge at you, so it's good that the bullet goes right to its brain. They have João jam its jaws open with a stick so everybody watching the movie can see all its teeth. And then he helps them rig a greased rope over a branch hanging out over the river, so they can run the camera while a chunk of pork belly is lowered into the water and it begins to boil with *piranha*. When João jerks the pork up there are a few of the little fish with their jaws still buried in the meat, and they put the camera up close to see some lying in the palm of his hand. He manages not to get bitten.

In the late afternoon Jim takes them through the rubber processing, the crew setting up powerful lamps to get enough light on the equipment. They are a little disappointed that the final product is just a thin sheet you could fold several times, which he explains makes it easier to handle and ship. But they get footage of it rolling out from the mangle, and decide there's not nearly enough piled up by the dock ready to ship to show in the movie.

"Not the message we want to send," says Phillips. It has been a relief to finally be shipping a few tons off now and then, though it's nothing like what was imagined back when they sent Jim here.

"Tomorrow we want to get some birds."

"Birds—"

"You know, exotic, tropical birds. Things you don't see back in the states."

"I suppose we can find some—there's toucans, there's *macaibas*, there's the *oropendola*, which is with a yellow tail, a red beak, and a patch of blue on its cheek—"

"Sorry," grins Phillips. "We're shooting black-and-white."

• • •

They run Kerry through the third degree like always when she wants to go out at night without them.

"Aren't you a little old to be watching cartoons?"

There is so little to do here that she knows they'd be going themselves if they didn't have to have a dinner with the Ford movie crew.

"And won't it be dubbed into Portuguese?"

"That's why I want to go. I want to hear Donald Duck jump around and squawk in Portuguese."

Paroled for the night, Kerry stands at the back of the dance hall till Flavio comes in, then settles one seat in from the aisle, putting the sweater it's too hot for down to save the aisle seat. He waits till the lights go down to sit and they can hold hands.

Her mother is sending her to Kalamazoo. Aunt Maxine has moved there, and there is a teacher's college, and even though Kerry isn't finished with high school yet her mother is convinced staying here will cause permanent damage.

"This is not the real world," is what she says but really just wants to get me away from Flavio.

Saludos Amigos hasn't even been shown back in America yet, but it has already played in Rio and got a lot of attention, so the hall is crowded, lots of people standing at the sides and in the rear. The movie starts like a newsreel, real live cartoon artists traveling around South America, probably the same trip that brought Mr. Disney here. Then stories about the different places start, Donald Duck as a tourist trying to ride a llama in Peru and falling off a suspension bridge into Lake Titicaca, a baby mail plane flying through a stormy pass from Chile to Argentina, Goofy as a gaucho with a very mischievous horse, trying to catch a running ostrich with a bola.

The one the crowd in the hall likes the best is *Colorado do Brasil*, where the wonderful song is sung while you follow the artist's brush, painting on the canvas of the movie screen along with the music—flamingos dance to the beat, colorful flowers turn into colorful birds and fly away, bananas on the tree turn into yellow-beaked toucans, and finally Donald Duck and a *papagayo* bird dressed in city clothes, José Carioca, are painted onto the screen. When José learns he has met the famous 'Pato Donal' he is overjoyed, talking a mile-a-minute in Portuguese and vowing to show him the city and explain the samba. Kerry has never been to Rio, and neither has Flavio, so the newsreel-type views of it at the beginning might as well be a painter's fantasy, and some of the local people have gotten up to dance along with the samba music, shaking their rear ends as if they had tail-feathers like Donald and José. José has Donald try a glass of *cachaça* which makes his breath so fiery it lights José's cigar, and finally we see Donald in silhouette, dancing the samba with a tall human woman whose silhouette looks a lot like Carmen Miranda.

They leave during the credits while the lights are still down, and take a long walk, stopping to kiss now and then. The song has been on the radio for a while but not in such a nice version with all the colorful images in the movie, and neither of them can get it out of their heads.

"Do you remember the words?" Flavio asks.

"Some of them."

"Then you have to sing it."

They are both in the chorus at school and sang *When You Wish Upon a Star* for Mr. Disney when he visited.

"I don't have the beat—"

"I can sing this," he says, and begins to make sounds like a tuba is playing them-

"Bump-bump-bummmmm—bum-pa-bumpabum—"

"Brasiiiiiil—" she sings-

"Meu Brasil brasileiro
Meu mulato inzoneiro
Vou cantar-te meus versos—"

As they sing, walking just out of the reach of the streetlights on the edges of the managers' compound, the images come back into Kerry's head, and it *is* like a watercolor, one picture bleeding into the next, and now in a lot of the pictures Flavio is there, smiling that beautiful smile-

"O Brasil do meu amor
Terra do nosso Senhor
Brasil! Pra mim! Brasil! Pra mim!
Brasiiiil!"

The lyrics are simple, I love my beautiful country, and the only ones that trouble her is at the beginning where they call Brazil an ignorant mulatto. She knows that's what her parents think Flavio is.

But he's not ignorant at all. He's just not white.

• • •

You've got to put them somewhere.

The Arsenal of Democracy business has been good for Detroit, shops that have been shuttered since the Crash reopening, lots of cash floating around, but all the new workers just arrived to crank out the trucks and tanks and boats and airplanes to fight the Nips and the Huns need a *roof* over their heads when they come home from the assembly line. And most of the folks who've been here for at least one generation might hold their noses and tolerate hillbillies, but they draw the line at colored. Right or wrong, that's just the fact of it, and Smitty is sure his neighbors down in Corktown, which started out all Irish, wouldn't be any more welcoming than this Improvement Project crowd waiting with rocks, clubs and **WE WANT WHITE TENANTS IN OUR WHITE COMMUNITY** signs to greet their new neighbors.

Black Bottom and Paradise Valley are already full to bursting, people crammed in firetrap buildings paying jacked-up rents, so the Housing Commission, in their wisdom, picked this spot to put up a grid of two hundred units and name it Sojourner Truth after a feisty ex-slave woman who spoke with a Dutch accent. A full mile from Hamtramck and the Poles, what could go wrong?

"Might be a few heads busted today," says Sergeant Tippett, Smitty's passport to the front line, "but not like the last time."

The last time there were not nearly enough Detroit cops assigned to handle over a thousand worked-up white folks lining the main road and blocking the entrance on a frozen morning in February, plus the colored families who were meant to move in on their own steam. A few of these had the sense to come in numbers, two or three families rolling up together in sputtering jalopies loaded with their children and their belongings, mattresses tied to the roofs, but even they had to retreat from the barrage of curses and projectiles hurled at them over, around and through the thin blue line of peace officers whose noses were already out of joint for being out in the brutal weather. Those who were able to get turned around with only a few broken windows were lucky, while the two cars that barreled through the human barricade were quickly surrounded and tipped over by the mob, their owners fighting or fleeing till taken into custody by the police—who somehow tear-gassed, then arrested over two hundred *col*ored trying to take possession of their homes and only three of the whites trying to keep them from doing it. Twenty-five families spent the night in city shelters, and one police horse suffered a stab wound.

"What kind of degenerate would stab a horse?" Sergeant Tippett generously supplied as the capper for Smitty's dispatch to the *Free Press*. "That is *low*."

Smitty is fond of Tippett not only because of his colorful phrasing, but for his bulk, the sergeant half a head taller and considerably wider than he is, a reliable mass to shelter behind when the feces hits the ventilator.

"The folks in this neighborhood have been jerked around," the sergeant says now, waiting with two-dozen men for the second attempt to house the families, all of them supposed to come together today and with an escort. "First it's colored housing, then the DHA backs down and it's white housing, then the Feds lean on them and it's colored housing again. You can't treat people in this neighborhood like that."

"The people trying to move in have been jerked around just as much," Smitty offers.

"Yeah, but they're *used* to it."

Smitty's believes that half the problem is the transit system. Since the war came to America it's been torture, streetcars jammed to the gills, either freezing cold or turned into metal sweatboxes, black and white rubbing up against each other belly to belly.

"I won't let my wife get on one of those things," he was told by a recent arrival from Kentucky, "it's not *de*cent. They got plenty money, what with the defense jobs, so they're in all the stores that used to be just for us. And now you expect us to *live* with them?"

Smitty covered the blowup up at the Packard plant, where it was the white women employees who came down onto the assembly floor to complain to their men that they had to park their fannies on toilet seats just vacated by colored women, leading to a walkout the UAW had to throw all their best people at to get back under control. And it's not even summer yet.

They hear the convoy long before they can see it, the protesters, fewer than the last time but still several hundred strong, muttering unhappily among themselves as the roar of dozens of motorcycles grows and grows, a skinny young man with a Louisville Slugger in hand declaring "At's jest like it must of sounded when them Nazis rolled into Poland."

Three huge cops on motorcycles lead the procession of top-heavy automobiles, table and chair legs sticking upward from the roofs, a few moving vans sprinkled in, more trios of motorcycle men along the sides, and then a truckload of National Guardsmen arriving from the east to clear a pathway through the crowds blocking the entrance roads to the Sojourner Truth houses.

"Back off, people!" shouts Sergeant Tippett. "We got plenty empty cells waiting for whoever don't behave!"

The stalwarts of the Improvement Project make way.

Neither Mavis or Whitley's wife came this time, just Whitley and Zeke and Maceo Suggs who owns a Ford pickup he won in a poker game and is willing to risk on this mission, a loaded shotgun slid tight inside a folded-up mattress in the bed of the truck.

"Something to impress your new neighbors with should they become rambunctious," he explained to Whitley when they loaded up.

Zeke just has an axe handle pressed between his knees as they ride up and park in front of the new-built government house.

The process is slow and ugly, the police and the rifle-bearing guardsmen there to discourage mayhem, not help haul furniture, maybe a quarter of the protesters wandering away but the others keeping up a stream of the usual bullshit while the folks move their stuff in. Nigger this and Nigger that. Zeke can hear that the women in the local crowd are slinging it as hot and heavy as the men. The women and children among the newcomers take all they can carry in their first trip inside, then only the grown men come back out for more, the Detroit cops assuring them they can stay parked in front of the house and their vehicles will be guarded.

For a couple days.

Zeke was here for the first try, turned back before they even got a gander at the place, and it looks nice, nicer than anything he's ever lived in. Whitley is excited.

"It's a *house*, Zeke. I got me my own *house*."

"Yeah, you do. Have fun sleeping in it tonight."

Smitty mingles for about an hour, collecting vituperative, mostly unprintable quotes from the local inhabitants, before asking Tippett if he can go inside one of the units.

"O'Halloran," the sergeant calls to an even beefier patrolman. "Escort this gentleman of the press inside and make sure he comes out in one piece."

The white-painted houses are in neat rows, simple one-story rectangles with a tiny patch of grass fore and aft, basic, but a hell of a lot better than anything available in Black Bottom or Paradise Valley or sleeping in your car. They come to an open door and Smitty knocks softly on it before stepping across the threshold. A family of six are quietly arranging their things here and there in the couple rooms, the man he assumes is the head of household standing up on a chair in the kitchen, screwing a lightbulb into an overhead socket.

"I'm from the *Detroit Free Press*," says Smitty, trying to sound professional though friendly to the cause, "and wonder if you might share your impressions on finally being able to move in here?"

The man with the lightbulb in his hand looks down at him for a long moment.

"White man," he says finally, "I got nothin to say to you."

• • •

At least they let her sit.

There are six of them, two new men in the cell, and four she knows, including Jeanette Virdon, who was part of the Wayne University crowd. Rosa wishes there was a wall for her back to be up against, only a little space and then the open door behind her, giving her the feeling that somebody is just out of sight, listening in.

"You were extremely critical of the Molotov-Ribbentrop non-aggression agreement—"

"You mean the Hitler-Stalin pact."

A moment of grim silence. "Call it what you will, at the time it was the Party line."

"Which I disagreed with—"

"You understand it was only meant to give the Soviet Union time to prepare better for-"

"It is *never* right to encourage Fascism."

She has decided to defend her position, though Ira told her they had already made up their minds and would accept only an abject apology, preferably after throwing herself prostrate on the floor. At least three of her inquisitors used to be reasonable people-

"Are you a military tactician?"

"No. I am, except in extreme cases, an anti-militarist."

"So you oppose an armed rebellion of the masses?"

"If it comes to that, after other possibilities are explored and found wanting, I will reluctantly pick up a weapon."

"As in the current struggle—"

"I haven't joined the WACS, and I'm not sure they'd have me, but I volunteer wherever I think I can be helpful, and I currently have a clerical job at Packard, where they're making—"

"Packard that struck when a handful of colored workers were promoted."

"An action I opposed, which did not make me popular with the majority of my co-workers—"

"You understand our commitment to the Popular Front?"

Rosa nods. "I support it whole-heartedly."

"Beginning with the edict that there be *no* strikes until the Nazis are defeated—"

"A promise the UAW has made as well."

"Yet there have been dozens of work stoppages and other actions."

"Wildcat strikes are just that—unauthorized reactions to unfair—"

"You've done quite a bit of work with Local 600-"

"-we were encouraged to aid, in fact to help *guide* the labor movement as it gained traction with the people—"

"You're aware that 600's allies in the Mine Workers union have gone out, despite the desperate need for coal to fuel our munitions factories—"

"I believe Mr. Lewis and President Roosevelt will work that out fairly quickly."

"You support the president."

Trick question here. The Party line on Roosevelt has meandered quite a bit since he was first elected.

"He has done some good and necessary things for the people in this country, but is still, I believe, a prisoner of his class and of the capitalist system."

"This is a recent appraisal?"

"No. I felt that way when the Party labeled him an enemy of the people, and I feel that way now that he's being presented as the savior of the so-called Free World."

"You have quite a few opinions, don't you?" Jeanette, blank-faced, joining the chorus.

"I should hope so. But I do try to examine them constantly, to test them against what I see in the world."

"You have a relationship with a young factory worker."

This is a statement, from the new man who seems to be leading the inquest.

"Yes—"

"By the name of—"

"Riccardo Donati. He's currently in basic training with the infantry."

"Not a Party member."

"He was in one of the flying squads during the Ford strike—"

"And your brother is—?"

"Ira. He's a 4-F because of asthma, but a friend got him into the Office of War Information."

"Making propaganda—"

"Actually, he reads film scripts from Hollywood. Looking for misinformation, military information that might be useful to the enemy, and—you know—anything that will discourage the people rather than inspire them to greater effort."

Ira is in heaven, of course, telling Rosa that some of the scripts he censors or rejects altogether are brilliant, and that he's made some good connections to the film industry-

"What distresses us the most," continues the point man, "is your attitude that the Party line, formulated with great diligence by persons with a much greater knowledge and analysis of the struggle than your own, is to be followed and passed on to others only when it meets your rather whimsical personal opinion."

Somewhere along the line she has stepped on someone's toes, and their identity will not be revealed in this session. Rosa knows that her face is flushed, as always when she is angry, and attempts to keep her voice level and calm.

"I am, perhaps, the *least* whimsical person I know," she tells them. "And if we as Party members give up our critical abilities, if we stop *think*ing, we risk becoming as easily led astray as any blind-faith religious or political sect."

A longer, grimmer silence.

"I don't believe I've ever refused to carry out an order," Rosa continues, "or even a suggestion to volunteer that has come down through Party channels. I understand that uniformed soldiers in combat are expected to obey their officers without question, but I am unaware that we in the political sphere are under that sort of discipline. If you have any specific suggestions as to how I might better serve our cause—the cause of humanity—I am entirely open and eager to hear them."

An even longer, grimmer silence, and then Jeanette lays it on the table.

"You won't be notified of our meetings anymore," she says, "and if you show up you won't be admitted."

Papa still has his IWW membership card in the top drawer of the old dresser they all share, and there is a joke between her and Ira about what happens, on the day the proletariat finally triumphs, to members who haven't kept up with their Party dues. There is nothing to turn in, no formal ceremony where you're loudly reviled by the assembled comrades or stripes are ripped off your sleeve. There have been rumors lately, reexamining the Moscow trials of a few years back, rumors Rosa has been careful not to pass on without more evidence. She was hoping to help build a better, less centralized Party here.

There are no goodbyes as she leaves the room.

Nobody in the throng filling John R Street, if they bother to look, can tell the difference. Just a dark-haired girl probably heading for her factory shift, one of hundreds now hurrying to catch the next passing public transport with enough room to squeeze in. Rosa feels dizzy. Her stomach hurts and she feels lighter at the same time. Rick, for one, will be glad, cajoled into attending one meeting, which he said put his brain to sleep. Rosa exaggerated her age to get into the Young Communists, and has been a faithful member, a true believer, for what—thirteen years now? She was a part of something so important-

It is not so easy to navigate the streets these days, not just in her Black Bottom neighborhood but nearly everywhere in the city, so much work at all the factories and so many newcomers to replace the young men who've gone off to war. These really are the People, she realizes, moving in every direction at once, in each other's way, jostling for elbow room-

"C'mon, honey!" calls a woman she recognizes from the floor at Packard, reaching out from the door of a loaded streetcar just easing away from the station. "Join the crowd!"

• • •

Edsel himself, thinks Harry Bennett, despite their many disagreements, would not resent him coming to his funeral. Edsel was a forgiving guy, a peacemaker, and understood that if you're going to have heat there need to be sparks. But Harry is so deep in the doghouse, fairly or not, with the widow and with the Chief's missus and for some reason with Henry Two, on leave from Navy training in his ensign's uniform, that the kindest gesture is to stay in his office and hold the fort during the ceremony.

The Chief is devastated, of course, never accepting what was clear to everybody else in the last couple months, riding Edsel about his drinking, which by Harry's standards was negligible, and his diet, as if going the soybeans and spinach route could cure cancer of the gut. There's always been a kind of mystical side to the old man, believing he was chosen or touched by higher powers to bring on the modern world with his machines, the Ouija-board stuff taking a firmer grip on him even before Edsel started to check out.

"We're still together, you know" he said just yesterday, gripping Harry's arm way too tight and staring at him with those steely gray eyes. "Me and Edsel. Whatever comes next, we'll be working together. I can *feel* it."

Whatever comes next is going to be a shitstorm unless Harry can get him to focus back on the business. The Chief jumped on that crazy pacifist wagon with Lindbergh, as if there was any way we could avoid being pulled into the festivities, and he never really liked the aviation business. So he let Edsel and Charlie Sorenson run the whole Willow Run deal, except for employment, of course, Harry saving their bacon more than once with his contacts down south sending up fresh recruits for the idiot jobs on the line. But now that you got the federal government breathing on your neck there's the danger of the whole thing slipping away. He'd nearly convinced the old man to give up on that money-bleeding crackpot Brazilian plantation when the War Department, starving for rubber, jumped in to haul it out of the grave.

Somebody's got to run this place, somebody with a pair between their legs. Charlie Sorenson is a good machine man, knows how to keep the system spitting out the most product with the least waste, but Charlie has no political skill—he just *yells*. And that fat boy in the sailor suit, Henry Two, still got peach fuzz on his face instead of a man's beard, knows more about running automobiles into *trees* than he does about making them. God help my Navy if he's the grade of officer they're sending up against the Fuehrer's U-boats. No, Harry's got to convince the Chief to sit back into the president's chair at the Company. Edsel was an excellent front for what—twenty years? Well-spoken, snazzy dresser, people liked him, didn't ruffle anybody's feathers just for the fun of it. But everybody knew the Chief was really at the wheel, so why keep up the pretense?

There've been some shaky moments, even before his son's health started to go south, when the Chief asked to see somebody who's been gone from the Company or even died years ago. Coming into Harry's office and saying "Do you know where I'm supposed to be?" But stick him in a room full of so-called engineers with a motor taken apart on a table and see who can slap it together and make it run. Sure, it'll get worse as he climbs into his eighties, but that's why Harry is here, that's why he's always been here. If Harry can explain it well enough, how the Company is bigger than family, how it's part of the lifeblood of the nation, and then get him to sign some sort of a document for when his ticket expires-

Harry hits the buzzer.

"Yes sir?"

"Mildred, I want the flag at half-mast over the—"

"Already been done, sir."

"Willow Run too?"

"They've been told."

"Terrific. Get the word out to my people at all our plants that after the lunch breaks are over, I want everything shut down, not a squeak, and everybody stands still for a minute of silence for Edsel."

"I'll call them now."

It was the Chief's order, but perhaps having it come from Harry will be appreciated. Bury the hatchet with the deceased. Harry was aware of some of the behind-the-back stuff, Edsel siccing Bugas on him about the theft ring at the Rouge, every Ford plant in the FBI's bailiwick now that it's all government contracts, till he finally had to hire the guy away at twice what Hoover was paying just to get him off his back. Poor Edsel, embroiled by birth in the intrigues of the court, but with no talent for the game. And he won't miss Edsel's bosom buddies—the colored people's rights crowd, Judge Murphy, Roosevelt—all thinking they had an in with the Company.

He hits the buzzer again.

"Mildred—"

"Yes sir?"

"Make it *five* minutes."

• • •

After they're told to shut the stampers down Kaz realizes that his ears are still ringing. He wonders if they just ring all the time now and he's stopped thinking about it, or if it's just the sudden silence in the factory. He's always heard guys say, especially at the Local, how good it would be when the Old Man passed and Edsel could take over the Company.

Not to be.

He never got to talk to the man but saw him now and then, just short of Tyrone Power handsome and always dressed to the nines—classy, not flashy. A gentleman, the one in charge of the Continental, which they say runs as great as it looks.

Five minutes is a long time to just stand and say nothing, especially in a building so huge that is usually a madhouse of noise and production. He looks over to Janusz Zybiki, the oldest man in manufacturing, who used to work with Pop on Model Ts way back at Highland Park.

There are tears running down his cheeks.

• • •

If you weren't invited they let you sit in the loft and look down at the people who run everything. Smitty and Portia stood outside as the long, shining automobiles rolled up, Smitty recognizing the heads of all the car companies, turning out war materiel now, while Portia filled him in on the high society types, Edsel's personal friends. They both recognized Ernest Kanzler, fired by the Old Man nearly twenty years ago but remaining Edsel's closest buddy, returned now as the federal government's representative in Detroit. He looks like he might not make it down the aisle.

"Their families vacationed together," Portia whispers to him just as the organ begins to moan. "And King Henry did not approve."

From the outside, Christ Church in Grosse Pointe is a formidable pile of sandstone, "neo-Gothic" Portia calls it, with a huge tower at the right front corner and a gleaming copper spire. Inside, the dull flagstone floor has been enlivened with what must be truckloads of red roses, while the altar is carpeted with white flowers woven into crosses. Long, stained-glass windows relieve the limestone block walls, and Smitty estimates about two hundred, two hundred fifty seats on each side of the center aisle, nearly every pew filled to capacity.

There is no eulogy. There have been plenty in the press, the body lying in state for a day at the Hamilton Funeral chapel downtown, quite a turnout from the citizenry, all happy to pass on their thoughts to Smitty. Edsel was always polite with reporters, measured in his responses, and not a liar. Lousy copy compared to the Old Man.

Portia points to a gray-haired gent sitting in the row behind the Fords. "Governor Edison of New Jersey. Son of Thomas."

Apparently the deal with Episcopalians is that all men are equal in death, so despite the floral tribute, the service is short and sweet. The bronze casket is covered with a blanket of white orchids, as befits a citizen who died with something close to eight hundred million dollars to his name and will soon be planted in the Woodlawn Cemetery, straight up Woodward from the old Highland Park factory. Smitty realizes that the young man in the Navy uniform at the end of the front pew is Henry Two, grown up now. Smitty followed a few rumors and wrote an article about the boy's adventures at Yale, failing in two majors and leaving after he was caught handing in a final exam paper he'd bought from another student. Fosdick read the article and said save your breath, anything short of a criminal charge and he's off limits. Smitty didn't kick too much—it was all true, but it wasn't *news*.

And here's the former frat boy, dressed like a sailor and looking lost. The King a withered stick, Harry Bennett in his ear night and day, Edsel gone, and his natural heir already at sea though he hasn't left the dock. If it is true that as Ford goes, so goes Detroit, thinks Smitty, God help us all-

Henry the Second has found a way to sit as far from his grandfather as possible.

Whatever the details might be, it was the Old Man who killed Daddy. No matter the problems at the plants—not enough workers, too many workers, unhappy workers, competition from GM or Packard or Dodge—the only ones that really got to him, the ones they'd hear him going over and over with their mother, was when the Old Man would treat him like shit. You couldn't ask for a better son, more hard-working, more loyal, than Daddy, and what did he get in return? Whereas, fuckup that I am, thinks Henry Two, Daddy was always behind me a hundred percent.

People coming up to him have been nice, they clearly loved Daddy, but the ones who work at the Company all have this question they don't quite say out loud—

Are you going to save us?

He was hoping to come back to the Company after the war is won, hoping to learn the ropes and make a contribution. But the Old Man isn't all there in the head, Bennett still has his fingers in everything, and Charley Sorenson clearly doesn't want to do anything but make the machinery efficient. The official from the War Department on his train here, clearly no coincidence, put it bluntly-

"We're not getting what we should out of the Rouge. Either we let you out of your commission and you go back there and straighten things out, or—well, we'd hate to have to *na*tionalize the Ford Motor Company."

And there was John Bugas, the Detroit FBI man who's now with the Company, waiting at the train station.

"I am so sorry for your loss, young man," he said, simple and sincere as a white hat cowboy in a Western. "I admired your dad. If there's anything I can do for you, *any*thing—"

"You work for Harry Bennett," he accused.

Bugas shook his head, looked him in the eye. "I work for your *fath*er. Always will."

• • •

It starts with the bumping. Alvin thinks that at first it was the white people just up from the South, used to colored people making way for them on the sidewalks, running smack into people like him raised in the north. Then all his friends start saying it was a protest campaign, like what happened at his father's factory, only this was revenge for what they did to the people trying to move into the Sojourner Truth houses. Anybody white—unless they were a cop—wandering around Black Bottom or Paradise Valley was just asking for it, and it was kind of funny to see how surprised they were. You did it when there were at least two of you and there were no cops or white soldiers and sailors around. The first time for Alvin was when they were walking on Saint Antoine, and Clifford suddenly bumped him sideways into a white lady carrying packages, almost knocking her into the street, and then he ran off just like Clifford did, people, including colored people, yelling angry at them.

It wasn't any fun.

But then it seemed like everybody he knew was doing it, and if you were out with the guys at some point somebody would announce "I see a cracker," and if you were the closest to the white person you had to bump or be a chicken. There was even an article in the paper complaining about 'Negro ruffians' and how somebody needed to be taught a lesson. So when Clifford said everybody was going out to Belle Isle on Sunday and there were some white gangs bragging they'd be there to do the teaching, Alvin said he wasn't feeling good and wouldn't go. But then in the morning it was so hot in their part of the house, hard to breathe even with the windows open, that he changed his mind and figured Belle Isle was big and if things started to get nasty he could get lost pretty easy.

But when he met the guys at the fountain there were so many people who had the same idea on the hottest day of the year that the island didn't seem so big.

"Little Willie says it's *war*," Clifford told him right away. "A bunch of crackers run him out of Eastwood Park last week and he says they likely to be here today."

Even just walking across the bridge, Alvin could see what was different—for once there are twice as many colored people crowding the island as there are whites. And the white folks don't look too happy about it.

It is a long day. They do a lot of the things they always do—make animal noises at the critters in the zoo, shoot dice and trade their little bit of money back and forth, have canoe races, two to a boat—but they are always on the lookout for white people they can mess with, butting in front of them in lines, running through and kicking over their picnic baskets, banging their canoes and not quite knocking them into the water. They see a bunch of white kids with the same idea and have a stone-throwing battle with them across the canal, working their way toward the footbridge so they can mix it up face-to-face, but then a couple cops come blowing whistles and they all have to scatter.

Alvin scatters as far away from the guys as he can, Clifford and another of them talking about robbing somebody, real trouble if you get caught. He makes his way back to the zoo.

There is an elephant and there is a bear, both of them alone behind walls, and then a pair of tigers and a pair of giraffes and a whole slew of fast little monkeys who never stop scurrying up and down the stuff they've been given to climb on. Alvin hangs there as people come and go, talking at the monkeys, and thinks about how easy it is in the zoo, none of the animals mixed in with things that aren't their kind, the ones that can eat you kept behind bars or in a pit so big they can't get out. There are countries where it's only colored people, all of them darker than Alvin, except maybe for Tarzan and the white hunters. Mostly the dark people get to carry stuff on their backs and try to fight with spears against guns like the Ethiopians and the Italians, which doesn't look like much fun.

It is nearly dark when Alvin and almost everybody else decide it's time to leave the island, and the bridge isn't wide enough for everybody at once, the cars in the middle barely crawling, and Alvin hears the fight before he can see anything over the crowd, then recognizes Clifford's voice yelling "Get him! Get him! Get him!"

He's almost knocked off his feet by three white sailors in uniform running past, pushing their way through to get into the action, and then he can see that the car traffic is totally blocked now, drivers leaning on their horns, as a battle has spilled from the walkways into the center road and before he can decide whether to go join his friends or turn back in the other direction there are two white guys beating on him, knocking him down and kicking him a few times before a colored man almost as big as his father lights into them. There is a Navy Armory just at the base of the bridge on the mainland side and pretty soon there are dozens and dozens of men and boys swinging and screaming at each other, police whistles blowing but no cops in sight and Alvin has blood on his shirt and more coming out of his nose and he hears glass breaking as people attack the cars, looking in through the windows to see if the people inside are friend or foe. Sirens wail but seem too far away to matter-

• • •

-Rosa crying "Let's go back!" She knows there is a curfew on the island, but everything ahead is just fighting, black against white, chaos-

"We can't let them get away with this!"

Rick is in uniform, back for two days leave before his outfit ships out to San Francisco, and has been itching to fight all day, furious at the gangs of young colored kids running wild-

"They're not getting away with anything!" she shouts, holding tight to his arm as the crowd around them pushes in both directions, hoping to get off the bridge. "The only way this is going to end is—"

"If I wasn't with you—"

"What? They're sending you to the Pacific to get shot at—you can't wait for that?"

"You think they care about you cause you rub elbows with them at your political meetings? All they see is some little white girl—"

She pushes him away, angry. He's different since the army training, all ramped up to kill and be killed-

"Hey, if you want to be an idiot, go ahead. I can take care of myself!"

Rick looks into the car they're pressed up against, then throws the rear door open, grabs Rosa by the arm and shoves her into the back seat, banging her head on the roof on the way.

"Get her home safe!" he hollers, then slams the door shut before hurrying up to the free-for-all as best he can, even climbing over a little Studebaker on the way.

Rosa sees a young girl with braces on her legs sitting beside her, a man and woman in the front.

"Lover's spat?" says the man at the wheel, looking at her in the rear-view mirror.

"Worse than that. This stuff's been going on all day."

The voice sounds familiar, and when he turns she recognizes him.

"Hey, you're—" he says, pointing at her-

"Rosa."

"Right. Shulberg?"

"Shimmel."

He looks to his wife. "I told you about her, from the Local. We run into each other whenever heads are being busted."

"Pleased to meet you," says the wife. "Are you okay?"

"I think I just broke up with my boyfriend, and he's going away to the Pacific," she says, and then starts to cry, furious at herself for letting the tears come. Goddam him anyway.

"Well you just sit tight, honey," says the wife. "The police will be here soon and then we can get you home."

She decides to wait to tell them where she lives-

-while the turnout at the Forest Club nearly fills the place. Mavis has been bugging Zeke for a night out for weeks and since he was still so bushed from work yesterday that he fell asleep by the radio during *Inner Sanctum*, it's the Sunday night crowd they're mixing with, all the factory workers and maids and nannies and pot-wallopers out to shake a leg, Cecil Lee's band playing on the stage and some kids who can do all that sliding and throwing around on the dance floor doing the jitterbug. A few zoot-suiters in the crowd, wearing their big hats tilted and their pants hiked up near their necks, and some gals showing it *all* when they start to high-kick.

On the way in Zeke found Sunnie to pay his compliments, the little man grinning just like he should be with his place jumping like this, everybody flush with war production money.

"Looks like you raking it in, Poppa-Stopper."

Sunnie was Mayor of Paradise Valley one year, an honor voted on in the colored papers, and it would be hard to find somebody, black or white, who doesn't like him.

"Come by tomorrow morning when I start handing it *out*," he grins. "Only Henry Ford got more Negroes on his payroll than I do."

The band swings into *Kalamazoo*, which is as fast as Zeke can handle, Mavis looking spectacular in yellow tonight—can't any white woman wear yellow and look that good—and he loves to watch her move to the music.

Years have gone by
My, my how she grew
I liked her looks when I carried her books
In Kalamazoo-zoo-zoo-zoo-

Things have been edgy at the foundry lately, the new ones up from East Pascazoola or whatnot feeling their oats and getting into it with some of the white guys, staking out territories on the lunch breaks, one bad fight at the time clock when somebody cut in front of somebody else, like you got enough energy at the end of a shift to trade swipes with some cracker. Zeke is still breathing hot gas all day doing shakeout, and can't get out into the open air fast enough. Mavis says if he hates the job so much why doesn't he quit and find something else, but there *isn't* much else, not for a black man his age. He took the exam for the post office and did real well on it, but nobody's come knocking on his door with a job there. Things could be worse. They've been socking away some serious money and just come up on the list for the Sojourner Truth housing—Maceo says it's because they got DeWitt down south training in a tank battalion, and that gives you points. If the damn war will just end before they want Alvin, who's slight and quick and always smiling and doesn't belong anywhere near a battlefield-

Zeke recognizes Hughie Gaines pounding the floor, and Tyrone Banks with a new girl who looks like she's up past her bedtime, and Mavis's brother Whitley with somebody definitely not his wife, like getting brained with a skillet by Lorena that first time knocked all the sense from his head, and two whiskies have got Zeke just as high as he wants to be. The song ends and some character carrying a briefcase steps up onto the stage and marches to the microphone.

"Ladies and gentlemen, if I could have your attention—" he begins, talking too close to the microphone so you want to put your fingers in your ears.

"I'm Sergeant Fuller, and I have some shocking news."

The shocking news, thinks Zeke, is that he recognizes the man as a guy named Leo who used to work for Sunnie in the coat room—neither a sergeant or a Fuller.

"There has been a rampage going on down at Belle Isle, and the whites have thrown a colored woman and her child off the bridge."

Screams and shouts then, Leo booming over them on the sound system-

"I need you men to go get your guns—there's free transportation outside."

More shouting and a rush for the doors then. Luckily there are a few ways out, so nobody is trampled, nobody listening to Sunnie, standing up on a chair at the far end of the long bar, shouting to wait a minute, wait a minute, aware that there's something fishy about Leo coming in here-

"You in for a piece of this?" yells Tyrone, a pool cue held like a club in his hand, looking ready to kill.

"I'm going home and check on my young ones," says Zeke, Mavis clinging to his wrist with both hands as if he's about to run away. "If what he said is true, you *know* this won't stay out on the island—"

-and Alvin hangs back when the police show up with a lot of patrol cars and get people mostly separated and on their way, cars stuck on the bridge and back on the island finally able to move. When he gets across to the mainland they have him stand in the headlights with arms and legs spread out while one pats him down for weapons, then tell him to go home and stay out of trouble.

He gets past the Navy Armory all right, then hurries down Jefferson all the way to Russell before cutting away from the river, and the craziness has already started. By the time Alvin gets to Hastings and Fort there are people—not just young boys—smashing windows on shops, mostly what Clifford calls Jew stores, though there are colored people who work in most of them. Sirens screaming from every direction, people angry or just excited, and it's clear that tonight there are no rules. He is hustled forward by a group running up the street throwing pool balls they've stolen from somewhere through the windows they pass, and bumps into something hanging from above and cries out at what he thinks it is, then can see it is only one of the plastic dummies they dress up in the windows of the clothing stores, stripped naked now and hung by its neck with some wire.

A white dummy.

Then one of the sirens gets louder and louder and there is a voice on a loudspeaker telling everybody to get off the street or be arrested and he turns to ease down Hastings, seeing a group of about twenty men and boys marching along together. Home is the other way, but he darts across the street to join them-

-Kaz slamming on the brakes, narrowly missing the colored boy. Rosa thinks she recognizes him, and sees that Rosen's Bakery has had its windows smashed and Snappy Menswear has people moving in and out of the busted-in door carrying armfuls of clothing-

"Where are you again?"

"Right here on Hastings," she says, "but we're way up between Division and Alfred."

"Don't think we'll make it going this way—"

"Maybe just find like an all-night diner that's open—"

"Don't be silly," says the wife. "We'll get you home or get you somewhere safe."

"I'll cut over to Woodward and we'll go up," says Kaz. "It should be under control over there."

The young girl in the back with her, probably their daughter, has been constantly shaking her head as she watches Rosa, who has decided it must be some kind of palsy and not disapproval. The girl speaks slowly and with some difficulty, asking a question Rosa can't understand.

"I'm sorry, I didn't get that—"

"That's not a very polite question, Sonia," says the mother. "She wants to know why you live where the colored people do."

Obviously wondering herself.

"It used to be mostly Jewish," Rosa tells the girl. "Then gradually the colored people moved in because nobody would rent to them anywhere else. And we know the landlord, who only charges us an arm instead of an arm and a leg."

The girl, Sonia, smiles at this. She has a beautiful smile, if a little lopsided.

Rosa listens hard and understands that the next question is if she's afraid to go out on the street there.

"No—not until tonight."

Kaz chooses empty streets, working their way up to cross through Grand Circus Park, looking normal for a late Sunday night, then heads north on Woodward.

"When my Pop come here from Poland he went through the same thing," he says. "The worst dumps to live in, charging the highest rent—"

"It's called capitalism."

Kaz laughs. "Listen to this girl, Sonia, you'll get an education. What was that thing you told me about on the picket line? Each one does the best they can, but—"

"'From each according to his ability, to each according to his needs.'"

"That's it—"

"It's the idea that the basic things—food, water, fuel—"

Sonia screams as a rock smashes the window next to her face, black men of various ages and sizes on all sides of them throwing things at the car as they cross Columbia by the Fox Theater, spider-cracks on both the side windows and something like a tomato plastering the windshield in front of the wife, Kaz stomping on the gas and swerving around a couple of them, passing an abandoned car that has gone up on the sidewalk and smashed nose-first into the light pole, running a red light to put some distance between them and the attackers.

"Jeez, they're all the way over here! You all right, Sonia?"

Sonia makes a noise and tries to sniff back her tears. Rosa takes her hand. "We got away fine," she says. "We'll be okay now."

But it isn't true. A half dozen white guys out in their T-shirts are standing across Woodward at the Vernor Highway intersection, waving them down and then looking in when Kaz rolls his window down.

"You people okay?"

"Yeah, except for the car."

"What are you doing out at this hour?"

"Trying to get home from Belle Isle."

"Some niggers raped a white girl over there today!" shouts one of the younger men. "Like twenty of them, taking turns. Fucking animals—"

"Where you trying to get to?"

"Hamtramck."

"Well get west of Woodward and circle around. They're all up and down this street, hunting for white meat."

"Thanks."

They don't speak as Kaz turns left on Vernor and goes all the way over to Cass Avenue before turning uptown again. At Mack Avenue a black man in a suit runs past the car, looking terrified, chased by a half-dozen whooping, joyful young white men waving clubs as they run, and just ahead a car has been flipped over onto its back and burst into flames, dozens of people circled around it like it's a holiday bonfire, sirens screaming from the east and a burglar alarm ringing loud and steady from some violated shop.

"You're staying with us tonight," says the mother to Rosa. "If we can get there—"

• • •

-and Alvin is not at home. Earline sits out in front of the apartment under the Blue Star Mother star they've put up, crying, and Zeke stops only long enough to grab the Smith and Wesson .32 he bought from Alonzo DuPree back when the Black Legion outfit was murdering colored men, barely listening to Mavis yelling that he'll get his fool head shot off. All he can think to do is to walk the streets angling down toward Belle Island, asking anybody he sees under twenty if they know Alvin.

Nobody seems much interested.

The streets of Black Bottom aren't quite as full as when Louis beat Schmeling, but it's well past midnight and people who were asleep have gotten up and out to join the party. An older colored man wearing a bathrobe and slippers is carefully painting **NEGRO OWNED** on the intact window of his shrimp shack, while the hardware store next to it has been raided, buckets of paint jimmied open and sloshed out on the sidewalk. A burglar alarm is ringing inside a pawn shop that has been thoroughly picked over, window glass and the Jew's three golden balls, revealed to be breakable plaster, littering the sidewalk in front of it.

Zeke catches a running boy by the arm.

"Alvin Crowder."

"Lemme go, man!"

"Do you know Alvin Crowder?"

"Naw, Mister, lemme go!"

He lets the boy go. There wasn't any 'transportation' waiting outside of the Forest Club, and the story about the woman and her baby on the bridge might not be true, but the thing that's been cooking for years has finally boiled over and he needs to find Alvin before the white folks come to make them pay. Come down to the crunch and you're always outnumbered.

Sirens are wailing, glass is breaking, people are running this way and that. A bunch of young men stand on a corner, offering bottles of stolen liquor for sale and sampling the rest.

"Yo, man! You want to get in on some of this?"

"I'm looking for my son."

"How old?"

"Fourteen."

"Hell, there's only bout two thousand of them little niggers running around tonight. Won't be no *school* tomorrow!"

The young men laugh, and one flips an empty bottle high in the air, sailing end-over-end, then it falls and smashes in the middle of the street.

"You know the police will seal us off," Zeke tells them. "Then they'll move in and start whipping colored asses."

"Let em come. All the tough ones gone off to war."

"Find out your own way," says Zeke and moves on.

Something is burning at the corner of Riopelle and Monroe, smoke clouding the street, and Zeke pauses to see what building it is and if anybody needs help. A patrol car screeches up, the headlights blinding him. They've got a microphone-

"Hands up and behind your head, kneel down!"

Zeke follows the instruction. He hears two car doors open, and a pair of cops step forward into the light, standing over him with pistols drawn.

"You packing anything, Rastus?"

"Front right pocket."

One of the cops yanks his .32 out while the other flicks on a flashlight and sticks it in his face.

"Ought to get a holster—you'll blow your dingus off carrying it like that. Got a permit?"

"No."

"Then what are you lugging it around for?"

"You see what's going on—"

"Yeah, you people are swiping anything that's not nailed down and throwing bricks at white people. Name?"

The smoke is stinging Zeke's eyes and he's kneeling on broken glass.

"Crowder. Ezekial Crowder."

"What you been up to tonight, Ezekial?"

"I'm looking for my son. He aint come home—"

"Well, maybe you'll see him at the station house. You sure that's all you been up to?"

"That's all."

The other cop starts to laugh, training the flashlight beam onto the sidewalk behind Zeke. He must have walked through the paint outside the hardware store, one footstep yellow, the other blue-

"We can check on that, Mickey," says the cop. "This fucker left a *trail*—"

• • •

-as Rosa discovers she is just small enough for the sofa. The wife, Molly, makes it up for her as Kaz and Sonia sit by the radio listening to the news reports on WMBC.

"Your father won't be worried?" she asks.

"Not really," says Rosa, amazed at how cool this house is compared to their apartment on Hastings. "I told him I'd be staying with Rick overnight."

"And Rick is—?"

"The soldier you saw me have a fight with."

"Ah."

Rosa forgets, sometimes, that she is in the minority in many ways, social mores being one of them. Kaz looks amused, but Molly—

"Did you have a date set?"

"A—? Oh. No. No marriage plans."

Molly tucks a sheet under the sofa cushions, pulling it taut.

Sonia, head still shaking, asks if Jews don't have sins. Kaz laughs.

"Sure," says Rosa. "There are things we're not supposed to do, though we—my family—are not particularly religious. I think everybody should have a moral code."

Sonia stares at her, trying to make sense of this.

"But your moral code might not be *my* moral code—"

Sonia asks, painstakingly, if Rosa can give her an example of something she wouldn't do.

"Well—if I owned an apartment building in Black Bottom, I wouldn't charge colored people three times what the same place would rent for in another part of town—a part they can't live in because there's a covenant—"

"Your landlord is white?" asks the mother.

"He's not only white, he's Jewish. And he goes to temple regularly."

"He's sticking you for that much?" asks Kaz.

"No, we only pay two dollars a week more than it's worth—religious discount."

Papa will hear the sirens and know to stay inside for a while—when he was a little boy in Würzberg he was hidden in a cellar during a blood-libel riot—and Ira is at the Great Lakes Training Base helping to make a recruiting film. They should have moved, really, but it seemed like a gesture of solidarity with their colored neighbors not to abandon ship-

Sonia asks why white people and black people fight.

"Oh—I suppose most people are afraid of what's different, what they don't understand."

I know all about that, says Sonia.

There are at least two hundred men of various ages crowded into the bullpen, all colored, and Zeke has been lucky enough to get a seat on one of the benches sticking out from the wall. They took his name, took prints, and photographed him, a new experience, and the one desk jockey who bothered to look him in the eye said he'd probably be tried for illegal possession of a weapon if the arresting officers couldn't come up with a more serious offense. The one toilet is broken and overflowing, and there are only a few drunks too far gone to take part in the war stories being swapped, the mood in the lockup alternating between rage and exhilaration. Every time someone new is thrown into the tank everybody is told to move away from the bars and Zeke stands on the bench to look over them and see if it might be Alvin.

Alvin isn't here.

"I don't give a *shit*!" shouts one young man, wound up so tight he paces quickly from wall to wall, smacking the wall with both hands when he reaches it, the other prisoners trying to squeeze out of his way and avoid setting him off further.

"I—don't—give—a—*shit!*"

A big man hanging on the bars, who looks near as old as Zeke, turns to call out to him.

"You don't give a shit about *what*, youngblood?"

The pacer stops for a moment to face the big man.

"I don't give a shit they lock me up for twenny years," he says. "I got some *back* tonight!"

• • •

-while the last show at the Roxy on Woodward, summer hours, doesn't end until four in the morning, and somehow the word has gotten around that a good part of the audience are colored. As they wander out from *Frankenstein Meets the Wolfman* there are gangs of white men and boys waiting with bats and clubs, and it's a good ten minutes before the night manager can get through the switchboard at the precinct to let the police know. Three patrol cars get there almost at the same moment, Smitty in the back seat of one of them with Sergeant Tippett and O'Halloran from the Thirteenth Precinct in the front.

Most of the whites clear out when the sirens get close, only a few stupid or drunk enough to annoy the cops sufficiently to spend the night on the city. Ambulances come a few minutes later, and the black men who've been beaten, most who can't stand up on their own power, are rolled onto stretchers and loaded up.

Smitty finds a couple teenagers, one with somebody else's blood smeared on his white shirt, leaning back under the Roxy marquee to admire their handiwork.

"The fight start inside or outside?" Smitty asks.

"I won't sit in a theater that lets niggers in too."

"So you don't see many movies."

"You heard what they done on Belle Isle," says the boy in the bloody shirt. "Raped a little girl and thrown her into the canal."

"And then they came here to see the show?"

"*Some*body's gotta fucking pay for that," says his friend.

Sergeant Tippett is sitting in the front of the patrol car, talking over the radio. He waves Smitty over.

"This is where you get off the tour, my friend. Just stick to the west side, you should get home all right."

"Something up?"

Tippett looks grim. "They just ambushed a couple of our guys up at Hastings and Alfred," he says. "What happens next you don't get to see."

• • •

Mavis only has so much patience. It's maybe two hours with neither Zeke or Alvin coming back, and she knows from the hospital that with a situation like this the switchboards will be jammed. So she walks down Beaubien to the precinct station at Macomb, zigzagging her way around the broken glass and unwanted or abandoned goods from looted shops and avoiding whatever looks like trouble, her sharpest kitchen knife ready in her handbag. The patrolman holding a machine gun out on the front steps allows her to pass, and the desk sergeant is angrily pulling a double shift.

"This is what we got," he says, pushing a clipboard with a list of juvenile arrests across the counter to her, "but I don't trust these young ones to give you their real moniker."

No Alvin Crowder on the list.

"And if he was too scared to say his name?"

"They keep the juvies in a separate tank. You need directions?"

At the jail, just a block north on Clinton, they make Mavis leave her handbag at the desk. She hopes they're too busy to search it.

There are only seven boys in a fairly big cell, none of them Alvin.

"This is all you got?"

"There's some at Receiving we got tagged for court," says the gray-haired turnkey, grinning. "If they don't bleed to death."

Receiving Hospital is back next to the police station and going full blast, people being wheeled here and there, nurses, orderlies and even doctors actually running down the hallways. Mavis knows that Darcy Wright, a nurse who used to be at Henry Ford, now works night shift here to keep the same hours as her husband out at Willow Run. She moves through the madhouse to track Darcy down, just inside where the ambulances pull up.

"Don't have anybody look like that come in so far," she tells Mavis, "but you can ask for the names at admission. What's it like out there?"

"Still crazy. You best not try to walk home when you're done here."

Darcy is light-complected, taken for Italian sometimes, and even white *cops* aren't moving around Black Bottom tonight unless it's in groups of three or four.

"If we had a bed open, I'd crawl in it right now," Darcy sighs. "Good luck finding your boy."

A steady stream of wounded, most still bleeding from somewhere, are taken past Mavis as she looks down the list at the front desk. No Alvin Crowder. She feels dizzy, then asks the woman in the booth if they have unidentified bodies.

"Bodies go straight down to the Coroner's Court, identified or not," the woman tells her. "Lafayette Boulevard over by Greektown."

Men are running on the streets, but whether it is to or from something, Mavis can't tell. She walks quickly down Saint Antoine toward the river, glad she thought to put on her work shoes, trying to focus on the thought that this is only to eliminate a possibility, that when she comes back home with no news Zeke and Alvin will be there to say she worries too much.

Whenever the running men are young, she asks about Alvin.

"Say again—"

"Alvin Crowder. He's about this tall, wears a—"

"Sorry, M'am, don't know him."

Twice she is stopped by white police in patrol cars, told to get off the street. She explains that she's going to see if her son has been killed. They tell her she'll be notified if he has and to get off the street. There are gunshots now, clusters of them, mostly from behind and to the east, and still the yowling sirens. She tries to walk faster.

A car begins to follow her, creeping forward, its headlights throwing her shadow out long in front of her. Mavis doesn't speed up or slow down. The car eases up beside her as they go under a streetlight and she has a glimpse of the driver, a white man with a red face smiling a terrifying smile at her. When they cross Monroe he slowly crooks a beckoning finger at her. Mavis can see that the car is crammed full with other white men, none in uniform, all of them staring dully at her. She suddenly turns and runs back to the intersection, hurrying down the side street toward City Hall, nobody else in sight until suddenly, almost magically, a dark figure appears in her path, spreading its arms and solid as a wall when she slams into it.

It is the Garveyite.

The Garveyite they used to see around Maceo Suggs's place in Inkster, dressed now like a band leader or a marine officer in a parade, a black-skinned man in a black uniform with loads of golden buttons, a high collar trimmed with gold, black boots, thick black belt with a separate strap running diagonally up over his shoulder, wearing a cap with a golden band and a gold medal attached to the peak. He has a long sword in a scabbard hanging from his hip.

"No fear," he says. "Cedric wit you now."

She lets him take her arm and they continue down Monroe. The car full of white men is not following him.

"Great consternation and hatred tonight. The bloods—white and black—they cyannot mix," he says. "Wheer you go, sister?"

"To the mortuary."

He frowns. "Wheer they maintain the dead."

"I'm looking for my boy."

The Garveyite nods solemnly.

"Cedric compny you theer."

They see not another soul on the way to the Wayne County Coroners' Court.

The offices and crypt are on the first floor. A young white man in a white coat who might be trying to grow a mustache writes her name on a sheet of paper on a clipboard and wearily leads her into a room with refrigerator coils along the walls from floor to ceiling. Mavis sees white puffs of breath coming out of her mouth, then sees that there are wheeled gurneys with bodies lying on them under white sheets, snugged up against the coils all around.

"Been a crazy night," says the young man. "We don't have names for most of them yet, but you're welcome to look. Think you can handle that?"

"I have to know."

He nods to a half-asleep police officer, who begins to follow them a few paces back as the young man first lifts the sheet up slightly at the bottom, checking the color of the bared feet of the corpses, before he rolls a gurney away from the wall and allows Mavis to lift the top of the sheet and look at the face.

"Coming in too fast to keep them separate," he says.

Mavis, still trying to convince herself that this is a waste of time, wonders if there is a room full of these people's shoes. They are halfway along the second wall when she finds Alvin.

"These colored ladies, you never know what they'll get up to," says the cop as he and the young man watch the woman cover the body on the gurney with her own and wail. "Wait till she wears herself out before you try to get his name."

• • •

It is the rainy season, and though the Tapajós has not spread wide yet to flood the surrounding jungle, they can feel the power of it pushing them upstream as they motor northward to the Mundurucú. Jim and Gomes wear rubberized slickers that make you sweat underneath. There are crates lashed to the narrow deck of the launch filled with things the Indians want—knives, fishhooks, cooking utensils, even some canned goods—enough to agree to tend a sizable rubber tree nursery and keep supplying seedlings.

"I don't know why we do this," says the *capataz*. Gomes has taken to wearing a white fedora, which he now has to clamp a hand on top of to keep it from blowing off.

"We're starting to produce rubber—"

There is a stinging rain, blowing hard from the west, an angry sky above them. It was calm and clear when they left Belterra.

"But this big war, this *matança*, is maybe ending," says Gomes.

Jim sits on a couple of the crates, holding tight to the taut rope that binds them to the deck, Miguelito in the tiny pilothouse wrestling the wheel to keep them aimed straight.

"Then we'll make cars again. Cars need tires."

"I think maybe I go to Rio," says Gomes, bracing himself in a crouch between tethered crates and the side of the pilothouse as the bow of the launch is blown to the starboard, veering perilously close to a huge boulder half submerged in the river. They are moving too fast, the motor on for maneuvering but the swelling river pushing them, its elevation dropping constantly on the way to the Amazon, branches torn loose and floating in the water banging against the hull-

"I go with Conceição."

Miguelito manages to steer them straight again.

It is no secret in Belterra that the two have taken up with each other, Connie popular among the mess hall workers and Gomes perhaps only a few years older than she. As for her past-

Jim tries to show the *capataz* a brave smile as the prow sends a sheet of water flying past them. "Any idea what you'll do for work?"

Gomes considers his answer, holding tight to his hat. "I believe," he says finally, "they are selling Mr. Ford automobile in Rio, no?"

Before Jim can respond it is like the bottom falls out from under them, then a shock as the hull comes down on something solid, followed by a blind toboggan ride, hitting both floating and rooted objects, hard water crashing over the bow, Jim sitting down on the deck with both hands clutching the tie-down ropes which are straining this way and that as the crates begin to shift with each impact, hearing the motor lift completely out of the water for a moment and then the launch plunges off-kilter and when it hits bow-down Gomes goes flying over Jim's head and into the river, Jim's grip broken for a moment by the wash, then the crates come loose on the tilted deck and take him overboard with them-

He is not a swimmer, but calm in emergencies, wriggling out of the heavy rubberized slicker while he is still under, then stroking hard for the surface of the swift-moving water. He gets a glimpse of the launch well ahead, riding low in the water, then is smacked on the back of the head by a floating crate. He comes up quickly, grabs onto another crate, but can feel it is quickly filling with water and won't float for long. He lets go of it, struggling to keep his head above the surface, his shoes feeling like lead weights, and thinks he sees the *capataz* not far ahead. But as he is swept closer he sees it is only the white fedora, floating-

• • •

Even with the hatch open, DeWitt wants to puke. The sailors who saw action said the ocean was much rougher the day of the invasion, said they watched several of the so-called amphibious tanks just sink in the waves with none of the crewmen swimming away. Their tank is in the front of the LCT, two others snugged in behind them, and DeWitt's portal isn't high enough to see over the bow. No Germans left to shoot at them from their bunkers now, which is a comforting thought, though the push into France must be pretty badly stalled for General Patton to eat crow and call in the 761st. They've seen thousands of white tankers pass through training and be sent over still wet behind the ears, have run rings around them in war games, and had just about given up on seeing any action-

"We'll be rolling onto Omaha Beach," Sergeant Amos told them when he got the word yesterday. "Where the worst of the slaughter happened."

Word is that the front is not too far from the beach, so they'll be in the shit soon enough, plenty of Germans left to kill. Otherwise, thinks DeWitt, this has all been one long prison sentence. He's done a month in the stockade—a mess hall fight with a white tanker after the letter with the news about Alvin caught up with him—and the rest of army training, including life in Fort Hood and that godawful Killeen next to it, was not much better. And after all the bullshit stories that've been hung on them, how colored troops are too slow, too scared, too stupid to fight in a modern war—well, now we'll get to show them, won't we?

Or die trying.

DeWitt looks up at the winter sky, no snow yet but threatening, then closes his eyes, tries to just listen to the waves slamming against the hull and ignore the movement—up-down, back-forth, side-to-side—without much success. The LCT pilot said they've blasted some channels in to the beach and there are markers to guide you now, so they're not likely to get hung up offshore and have to roll through the surf. DeWitt used to go in the river all the time, salvaging things or just fooling around, but he doesn't really know how to swim. The idea of those crewmen on the day of the assault, buttoned up inside their tanks on the amphibious craft, water starting to pour in from above-

DeWitt is jolted out of the thought, momentum stopped, all the wave sound from behind now. As the ramp comes down he can see the top of the low green hills where the Germans were dug in, then rocky cliffs, then the beach itself—crowded with several companies of infantry who have just been hustled onto the sand, NCOs herding them into formation. Signal flags have been put up to outline the path for armored vehicles to take, and DeWitt, driving today, puts them into forward gear.

"Move it out, Crowder," calls Sergeant Amos, standing in the turret above. "Nice and steady."

DeWitt has not bothered to imagine what this would be like, rolling onto newly liberated French soil in Sherman Easy Eights, a class above the Stuarts they were given to train in. The one letter Alvin wrote all himself, he was so excited that the outfit had taken their motto from what Joe Louis always said when asked for his strategy.

Come Out Fighting.

DeWitt eases it onto the beach and then up along the marked pathway, white troopers on both sides turning to stare. Probably never seen a colored man with a rifle, much less one in charge of thirty-two tons of trouble-

With a Ford V-8 engine his daddy might have had a hand in making.

One beanpole of a private walks alongside them for a bit, just shaking his head, and finally calling up to the turret.

"Hey, where you boys gonna deliver them tanks?" he calls over the engine noise.

"Berlin," answers Sergeant Amos. "We'll be waiting when you get there."

Smoother than ever—
it's a new ride!

The 1945 Ford car—so big and smartly styled—offers more new developments than most pre-war yearly models . . . New multi-leaf springs—long and slow acting—give you a velvety ride that's smooth and level . . . Brakes, too, offer major new advancements. They're oversize, self-centering hydraulics for "cushioned stops"—quick but quiet. Less pedal pressure needed . . . Under that broad hood there's stepped-up power, and with it a new thriftiness in gas and oil . . Inside, new luxury awaits you. Colorful fabrics and trim in pleasing two-tone combinations. Seats that are wide and deep . . . Take your choice of two great engines. The V-8, increased from 90 to 100 horsepower; the 90 horsepower Six . . . Yes, everywhere you look, you'll find advancements in this youthful new car . . . Ask your Ford dealer about the smartest Ford cars ever built.

THERE'S A

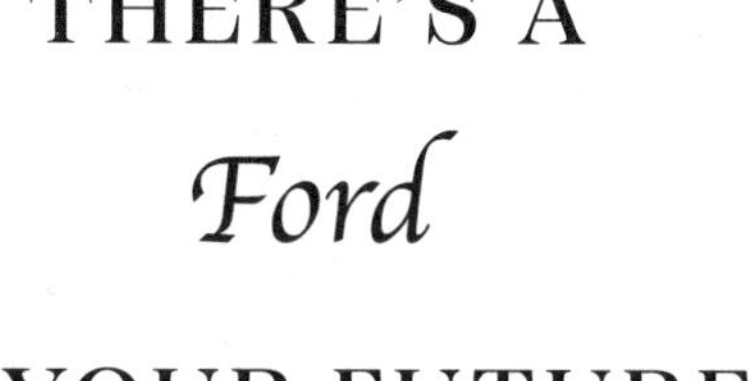

IN YOUR FUTURE

IF HE'D ONLY GOTTEN THE Chief to sign it then and there. Harry read the codicil out loud to him, slowly. Capizzi had looked over the will and made sure all the language was right—when the Chief passes, the Company will be run by a board for ten years, a board made up of solid guys Harry knows he can trust, with him as the secretary. No increase to the seventy-five grand he's pulling in now, no change to where the Chief's stock is going. This is not about money, it's about control of an important business enterprise, an outfit that helped win the war.

"Sounds okay to me," said the Chief, taking the document and stuffing it in his pocket. "Let me sleep on it."

From the amount it's been folded and crumpled he may literally have done that, holding onto it for at least a month, sometimes needing to be reminded that it lacked his signature, then finally, on one of his good days, slapping it down on Harry's desk.

"You wanted this," he said, grinning. "Complete with my John Hancock."

Not wanting to complicate this increasingly rare good mood, Harry didn't inform the Chief that his signature was supposed to be witnessed by at least three persons. Capizzi, who will be on the board, says this might squeak by, but declined to sign on as a witness, so Harry got his driver Frank and Chief Brooks and Sam Taylor to add their names *post facto*. More problematic, says Capizzi, is all the stuff the Chief scribbled on the document while it was in his possession—ideas for suspending pistons on top of the V-8, reminders for errands, quite a few spot-on quotes from the Old Testament-

Know the plans that I have for you, plans for welfare and not for evil, to give you a future and a hope

"Not convincing evidence," said Capizzi when he got a look, "that the old gentleman is in his right mind."

But the Chief heard it read to him and he had plenty of time to read it himself and he signed it, that was his *will*, and unless that fat little fuck Henry Two or Edsel's widow get close and take advantage of the poor old guy, it will stand. Which is what he'll tell Bugas.

Bugas has been a disappointment, worse, a traitor. A tough cowboy from Wyoming turned G-man, he and his wife excellent company when invited to the Castle, he seemed genuinely grateful when Harry brought him on board at twice what the FBI was paying. But too much time hanging around Edsel and his fancy-pants cronies must have turned his head, and now he's sticking his beak in where it doesn't belong. He's been cooling out there for forty minutes, and Mildred would have buzzed if the guy had given up and crawled back in his hole.

Harry hits the button.

"Tell him he can come in."

Harry sits back behind his desk, the man in charge. How Bugas even learned about the codicil—there must be a rat and it can't be Capizzi-

John Bugas steps in. He isn't tall, but taller than Harry, big deal, and tries to drill you with his eyes if he thinks it will give him the upper hand. But Harry has lunched with half of the Purple Gang, may they rest in peace, and is not impressed.

"John. What's on your mind?"

"You know what. I need to see it."

"On whose authority?"

"Henry Junior."

"You work for him now?"

"He's the Executive Secretary of the Ford Motor Company."

"You know what the Chief thinks of titles."

“Fine. We’ll call the Chief here and go over it together.”

There is no bluff to Bugas. Harry thought that when he had the disloyal bastard’s office moved into the washroom, the toilet just on the other side of a flimsy panel, he’d either go crying to Junior or quit. But he just moved his papers to the new, smaller desk and borrowed a hammer from the janitor to tap in a nail to hang his hat on.

“I’ll read it to you.”

“You don’t trust me to touch it?”

“You don’t trust me to read it?”

A Mexican stand-off, just like in the pictures.

“I’ll be back tomorrow,” says Bugas after some more staring at each other. “If you don’t cough it up then, I’ll come with some lawmen. Ones you don’t control.”

He is gone then, and Harry considers his options. The Company, apparently, is not doing well as the war in the Pacific winds down, several departments in chaos now that Sorenson has retired, the best men at Willow Run threatening to desert to rival companies. All the more reason for Harry’s board to take charge. You can always hire engineers—the universities spit out a new crop every year—but men who understand how the world works, how to be approachable and ruthless at the same time-

If only the Chief hadn’t scribbled all over it.

• • •

Kerry has only been on a plane once before, a cargo plane to Manaus with Mom, where there was a bench in the hull you could sit on but no way to look out. The nice Brazilian lady beside her gave up the window seat when she learned this, and now Kerry sees the shadow of their plane racing over the jungle canopy below. It is a flat green mat with the occasional glint of river—beautiful, meandering river that doesn’t look like it could kill anybody.

The pilot made it back two days after, the launch battered but still afloat, having searched the banks all the way upstream to the mission. He said he was so busy trying to keep off the rocks that he didn't even see the men go over. Kerry didn't believe it was true, Daddy couldn't just disappear, so they waited and waited, still hoping-

No body was ever found.

With no body, her mother has decided not to have a ceremony, insisting that Kerry not miss the beginning of her first college semester, that she will stay behind to settle things, then fly to Detroit to meet with the Company about money.

Just after takeoff Kerry saw flamingos take flight, their wings moving incredibly slow, a wash of light pink against the dark green of the jungle trees. Jocko is down there, wild now, at least trying to be. The first time she and Flavio took him to the spot where the troop came to eat and let him loose, he kept climbing up to get fruit from the high branches, then scurrying back down and leaping into Kerry's arms to cling for a few minutes before the next foray. When the troop came, maybe a dozen of them all together, he went up fast, curious, and there was a lot of chattering and stiffened fur and bouncing on branches till he was driven away without being touched. The next time, a few days later, the troop was already there. Jocko climbed a tree not so close but within sight of them, his eyes never off them as he picked and ate. There was a little chattering, probably all the males, but it's hard to tell with squirrel monkeys, and eventually they settled in, Jocko lasting only a little while before rushing back down to Kerry.

"He is more nerves than hungry," said Flavio.

"Nervous."

They had continued to correct each other, Flavio's English just as adequate as Kerry's Portuguese, with lots of sounds they still have trouble making.

Flavio is down there too.

It was on the fifth trip that Jocko ended up in the same tree as some of the troop monkeys, engaged enough that she and Flavio were able to slip away without him seeing. Kerry barely slept that night, up several times to look out the window to the yard, but he never appeared, leaving her half satisfied that she'd done the right thing and half disappointed that he could forget her so quickly.

You have to grow up some time.

It will be a little scary being with real American kids again, no telling how many years it takes for songs and movies or ideas about what is swell and what isn't from there to penetrate the Amazon jungle, but she will just stay quiet and pay attention, like she did the first year in Fordlandia. There won't be a school uniform, so she'll have to see what the girls are wearing and buy some new clothes.

Jocko came back the next evening, playing loudly on the trapeze setup her father had made, till she came out and he jumped into her arms. She left him out there untethered, and he was gone in the morning, this morning. Her father said he'd be the smartest monkey in the jungle and Mom said good, you're supposed to stay with your own kind, and Flavio said he would go to the spot sometimes, but wasn't sure he could pick out Jocko from the rest.

Kerry doesn't know if she'll write to Flavio. He said goodbye last night, saying love things that made them both cry. Mom says this is what Daddy wanted and that it will be a great adventure, but it's only a teachers' school in what's most likely a boring place.

"You are going home now?" asks the nice Brazilian lady beside her.

"No," she says. "I'm leaving it."

• • •

Bugas straps his piece on for this one.

With Harry you never know, so much of it is just show, tearing the coat off and announcing he's ready to mix it up right when there's somebody to step in between and pull the other man away. But he does have a temper and he's been letting it run rampant lately, confident that he and Mr. Ford are so visibly inseparable these days that people will jump whenever he barks.

This time Harry makes him wait for an hour. Nobody else comes in. When Myrtle finally gives him the nod he steps in to find Harry standing behind his desk, grinning and holding an oft-crumpled sheet of paper up by one corner.

"Afternoon, John. Sorry to keep you waiting."

"Just one page?"

Harry pulls his gold cigarette lighter from his jacket pocket, flicks it and holds the flame to the lower edge. They lock eyes as the paper browns, then burns, wispy bits of black floating down to the space that Harry has cleared on his desktop. When it is done he pushes the pile of carbon gossamer toward Bugas.

"You can take that to Junior."

• • •

TOGETHER WE WILL WIN THE WAR

By Sonia Pilsudski

War is a terrible thing. But once we have been forced to engage in it we must all play our part. Even in the armed forces, many more soldiers play support roles than engage in actual combat, while here on the home front we agree to rationing of vital materials that are better employed in the effort to defeat our enemies, and many of us are engaged in the production of vehicles and weapons needed to continue the fight. My own mother and father work at the Willow Run facility, making B24 bombers, airplanes which will rain death and destruction on our enemies—

Sonia loves the dash. It is so unfinal, if that is a word, so like the way she thinks. Maybe because she is always a bit behind everybody else, walking slower, talking slower, never quite getting to the finish line. Like her typing, building a word one careful push—she doesn't strike the keys, needing to have her finger actually touching the surface before she pushes or she might miss it—at a time, having to stop her racing mind as if at a red light until her fingers can crawl back in touch with it. If there was a way to connect a typing machine with her thoughts it would fly—

> After the attack on Pearl Harbor, which was in our territory of Hawaii, we have not been bombed again on US soil. Other people are not so lucky, including, now, the Germans and the Japanese. It must be a terrible thing to go to bed listening for the whistle of explosive bombs falling upon you from the sky.

It is a terror Sonia wrestles with every night now, ever since she saw the newsreel where they showed the bombs falling one after another from a squadron of Liberators, adding the whistling sound they make and then seeing the flashes below that you know are explosions that could blow up an entire block and kill everybody living there. Stan says things are going our way now, the tide has turned, but that doesn't mean enemy planes can't sneak overhead somehow, and with all the war production in Detroit, what would be a better target?

> The people who die in wars are not always the ones who start them. The best way to deal with a war is to win it as quickly as possible. This is why we all have to do what we can to support our boys in uniform.

Stan is dying to sign up but isn't old enough yet. Sonia hopes it is over by the time he is, or that the Army or the Navy give him a job where he doesn't get shot at or have to kill anybody. She is *will*ing to do whatever she can, but not very able—so far mostly not complaining about the rationing and helping to Save Scrap for Victory—collecting metals, paper, rubber, and rags to be made into war things and even going from house to house asking if people have old records they don't want anymore, valuable for the shellac. For this she has typed up a card stating her mission, pasted it to a square of cardboard, and shows it when people come to their doors. They assume she is deaf and talk really loud, but she feels a little bit useful when she gathers enough to bother handing it in at the collection center.

In a movie about war she would be the one who says "I can't keep up, leave me behind and save the others!"

I pray for our soldiers every night, but I don't think God is involved in battles one way or another, because there must be people on the other side praying for their people. I hope that when this is over we won't need armies anymore, or jeeps or tanks or battleships or bombers, so we can go back to just making Fords to ride in. Maybe somebody will learn how to make a bomb so big and powerful that people will have to stop fighting or all be blown to smithereens.

If this happens, Sonia hopes America will invent it first.

And yes, 'smithereens' is even in the dictionary.

• • •

The stockholders' meeting, though short as usual, has a touch of drama. Eleanor Ford, holding all of Edsel's shares, nearly half the Company, has promised to sell it to outsiders, most likely auto business rivals of her father-in-law, if changes are not made. Henry Ford, for maybe the second time in his life, has surrendered to the inevitable. Rail-thin and ghostly pale, he sits quietly listening to lawyer Capizzi reading the statement of his resignation as president that he dictated this morning. Halfway through it Harry Bennett jumps to his feet, says the hell with this and heads for the door. When Henry Junior stands to say something he turns on the young man-

"You're taking over a billion-dollar organization," Bennett snarls, "that you know *no*thing about."

He slams the door but Henry Ford seems not to notice. His grandson looks meaningfully to John Bugas, then to Capizzi, who resumes reading the letter of resignation.

Bugas leaves the room, checking his pistol before starting downstairs. Myrtle seems to be in shock, saying nothing as he marches past her and into Harry's basement office-

Harry is piling folders from his file cabinet onto his desk. Bugas has one of the Little Man's paintings, a tiger crouched to leap, from when they were still palling around together.

"You treasonous son of bitch," says Harry. "You engineered the whole thing—"

Before Harry can clear his .38 from the drawer Bugas has his own pistol out and aimed.

"You touch that trigger and I'll kill you, Harry. You know I won't miss—I'll put one right through your heart."

There is no bluff to Bugas. Harry grips the .38 but doesn't raise the barrel.

"Henry Junior wants you to have a pension. Against my advice."

Harry starts to laugh. "Give me a day to clear out."

"You can keep anything in this room," says Bugas, backing out of the office.

Harry stashes the pistol. A smart fighter, one who wants to quit before his brains are mush, knows when to stay down for the count. He begins to make two piles, one for home and one for the fire.

• • •

The old steamer that goes to Belém is coming up from the south, and late again. Since VJ Day the military have moved all their aircraft out, and both of the Company planes are being worked on in São Paolo. Norma stands waiting at the dock with her luggage around her. She's gotten rid of all her black clothing over the years here, and so only wears the black armband. The woman Jim always called Connie and was some kind of a prostitute is waiting as well, with only one small suitcase by her side. The other Fordlandia people waiting for the boat stand away from them, recent widowhood a disease that might be catching.

Connie came in for an exam only a month ago, hoping that she was pregnant, but it was only a urinary tract infection. Dr. Niles tried the new penicillin drug on her and she recovered quickly, but she was badly disappointed. She told Norma the names she had chosen, one for a boy, another for a girl.

Norma tries to think of something here that she'll miss.

The work—she'll have to study and be certified, of course, but she'll want to work as a nurse no matter if the settlement means she doesn't have to. It made her feel real here, necessary in some way.

There is shouting on the dock now, but people are looking upstream so it can't be the steamer. Indians rowing a boat. They do a little trading with the locals, but Jim always liked to call them "Mundurucú tourists."

One of the Indians isn't rowing and doesn't have paint on his face. Not wearing the robe, so it isn't a missionary-

Jim.

Norma screams and then covers her mouth and then people are around her, helping her to her feet and he is there, wearing somebody else's clothes, there and holding her as she weeps.

None of this has ever been her real life.

People from the Company must have been run for and told and they are here now, smiling and thumping Jim on the back. It takes a while for him to see Connie.

"*Ele se foi?*" she asks.

Is he gone?

Jim shakes his head sadly. "*Sinto muito.*"

The woman only nods, then looks downriver, waiting for the steamer to come.

• • •

The deal with getting hitched, thinks Smitty, is that you don't get to just marry the other person, but now have to deal with their whole family. Portia gets off light with that, Smitty's living relatives few and far away, while he has to deal with the Grosse Pointe von Dusenbergs, here to check him out, and, today, tour the Sage of Dearborn's nostalgic folly. Sister Daphne, with her hint of an English accent though Portia assures him they grew up a stone's throw from Lake St. Clair, is enough of a pill, but her husband Milo is an estate lawyer with a bone-crunching handshake who fills every space he enters with his stentorian commentary.

"It's an attempt to render history as industrial and scientific evolution, you see," he announces as they gaze upon an early dynamo in the Armington and Sims machine shop, paraphrasing the printed guide they were handed at the information desk. "Which, from the viewpoint of a clever mechanic, it might well be."

Milo also relieves them of the burden of reading any of the plaques and explanations posted next to the exhibits, singing out the texts when discovered, and whenever he spies a familiar household object, announcing that "My grandmother had one of those!" When Smitty remarks that his grandmother must have had a very large house, Milo proceeds to describe it in stultifying detail. When this travelogue reaches the second floor, Smitty fakes a violent coughing fit and excuses himself.

Portia, being the gal she is, gives him a subtle thumbs-up.

It is far too windy outside to light one of his secret stash of Camels with a match, so he ducks into the Edison laboratory, which is empty today if you don't count the new addition, a wax figure of old Henry Ford in a white suit and a '20s skimmer hat, staring intently at the set-up illustrating the invention of the carbon-filament light bulb.

Only it isn't wax.

Smitty tucks the cigarette and matches away, stands next to the old gentleman for a while and stares at the single, glowing bulb until he is noticed. Ford looks at him, puzzled.

"Do I know you?"

"We've spoken over the years. I'm a reporter."

The Old Man grins and waves his hand back and forth in front of his face.

"Blowflies. They cluster wherever an animal drops a turd."

"We're part of the cycle of life."

The Old Man waves at the room around them. "This was Edison's shop. Nothing fancy. Just what you need to work."

"Like our newspaper."

"Hell, you boys upstairs just *scrib*ble. The real work is down under, where they crank out the papers. It's a *fac*tory down there."

"I'll accept that."

"I was born before the linotype was invented. Wonderful machine—no waste. The lead that's pressed into the letters goes right back into the hopper to get melted down. Revolutionized the printing business."

The Old Man looks back at the glowing light bulb.

He's not really a story anymore, now that the grandson has taken over. They trot Henry out for honors and occasions or say he's not feeling up to it. Word is that he's gone a bit dim-

"I'm just a vessel, you know," he says.

"A vessel—"

"I never in*vent*ed anything, it was all *there*, waiting. I just connected one idea to the next—"

"But you had the ideas—"

"Yes, I was chosen, just like Tom Edison. There's a—a *pow*er—whatever you want to call it—that wants us to move forward, and I was chosen to help bring it about."

"Chosen for wealth and fame—"

The Old Man shakes his head. "It was never about the money. People don't understand that. I was trying to show them how to *live*. But—"

The Old Man shrugs his shoulders. He looks lost.

"Maybe they did understand," says Smitty, trying to help the old guy feel better. "But—you know—wanted to live their own way."

"Maybe," says Henry Ford, staring at the glowing bulb. "People aren't machines."

• • •

Once you get used to the heat it isn't so bad. Good to be back at the Rouge and off the metal presses before his hearing was totally shot. The union kept pushing for some foremen who weren't ex-pugs or parolees from Jackson, men who had put in some real time on the floor, and Bennett, before he left, gave in with the proviso that they started in the foundry. Kaz was surprised that not only was his name was near the top of the seniority list, but that none of the half-dozen bumped up were colored.

So he feels the resentment.

Nobody has said anything, but it's there. The bunch he watches over in shake-out all know their jobs and do them well enough, so there's no point cracking the whip the way they used to in Assembly—the temperature of the metal has to be just right for each step of the process and there's no point hurrying it along. There are days when Kaz wonders what they're paying him for, just a little paperwork and making sure nothing gets clogged with sand from the molds. There's no sitting down, of course, and you never want to get caught with your hands in your pockets, but he's pretty sure that if he didn't show up most days the engine blocks would get made without him.

There is only one man he's afraid of, Crowder, who's been with the Company as long as Kaz and probably should have been made foreman. But he was with the bunch who didn't come out the first day, so the union didn't go to bat for him. Crowder never says a word, not to Kaz or anybody else as far as he can tell, just cracks the molds off the blocks. When he bothers to look at Kaz it's like he wouldn't mind picking him up and carrying him back to the open furnace to add to a charge. Big enough to do it too. Word is that he has a son, back safe from fighting in Europe, who has a spot as a draftsman over at Engineering.

Kaz asked Gamble, the one who lost some toes on the job and is friendlier than most, what the deal was.

"Zeke gone through some seriously nasty shit," the pourer said, growing solemn. "Man don't have time for *nobody.*"

Kaz watches the man from behind a pillar and marvels at the economy of his motion, something they always harped on back in Assembly—don't fight the machine, be*come* the machine. Give yourself up to the routine and the rhythm of the task as if nothing else exists, over and over and over and over and over—

• • •

She misses Ira. Almost single-handedly running the little radio station up in Bemidji, he sounds like he's happy and reports a romance with a girl recently out of the WACs who sells advertising time to local merchants. Rosa knows he'll be listening to the same broadcast, thinking about her and Papa, the last white people on their block of Hastings, tuned in to the big game. It has been a real nail-biter—the Tigers, depending on the outcome, either going to the World Series or back to their homes to mope, but Rosa has had a hard time concentrating on the play-by-play. Rick back home from the hospital in San Francisco last week, his left arm intact but basically useless, not wanting to talk to anybody. And then the scene this morning-

Virgil Trucks got them to the sixth inning giving up only one run, amazing considering that he's just out of the service and hadn't thrown a pitch all year, but then lost his steam and Hal Newhouser came in and the Browns have been getting to him, one out when Finney singles and then Pete Gray, the One-Armed Wonder, hits a grounder that with a slower runner would be a double play, but he beats the throw to first.

Of course Gray is only in the major leagues this year because of so many young men still away at war, able to catch a ball in center field and somehow quickly roll it across his chest, ending with the glove wedged in the crook of his right arm stump and the ball in his left hand to throw. He was a decent one-handed hitter too, till the big league pitchers realized he couldn't adjust his grip to handle a curveball and have thrown him nothing but breaking stuff ever since. He is a model of determination, generous with photos and interviews, held up as a hopeful example for GIs coming home with missing limbs.

Rick calls him a freak.

A *fuck*ing freak.

But when the next batter lines one between left and center, Pete Gray is swift enough to race all the way home, putting the Browns ahead three to two and causing Papa to grab onto the few tufts of hair left on his head and begin to moan.

"Here it comes," he says. "They tease you with success, then they yank it away. I should have quit in August."

Papa had the second heart attack in August, dead as a doornail when the ambulance finally came, but reviving on the way to tell them he'd rather perish than spend a night at Henry Ford Hospital. He spent two nights in bed at Receiving before they sent him back, lucky to escape, he said, "before they had time to sew my foreskin back on."

If the Tigers blow this game they have to face the Senators in a special playoff, which Papa is certain they will lose just to torment him.

If the Tigers blow this game it will be officially the worst day of Rosa's life.

Unemployed again, Rosa has been volunteering to do clerical work at Local 600. First thing this morning Leary, over from UAW headquarters, stopped by the pension desk she was holding down, bending low to speak confidentially.

"Schimmel, right?"

"Yes?"

"I have to tell you, you're on the list."

"What list?"

"The one they'll deny exists if you ask about it. The list of subversives."

"I'm a subversive? I come here, I answer phones—"

"It's not your actions, it's your associations."

Roosevelt dying was a blow to everybody, but it has been surprising how quickly certain things have changed without him. Perhaps the United Front was always an illusion-

"I'm not in the CP anymore."

Leary raises his eyebrows. "So you admit that you were—"

She doesn't let him finish. "In 1932," she says, "if you weren't in the Party, you weren't paying at*ten*tion."

600 is considered a rogue outfit, the local that still kicks the hardest, and she imagines she will be welcome there. But if at any point her presence becomes a liability-

Newhouser strikes out Gene Moore to end the inning.

The announcer glides into an ad for the new model Ford. She has asked Ira how he can countenance reading these paeans to toothpastes and cigarettes, but he tells her that without them there would be no radio, no Bing Crosby, no Bob Hope, no *Duffy's Tavern*-

Before Rosa left the Local office she made one last phone call, to Rick. When he heard her voice he hung up the phone. Rick stopped writing even before he was wounded, and she doesn't blame him. It's one thing when you're still in training and lonely or just shipped overseas, where they read and censor all the V-mail, but when you're actually in *com*bat, she imagines-

No, she can't imagine.

He's a different person now, not just the arm but how he sees the world. Saying they should have dropped more of those bombs and killed every Japanese, man, woman, and child—the Rick she knew before would never have said that, said it like he meant it from the bottom of his heart. Seeing friends killed right beside you, nearly being killed yourself more than once—would she want to have people who never even picked up a gun burned in a nuclear storm?

She won't judge him, but it's clear she can't be with him.

Potter is still on the mound for the Browns, and Hub Walker, first man up for the Tigers, singles off him.

"Signs of life," says Papa.

It has happened gradually. Papa and Ira always with the games on the radio, then finding herself going straight to the *Free Press* sporting pages to see how they'd done, pausing to listen if she passes a house or a store with the game on, and following Hank, a Jew in a Gentile game hitting nearly as many home runs in one year as the great Ruth. Hank volunteered even before Pearl Harbor, went away with the Army Air Corps to the China/Burma theater of operations—but still she followed the team through some very rocky years.

Rosa Shimmel, the Rebel Girl of northern Michigan, a baseball fanatic.

If sports are not exactly the opiate of the people, they are *something*—and it is addictive. The saving grace of baseball for her is that you go to Navin Field and see people of every race and class in the seats, pulling for the Bengals. And if the petition she and Ira put into circulation reaches the right people, someday soon you might see all colors and classes *play*ing together on the field as well.

Skeeter Webb lays down a bunt and they try to get Walker out at second but fail. Two on, no outs. Eddie Mayo comes up and *he* bunts, thrown out at first but moving the runners to second and third with one out. The Browns manager comes out to the mound to talk, and then Potter walks Doc Cramer intentionally to fill the bases.

"They've got to be kidding with this," says Papa.

She understands the strategy, how a ground ball could get you a double play, out of the inning, game over, especially as the batter is no speedster. Common baseball knowledge, drilled into her by her father and brother.

But the next batter is Hank Greenberg.

Hank who came back from overseas and changed uniforms to play almost half the season, batting like he's never been gone. Hankus Pankus, who as a boy would stay in the sandlot hitting balls from whoever would throw them till his hands bled.

The Hebrew Hammer.

Rosa is holding her head in her hands with fingers crossed and knows that thousands sitting by radios all over Detroit, all over the state of Michigan, are doing the same, and the verses Ira used to torture her with come into her head-

> *Then from five thousand throats and more there rose a lusty yell;*
> *It rumbled through the valley, it rattled in the dell;*
> *It pounded on the mountain and recoiled upon the flat,*
> *For Casey, mighty Casey, was advancing to the bat-*

Hank takes the first pitch for a ball.

> *Ten thousand eyes were on him as he rubbed his hands with dirt;*
> *Five thousand tongues applauded when he wiped them on his shirt;*
> *Then while the writhing pitcher ground the ball into his hip,*
> *Defiance flashed in Casey's eye, a sneer curled Casey's lip-*

Only Hank would never sneer.

Potter winds up, lets the pitch go-

Henry Benjamin Greenberg lines the ball down the left field line and into the stands, just fair of the pole. Grand slam home run, everybody trots across the plate, Tigers suddenly ahead six to three. There are three Browns to get out in the top of the ninth, but they won't come back from this, impossible, Rosa whooping and jumping to her feet and Papa holding his cane over his head like Moses about to part the Red Sea.

"It's settled then," he announces. "I don't kick the bucket till the Series is over."

• • •

They are pulling out rubber trees. Santos and Flavio chopping down with their mattocks, João dragging the trees, only six feet tall in this section, to the big pile for burning. Dom Fernando is paying them, saying that the Fordlandia trees draw insects and disease that will spread to the good Brazilian trees still standing, scattered in the forest beyond.

They can hear the noise from the shop buildings near the river, former plantation workers and new people who have come to strip whatever might be valuable.

It isn't right, says João. Mr. Ford gave all this back to our government, not to those thieves.

If we don't take it back, says Santos, the jungle will. Soon enough.

Still, it's wrong.

"Think of it as back wages.

I was paid every week. For years.

So you broke even.

No, we still have the house they gave us in Belterra.

There's no work down there.

There's no work anywhere, says João. Once this is done.

They came, says Santos, they tried to beat the jungle, they lost, and they left.

They left some good things.

Tell me one.

They educated my son here. He can speak English.

Santos, who has come only for the destruction, lets his mattock rest and looks over to Flavio.

Let's hear some.

Flavio—show him.

Flavio, a powerful young man now, does not break the rhythm of his work.

"A, B, C, D, E, F, G, H—" he chants, "I got a gal—in Kalamazoo—"

-singing now-

"Don't want to boast
But I know she's the toast of
Kalamazoo-zoo-zoo-zoo-zoo-zoo— "

ACKNOWLEDGEMENTS

Crucible covers over fifteen busy years of life on this planet, and there is a pile of books that I found useful in setting a story within them. Greg Grandin's *Fordlandia* got me started on the idea, his legwork and writing bringing the fascinating story of Henry Ford's abortive Brazilian adventure out of obscurity, and Al Hirschfeld's *The Speakeasies of 1932*, full of his terrific drawings, gave me a nice feel for the vibe of the Prohibition days. *Diego Rivera and Frida Kahlo in Detroit* by Mark Rosenthal is a detailed account of the muralists' sojourn in the Motor City, while Pete Hamill's *Diego Rivera* provides a critical view of the man and his art. *Toast of the Town* by Sunnie Wilson, makes you wish you knew this unofficial 'Mayor of Black Bottom,' while *The Making of Black Detroit in the Age of Henry Ford* by Beth Tompkins Bates delves into Ford's complex relationship with his African-American workers. *Black Detroit and the Rise of the UAW by* August Meier and Elliott Rudwick, and *Layered Violence: The Detroit Rioters of 1943* by Dominic Capeci, Jr., and Martha Wilkerson are very useful in understanding the causes and consequences of the first terrible Detroit race riot, while former mayor Coleman Young and Lonnie Wheeler's *Hard Stuff* gives a colorful picture of growing up in that city's black neighborhoods and getting involved in its progressive politics. The 1936 *Detroit Street Guide* and dozens of period photos helped me understand neighborhoods that were very pointedly destroyed by urban renewal, while *The Color Line and the Assembly Line* by Elizabeth Esch is another strong source, among the many books whose cover art is taken from Diego Rivera's *Detroit Industry*

Murals- if you ever get to the city be sure to visit the Art Institute and walk around in the mural. Histories and biographies of the Ford family and the Reuther brothers are too numerous to mention and well worth delving into, while Harry Bennett's *Ford: We Never Called Him Henry* is a snappy bit of self-justification by the larger-than-life 'Little Man' who policed the River Rouge factory complex like an island dictator. Radio broadcasts of Father Coughlin's screeds and play-by-play of Detroit Tiger ballgames can be found on YouTube. James Buccellato's *Early Organized Crime in Detroit* (Harry Bennett makes the cover) has a good account of the Jerry Buckley killing, as well as the complicated shifting ethnic ties and rivalries that began even before the Prohibition amendment and its position on the border with Canada made Detroit a violent hub for racketeers. As the novel displays, enormous social and economic forces rushed together in that city, making it more a high-pressure crucible than a genteel American melting pot-

JOHN SAYLES